Apparently, Sir Cameron Needs to Die

GREER STOTHERS

Titan BOOKS

Apparently, Sir Cameron Needs to Die
Paperback edition ISBN: 9781835413807
Australian edition ISBN: 9781835418086
E-book edition ISBN: 9781835413814

Published by Titan Books
A division of Titan Publishing Group Ltd
144 Southwark Street, London SE1 0UP
www.titanbooks.com

First edition: February 2026
10 9 8 7 6 5 4 3 2 1

This is a work of fiction. All of the characters, organizations, and events portrayed in this novel are either products of the author's imagination or are used fictitiously. Any resemblance to actual persons, living or dead (except for satirical purposes), is entirely coincidental.

© Greer Stothers 2026

Greer Stothers asserts the moral right to be identified as the author of this work.

No part of this publication may be reproduced, stored in a retrieval system, or transmitted, in any form or by any means without the prior written permission of the publisher, nor be otherwise circulated in any form of binding or cover other than that in which it is published and without a similar condition being imposed on the subsequent purchaser.

A CIP catalogue record for this title is available from the British Library.

EU RP (for authorities only)
eucomply OÜ, Pärnu mnt. 139b-14, 11317 Tallinn, Estonia
hello@eucompliancepartner.com, +3375690241

Designed and typeset in Kristal by Richard Mason.

Printed and bound by CPI Group (UK) Ltd, Croydon, CR0 4YY.

"From the very first page, I knew I was in for a good time. With vibrant characters, delightfully weird worldbuilding, and an absurd plot, this was one of the most entertaining stories I've read this year. If you like outrageous (complimentary) science fantasy, you're in for an enormous treat."

KEMI ASHING-GIWA, *USA Today* bestselling author of *The Splinter in the Sky*

"Full of cozy heart and charm, with a delightfully hilarious main character—I kicked my feet all the way through."

CHARLOTTE STEIN, author of *When Grumpy Met Sunshine*

"A delightfully unpredictable fantasy adventure that turns familiar tropes on their heads in increasingly hilarious ways, Stothers perfectly blends heart, humor, and charming absurdity into your new favorite read."

CAMILLA RAINES, author of *The Hollow and the Haunted*

Praise for

APPARENTLY, SIR CAMERON NEEDS TO DIE

"Come for the silliness, stay for the twists."

CAITLIN ROZAKIS, *New York Times* bestselling author of *Dreadful* and *The Grimoire Grammar School*

"When times are hard, comedy feeds the soul. I *promise* this book will make you laugh. The only way it could be improved is with more man-on-vulture action. Five stars."

ALEXANDRA ROWLAND, author of *Running Close to the Wind*

"Sir Cameron is one of those heroes that you not only want, but need. Is he brave? No. Smart? Not really. Talented? Absolutely not. Did I relate to him? One hundred percent. He just wants to stay alive, and his antics to do so—like throwing in his lot with an evil sorcerer—lead to a story full of humor, warmth and depth. Stothers takes a fresh slant on time honored tropes, gleefully using them to skewer concepts of identity, gender, class and religion. The result is a hilarious romp full of satire, heart, and the overriding question: who gets to decide what's evil and what's good anyway? I thoroughly loved it and recommend it to anyone who enjoys fantasy that makes them laugh."

LISH MCBRIDE, author of *Hold Me Closer, Necromancer*

"A rollicking blend of whimsy and madness that kept me on my toes the whole way through. This tale takes the cookie cutter ideal of heroes and villains and twists them into all sorts of new shapes (sometimes quite literally) with delightful results."

MAIGA DOOCY, *Sunday Times* bestselling author of *Sorcery and Small Magics*

To Anzu.
You weren't good at laying eggs, which is the primary duty of a chicken, but you did have very pretty feathers. I'm sorry that rats dug into your grave and ate you. That was unfortunate.
I would say rest in peace, but alas. The rats.

PROLOGUE

In Which the Mad Sorcerer Merulo Announces His Nefarious Intentions to the World, Expecting Some Nonspecific Mixture of Fear and Awe, but Is Instead Ridiculed for His Clothing, Which He Chose on the Basis of Wanting to Look Intimidating and Is Thus Rather Sensitive About.

The man in black waited in line.

He did not look happy to be waiting in line. But then again, few people did.

Chancellor Felix Noor found his eyes drawn to the man, time and again, as he performed his own duties. *His clothing is just awful*, he thought, straightening his own ermine-lined sleeves. *Though what's worse—to be awful, or to be dull?*

A seemingly endless crowd waited in the audience chamber, their murmurs overlapping in a background babble. Their modes of dress varied, but none belonged to the noble lineages of New Albion, represented by the banners that hung from the walls: the eagle of Nasr, the salamander of Falade, the lion of Vaillancourt, and so on.

Nobody, then, worth paying much attention to.

The chancellor sighed and threw back his wine. When he slammed the goblet down against the arm of his chair, the serf at the front of the queue hopped, turned several shades paler, and choked on his tongue. The chancellor's knights urged him forward, but the serf failed to recover, and his speech stumbled.

This brought Chancellor Felix Noor no amusement; it made the process drag on intolerably. Still, he couldn't shun his duties. Not with the Church watching.

The man in black was next. He'd jumped the queue somehow, the family of farmers behind him appearing oddly frozen. Without waiting for a summons, he marched forward, his pinched, weaselly face jutting forward with unearned haughtiness.

Chancellor Felix Noor leaned in for a better look. The man's black robe blended with his dark, limp hair to give the impression of a cowl. Perhaps it was a purposeful perversion of an Elder's white gown—the chancellor glanced at the Church representative seated to his right, curious to see her reaction.

Elder Beth was busy with a drinks order. A stooge hovered, bent nearly double to better hear the woman, peppering every pause with compliments as to her taste.

"I am the sorcerer Mer—" the man began, his voice raised imperiously over the merchants, farmers, and freshly washed peasantry who waited to be seen behind him.

"Hold on." Chancellor Noor raised a hand heavy with rings. "Elder Beth. Do you have any thoughts on his robe?"

Elder Beth frowned, clearly annoyed by the interruption. "The shade is unpleasant. What does black symbolize—death and wickedness? And that cut—does he pretend to be a monk?"

The man glared up at the Elder with undisguised hatred. He was lanky and tall, but he stood some feet beneath them, a dais keeping the chancellor and his guest clear of the masses.

"I don't *pretend* to be anything. I am the sorcerer Merulo, and I have come to announce my intentions!"

At his proclamation, a hush fell over the crowd. Chancellor Noor thumped his goblet meaningfully against the arm of his chair. In answer, the knights guarding the dais ceased their yawning and scratching of armoured asses, and stiffened, ready to advance.

"Insolent creature. What are your intentions?" The Elder's words rang clear and strong across the audience chamber.

"I will, eugh—" The man's voice broke, and he cleared his throat, blinking. His eyes matched his attire, chips of flint in a ghoulishly pale face. "I will kill your God," he continued, clearly trying to match the Elder's volume and charisma, "and destroy the world's magic!"

Laughter came from the queue, some of it nervous, some genuine. The chancellor hid a smirk behind a broad hand. "Now, most people come to me about property lines, or conning merchants. He's obviously insane," he added to the Elder, who'd leaned so far forward in her carved seat that it threatened to topple. She looked like a dog pulling at an invisible chain. "Shall we take pity on his lack of faculties?"

"Doing so would be an insult to Order itself," she growled. Then, louder: "God is everlasting. We shall give you ample time to reconnect with Him through prayer. Escort this man to a holding chamber!"

The chancellor bristled at her giving orders to his men, but such was the way of the Church. To contest its representatives' will would be akin to blasphemy. Wearily, he swung his attention back to the supplicant—and exhaled sharply. The man glowered up at them without fear, his thin lips pulled back in a flash of teeth.

Of course, the poor idiot lacked all sense. Still...

"He did claim to be a sorcerer." The chancellor glanced sideways at the Elder, fingering an opal in his ring. Projecting his voice, he called: "Hold up, hold up. You can arrest this man in just a moment."

His knights paused, all but rattling in their armour at the conflicting commands.

Elder Beth's eyes bulged. "You—"

"I only mean to better evaluate this threat to the Church. Say, sorcerer, do you know any spells?"

"Do I—" the sorcerer spluttered. *"Do I know any spells?* I am the great sorcerer Merulo—"

"So you've said."

"My magic could have you weeping on your knees!"

"Oh?" said the chancellor, not hiding his yawn. "Could it?"

A poisonous look crept over the man's face. "Would you like a sample?"

"That's more like it." The chancellor sat up and beamed at the Elder, who had turned an interesting shade of maroon. "Shall we see a spell, Elder?"

Before she could respond, several figures stepped forward from the queue, their motions stuttering and faces blank. The knights paused—they had clearly readied themselves for a day of sweating monotony—but the figures showed no such hesitation. Accelerating to a run, they crashed into the line of knights, mouths gaping into splinter-lined cavities. All illusion vanished as they fought. It wasn't men the knights grappled with, but sickly, twisted trees, given a freakish semblance of life.

The Elder rose, whipping out a wand of carved ivory. She spat an incantation at the sorcerer, and gleaming ice swords condensed out of the air, leaving the chamber dry and staticky. They encircled the black-robed man, stabbing inward—only to shatter into a cloud of refracting droplets at a single barked word.

"Damn." The chancellor sat back. "He's good, eh?"

The sorcerer's next word sent the Elder sailing backward in a billow of white cloth, like a giant swatted dove, to crash against the tapestry-draped rear wall. The chancellor winced in sympathy, but made no move to assist.

"You understand, then?" shouted the sorcerer, panting not from exertion, but from what seemed to be anxiety. "I'll kill God. Destroy the magic. Yes? I anticipate a timeline of"—he ducked a thrown dagger, one of his wooden servants dashing forward to maim the source—"five years, give or take, so if any infrastructure changes are required—Oh, for fuck's sake."

A burly knight had broken through the wooden monsters with great rending sweeps of his axe. He roared, lunging at the sorcerer, who hastily flicked his pale fingers—and the knight collapsed in a clinking heap. The crowd screamed, trampling each other in their rush to escape through the great double doors, forcing the sorcerer to shout at an ever-higher volume.

"Look, you've been warned, yes? This is a warning? I have twenty-three more stops to make and can only hope that *other rulers* treat me with more *grace*. Goodbye, your Royal . . ." He trailed off. "Why are you shaking your head?"

"Your mistake is flattering, but I'm the chancellor. Felix Noor, advisor to the king. I'll pass on the bit about infrastructure."

The sorcerer settled for grimacing in response. Looking somewhat defeated, he muttered a portal into existence, an unfurling hole in reality through which he stormed with an imperious flap of his robe. His wooden servants followed, crawling and leaping, the portal folding shut behind them like the closing petals of a flower.

"Well," said the chancellor, taking a sip of his wine. Then again, "*Well.*"

Bodies jammed the double doorway. Too lost in their panic to notice the sorcerer's departure, the crowd pushed and shouted, worsening the clog. Trampled citizens lay scattered through the room, dead or unconscious, alongside a number of prone knights, while pieces of shattered monstrosities lay twitching in their desire to follow their master. Blood speckled the tiled floor and smeared the tapestry where the Elder had slid down it.

The chancellor took another deep draught from his goblet. "He's definitely mad," he murmured, pulling thoughtfully at his beard, "but good show, nonetheless."

CHAPTER 1

In Which Forty Years Have Passed and We Meet a Handsome Knight, the Hero of Our Story, Who Is Over Six Feet Tall and Has Straight Teeth and Nice Hair and Wonderful Musculature and Who Is Only a Little Bit Frightened. Not Even Frightened, Really, Just Reasonably Worried. Or Rather, Alert. Yes, Let's Go with Alert.

I tried to keep my grimace on the inside, and very nearly succeeded.

In a miraculous act of stupidity, the last scouting group had caught a construct and brought it back to the Order outpost. They'd cleared out a pen of unicorns, locking the peevish mounts into their stalls, and tied the thing to a stake typically used for breaking yearlings.

It glowered. Its eyes spat green flames. Hopping on its remaining leg, it swung the stumps of its wing-arms and seethed at us all.

A crowd formed about the pen, men sitting atop the bars to laugh and throw stones. With ale dispersed and skewered rabbit sourced from the kitchen, the scene had a carnival atmosphere.

I was the only one not caught up in the mood. The construct's wooden beak jabbed at the air in sudden, unnatural movements that accentuated the artifice of the thing, but that wasn't the worst of it. The worst was the way it quieted all of a sudden and looked at us—really looked at us, one by one, as though memorizing our faces. For what purpose, I couldn't say—it would be dead and burned by sundown, and had no means of communicating with its comrades. Still, as those flame-eyes flicked from knight to knight, I found myself shrinking. And when its eyes met mine, the boiling hatred in them made me cry aloud.

Maybe I fell back a little. Maybe the knights behind me provided support until my knees regained their solidity. Who can say? By the time I was paying attention again, those terrible eyes had moved off me, while the eyes of nearly everyone else turned my way.

"Perhaps Vaillancourt can give it a try?" a voice called out, and cheers rang about me.

"Eh?" I said—and then hands shoved at my back, propelling me toward the pen gate. Finally, my brain translated the crowd's babbling; they'd been talking about fighting the thing, for sport!

My legs locked, and my heels dug channels into the soil, but my fellow knights were all shouting my name now: "Sir Cameron! Brave Sir Cameron! Cameron the lionheart!"

Warmth bloomed in my chest. I could hardly disappoint my peers, who—doubtless in awe of my size, and my flawless golden curls—had elevated me to a status that frankly, I wasn't so keen on. "Thank you, thank you," I said, flashing teeth I knew to be a dazzling white. "But I haven't a sword!"

Something jabbed at my gut, and reflexively I flinched from it. "Take mine," said the grinning knight, offering the sword again. This time, I accepted the hilt before he could poke me with it.

"Ah." Sweat was gathering on my forehead. "That's so generous, really, but what if I chipped it? I really can't—"

"No bother." The knight's smile was too fierce, and too yellow, and stank of onions. "Chip away."

"Oh God," I muttered. A final push sent me stumbling, then a click sounded behind me. I was in the pen. And they had closed the gate. "Gentlemen," I tried, still holding the sword out for someone to take. "I, ah, love the spirit of this, really, but I don't have my armour—"

"It doesn't have any arms," someone shouted, and laughter rippled through the knights. "You make a good pair!"

"I have an upset stomach!" I cried. "I ate a bad trout. Something might happen!"

"We'll stay upwind," another voice called.

Slowly, very slowly, I turned to face the construct. My tight-laced jacket—though it looked *fantastic*—restricted my motions. The stylish sleeves scarcely allowed me to raise my arms above the shoulders, and they expected me to swing a sword?

I mean, I could. Very well, in fact. Just . . . not now. At any other time, though, certainly.

Shouts rose from behind me, taking on a sharper edge the more I hesitated. The pen, already clipped clean by unicorn teeth and trodden into mud, now contained a small ditch where the construct hopped and twisted and clacked its beak. The thing, in its fury, was digging itself into a hole.

I swallowed and marched forward, stepping around heaps

of unicorn dung mottled with flies. Their buzzing reflected the keening in my skull as I drew closer and closer.

Twin green flames fixed on me. A chain hooked through the construct's gut, the other end securing it firmly to the pole. My sword gave me a longer reach than the beast, but if it were to seize me and close that shear-like beak across my face...

Sweat loosened my grip on the sword. I clenched my fingers, determined not to fumble.

"It isn't worth it," I mumbled, too quiet for anyone else to hear. "Just leave and be humiliated. This simply is not worth it."

The construct tilted its head, flames wavering with the motion.

I circled it, eyeing the carved-up soil, judging how much leeway the chain gave. On my third circuit, the construct lunged. I fell backward with a shriek, and scrambled away, scarcely keeping hold of my weapon, while on all sides my fellow knights jeered and hooted.

Standing and brushing myself free of dirt, I smiled and waggled the sword at them. Just to make it clear I was a participant in the fun. Then, the construct twitched a claw—I swung back to it, holding the sword at a practiced angle. Noise no longer carried past the pounding in my ears.

Lunge, and swing. Lunge, and swing. That was all I had to do. "Easy peasy," I babbled.

The construct darted forward, its foul beak stretched in a silent scream. A non-silent scream tore from my own throat. I lunged and swung, impact jarring my elbow.

The construct's head bounced, twice, before rolling to a stop before my feet. As I stared, the green glow of its eyes faded.

"Oh." I took quick steps backward, away from the broken

thing. Belatedly, it occurred to me that I should wave at the crowd and have them cheer. I held the sword high, where it vibrated with my arm's trembling. "Huzzah!"

If I didn't know better, I'd say the men looked disappointed. "Let's go," someone muttered, and the crowd began to disperse, knights hopping from their bars and tossing rabbit skewers. It didn't take long for the area to clear—except for the knight who'd lent me his sword, who waited, palm out. When I placed it in his hands with gracious thanks, he simply grunted and left.

Which left me alone in the pen with the decapitated construct. Deprived of life, it looked no more dangerous than firewood. Yet I could still make out the contours of its empty eye sockets and the gape of its beak. I shrugged off my unease and left, unhooking the gate with only minor difficulty. "They called me a lion," I muttered, as I followed my stomach to the dining hall. "That was nice. I am a bit of a lion, aren't I?"

The long, dreary room was already full by the time I filed in, the torchlight flickering with the force of the noise. I slid in beside Sir Babbet, whose silence I could usually rely on. It'd be best if my jangled nerves weren't rubbed upon any further, at least for the evening.

"Lads." I nodded in greeting, then leaned over to grasp a plate of roast beast. My fingers brushed the edges of it but couldn't quite hook on. "Could someone, ah . . ."

A thickset knight pushed the dish toward me with enough force that I flinched. "Sir Cameron," he boomed. "I caught your performance."

"Thank you!" I said, before realizing that he'd forgotten to add a compliment.

The knight chewed slowly, flecks of meat occasionally making their way down his chin. "Anyway. Didn't think we'd be seeing you today."

"Oh? Why is that, Sir Galahad?"

A nasal voice pitched in from across the table. "When battles brew, you always seem to go missing."

"Do I?" I filled my plate carefully with slices of roast griffin-duck. The gravy dripped abominably, and I was wearing my best jacket—a scarlet that set off the rosiness of my cheeks, slashed along the sleeves to reveal an underlayer of Vaillancourt gold. "Anyway, who's fighting?"

A hush fell over the table, and too many heads once again turned my way.

"Cameron," called that nasal voice again. "We are. With the mad sorcerer."

I craned my neck until I found the source: Sir Regulus, gravy dripping down his fingers, and splashed liberally through his curling mustache. "Good God, man." He laughed in a spray of meat. "Did you not know?"

"I only meant"—my face warmed, but my smile remained unwavering—"that I did not know whose squadron had been, ah, singled out for the honour."

"No one knows." He shrugged broadly. "But with Elders here, something must be going down. I hear your elf's been walking about with them."

"Glenda? She mentioned a meeting, but—"

"Then you don't know anything?"

"No," I started—but in confirming my ignorance, I lost their attention. Sir Regulus turned to shout at another arriving knight, and voices rose in an impenetrable wall.

I sliced the griffin-duck into smaller and smaller ribbons while I waited for the noise to subside. A battle . . . usually, I was more on top of those.

Granted, my best source of information had recently been slain in combat: Sir Hamlin, who'd put up a great show of *'Oh but we can't do that, we're both men,'* only to stick his hand down my breeches behind the unicorn stable.

A bead of sweat trickled down the tip of my nose to splatter among the desecrated meat on my plate. I'd been sent here by my father with the expectation that I fall in combat, joining Sir Hamlin, and Sir Wilkin, and Sir Xiu, and . . . whoever else numbered among my dead comrades. Too many to have them memorized. God bless them, and all.

Point was, avoiding that particular fate had become a full-time job.

"Lads," I said, standing with a screech of my chair, "it's been a pleasure, but I do think that I, ah, have somewhere else to be."

Sir Babbet leaned to look at my plate. "Did you even eat any of that?"

"What?"

"Your food."

"What about it?" I tapped impatiently on the head of my chair. "Look, I'd love to chat, let's catch up some other time, but for now I've got to go. Alright?"

His face screwed up in a sort of bafflement, but I was already on my way.

My first thought was Glenda—but no, she'd still be in her meeting. I sometimes bribed the outpost scribe for intel, but then, the Elders had commandeered him for notetaking, hadn't they?

Paralyzed by my lack of options, I sprawled across a bench in the common room beneath the banner of the Vaillancourt lion. We'd eaten while the sun was still high in the sky, so the room remained muggy with warmth. Even as I plotted, even as stress ate at me like hunger—as a matter of fact, it probably *was* hunger—I couldn't help but succumb to the heat. My eyelids grew heavy, and I yawned.

"Cameron."

I nearly fell off the bench. "Glenda! You're back! How was the meeting?"

The elf stood too close, her blue face twisted into a strange expression. "Pack your things," she said. "We have to go. Now."

CHAPTER 2

In Which Our Handsome Knight Is Very Confused as to Why We Had to Leave So Abruptly but Is Committed to Being Charming About It. In Which Charm Might Come Easier if I—I Mean, if He—*Knew What the Fuck Was Going On.*

The closer we got to the mad sorcerer's territory, the more malevolent the trees looked. They crowded about us, roots bulging from the soil and daring us to trip.

Glenda walked in silence, avoiding any leaf or twig that might crunch underfoot. It was a wasted effort, as I stumbled over the uneven ground and caught myself on branches with apologetic grunts, but I tried not to fret over the noise. With Glenda at my side, the borderland woods felt relatively safe. The sorcerer's constructs always fell easily to her flashing blade, and her condescension toward humans meant she thought nothing of me hunkering back while she fought.

Securing her friendship had kept me alive while other, better knights took their rest in the soil—so her current moodiness put me on edge. Since her meeting with the Elders and our hurried departure, Glenda had barely spoken two words. Though when I'd walked out in a padded gambeson (secured with buttons of polished unicorn horn), she'd shaken her head, violently, and told me to change into something lighter.

Had I pissed her off? I always tried not to, elves being a class above even petty nobility such as myself. I peered at her as we marched beneath the bristling trees in the fading remains of daylight. She didn't seem angry. She looked . . . sad. Loose hairs stuck out from her normally meticulous braid, and she chewed fretfully on her lip. Feeling my gaze, her eyes flicked up to meet mine. I reeled back, pretending to study the flight of a bird overhead.

I did consider, briefly, that her mood might have nothing to do with me; that she might have a life of her own, independent of my existence. Only briefly, though.

"Glenda," I said, after we'd settled on a spot to spend the night. "I suppose the meeting went . . . ?" She looked at me with red-rimmed eyes, and I lost my nerve. "Ah. Never mind."

Had she found out about Sir Hamlin? Anxiety filled my mouth with saliva, which I swallowed. Glenda was so . . . *passionate* in her adherence to Order. Though perhaps it could work in my favour, if I allowed her to guide my 'repentance.'

With increasing agitation, I built a campfire, cooked her a vegetarian broth, gnawed at my own rations, then dove into my sleeping roll. Roots poked at me through the burnished leather and rabbit skin; it felt like I'd lain across someone's bony feet. "Glenda," I tried again, shuffling to get comfortable. "Is something wrong?"

She gave a hiccup of laughter. It had an oddly hysterical tinge.

"Come on." I raised onto an elbow to squint in her general direction. "I know something's wrong. My brother sulked just like this when he had to kill one of his fancy goats for Descentmass."

"Oh." She sighed, and I heard her rolling to face me. "That's horrible! If he had a bond with that animal, it should have been respected."

"Glenda, I won't let you change the subject. You're upset about something non-goat related, and I'd really like to hear it."

Silence stretched, long and tense. Eventually, I gave up and snuggled back into my roll. Too full of nervous energy to sleep, I listened instead for the creak of constructs. They rarely struck at night, and Glenda's hearing surpassed mine regardless, but logic could only put small dents in my fear.

Then, she spoke, in a whisper so soft I nearly missed it. "Cameron. You're going to die."

"Sorry?" I scratched at a bug bite. "I'm sure I misheard you. I'm going to *what*?"

In response, sniffling, and the crunch of a small body curling inside a hemp bedroll.

I threw back my covering and sat up. "Glenda, come on. Why am I going to die? What does that mean? That's such an alarming thing to say. Do you mean in terms of our respective lifespans, I'll die first? Or do you think I have a disease, or . . . ?"

I couldn't complete my sentence. The Order didn't *execute* people for minor sexual deviancies—and certainly not someone of my station. Right? They wouldn't. They couldn't.

The shadowed lump, barely discernible as Glenda, remained mute. Of course, with her elven night-vision she could see me perfectly as I gaped at her. "Glenda?" I said again, groping about for a stick to poke her with.

"I'll tell you in the morning!"

I waited a few beats. "You promise?"

She wailed, then muffled it. Like she'd clamped a hand to her mouth. I fully intended to press, but then the sound of weeping reached me, and I lay back in baffled silence. Glenda's crying continued for a good while until, after a round of loudly sucking in snot, her distraught breaths evened out. Soft snores filled the air.

Frustration heated me as I lay in the dark. She'd left me to wallow with such a horrible notion while she escaped to dreaming!

But I relied on her. I couldn't afford to be anything but charming.

All attempts to empty my head proved useless. I cycled in and out of a half-awake state, always conscious of the roots beneath my back, and the itch of mosquito bites, and my own impending death. Especially that last one, if I was being honest.

When the dawn chorus rose, robins and blackbirds and hedge-griffons all chortling and whistling in competition, I wanted to cry aloud. Instead, I began the day.

It made for an easy routine: put the fire back up, comb my golden hair to perfection, and heat Glenda's breakfast in a little pot—mushrooms and seaweed, with a decadent slice of ginger. For myself, I had a fistful of dried meat. It tasted like shoes.

Eventually, Glenda woke. The morning light filtering through the branches cast dappled spots across her blue skin as she stretched.

I chewed at her, open-mouthed. "So, I'm going to die?"

"Please," she said, rubbing her eyes. "May I have something to eat first?"

I gestured at the pot, then shoved the jerky into my mouth, whereupon I choked. While Glenda sat cross-legged on her bedroll, weaving her silver hair into an intricate braid, I spat the jerky into my hand and had at it again in smaller, rodent-like bites.

Having made herself decent, Glenda joined me by the fire. She took the bowl I offered, and added something from her pocket—flavouring, I supposed.

I waited impatiently for her to slurp it all down, then tried again. "Why am I going to die?"

Carefully, Glenda set down her bowl. Her overlong eyelashes shuddered as she stared into its empty depths. "Because of the prophecy."

My first thought was: thank God this wasn't about Sir Hamlin. With unearned relief, I bumped my leg against hers in a comradely manner. "What exactly is 'the prophecy'?"

"They made me promise not to tell."

"But you've already told me. You might as well finish the job."

She tilted her head back, so that her braid hung straight like a noose. "This isn't a scouting mission."

Was she looking for a reaction? "Oh!" I provided.

"We're traveling to a battleground, where our men will fight the sorcerer's foul constructs, and you—" Her voice cut off in a choking gasp. A fleck of her spit landed on my knee.

". . . will die?" I completed, wiping it off with a thumb. "Wonderful. Good to know. Obviously, I won't go, then."

She burst to her feet, and I flinched back, startled. "You don't understand! If you don't die, then none of the rest will come to pass!"

"Oh?" My heartbeat picked up. "And what's the rest?"

Glenda began to pace tight circles around our clearing. "The Elders," she said, deftly avoiding a root, "burned the last dragon heart to fuel a powerful magic. In the prophetic vision that resulted, they saw the mad sorcerer defeated, and the world saved."

"Hey, that's fantastic!" I said, and succeeded in swallowing *'Now what the fuck does that have to do with me?'*

She nodded, confirming that yes, it was fantastic. I wondered if I should stand too, or if she might perceive that negatively. For a human woman, a man towering over you during a tense discussion might prove intimidating—but for an elf, with their superior strength and magic? I wasn't sure, so I stayed seated, twisting my torso to follow her movements.

"And they saw the death of a tall, golden-haired knight." She stopped with a pursed, lemon-sucking mouth. "They saw you."

"Ah," I managed. "But how certain can they be? It can't be completely conclusive, can it? Is it?"

She nodded gravely. "It is. You die in this prophecy with a sword through your throat."

"No," I said. It came out like a belch, unbidden. At the look on Glenda's face, I quickly amended to: "No . . . way! How incredible that . . . what I mean is that . . . that's such a fantastic amount of detail!"

"Oh yes, the prophetic vision was clear in every particular. The method of your death, the meadow it happens in, even down to the length of your eyelashes. You do have such long eyelashes for a boy."

No longer able to manage words, I simply nodded with enthusiasm.

The twitchiness of her excitement brought bile to my throat. On some level, the drama clearly appealed to her. "At the meeting with the Elders, they shared the prophecy with me at great magical expense. That's how I know all this . . ." She spoke in slow, deliberate fragments, drawing it out. "I was even able to assist them in identifying you as the golden knight. Sorry, did you say something?"

I'd let out a small noise. "Nothing. Please . . . please continue."

She did, frowning. "A prophecy is like a recipe. In order to get the end result, you must follow each step."

"And I'm one of those steps. What an honour, that it all hinges on my . . . on me." I cleared my throat, but the lump remained. "And what an honour for you, too. Considering the role you played."

"I'm so happy you see it that way! Because it is. It is such an honour." Glenda wiped delicately at one eye. "Once the war is over, I was thinking I could dedicate myself to the arts. And like, sculpt a commemorative statue of you, for people to leave flowers at! That's why I keep looking at you. It's to memorize your expressions. How your lips move, how your forehead creases . . ."

"Wow!" I said. "How fantastic that my forehead creases will be preserved."

She giggled, leaning back against a particularly gnarled and menacing tree. "It's such a relief to have told you. We should pack up now, if you're ready?"

How could I ever be ready? Even so, I rose on wobbly legs and obediently kicked dirt over the fire, choking its embers. Scraping out a piece of seaweed from the pot, I carried it to be packed.

"I mean," I said, finagling the damp metal into my leather bag. "I guess there's no possibility that I survive this? I'm just concerned, you know, that the sorcerer's reign of terror might continue unabated."

"Please don't worry about that!" Glenda looked up from compacting her bedroll, her mouth open in alarm. "We'll ensure it comes to pass. If the enemy fails to strike you down, I—that is, *someone* is assigned to the task. So don't worry about rushing into battle or standing in a certain position." She rolled her eyes to show the silliness of the idea. "Just show up and leave the rest to us!"

The muscles in her slender arms flexed as she tightened the drawstrings. I bundled up my own bedding, securing it into the belts of my pack, waiting until I felt certain that my voice would hold. "I suppose *you* could even be the person who . . . I mean, I won't be mad or anything, but maybe you, uh. Have further instructions?"

Despite my stumbling, I saw understanding on her face. "It might be better if it's someone you know. A-and—" she stuttered, and the tears that had threatened all morning spilled down her cheeks. "It should be someone who loves you!"

"Thank you, Glenda. I appreciate you telling me. Now I won't be scared at all when you stick a sword through my throat."

She frowned, as if finally detecting my lack of sincerity.

"I mean that sincerely," I added, shouldering my pack. "Thank you, Glenda."

CHAPTER 3

In Which I Am Very Scared of Death and Feel Very Small and Shaky and Would Like to Bite at My Hand so as to Focus on the More Manageable Sensation of Pain, except that I'm Certain Glenda Would Look at Me Funny.

I hadn't always been afraid of death. Or at least, not so obsessively.

It was like complaining of a disease—*'I wasn't always stumbling about and covered in sores!'*—except that it existed only in my mind, where nobody could see it to spit in disgust. Why I proved weak enough to catch this fear while others seemed immune, I didn't know.

The moment of infection . . . *That* I could pinpoint with certainty. It happened during a childhood tutoring session on the Descent. I was sitting in the shadowy depths of our manor's great hall, while outside I knew it to be sunny and warm, my eyes not quite focused on the man across from me.

At first, I struggled to pay attention. It didn't help that my tutor-priest spoke wetly, like he was holding a mouthful of saliva. I already knew the broad strokes of his lesson: the ancients, with their heretical devices, pumped poisons into the air and water, and instead of seeking a solution, they simply retreated indoors, leaving the outside world to rot and die. You might imagine that watching all this, God would grow rather fed up, and so He did!

One day, He snapped. Or rather, He Descended. Like a parent storming into a child's room with a brush, He purified the world, blasting away the blasphemous devices with their gaseous emittances, and banishing the knowledge that had brought them into being. With blue skies and fertile lands restored, His true believers inherited Larnia, and all was paradise, forever and always.

At least, that was the version of events taught to young children. Having recently turned six, and thus passing some necessary threshold of sentience, my teacher could now detail how the ground had cracked and churned beneath the ancients' feet, and how all who looked skyward saw Him. How, in reshaping the landscape to His Design, vast chasms formed and sealed, the raw fire of Larnia's core exposed. And how, though all survivors received His Design, not all chose to abide by it, necessitating the hasty formation of the Church of Order, to keep the world on its ordained path by way of sermon and sword.

And despite my tutor's squelching delivery, and the worn familiarity of our hall, all those ancient deaths linked to the inevitability of my own in a rapture of emotion, like a saint awakening to religion.

The diseased knowledge entered me that every person burned or crushed in the Descent was once a fully realized human being. And that very little, aside from time and luck, prevented me from joining them and becoming similarly nameless and forgotten. From becoming *nothing*.

Digesting that all, I excused myself from the lesson politely, walked up a flight of stairs, hid inside a wardrobe, and got properly hysterical.

From that day onward, the Fear would descend periodically like the maw of an animal. Caught in its teeth, I'd curl up and sob.

And now, I had not years, but hours before my greatest fear came true. My skull felt tight, tingling, as though in the grip of a hand. Even the whistling of birds overhead sounded mocking. "Are we close?" I asked, hearing my own voice only distantly.

Glenda rearranged the pack on her shoulders. Despite her small size, she carried more than I did—a testament to her elven strength. I'd wasted precious time fretting, wondering why the Order hadn't drugged me, or at the very least, marched me with a proper escort, but when understanding finally hit it was unwelcome. The short girl walking at my side had nearly a century's practice in warfare and magic. Add to that her elven sight, speed, and instinctive ability to track . . . If it came to combat, I'd be greatly outmatched. If I fled, she'd be on my ass like a wolf after a three-legged doe. They may as well have hauled me to the spot in shackles.

Besides, the Order probably had precautions in place. Spy animals, hidden troops, spells waiting to be triggered . . . They wouldn't do it halfway. Not for something this important.

"We are," Glenda answered, and I started.

My mind buzzed with increasingly ill-advised schemes. She'd said she loved me. Clearly, she didn't love me *enough*, given that she planned to butcher me like a goat, but that could change. Perhaps a passionate dalliance on the forest floor would tip the scales in my favour?

I didn't particularly want to—but then again, I didn't particularly want to die.

And she liked me *like that*, she had to. She was always cooing about my looks—about my eyelashes, for God's sake—and now this love confession. Yes, I had a good shot. All that remained was to execute this plan with maximum skill and charisma.

"Hey," I said, all light and sexy-like. "Why don't we take a load off?"

Glenda, who'd been walking ahead for some time while I dragged my feet, glanced back. Her eyes looked sore and red from crying.

"Stop and rest," I clarified. "Or stop and . . . ah, other activities."

"We have a schedule to keep," she said, but something in my face must have convinced her to pause. "If you're not feeling well, we can rest. Sorry, I sometimes forget how quickly humans tire."

"I mean. There are *some* activities where I never tire."

"Certainly. I didn't mean to imply otherwise." Glenda removed her pack in a fluid motion and sank to the ground. She frowned at me. "Cameron, why are you undressing?"

I paused with my shirt half-off, my arms trapped in the sleeves above my head.

"Are you feeling overheated?"

"Yes!" I shouted gratefully. "It's a hot summer day, isn't it? And I was just thinking, well, it might be more enjoyable with our clothes off."

I didn't typically take the lead in these things. It felt cosmically mean that my life now depended on it.

"That's..." Her face was unreadable. "That's an interesting thought."

Dropping my shirt to the ground, I casually flexed one arm to push back the combed waves of my hair. "How interesting a thought is it, exactly?"

"I think there's a cultural barrier here. I'm not really following."

Aware of my clenched teeth, I relaxed my jaw. I was a golden lion. Everyone wanted me. Confidence was key.

Loping closer in a leonine fashion, I sank to my haunches and dropped a muscled arm around her shoulders. "I'm sure any barrier can be overcome."

I moved in for a kiss, and Glenda yelped, her head shooting back so fast that, if not for my arm, she'd have toppled to the ground. I froze, lips puckered.

"I'm so sorry. I've, uh, it's not you. I've just never been that attracted to humans," she said, looking anywhere but at me. This close, her breath smelled strongly of seaweed.

Realizing that my arm still trapped her, I recoiled, leaping to my feet. "But you ... I mean, don't you love me?"

"I do! I do love you." Glenda hugged her knees. "You make me laugh every day. And I've had such a wonderful time serving the Order with you at my side. My friends back home, they're always asking me how to get a human of their own." She tried to smile, but it wobbled and failed. "They love hearing about you."

A human of their own? "Isn't that somewhat bigoted?" I asked. It came out sharper than I intended.

Glenda rocked back like she'd been slapped. "I didn't mean—that's not—Cameron, I am going to miss you so, so much, and I will never forget you, I promise!" Her head sank into her hands, her breath coming in gasps.

I realized, as the noises became wet and clogged with snot, that we had entered another round of crying. And back came my anger. I was the victim here. I ought to be the one in tears, and yet here she was again, emotionally incapacitated by the slightest...

Hold that thought. She was incapacitated, wasn't she?

Something despicable occurred to me then, and I immediately accepted it as my best course of action. "Glenda," I said, fingering the hilt of my sword. "This is my last day alive, and you've already ruined it. Would it have been so difficult to peck me on the cheek and lie? Or am I too lowly even to touch?"

Her damned elven hearing could ruin it all... but Glenda had her pointed ears covered to better blunt my words, and her own swallowed cries likely drowned out some level of noise.

"You shouldn't have told me *any* of this!" I timed my shout with the oh-so-gentle snick of my unsheathing blade. "You broke a promise to the Elders, and for what? Just to scare me before I die?"

This outburst must have been shocking to her—we'd never had so much as a disagreement. But I couldn't spare any pity.

She belched something that sounded like an apology into her knees, her body quaking. I stood behind her, lining up a shot with the flat of my blade.

"Sorry, Glenda." And I swung.

Chapter 4

In Which an Elf Is Concussed, but It's Not Really My Fault because What Would You Have Done? Would You Not Have Concussed the Elf? No, Of Course You Would Have. We All Would Have Concussed the Elf. Besides Which, I Am Very Sorry for Concussing Her and Will Try to Make Amends Later if She Stops Trying to Kill Me. And Also, Her Intent to Kill Me Was a Highly Relevant Factor in My Decision to Concuss Her.

My plan of traumatizing and concussing an elf was a great success.

After she crumpled forward, I thought about giving her another whack, but decided against it. The smear of blood on the blade . . . had I really hit her that hard?

"You were fully planning to murder me." I rolled her onto her side in the dirt and checked her breathing. She looked like a newborn calf, all gangly limbs. "Fair is fair."

But still I stood there, peering down at her sadly—until her finger twitched, at which point I bolted with a choked screech. I did not want to be there to receive her bloody rage when she woke.

Some indistinguishable length of forest passed before I realized, with a nasty jolt, that I'd forgotten my pack. But it was useless weight, I reassured myself, full of pointless things. Like food. And water.

I'd also left my shirt, which the heat of my run made me temporarily grateful for. And my sword, God damn it all.

Well, there was no point obsessing over errors. All I could do now was run.

A root caught my foot, sending me crashing to my hands and knees. I scrambled up, panting and swearing, feeling the wetness of my scraped palm but not the pain. My body shook with the urge to keep moving, but instead I pressed myself flat to the trunk of an oak and tried desperately to *think*. Every second mattered. I had to keep running. But to *where*?

In early summer, the sun rose in the northeast. Using that as a compass point, I could roughly guide myself to any number of places. But the Order wouldn't waste time in broadcasting my fugitive status, and their influence extended, well, everywhere.

It felt like probing a fresh wound, but I had to think this through. My only friend wanted me dead. My lord father had *always* wanted me dead. No God-fearing citizen would shelter me, which wrote off all of humanity and the vast majority of elves. The dragons opposed the Church but, quite selfishly, they'd gone extinct.

Who then, in this entire world, could possibly grant me shelter? I knew who stood to benefit from my death, but from my continued survival, there was nobody, with the obvious exception of the . . . *oh*.

What a terribly interesting idea.

My paralysis broke, as my feet took me southeast—toward the sorcerer's territory. I tried not to overthink, focusing on my footfalls even as my breath burned. Every flap of wings overhead, every snap of a twig, sparked fresh surges of adrenaline. I tried not to think of the spy animals that the Order seeded through these woods, or the troops that likely lay in wait, or the knights who could even now be positioning themselves for an ambush thanks to squawked and chittered intelligence.

A robin zipped past my face, its breast an alarming slash of scarlet. Was its flight path unnatural? Had it come too close?

And if the Order had eyes on me, what about the sorcerer? This deep in the border woods, he certainly had spies of his own.

"Hey," I rasped. I slowed to catch my breath, only to startle back into motion at the whistle of a too-near grackle. "HEY!" I shouted at full bound, sweat-soaked hair matting my forehead. "HEY, MAD SORCERER! HEY, I'M HERE! HELLO!" Every yard brought me closer to his lands, with more chance of passing a construct. "SORCERER, YOU'RE GONNA WANNA HEAR FROM ME!"

If he did appear in a flash of foul smoke, my huffing and wheezing would immediately put the man off. A brief respite seemed more and more appealing, a chance to lie in the dirt and let my heartbeat return to a normal pace. Stripping me of the decision, another root caught my foot.

This time it hurt, my knee crunching hard into the dirt. A wail escaped, not of pain but of frustration. Okay, so I wasn't particularly valiant, but had I ever done anything *that bad*? Ignoring the events of earlier (best wishes to Glenda and all that), had I ever done anything remarkable, of any sort, to merit a singling out?

Grasping a nearby trunk, I hauled myself up, testing my leg. Sharp needles ran down my shin, and my eyes prickled with tears. I could run on it, but not fast.

"SORCERER!" I hobbled at a decent clip, grabbing branches and trunks anytime my knee threatened to give. If only I'd given Glenda that second whack to grant myself more time. If only I hadn't run off blindly like a prey animal. "SORCERER, I NEED A WORD WITH YOU!"

What was his name... it started with M, didn't it? Margaret? Malady?

"MALODOROUS!" I shrieked. "MATTHIAS! MAXIMILLIAN!" Damn it, why did everyone call him 'the mad sorcerer'? Nobody in recent memory had referred to that blasphemous man by anything but derogatory titles. "MADDOX!" And my knee throbbed so angrily. "MAURICIO!"

Shapes moved in the distance. A pair of armoured men, gleaming visions of death, emerged from the brush. They wore the balancing scale insignia and pristine white of the Knights of Order. Four more appeared, mercenaries or foot soldiers, indistinct at this distance.

They might not have seen me. I sank down, edging toward a trunk. Then a red-breasted robin landed on a knight's shoulder, all eyes turned toward me, and the last of my hope departed. It was a feeling of increasing familiarity.

The knights didn't shout as they advanced—they at least had the grace to pretend this wasn't a hunt. Released from its magic, the robin exploded into the air, disappearing into the canopy with a series of aggrieved cheeps. Having no similar powers of flight, I settled for sagging in place.

"Massimo," I said weakly. "Malodorous." No, I'd already tried that one.

As the men drew closer, I recognized a knight from my outpost: Sir Percival, a square-jawed carrot top with an infectious laugh. He looked deadly serious now, his strong features tense.

"Merulo," I tried. No, not that either. Or—wait. "Merulo!"

The men broke into a trot, reaching for their weapons.

"MERULO!" My voice sounded high and girlish. I suddenly saw myself through the knights' eyes, shirtless and flushed, with a buckled leg and too-wide eyes. I looked stupid and, despite my size, quite helpless.

Sir Percival brandished his sword, sprinting. They couldn't kill me here, I knew that, but cutting me to ensure I couldn't flee . . . ?

"MERULO, GREAT SORCERER, COME TO ME NOW, AND I WILL HELP YOU SLAY OUR GOD!" I roared at the sky, standing as tall as my bad leg would allow.

Sir Percival seemed to trip forward and fall backward simultaneously. I blinked, and his upper body separated from his lower, crashing face-first into the soil as his legs fell comically behind. The other men shouted, swinging at the air.

Constructs. The monstrosities rushed the men with no regard for their wooden flesh. A winged construct plunged with joyful frenzy onto a knight's sword, writhing down its length to peck at the soft tissue of his eyes and nose. Before his features disappeared entirely, I recognized him as Sir Galahad. He'd been terrible at card games—a deficit I supposed no longer mattered.

"Merulo, Merulo, Merulo," I moaned as a lupine construct with sharp wooden legs stabbed into a foot soldier, splattering his chainmail red. "Merulo, Merulo..."

A construct approached where I clutched, leaden, at a tree trunk. I stared up at the humanoid creature, its scythe dripping Sir Percival's gore. He wouldn't be laughing anymore.

"Merulo, Merulo..."

The construct hoisted its scythe and like a dam breaking, sense returned to me. My hands shot up in surrender. "I HAVE A MESSAGE FOR MERULO, IT IS OF GREAT IMPORTANCE!"

The scythe did not descend. The construct's face, a mess of knotted burls and cavities, seemed a deliberate mockery of human features.

"Uh, this is going to sound silly, and honestly unbelievable, but—" I stopped as the scythe moved upward, resuming its swing. "OKAY, short version! The Knights of Order—or rather their Elders—performed a prophecy ritual. Something to do with dragon hearts? Or a singular dragon heart? And it predicts the downfall of the mad—I mean, the Great Sorcerer Merulo, but only if I die. Hence why these knights are, ah, out to get me." My injured leg shook as I rose slowly, using the tree for support. "That's why, Merulo, your boss?" I waited for a confirmation that didn't come. "Well, he should want me alive and perky. It's in his best interest, after all."

The construct made no acknowledgement of my words, aside from not killing me, which I did appreciate. The copper smell of blood wafted from feet away, where bodies lay in pieces. Supplementing it was the stench of opened bowels; it summoned memories of a battle I'd deliberately arrived too late to participate in. I'd been surprised then, that a killing field could stink like a latrine.

At some unspoken order, two of the winged constructs erupted into the air, flapping toward me. Talons like tree roots closed around my arms.

I might have screamed and wiggled a bit, fighting their attempts to get me into the air, because the scythe-wielding construct raised its weapon meaningfully.

"Okay!" I said, going limp. "No, for sure, go ahead." And my feet lifted off the ground.

The constructs smashed through the canopy, drawing me upward. I spluttered, blinded by the wet slap of leaves—then we were out, the trees sinking beneath us into a green patchwork.

With the ascent came rising pain as my shoulders took the full weight of my hanging body. "Please," I cried. "This actually hurts a lot! Don't you want me alive, isn't that the point of this?"

If the constructs understood, they showed no sign of it. I dangled like prey between them, my shoulder sockets crunching, while their leaf-and-mud wings buffeted my hair into disarray. I couldn't do much but kick my feet and take in the view. Miniaturized in this way, the forest looked like a bed of moss, all puffy greens with the occasional shadowy gap.

Somewhere down there lay Glenda. I'd seen the aftermath of blows to the head; if she woke at all, she'd be aching and nauseous. Assuming she overcame her infirmity, she would follow my frantic, sloppy trail to arrive at its gory termination all alone, with her emotions already a ruin. Ah, poor Glenda.

"Poor me," I corrected, then frowned. The ground was rising beneath us.

We'd reached the sorcerer's cliffs.

The infamous fog rose in a white wall before us, which the constructs flew into without hesitation. It closed about me, cold, wet, and blinding. Without warning, both sets of talons released my arms, and I fell shrieking... only to land a second later, the ground a mere foot below. Even so, it jarred my knee.

Favouring my good leg, I stood carefully and rolled my shoulders. The constructs circled once, before vanishing upward, leaving me alone in the fog.

"Hello?" I called to nobody, rubbing my arms. Red punctures ringed them where the claws had gripped too tight. I stayed there, rubbing away, for longer than strictly necessary; anything to avoid my thoughts. I'd never been this far into his territory before. Coming within sight of the fog—let alone *entering* it—was suicide.

Nobody knew what spawned it. Nobody knew what effects it caused when inhaled; nobody had ever come back alive. And here I was, filling my lungs over and over!

A sound broke through my hyperventilation. Distant hoofbeats, growing closer and louder, until a head broke through the fog. Another construct, equine this time, with a body of interlocking driftwood and glowing eyes that cast the fog in green. It clattered to a halt, a steed from a nightmare, and I swayed on my feet in acceptance of my doom.

Nothing happened.

Nothing continued to happen, until I broke. "Did you want me to, uh, ride you?" I asked, evaluating the construct. While I stood a good six feet, it was the height of a war-unicorn. "You're too big. Could you bend down or something. Please?"

It didn't move. With some reservation, I approached,

pressing my palm flat against its shoulder. It was smooth wood, without any of the warmth or reactivity that would signal life.

"How do I . . ." Usually I had a block, or a convenient stable boy with cupped hands. Tentatively, I dug my fingers into the crevices between its woven branches, then with more confidence at its continued tolerance, I hoisted myself up, up, only to overshoot and half fall down its other side. I'd effectively beached myself across its back. "Shit, hang on, WAIT!"

The construct creaked into motion. I groped at its driftwood ribcage, hooking a foot around its gut so as not to slide off the trotting creature in either direction. Blood rushed to my head, the wood rubbing against my bare chest. "Come on, if I die it's bad for Merulo. This has far too much potential for bodily harm. Please!"

I bounced, griped, and chafed as the mulch of hooves on grass became the clatter of wood against stone. After an eternity (which felt more and more like divine punishment), the construct slowed to a halt.

I unclenched my fingers from the wood, allowing myself to groan at their stiffness, then pushed backward, sliding down the construct to fall ass-first onto the cobblestones. The blow drove a sick blossom of pain up my tailbone. "Ahhhhhhhh!" I exclaimed, and it helped a little.

Stepping over me with surprising delicacy, the construct clopped away, disappearing into the fog.

"Merulo?" I called, sitting huddled in the featureless space. Slowly, as though sucked in by a giant breath, the fog pulled back to reveal my location. From the escarpment before me rose a castle. Instinctively, I gasped—though my reaction came too early, as the sight was far less awe-inspiring than I'd hoped.

The mad sorcerer's castle was scarcely larger than a lord's manor house. Moss blotched its ugly stonework, gashed through by thin windows. If placed beside the castle I'd served in as a squire, it would've collapsed from embarrassment.

Occupied with my criticism, I nearly missed the constructs. Pinpricks of green light betrayed their presence first. As my eyes adjusted, I saw dozens of unnatural bodies clinging to the walls and battlements, crawling over one another like maggots on a carcass.

I reached for a sword I didn't have.

"And who might you be?" came a haughty voice.

My knee nearly gave as I leaped to my feet. Cursing, I limped around to face the man. "Ah, Cameron! I'm Cameron Vaillancourt. Sir Cameron actually, being a knight and all, except I've probably been excommunicated on account of not dying."

This unspectacular man couldn't possibly be Merulo. He stood about my height, but thin and bent, greasy black hair falling in curtains around scooped cheekbones and white flesh. From the frown lines carved into his brow, he was clearly my superior in age, but inferior in most other respects. A thorough victim of famine and poor hygiene.

"Your robe looks nice. Is that tailored?" I asked, complimenting what I could. It did fit well, a richly dyed black that provided a suitable backdrop for his threatening leer. One of the man's eyes gleamed oddly. I realized, squinting, that it was stone.

When he didn't answer, I continued, "Is Merulo around? Do you reckon you could call him?"

"I am Merulo." With a scowl, he looked me up and down,

pointedly evaluating. Perhaps taking in my physique, toned from years of swinging a sword. Or possibly my erect nipples, brought to attention by the recent cold and friction. "I suppose you think very highly of yourself." His voice held nothing but contempt.

"Absolutely not, I am a worm!" I protested, attempting a military posture. Somehow, he looked even angrier. Should I be addressing the sorcerer by a certain title? "Er, do you prefer 'sir' or 'my lord'?"

"Shut up." Merulo looked distracted, his inhuman eye flashing.

"Okay," I said. Then, after a pause, "My lord."

The thin man muttered, his eye flickering, and his attention diverted from me completely. Occasionally, one of his constructs would swing to glare at me—and the sorcerer would twitch his head in an echo of the movement, his stone eye flaring to mirror the construct's sickly green.

We'd all wondered at how his constructs took instruction, even shouting in argument over it on many a drunken night. Now, I watched as the mystery became unmysterious, and felt nothing but annoyed. This was top-shelf intelligence! He had a magic rock eye! And the people who'd most like to know would congratulate me for the discovery, pat me on the back, then push a sword through my throat.

Waiting for the sorcerer's scrutiny to return to me, I stood at straight-backed attention for as long as I could manage. Which, as it turned out, was about four minutes, after which I gave up and sat on the cobblestones.

Merulo glanced at me sharply, though he didn't cease his muttering or flashing.

"I'm injured," I explained, pointing to my leg. "But take your time."

With the sorcerer attending to his business, I held an internal strategy meeting. The man obviously lived a lonely, ill-cared-for life. Certainly, he couldn't have had his body touched in God knows how long—could I work that angle? He'd taken a nice long look at me, and I wouldn't mind, if it meant a stay to my execution. And though the Church enforced a certain traditionalism, I couldn't imagine a *mad sorcerer* would feel himself constrained.

While I scratched my head, considering, the sorcerer turned his hateful eyes on me, flicked his fingers, uttered something foul, and everything turned to black.

CHAPTER 5

In Which I Have Been Cruelly Robbed of My Consciousness, In Which That Bastard Has Laboriously Delivered My Large and Muscular Body to Whatever Shitty Room This Might Be When I Could So Easily Have Walked, and In Which, Dare I Say It, I Am Beginning to Doubt My Own Sexual Appeal.

Alright, so the mad sorcerer did not want to sleep with me. My clothes had been swapped at some point during my unconsciousness, though I couldn't imagine he'd done it himself. Not with those frail, anemic hands; I'd be too heavy to manipulate. Possibly a construct had changed me, pulling on fresh pants with its evil wooden claws. They fit loosely, and the metallic stain over one hip made me suspicious as to their origins.

"Did you pull these off a corpse?" I shouted to the empty room. "Why did you take off my moderately clean things and put me in unclean things?"

At least I had a shirt again. The fabric felt cheap, but I couldn't complain given the reprieve from my prophesied death.

"Might I suggest a wealthier corpse next time?" I guess I could complain. The wooden cot was unbearably hard, so I hopped to my feet, turning anxiety into motion.

Pacing the featureless room, the absence of pain struck me. My knee felt sore, yes, but not with the shooting agony that had left it trembling and weak throughout my escape. Ignoring the panic that fluttered through my gut, I felt curiously refreshed. Even my bowels felt taken care of. Had that excessively thin man healed me with magic?

I couldn't help a smile. This so-called 'mad sorcerer' might not be so bad, even if he had dressed me in corpse clothes for no discernible reason.

Still, I couldn't compliment the man on his accommodations. Only a slim beam of light, falling through a window slit, kept the room from darkness. Outside, impenetrable fog coated the grounds.

"Is breakfast a possibility at all?" I called to nobody, then started as a previously unseen door slammed open. A wooden arm emerged from the doorway, beckoning. Packing my fear into a little box at the back of my head, I followed.

Our footsteps echoed in the corridor. I'd hoped to learn more about the sorcerer from his household decorations, perhaps pass a painting or relic I could drop into conversation later—like, *'Oh your favourite lancer is Sir Bartimaeus, mine too, let's pour some grog'*—but dust buried the ancient furniture, and the walls were plain stone. All in all, the castle interior looked as shitty and dismal as its master.

Distracted by my observations, I smacked into something hard: the construct, which had stopped at an entrance. "Sorry," I said, backstepping hurriedly. "Do I go in there, then?"

No response. Hesitantly, I squeezed past the wooden beast through the open door. I'd barely entered when the creature came after me. I whirled, shielding myself with my hands, a memory flashing of Sir Galahad's face torn to a red soup.

"Relax," commanded a voice from the corner as the beast curled its talons around my shoulders and shoved backward, forcing me to trip over my own feet until I hit the rear wall. "I had them adjusted while you slept. They should fit as though tailored . . . just like my cloak."

I failed to understand, until the construct pulled my arm up and, with a clink, closed cold metal around my wrist. An experimental tug produced the rattle of chains. The construct maneuvered my other arm into the same indignity and—needing someone to protest to—I scoured the dimly lit room for the sorcerer.

Merulo stood under the dancing shadow of a wall-mounted torch, witch-light burning in his stone eye. He looked simultaneously pleased and annoyed.

A creak sounded as the wooden construct bent, pressing metal around my ankles, and leaving me jailed against the stone. Alright, so the sorcerer hadn't liked my comment about his cloak. Well, noted. I'd be stingier with my compliments in the future.

"Why am I wearing poor people clothes?" I asked, trying for some class solidarity. He lived in a castle, I was a lord's son, I reckoned we could get along.

The sorcerer looked away, clearly uncomfortable, which only piqued my interest. "It's a bit saucy, isn't it?" I pressed, giving him a smile. "Stripping me while I was laid out flat? At least let me be conscious so I can enjoy it."

"Oh, shut up," said the sorcerer, but he still looked ill at ease. "This doesn't usually happen, but the command word caused your body to slacken too . . . completely."

I cocked my head, not understanding.

"You shat yourself," said the sorcerer.

"Ah." Extending my awareness, I tried to mentally examine my rear. It didn't feel especially crusty, nor had there been an odour.

"The constructs"—Merulo cleared his throat—"attended to you."

"Well, seeing as you flung a 'shit-yourself' spell at me, that seems warranted." I peered at him, wondering if another round of my 'verbal abuse' technique was in order. It had worked marvellously on Glenda, with the negligible side effect of making me feel like scum.

His face darkened, stone eye flashing, and I decided to change tactics. "Thanks for patching me up, my lord, that was a nice surprise." I tried to flex my body in a healthy, grateful way, but mostly succeeded in jangling the chains.

"Well," he said, stepping closer and casting a significant look at me. "If your claim was truthful and not some desperate fabrication, any injury that endangers your life may also threaten mine."

It suddenly seemed of immense importance that I recall what, precisely, I'd said to that scythe-wielding construct. No doubt some of it had been embellishment and half-truth, but he didn't have to know that.

"Obviously, a truth spell is in order," the sorcerer drawled, and my stomach dropped into my nether regions. His spidery white hand disappeared into the dark interior of his cloak, emerging with something small and sparkling. A geode, with roughened rock on the outside and crystalline beauty in its exposed core. Someone had hacked the purple stone into a strange shape, its curls and loops somehow malevolent.

Merulo brought the geode to his lips and whispered something soft and slimy, raising a blue glow that spilled across its surface like fluid. Approaching my chained form, he shoved the precious rock under his armpit and, in a shock of contact, began unbuttoning my shirt.

I watched silently, enjoying the slow reveal of my chest hairs until, roughly, he yanked my shirt up and over my left shoulder. Retrieving the geode, he stamped it into my chest. The rush of cold energy made me gasp; it felt like the icy twin to a cattle-brand.

It was a seal, I realized. He'd pressed a spell onto me.

"And now," Merulo spat, teeth bared and face too close, "you will tell me of this prophecy."

I flushed. His breath, warm and odourless, was decidedly more pleasant than Glenda's seaweed-scented emittances. Did I enjoy being strung up like this, the constrained helplessness of my position, the cool shackles on my skin? Every day, we learn something new.

"Well, my lord, it's like I told the construct," I said, praying half-truths were permissible. "Our Elders performed a something-or-other ritual with 'the last dragon heart,' and in the resulting vision of the future, several steps were detailed. The person who, uh, disclosed this to me described them as 'ingredients in a recipe.' Every requirement has been fulfilled but the last one." At this I raised my eyebrows, feeding the drama. "My death. And the outcome, once it's all wrapped up, is said to be your defeat." I made deliberate eye contact, my confidence growing as the spell failed to compel the full truth. "They win, my lord. But only if I die."

"And that's all there is? Nothing more?" Merulo asked, his voice a deadly silk.

"Nope!" I said, then gagged.

The sorcerer leaned closer, grabbing my chin with a slender hand. His grip tightened, clearly trying for uncomfortable pressure, but he lacked the strength to make it anything but sensual. Could he feel my pulse, thundering beneath my skin?

"It seems," he purred, and I focused on the rich darkness of his human eye, "that you are withholding information from me."

"I am," I tried to deny.

With an animalistic noise, he shoved my head back against the stone, clenching his hand around the stubble of my throat. His body pressed close enough for me to feel its heat. The smell of pungent herbs and burnt wood overloaded my senses.

I let out a little sound of something that wasn't fear.

The mad sorcerer froze so completely that he resembled one of his constructs. With agonizing slowness, his gaze traveled downward. "Are you . . . What is *wrong* with you?" He leaped backward, nearly tripping over his own robe. "How could you possibly be erect right now?"

I jingled my chains helplessly, knowing any words that left me would be compelled truthfulness. "Well listen, Merulo, you're an extremely powerful man, and here I am all, you know . . ." I tugged my restraints in demonstration. "Seems like you could have your way, and little ol' powerless me, what am I to do but take it?"

His face twisted into something that even an optimist like me would struggle to read as lust.

"If it's an issue of consent, I absolutely do consent," I clarified.

"*It is not an issue of consent,*" he hissed, rubbing his hands, as if the brief contact had made them dirty. "I mean, not that I would violate someone's . . . but that's not . . . I don't want . . . I am INTERROGATING you!"

It killed the mood, if I was being honest, and I was magically obligated to be honest at the time.

Recognizing his loss of control, Merulo beat a tactical retreat. He stormed from the cell, yanking the wooden door shut behind him, leaving me alone under the torchlight with nothing but my thoughts.

An itch developed on my ribs. I stretched my fingers to combat the tingling. With each passing breath, the loss of sensation in my elevated hands became more worthy of attention.

The discomfort wasn't solely physical, either. In the stagnant quiet, something foreign to me grew hot and coiling in my chest: *shame*. These last two days, I had performed poorly, charmed nobody, and had certainly not been carnally desired. The prophecy obligated Merulo to keep me alive, yes, but a man could persist in many physical conditions that still qualified as 'alive.'

In truth, he didn't even need to maintain my life. He need only keep me from dying in that certain place, in that certain way. The truth seal felt bitterly cold against my skin, and I pulled my lips tight in hatred of its magic.

The door creaked. Pricks of sick-green light emerged, set deep in the canine face of a construct. Branches and twigs, shaped like something a cat might throw up, formed the mass of its body. It approached on tapping wooden claws, those green flames lowering to focus on . . . oh, for God's sake.

Apparently satisfied with my flaccidity, the construct clicked its way to the corner, standing to attention as the door opened once more. In strode the sorcerer, cool, composed, and pale as ever. I fought back a snort as a flaw in his careful persona became apparent: he could no longer look me in the eye.

"This is Benedict." Merulo gestured haughtily at the dog-faced construct that stood, statue-like, behind him.

He names them, I thought in wonder. "Hello, Benedict."

The sorcerer let out a long breath, as though I'd already acted poorly. Should the constructs also be addressed by a certain title?

The itch had returned to my ribs; with some effort I ignored it.

"Benedict," said the sorcerer in a strangled voice, "likes teeth. I'm sure he'd like your teeth very much."

I grinned, open-mouthed, indulging the construct as best I could.

"He likes to remove them for personal consumption," the mad sorcerer continued, and I shut my mouth with a snap.

"My lord," I began. "Is there a chance Benedict could, um. Have his needs met elsewhere?" Despite the cold stone at my back, a bead of sweat rolled down my forehead.

"That's up to you," said the sorcerer, and I heaved a sigh of relief. He didn't want a lover, being either deeply repressed or lacking a libido, but perhaps I could play another role. Servants he had plenty of, and could craft more at a whim—but what about friends? The castle looked curiously unlived in. Where was the mad sorcerer's family? Who raised him? What, above all else, did he need?

I eyed him, evaluating. "Well, I'm here to oblige. Say, I can't help but notice your, uh, dressing robe situation. If you need another man's help to assemble a wardrobe, perhaps I could walk you through the current fashions, teach you how to belt a tunic, you know?"

"Benedict, please remove a tooth."

"What am I doing wrong? Please stop, please stop," I begged as the construct clicked with slow menace toward me. "Merulo, come on, I'm here to help you, ah, to foil the prophecy and, er . . ." What had I said that had brought his constructs to my aid in the woods? "TO SLAY OUR GOD!" I shouted, chest heaving with effort.

Merulo signaled the construct and it stopped, taloned hand inches from my mouth, fingers already curled to pluck.

That's what he wanted, a fellow heretic! I scolded myself for ever doubting my ability to charm.

"The seal forces out what you perceive as the truth." The sorcerer seemed perturbed. "But an ordinary man wouldn't vow to kill God just to save himself."

His assumption surprised me, but I didn't contradict him.

The construct withdrew to its place in the corner, keeping those nasty twig claws to itself for now. Merulo looked at me sideways. "Cameron." The use of my name shook me, though of course I'd introduced myself the day before. "Did you only declare that . . . to save yourself?"

"Why yes, of course," I replied cordially—then wanted to swallow my own tongue. "Damn it. Please, please don't pull out my teeth, I'm absolutely willing to cooperate with anything you want."

The sorcerer's artificial eye hadn't flickered for some time. His attention, with the coiled menace of a too-still serpent, was fixed solely on me. "Then let's go over the prophecy one more time. And no more ridiculousness. I want short, concise answers."

"Yes, my lord, of course. I'm not entirely sure what you mean by ridiculousness, but I swear—"

"In fewer words," Merulo snarled.

"My lord, I'll do my best!" A gurgle sounded from my unfed stomach. I closed my eyes, feeling abruptly overcome by it all.

"There are details you've kept from me?"

My mouth twisted with the need to frame the word *no*. "Yes, my lord."

"Then you'll tell me everything now, and if afterwards I ask that question again and receive the same answer, my good friend Benedict will have the time of his wooden life in your mouth, and no amount of *'please, my lord*'s will stop it." The sorcerer seemed to enjoy mimicking my voice, though there was no way I sounded that high-pitched.

With reluctant nausea, I relayed everything that Glenda had shared the previous morning. I even included the bit about my eyelashes. At the end of it, the mad sorcerer assumed a thoughtful, distant look. His jaw moved as he chewed the inside of his cheek. "And that's everything?"

"It is," I confirmed warily.

Merulo surprised me first by giggling, then convulsing with shrill laughter. He wiped at his eye with a long, pale finger. "So I don't need you alive at all."

"Oh, that is entirely the wrong conclusion," I cried, spine rigid against the stone wall. "My lord, here you have a strapping young knight, completely ostracized from everyone who might oppose you, at your beck and call. I'd be loyal until the day I die because, quite frankly, everyone else wants to slit my throat and sculpt me a statue! And I have no strong feelings about statues, all that time and effort for something birds shit on, no thanks, so please, consider allowing me to assist in your assault on God."

Time passed with torturous slowness as the sorcerer stared into nothing, his eye flashing, muttering instructions under his breath. When he returned to me, Merulo's voice sounded distracted, dismissive. "You'd betray your comrades, your family, your . . . entire world and civilization? Even that elf girl, what's her name—Glenda?"

"Absolutely." I nodded with enthusiasm, dismissing thoughts of my animal-loving brother.

"Then there's a situation in which you'd betray me. It probably wouldn't take much. Answer me now," he commanded, "or I'll bring Benedict into the conversation."

I grimaced and spoke in as quiet a voice as the seal would allow. "I would . . . betray you. To save myself."

"Then we're done talking." He swirled that expensive black cloak and marched to the door.

Metal cut into my wrists and ankles as I pulled, frantic. "No, no, come on—Merulo, please, you owe me, they would have defeated 'the mad sorcerer' but I came to you instead, you OWE ME!"

Merulo halted. He may have been genuinely moved by my invocation of 'tit for tat,' but I suspected it was pre-planned for dramatic effect. This suspicion strengthened as his sickly face turned in the fire-lit gloom, and I saw nothing but malice. "Well. I can't exactly send you back into the woods as you are. Hmm." He smiled then, all oily and pleased with himself, and I felt sick to my stomach. "Your physical description, in this vision of the future, came quite detailed. Down to the 'girlish' eyelashes. I can't help but think . . ."

CHAPTER 6

In Which Glenda the Elf Has a Lovely Cup of Tea at Her Friend's Cottage and Most Certainly Isn't a Bigot Regardless of What Anyone Says, because Honestly, That's Such a Serious Word to Throw Around, and Anyone Who Understands the Situation Would Recognize It Was Unwarranted, and Really, She Should Just Stop Thinking About It because She Doesn't Need that Stress in Her Life Right Now.

"And then he called me a bigot," Glenda said in a hushed voice. "Can you believe it?"

Her elven companion raised a teacup to her lips and slurped delicately. "That's so stupid. People are attracted to the sort of people they grow up around, and like, can we help being raised with other elves?"

"Exactly!" Glenda slammed an open palm on the table, rattling her own teacup. Sunlight pooled honey-like beneath the cottage window, illuminating the veins in her pale blue skin. "And what's wrong with having a preference? If he said *'Oh, I only like girls with brown hair,'* nobody would give a crap. But publicly state you don't date humans, and people lose their minds!"

"You can't help who you're attracted to," Cerulina soothed, silver bracelets tinkling as she took another sip. "And it's not like we think they're inferior."

"Right, right. Like, I have so many human friends. You can think people are different from you without it being a negative thing. Like, take education." The elf's ringed fingers hovered over the plate of sugared biscuits that rested on the table between them.

"Education!" Cerulina echoed. "It's not their fault, obviously, but how can we be expected to relate to someone who can't play a single woodwind instrument? Like, at least string a lyre or something."

"I don't want to be rude, but the guy is barely literate." Glenda lowered her voice to a whisper. "He can't read *any* of the forbidden languages. I asked him once, and get this, he said, 'Which ones are forbidden again?'"

Cerulina brought a hand to her mouth in faux shock. "Oh my God, he didn't. That is hilarious."

"Right? Like, for attraction, there needs to be some level of . . . of feeling like you're with a peer. Not that I think any less of humans," Glenda added hurriedly.

"Of course not."

Both elves sipped their tea. In the calm cottage air, far enough from the outpost village to keep noise to a minimum, but close enough for morning walks to the market, birds cackled and sang.

"It's not their fault. It's just how things are. And that doesn't make me a bigot, for God's sake." Glenda considered the confectionaries. The plate was cleverly shaped like a leaf, and this time she chose a biscuit from its stem. She nibbled at it, a hand cupped underneath her chin to catch crumbs.

"Of course not. That was a stupid, stupid thing for him to say." Cerulina lowered her teacup to the table with a clink, scrunching her brow in exaggerated concern. "So, how's . . . ?"

"Cerulina! I don't want to talk about that right now," Glenda squealed, pushing her chair back as if she meant to leave.

Cerulina leaned forward, clasping her hands. "You promised you were going to quit."

"I know, but . . . Without Passionweed, I feel nothing. And I can't stand that. It's suffocating." Feeling the budding pressure of tears in her throat, Glenda turned her attention to the window and the gently waving branches outside.

Cerulina raised her brows. It had little effect on her unlined forehead. "You're so traditional in other regards. It just surprises me, is all."

"Oh, come on. I had a bad trip. One bad trip. And Cameron got the best of me. But I'd doubled up that morning anyway, so it wasn't a normal situation."

"You took *double*?"

"Oh, close your mouth. Yes, I took double. Because I was going to put Cameron down that afternoon, and the *emotions*. It would have been next level." Glenda glanced at her cup. "Is there any tea left?"

Cerulina lifted the pot and poured steaming amber into each of their cups. "And now?"

"I mean, I'm lowering my dose."

"Glen! You are *totally* addicted. And do not say 'I'm in control,' not while the back of your head is all scabbed. Can you go a week? Prove you don't need it for one week, and then at the end I'll do it with you." Cerulina drank from her freshly filled cup and closed her eyes in satisfaction. The scent of ginger and honey filled the room.

"Are you serious?" Glenda curled her hands around the warmth of her own teacup.

"Yeah, totally, we can party like back in school. But only if you go clean for a week."

Glenda groaned. "But I'm feeling so much good stuff right now. Like Cameron's betrayal, it'll feel way less sharp after a week. And I swear, right after everything happened, it felt amazing. So strong. I cried so hard it literally dehydrated me."

"You see, that's what worries me. Your health!"

"One week. Okay, I can do better than that." Glenda blinked dreamily. "If I stop using until we find Cameron . . . If I take it right before cutting his throat in that field . . . the hit of all those neurochemicals at once, after *days* of numbness, it's going to be like nothing I've ever felt. It's going to blow my mind."

"Yeah girl, that's the spirit. It'll serve him right, too." Cerulina drained the remains of her cup, smacking her lips. "*Bigot*, honestly. Who even talks like that?"

CHAPTER 7

In Which I Have Possibly Become an Atheist, because What Loving God Would Allow This to Be Done to a Man? I Mean I Remain Exceedingly Grateful Not to Be Dead, Not Meaning to Discount That, but This Is Otherwise a Completely Reprehensible and Fiendish Response to a Single Accidental Erection.

The sorcerer turned me into a fucking vulture.

"This is so mean," I wanted to say, but birds can't talk. Bastard that he was, the sorcerer relished having a construct bring me my first rabbit, its head dangling loose on a broken neck. He brushed off a dusty seat, dragged it screeching across the floor for a prime viewing angle, then sat, pointed chin in his hands, with an open-toothed grin that would have delighted Benedict.

Considering my hunger, there wasn't much inhibition to break through. If the sorcerer expected a show of *'Oh, I couldn't possibly eat a bunny rabbit with all its skin and fur still on,'* he should have transmogrified an elf. Admittedly, using the beak took some practice, as did learning the entry points of the body where meat would prove most accessible—pro tip, it's the soft, gummy organs of the face.

Merulo grew paler than usual watching me gore out the rabbit's eyeballs, and for my subsequent feeding sessions, he was absent.

At least the sorcerer didn't immediately boot me out of the castle. Not until I'd proven I could fly, on my admittedly majestic new wings. Now here I was, a bird in my prime, soaring over the sunken fog of the escarpment. From above, the sharp delineation between roiling white and normal forestry looked distinctly unnatural.

Past the fog line, the view became spectacular, a toy set of bushy treetops and the tiny black movements of animals. With the sun warming my back, the swelling of thermals beneath my wings, and the scent of a fresh carcass in my nostrils, life was good. It could almost be great, if not for that stupid, insidious question: What was the lifespan of a vulture in the wild?

A man could live seventy, maybe eighty years, if he had good teeth or someone to chew for him. My brother's fancy-feathered hens, however, had been lucky to live half a decade. Foxes took them, or bad weather, or they simply collapsed into a feathered puddle, having succumbed to one of an endless assortment of chicken maladies.

This body had the mass and nobility of a grown bird, so I was what, already halfway through its lifespan? How many years did that leave me? The Fear that once lived politely in my periphery had more of a presence than ever before, churning my gut, spoiling my food, fattening into a tumour of such nauseating weight that sometimes I felt my wings might give.

A passing crow shot me a look as I hovered and trembled. *'What, you've never seen a vulture with anxiety?'* I wanted to shout back.

I had to get out of this body. Step one would be re-learning speech. Step two would be to find a magic-user willing and able to restore my humanity. Scrawny, slouching assholes like Merulo couldn't hoard *all* the power, now, could they?

Circling downward, my telescopic vision locked onto a suitable perch. Surely, a selfless and beautiful mage waited for me in the great beyond, someone with a heart of gold and a convenient fount of magic. I pictured her—with her kindly eyes, and her willingness to do a bird a solid—and I knew that she existed.

Thus absorbed, I overshot the branch. My wings slapped at the air, a second tree was narrowly avoided, then the ground slammed into me.

I lay stunned, a feathery bundle staring up at the distant interlocking canopy. The forest floor, with its shifting shadows, felt dangerous in a way that it never had as a man. Any manner of beast might be stalking closer on gently padding paws, ready to sink sharp teeth into the clumsy, grounded morsel I'd become.

Shaking off dirt, and definitely not in a panic, I launched myself and, flapping frantically, managed to seize a branch. Time for practice.

"Herrrrraaaaooo," I squawked, vibrating the cords of my elongated neck. "Hehhh, hehh, heerraooooa. Healllrrooo. Hello."

Did the sorcerer understand what he'd done in granting me this form? I'd had the misfortune of encountering Strix vultures in the aftermath of battles, picking at whomever had bad enough luck to be lying around dead, and laughing in their voice.

My hope, carefully nurtured *away* from the twig-limbed sorcerer, was that Strix mimicry didn't start and end at malevolent chuckling. And, after days of frustration, progress was beginning to show.

"Heelllrraaaoo, mah, my nnnennnnnaaa naewk, my nayme is Camraahhhwk." I shook my bald head, talons shuffling along the branch. "Hello, my nahyme is Cameroawn and I betrawyed humanity!"

Alright, so maybe I wouldn't use that line.

It took a few more days to get the consonants down, in between prying at the ribcages of rotting deer and pointedly ignoring the odd construct that loped through the woods beneath me. Once I had a good grasp on vowels, my first point of order was returning to the sorcerer to bother him.

He wasn't on the battlements, casting his daily spell to renew the fog. Inside, then.

The castle windows, which had proved too narrow for my muscular man-body, suited my bird form perfectly. I wriggled through the aperture and, dislodging dust with each flap, began my hunt through the various lonely corridors.

The rooms that served as storage for bizarre metal objects, I ignored, as they had never in my time here been occupied. The dust lay thick and grey, with the only sign of life being exploratory vulture footprints from days prior.

I considered checking the cavernous library, with its imposing rows of shelving, but he'd gotten *so angry* the last time I fluttered in. Couldn't disturb his precious texts. If the mad sorcerer was in there, I'd have to wait for him to exit of his own accord.

After a few dead ends, and a surprisingly tricky descent

down a spiral staircase (I ended up hopping, rather than risk the tight space with my wings), I found him. The sorcerer sat shaving branches by a roaring fireplace, a stack of stripped wood piled at his feet. He rose to leave as I flapped in for a landing, forcing me to take off again and follow his imperiously retreating form. We arrived shortly in the castle's kitchen, where small humanoid constructs rolled dough and stoked the flames of a brick oven. Herbs hung from the rafters, tickling my back as I swooped to avoid them.

Plucking a handful of fresh scones from a tray, Merulo leaned against a wall and gestured for me to land, which I did with an extravagant flap and shuffle. I didn't bother trying for a scone. Not that I had any teeth left for Benedict to examine, but the sorcerer was clearly baiting me with some other torturous scheme in mind, and rabbits were good enough, thanks.

"Why a vulture?" I squawked as he chewed. "Honestly, I'd rather be an eagle. One of those brutes could nab me right out of the sky, if it wanted, and I've seen how the other birds respect them. Lovely feathers, too!"

I braced myself, anticipating shock, and yes, even begrudging admiration for my new vocal abilities. Instead, the sorcerer continued his slow mastication, a slimy sneer settling over his face.

"Why a vulture?" I asked again.

"An idiotic clown bird," Merulo spat. "A virtue-less animal that feasts on refuse. I think it's quite appropriate." He bit aggressively into the scone.

"Did a vulture fuck your mother or something?" I squawked, then ducked as a high-velocity baked good flew past my head.

"Now, how come you're so scrawny, if you've got all this food to chuck around?" I asked, and caught the next hurtling scone in a talon grab that was more luck than skill. Cackling to myself as only a Strix vulture could, I flapped from the room before the sorcerer could do anything more.

It took a couple of too-tight turns and some scuffed flight feathers before I found a window to squirm through. It was only then, out in the open air, that I realized nothing had pursued me.

Settling atop a battlement amid swirls of white fog, I ate my scone in peace. I pinned it with a taloned foot, prying with my sharp beak, until the inner bread, warm and fluffy from the oven, was at my mercy. Between beakfuls, I shat carelessly down the castle wall, another smeared white gob to join the rest. A construct flapped by, and I mantled my wings warily about the scone, but it didn't so much as glance my way. If any started trouble, outmaneuvering them would be simple; these half-alive constructs flew with less grace and intelligence than an arthritic sparrow. Less certain, however, was my ability to outpace them, as something told me that mud and leaf wings didn't tire like flesh.

A shiver of dread put my feathers on end.

"Why should he be mad? He's the one who fucked me over," I grumbled, then winced, hoping the construct circling some distance below hadn't caught my words.

Another swallow, then I was off again.

It took some questing wing flaps to find the billow of a thermal. Soaring high, I returned to my musings about that hypothetical mage. 'Limited' was the best descriptor for my magical knowledge. 'Humble.' Children from all but the most isolated homes had their magical reserves tested at an early age, and I, like the majority of humans, had exceedingly little. I could barely levitate a pebble.

Even for those born gifted, magic had harsh limits. A wellspring of set size existed in each person. That power could be siphoned out, either in small trickles or roaring torrents, but once drained it did not replenish. Hence the tendency toward magical miserliness. When every good deed sucked you dry just that little bit more; when on some fearfully anticipated day, you'd speak a spell only for it to crumble on your lips, leaving you with fading memories of a power that once came like breathing . . . well. It meant that finding someone with not only the magic to shift my form, but the willingness to expend that precious resource on me would be difficult, to say the least.

I myself had been drained as a child, in a standard Church tithe. What scarce, pitiful magic existed in me had been extracted for the construction of a levitating cathedral. And not just mine—they'd gathered a group of local children for the ritual. An Elder gave us the words along with directions for how to void our power. As a choir we'd chanted and been rewarded with an impossible sight: a heaping mass of stone becoming light, tearing free from the earth that still gripped us.

One girl fainted, and my nose had bled, but mostly I remembered the wash of relief at never having to memorize those strange words again. Magic was a burden that all but the most gifted or wealthy disposed of in childhood.

This, of course, was what made the mad sorcerer so terrifying. He cast spells frivolously, wastefully, with less consideration than you'd give to preparing a pot of tea. And the enormity of his magic. How it showed no signs of waning, after decades of expensively maintained warfare! He drew from a colossal ocean of power, a single, scrawny man who could challenge God Himself.

He was an, uh, *inadvisable* enemy to have made for the sake of a mediocre scone.

No, I couldn't lie to myself. It was a fantastic scone. All buttery and warm.

Glenda knew some magic-users, didn't she? I flapped my wings idly, passing through the mist of a low-hanging cloud. She'd been bad-mouthing one last week, some 'who does she think she is' bog witch who'd made a hobby of calling forth undesirables and patching their scraped knees.

Well, I was plenty undesirable, and happy to wait in line!

Really, it was in Glenda's best interest to facilitate my return to man-shape. Merulo had acted with undeniable cunning: the prophecy clearly stipulated a golden-haired knight, not a vulture. Regardless of how she felt about our less-than-ideal parting, the elf should be willing to fork over the address of this helpful witch—or at the very least scrape a map into the dirt. And if, for whatever reason, she did react poorly, I had these lovely new wings to carry me away.

Still, I wavered in indecision until an incident at the bank of a stream. Birds have little ability to suck or lap, so I drank by filling my beak with the cool flowing water, and then ducking my head back, and letting it trickle down my throat. For all that it was an unnecessary amount of labour, I did find it relaxing. So much so that I nearly missed the crunch of a dead leaf. Animal instinct shot me forward, nearly spilling me into the stream before my wings managed a desperate downstroke. Flapping wildly, I spun in midair to see a black shuck-hound, tilting its head as though attempting a difficult math problem. It could almost be mistaken for an ordinary dog, if not for the vertebral ridges pushing through its wiry fur.

"That's it, fuck this. Fuck the sorcerer. Fuck you," I shouted, circling out of reach of the shuck. It sat back, watching me with lazy yellow eyes. "I'm finding Glenda. Fuck it! What's a vegetarian going to do to me, anyway? She eats seaweed, for fuck's sake. Fuck you!"

The hound yawned, giving me a generous view of its sharp white teeth, which just set me off again.

All this shouting proved tiring. Eventually, I ceased my wheeling and flinging of abuse, and set off to find my former friend.

I'd begun my quest rather late in the day, and the clouds soon darkened to a blood-soaked cotton. Before night fell completely, I found a tall tree to touch down on, and, with the sounds of nocturnal creatures scratching and snuffling in the woods below, I tried to sleep without fear.

The dawn song of smaller, lesser birds brought me back. With a great shuffling of feathered shoulders, I returned to the air.

It took me all morning to reach the outpost, and almost immediately I wished that I hadn't. It hurt, drifting over those familiar streets. There'd be no more patrolling in my armour, collecting swooning glances. No more drunken caroling. No more prying for information about upcoming battles to avoid. I missed my old life, but couldn't see any path to regain it.

Another problem: of all the people who milled through the

town, haggling over fried rabbit haunches or edging their way past the dung of carriage-beasts, none had the blue skin and silver hair of an elf.

I perched on a church spire with a great puffing sigh, and tried to think. What duties did Glenda favour, and where did they take her? Not hunting—she couldn't bear to harm an animal, and using her physical strength to gather resources would be beneath her. Sentry duty, then, somewhere on the outskirts.

I resolved to fly diligently over the forest, until either hunger or fatigue took me down.

The sun shifted overhead, and I searched. A patch of dark cloud threatened rain, and I searched. A mean-spirited robin chased me for a time, chirping insults, and still, I searched. Just as I'd convinced myself to give up for the day and find a nice carcass to tear into, a flash of silver caught my eye. I wheeled down for a look.

Glenda sat daintily by the edge of a brook, one foot tugged by the gentle current, the other folded beneath her. A sheath of arrows kept her spine straight, her long, meticulous braid falling in among them. She glanced up as I landed in a graceless splat of feathers, her face curiously blank.

I eyed the bow in her grip. *'How's the concussion?'* seemed a bad opener.

"First off," I squawked. "I'd like to sincerely apologize. I acted poorly, and do not expect forgiveness." Pure bullshit: this entire plan depended on me being forgiven immediately.

Glenda looked at me, unbothered to a degree that struck me as eerie. "I don't know any vultures," she said, cold and clipped.

"Well, it's your lucky day!" I cried. "Here I am, a surprise vulture pal!"

With her lack of reaction, it felt like speaking to one of Merulo's constructs. Slowly, she retrieved her foot from the brook, rising to her feet like a cat readying to pounce. It drove in how small I was, that even tiny Glenda could look down at me with menace.

"Promise not to get mad," I hurried, in the alien screech of my new voice. "But it's me, Cameron. And I am, again, so sorry for how we parted, violence is never justifiable, and—hey, hey, let's put down the bow, eh?"

She pulled an arrow from her back and notched it at an unhurried pace. Where were the waterworks? The joys and sorrows of reunion?

"You must be wondering, *'Hey, Cameron, how come you're a bird?'* Well, completely against my will, I was kidnapped, or rather man-napped, by the mad sorcerer. He cast some tricky magic, I fought back the best I could, blackened the bastard's eye, even! But uh, um . . . Anyway, he knows everything about the prophecy, and this," I raised my wings, "is his solution. Kind of clever, right? Because it's not a prophecy about a vulture."

"You . . . told that maniac about the prophecy. The enemy of humanity, the man who vowed to kill our God, *the mad sorcerer?*"

"Well yeah, I might have. The guy is a total asshole," I confirmed. "Sadistic prick. Honestly, can't stand him."

The arrow flew. I snapped backward, pinned to the earth, my wing first numb, then hot with a pain that blazed out concentrically, lapping at my nerves and flesh. "Glenda, Glenda, Glenda," I heard myself plead. "Come on, we're friends, let's talk this out. Glenda, NO!"

Glenda's foot descended on my prone body, pressing too hard for my hollow ribs to handle. Almost lazily, she bent to grip the arrow's shaft, and pulled.

Fiery pain erupted. I shrieked, my other wing beating uselessly against the soil. Without removing her foot, Glenda wiped the stone head on the grass, once, twice, before replacing the arrow in her quiver. Some vegetarian!

"These are expensive," she said, her eyes glassy and lifeless. "Can't waste one on trash like you."

Trash?! What happened to '*I love you*'? She had said that, hadn't she? Who was this person?

"You're my friend," I squawked, wetness spreading from my pierced wing. "I thought—"

"You thought." She laughed, a passionless bark. "That's a first."

"What the fuck, Glenda?" The weight on my chest increased, accompanied by a crunch somewhere deep inside me. Words flew through my mind, but not the right ones. Nothing linked into a rope that could save me.

I had failed at being a man—but I was still a vulture. My beak, long and cruel, a handy pick for opening deer hide and prying marrow from spinal cords, plunged with desperate force into Glenda's leg. She cried out, staggering backward. Elven blood in my nostrils, I shot to my talons and launched, up, up, branches whistling past. The next arrow caught me in the gut, punching through my back. I felt the impact, but didn't stop.

The protruding arrow dragged in the air, and the motions of my injured wing felt wrong, but still I flew, panting wildly, trying to ignore the blood that fell from me like afternoon rain. I didn't have to make it to the castle, just to a construct. The sorcerer would fix me, he'd healed my leg and magic was nothing to him. *Why* had I taken that scone?!

Either I blacked out or disassociated, because when I next came to, it was twilight. My wings, locked into position, felt like taxidermy. I tried a test flap, and found they no longer took instruction. Another attempt, and my pierced wing crumpled. The world rolled as I fell, spinning head over feathered ass.

It could all be over, no more struggle, if I just shut my eyes. Instead, muscles shrieking, I forced my good wing out, righting myself into a half-glide as the ground rushed closer. Branches broke my descent. Their leaves received me like groping hands, catching stomach-churningly at the arrow that impaled me, but I thumped into the muck-strewn ground both conscious and alive.

It didn't feel like I lay there long, but when at last I struggled to my feet, darkness had stripped the forest of colour. No possibility of flight remained, with my bad wing now completely numb.

How, how could I save myself?

I raised my serpentine neck to sniff at the air, enlarged nostrils filtering out the smell of soil, animal dung, and rotting wood, until I found what I needed: death.

The gore of opened organs and smashed meat wafted from a distance. It smelled substantial. Not a mere animal kill, then, but—hopefully—the result of constructs meeting men. I shuffled, limped, and hopped across the brush and dirt, every movement a pulse of agony, each step leaving more of myself behind in puddled red. I let that hot squeezing Fear spur me, as I dragged my body onward.

Ahead, light pricked the woodland murk. Stars fallen to the earth, twin fireflies. I approached them, or they approached me, I didn't know which, but suddenly they burned close and large.

"Merulo, help," I croaked as black swallowed my vision and construct claws descended upon me.

CHAPTER 8

In Which I Might Be Warming Up to the Sorcerer despite Him Being an Absolute Bastard with Terrible Fashion Sense, because the Shittiness of His Behaviour Makes the Occasional Non-Shitty Action Stand Out in an Almost Heroic Light, and Also, I Definitely Had a Sexual Awakening in that Interrogation Chamber.

"How you survived to adulthood is a mystery," said the sharp-faced man, as the construct hand-delivered me to the castle gate. I didn't have the energy to respond, instead choosing to black out again.

I awoke cradled in a soft material. Groggily, I snaked my head out. This room, lit by fog-dimmed light, and furnished only by the cot beneath me, looked familiar. I'd woken here before, on that first morning. And the nest of fabric . . . of course, the corpse clothing! Someone had washed them, thankfully, as they lacked the former bloodstain.

Shuffling my wings experimentally brought no pain, though extending the right one did produce a twinge. Tucking them back in, I gaped my beak in a yawn. Nothing demanded my immediate attention, so squirming further into the nested clothes, I retracted my neck and closed my eyes.

Upon my next waking, the door was open, with a dead rat deposited on the floor. Something, likely a construct, had torn its head off.

"Now what's with all this pampering?" I squawked in wonder, shaking my feathers and hopping off the cot to eat.

After hollowing the rat and preening thoroughly to remove the flecks of flung meat from my golden-brown feathers, I waddled out to find the sorcerer.

The click of my talons against the stone made for a lonely noise. Since the mad sorcerer was a creature of habit, I knew the route to take: right, left, left again, hopping down that spiral staircase, right, and here we go. The crackle of the fireplace from the wood-carving room confirmed my guess.

Gritting my beak, I pushed from the stone in a burst of noisy flapping, and swept through the doorway, flaring my wings to slow before touching down on a stack of wood.

"You've gotten better at landing," the mad sorcerer noted. He sat weaving cut saplings around a bleached-white core, forming the messy approximation of a limb. Behind him, neatly piled, lay more of the smooth white branches—no, bones. He had a stack of bones. *Human* bones, I corrected, spotting the cracked ruin of a skull. It was oddly poignant, watching the construction of an enemy I'd fought for years, their secrets bared to me so casually. All the constructs I'd seen hacked apart in the aftermath of battles had been wood throughout—but a fleshy, unnatural wood that flowed seamlessly into teeth and fingers. There must be a merging process between the bone and branch, one that imbued them with demonic half-life and connected their senses to Merulo's eye.

Finishing one limb, the sorcerer moved to another. He reached behind him to pluck one, then two long bones from the stack, then twined a thin, flexible strip of wood around the joint, connecting them. I grew less content to watch.

Probably shouldn't ask. It wouldn't lead to anything good.

"Why did you save me?" I asked. "I'm pretty sure you hate me, so it doesn't make much sense."

The mad sorcerer sniffed. "Because you are a pathetic jester. You'll suffer far more alive than you would dead."

Okay, so I really shouldn't have asked. I sighed, shuffling on my talons, then sighed again.

At my third sigh, Merulo looked up from the half-formed leg with a grimace. "What?"

"Don't you want to know the circumstances of how I got shot?"

"Not particularly." The flicker of firelight shadowed his hollow cheeks, making him look even more sickly. I wondered at the lack of muscle on his arms, given he seemed to spend a good amount of time manipulating weighty blocks of wood.

"Okay, so there's this elf named Glenda," I said, and then, in a quickening spill of words, told him everything about our second-to-last encounter, the one that culminated in my sword bashing her skull. I told him about our friendship, about my Fear, about attempting to put 'the moves' on her, the crying, how I'd left her crumpled on her side, skinny limbs askew in the dirt. And how that led to the unexpected violence of our reunion.

The sorcerer, for his part, seemed to listen as he worked,

and waited until I had exhausted my torrent before putting the woven leg aside and turning to consider me.

"So this . . . harassment." The sorcerer gestured broadly. "It's a pattern for you."

Of course that's what he'd focus on. "In no way did I harass her," I sputtered. "And I didn't harass you either, that was—that was a bodily reaction under circumstances outside of my control. In fact," I continued, gaining confidence, "some would say it was *you* who harassed *me*, with those tight chains and getting all up in my space till I was hot and ready to pop. Oh yes, I definitely feel like the victim of, what's the word for it, *inexcusable sexual harassment*."

"Are you done?" Merulo said calmly. I didn't trust the change that came over his face.

"Yes," I said, puffing out my vulture chest.

"Alright. I am going to kill you now."

"Ah, I can't win!" I shrieked, sinking into a quivering bundle of feathers. An unexpected reprieve to my Fear had come in the form of utter exhaustion. "I can't ever win! The world is out to get me, so go ahead. If it isn't you, it'll be something else tomorrow."

Squeezing my beady eyes shut, I waited for a blow that never fell. Instead, I heard the steady scrape of metal on wood. When I felt brave enough for a peek, I saw that Merulo had pulled a knife from the depths of his robes and was carving at a minuscule stick, the construct limb lying forgotten at his feet.

Some time passed, me watching and him whittling, before he spoke.

"The world is not 'out to get you,' Cameron. On the contrary, it's given you wealth, affluence, a comely physique"—

the sorcerer smirked—"though not anymore, vulture boy." He raised a hand to silence my protests. "You were given rank, without any merit or demonstrable talent, born into an undeserved social standing. One of the fair folk selected you for companionship, despite their noted disdain for humans. A prophecy inexplicably singled you out among millions, bringing the chance for a more significant death than most men dare to dream of, which would certainly have been followed by fame and folk songs of your 'heroic sacrifice.'" He imbued the words with the maximum amount of disgust. "And, when you chose to renounce that fate, assistance came from a former enemy, who gifted you a transformation that excused you from this prophecy, allowing you a free and undisturbed existence. At what point"—slashing at the twig in his hand with strokes that threatened to split it, his voice rose to a shout—"has the world *ever* been against you?"

"Oh fuck off, you turned me into a vulture," I muttered, though the 'former enemy' part did stick out as hopeful phrasing. It raised my spirits a touch; if the mad sorcerer wasn't an enemy, perhaps another sort of relationship wasn't out of the question.

In response, more frenzied whittling. I had never seen a man carve wood with so much fury. If he kept up this pace, I wondered how fast he could make a chair.

"There!" Merulo exclaimed, startling me. He brandished the carved splinter and, bringing the jagged thing to his lips, whispered to it like a lover. The wooden needle blossomed, its head puffing into an intricate net, until it resembled a key without teeth.

Grinning, the sorcerer beckoned me closer. "Come here,

little birdy." Obviously, I stayed put. "Come of your own free will, or I will make you come."

It should be held endlessly in my favour that I did not comment on the innuendo. Reluctantly, I hopped from the stack of wood and waddled across the room, stopping by his stool. The sorcerer patted his lap. I cocked my head in disbelief, before launching with a single flap and settling onto his bony knees, carefully, so as not to pierce his robe with my claws.

"You," the mad sorcerer began, placing a gangly hand across my back, "have become shockingly disrespectful of late. Without fear of me, and with no thought of consequences." In his other hand, he raised the carved needle. "This, my carrion-eating wretch, is a consequence."

"My lord . . ." I widened my pebbly eyes in my best puppy-dog impression—then shrieked as he jabbed quick as a viper, the needle sinking into my chest.

Oddly, I felt no pain. Looking down, my beak open in horror, I saw the needle's elaborate head protruding from my feathers, the remainder buried in my flesh. Something hung sparkling from the hateful thing. A translucent chain, of which Merulo held the other end.

"Now," said the sorcerer, with malevolent glee. "I am expecting visitors. Why doesn't my pet join me? You can perch on my shoulder."

"Sure thing. Only problem, are you going to grow broader shoulders with magic, or . . . ? My lord, I'm a big bird and there's a surface area issue with—AH!"

Ice stabbed out from the embedded needle, cold ruptures of pain that chilled me to the bones. *'Consequences,'* the mad sorcerer mouthed.

Fighting back a few choice curses, I launched myself onto his shoulder. *As I'd tried to explain*, I didn't fit, and after some scrambling and flapping, mussing of his robe, and grunts of frustration from both of us, Merulo shoved me off. "Just . . . just follow behind me, alright?" he said, flustered. "And stay mute. If you attempt to provide any assistance to the knights we are to meet, I will end your life with one twist of this chain. That is not an idle threat."

"Why would I do that, my lord?" I asked, watching him try fruitlessly to smooth the ruined shoulder of his robe. "I'm not being facetious. The Knights of Order would bleed me out like a goat if they could. They can rot. Although," I added, "if my lord would like me not to betray him, perhaps he could treat me a little more *kindly*."

Merulo raised his end of the chain in threat, and I shut my beak.

The sparkling chain seemed to expand or contract not according to any physical rules, but stretched to cover what ground it needed, so that I was able to fly at a comfortable distance ahead of the sorcerer as we moved through the castle. I did incorrectly guess which turns he'd take a couple of times, forcing me to backtrack.

On the third wrong turn, he shouted, "Just fly behind me!" in a surprising burst of rage.

"But, my lord," I said, blinking. "You're very slow." The sorcerer moved to twist the chain; before he could complete the action, I circled back and landed beside him. "Which is why I'll walk, of course."

That didn't work either, as a vulture can't waddle at the speed of a lanky man's strides, so I settled for occasionally surging into flight whenever I fell too far behind, a thoroughly tiring process. By the time we reached the castle gate, I wanted to go back to bed.

The equine construct waited, pitted eyes glowing green in the fog. It knelt as the sorcerer approached, allowing him to sit in a twisted but somehow elegant manner, with both legs dangling from one side. Side-saddle, like a lady. An accommodation for his robe, I supposed.

"Oh, so you do know how to bend down," I griped to the construct, landing on its rump. I didn't bother minding my claws.

As we left the gateway and began a bouncing trot down an escarpment pathway, I thought it safe to angle my ass over the side of the construct and let out a quick white gob that fell harmlessly into the fog.

A pained sigh came from the sorcerer. My emittance had not been as soundless as I'd hoped.

"My lord," I explained. "Birds don't exactly have bowel control. When you gotta go, you gotta go."

"You didn't have bowel control as a human either," the sorcerer said wearily. "And anyways, be silent."

"I will be silent, my lord, quiet as the grave, you won't hear a word from me, except that first I have to ask . . ." My grip on the construct's knotted back tightened as we descended at a steeper angle. How this thing could orient itself in the blinding fog was anyone's guess.

"You have to . . . ?" the sorcerer echoed disdainfully.

"My lord, we will be encountering the Knights of Order, yes?" I stared at the back of Merulo's oily head, wishing he'd turn so I could better gauge his expression. One of his hands gripped the bristle-twine mane of the construct, the other resting in his lap.

"Yes," the mad sorcerer replied.

"Well, my lord, not meaning to cause trouble, but if they have arrows, I'm outta there." I drove my talons into the construct, intending to remain perched even if a bolt of pain sprung from the needle, but my fear was misplaced. The sorcerer seemed too distracted to get properly angry.

With his free hand, Merulo reached into the depths of his robes. There came the clinking and shuffling of objects, then he withdrew a large metallic black leaf.

"Dragon scale," he said. I stifled a gasp. Could this be the key to his seemingly unending magic? The body parts of dragons could be burned in place of a person's own magical reserves, leaving the spell-caster undiminished, but they had a ludicrous price tag. For all of post-Descent history, slaying dragons had been a significant source of revenue, but nobody had seen one alive in at least a century.

If the sorcerer had stumbled on a dragon corpse, perhaps curled and mummified in some ill-explored cave, and entombed it in that fog-choked castle . . . Again, precious intel that could not be used. It would explain a lot, though. Everything but his hatred for God.

While I sat open-beaked, bobbing with the motion of the construct, the sorcerer crumpled the scale in a careless motion and recited what sounded like a whispered prayer. Before I could react, Merulo opened his hand and, swiveling, blew the dust at me. I sneezed.

Apparently satisfied with his work, the sorcerer returned to his original position. "Any weapon capable of cutting through dragon scale can still strike you down, and the protection expires at sunset—don't think this leaves you immune to injury."

"Only me?" I squawked, dumbfounded. Did the sorcerer already wear dragon scale protection? And why waste an item of such unthinkable value on, let's face it, a hated nuisance?

"You forgot the 'my lord.'"

"My lord," I amended. The clatter of the construct's hooves against the stony escarpment slowed.

"Silence now," said the sorcerer. "We've arrived."

In the fog around us, glowing pinpricks of light materialized. The bobbing eyes of constructs, their bodies still shrouded in mist, gave the impression of a firefly swarm. This sight grew more disquieting as they closed in and their wooden features came into focus: false birds, great horrible cat-things, branching trunks that lumbered on reptilian legs—but the constructs that resembled men twisted my gizzard the most.

I fought the urge to flee, spurred by memories of past skirmishes, but no sooner had the constructs reached us they fanned out behind the riding sorcerer, slipping into formation. Their many footfalls, timed as one, made for a rhythmic thudding. It disturbed me greatly to see their poor simulation of life, but with any luck, they'd have the same effect on the knights we were to meet.

The thinning fog told me we'd reached the borderlands. Ahead of us, the silhouettes of men appeared. These resolved into an escort of knights, fog lapping around their ankles, clad in the white cloth and balance scale insignia of Order.

At their head, a richly dressed figure loitered indolently.

The equine construct halted, and they faced off: Merulo and his constructs against the wealthy man and his knights.

The sorcerer slipped to the ground, landing with surprising finesse for a man of his muscle tone. The equine construct, having fulfilled its purpose, turned and trotted back the way we'd come, carrying me with it. A little too late, I realized some action on my part was required and took off into the air.

As I circled down for a landing, the sorcerer's stone eye flashed faster and faster, flicking from view to view to view.

The wealthy man stood with a self-assurance that did not fit his current circumstance. Perhaps he'd attained tranquility with age; his white cloud of hair glowed against the dark brown of his skin. Lavish fabric framed him expertly, his embroidered red cape hanging over, unbelievably, a *violet* shirt, making even his paunch look deliberate and masculine. Time had treated him kindly, carving few wrinkles but for those that bordered his eyes and mouth, giving him a look of permanent amusement.

In accordance with the Church of Order, all the bordering kingdoms had combined resources in their war against the sorcerer. Was I looking at the king of one such region?

A stack of strange books lay at the maybe-king's feet. In what anemic light the fog allowed, the covers shone glassily, a peeling film overlaying what appeared to be exquisite paintings. Staring at the tomes, stacked directly onto soil and grass, the sorcerer's face scrunched with pain. It almost brought a chuckle to my beak; he treated his own books as delicately as newborns.

"As you can see," said the maybe-king, "the materials you requested."

"Seven books," the sorcerer snapped. I made a note to advise him later that it was best to conceal emotion at times like this. "I requested seven. If you are capable of basic addition, then please, tell me how many there are. Go on—or should I count for you?"

"We couldn't find the final volume," he said, without a hint of strain. The man must have practice dealing with Merulo's temper.

"Let me remind you," said the sorcerer, "what the terms of this exchange were." He stalked forward, black cloak flowing like a spill of ink, until exceedingly little space separated him from the shorter man.

Knights clanked into motion behind, but the maybe-king raised a regal hand to halt them. Gold rings shone on his fingers. His sleeve fell open slightly, and I spotted a timepiece clasped about his wrist. This man *must* be royalty, to adorn himself so casually with a relic!

"Within these texts is ancient wisdom. I could occupy myself with the translation and analysis for months, if not years. They are my stepping stones. Without them, I have no means to progress. Meaning . . ." The sorcerer leaned right into the man's noble face. To his credit, he did not so much as flinch. "Without further knowledge to consume, I am left to act. And my actions, ignorant as they are at this stage, will be raw and untempered. I will crack this world open, Felix, and pry your God out like a snail." The sorcerer was spitting in rage. "*Escargot*, Felix. Do you understand?"

God bless the memorization they'd put us through as pages. This must be Chancellor Felix Noor, advisor to the King of New Albion. In my opinion—completely uncoloured by where I happened to have been born—this was one of the foremost kingdoms of Larnia.

"We will find your seventh text," said the chancellor. "But such a task will take time, and resources."

The sorcerer's bony form bent comically in menace over the healthier-looking man. "Resources," the sorcerer repeated, incredulous. "More payment?"

"They are forbidden relics, full of heresy. Near priceless, and dangerous to ask after. It's a wonder we even found six."

I thought Merulo would lose it then and there. Instead, the sorcerer spun, his cape a billowing shadow in the fog, leaving his back exposed to the knights with an insulting lack of caution. His stone eye flashed. From the fog, a humanoid construct emerged, carrying a rectangular metal object. At the sight of it, my feathers stood on end. Another relic. The device was of pre-Descent craftsmanship, sporting a glass front with a curved opaque handle beside a grid of neatly aligned squares. An odd rope dangled beneath the object, like a grotesque umbilical cord.

"Oh yes," the chancellor breathed, his composure finally breaking. "Yes, this will do well. Does it work?"

Merulo scoffed. "Of course not. None of the ancient technology has ever worked." His voice had pitched curiously high on the last words, and I narrowed my eyes, wondering if I'd caught the sorcerer in a lie.

Regardless, the exchange took place. After the construct passed the device to a nervous-looking knight, it moved to the books, piling them in its arms with careful precision. Both the chancellor and the sorcerer stepped back to allow this.

Jovial now, Chancellor Noor waved my way. "It's rare to

see you with a creature not made of wood. Tamed yourself a pet, hm?"

"Oh no," said the sorcerer, with all the satisfaction of someone biting into ripe fruit. "That would be Sir Cameron."

The chancellor went rigid. With obvious effort, he smiled. "That wouldn't happen to be—"

"The Sir Cameron of the prophecy? The Sir Cameron your forces were hoping to use as—how did he put it—the final ingredient in my defeat? Yes, that is him." Merulo could not have looked prouder of himself if he tried.

"Hello, your excellence," I squawked helpfully, before remembering that Merulo had commanded me to stay mute. Ah, well, I'd already broken the order. "So sorry that you nice folks don't get to kill me."

"Given your current position," the chancellor said, recovering from his stunned silence. "I'm not sure that I would not prefer death."

Double negatives confused me, so I did not respond.

"You could have saved the world, Sir Cameron." The chancellor regarded me with hooded eyes. "Enjoy being the plaything of this, this . . ." He let a gesture complete his words.

"Well thank you, your excellence, I sure will," I shot back, then winced in anticipation. But no pain came from the embedded needle, and when I chanced a glance at the sorcerer, he seemed to be hiding a smirk behind one bone-white hand.

My father would have been incandescent with rage, hearing me talk so discourteously. It said something about Merulo's power that I could taunt a chancellor and his knights without repercussions.

A familiar clattering sounded, and the equine construct

emerged from the fog. It came to a halt before the sorcerer, glaring its witch-light eyes at the assembled knights. One of the constructs broke formation, stomping over, then lowered to all fours beside it, as if prostrating in grief or supplication. Merulo used it as a stepping stool.

The knights dissolved back into the fog as the sorcerer mounted, apparently eager to flee this cursed setting.

"Come along then, plaything," Merulo called.

"And you get mad at *me* for making things sexual," I squawked, before remembering myself. "My lord." I pushed off from the rocky ground to land once more on the construct's rear end.

Again, no pain from the needle. I wondered if he'd forgotten about it.

Fog closed around us, granting a semblance of privacy. I decided to push my luck. "My lordship, I've been meaning to ask. Since you're pretty much at war with the whole concept of 'order,' I don't suppose you have a problem with . . . how to put this . . ."

At the trepidation in my voice, the sorcerer looked at me with interest.

"You know . . ." I waggled my head on my serpentine neck, wishing I had eyebrows. "Men being with men?"

"Enough," he hissed, and I snapped my beak shut.

The mad sorcerer twitched with impatience as we rode. The reason for this soon became clear, as the book-laden construct marched closer and handed over the top-most text. Bouncing as we were over the uneven ground, I feared he'd drop it, but his bloodless grip proved strong. He swiveled in his seat to brandish the relic at me. "Do you have any idea what this is?"

The glassy cover looked worn, peeling at the edges. A shiny red apple served as the focal point, beneath a shooting star. Two youths completed the scene, their mouths open in exaggerated awe, hands clasped to their cheeks. Though terribly ugly, the painting was extraordinary in its realism.

"Do you have any idea?" the sorcerer repeated. "No, of course you don't. Physics. The ancient mysteries of time and space. The primordial forces that ruled our land before the Descent of God." Passion left him breathless, and I was struck by his eagerness to share. The sorcerer typically didn't talk to me with this level of enthusiasm.

"I thought the heretical texts were purged, my lord," I said, with some hesitation. Glenda had told me that, after I'd accidentally admitted to my ignorance of, well, everything. I knew this much, though: "Reading one would be a crime against, like, humanity itself. Who in their right mind would have protected these books for so long?"

"Historians. Librarians. Merchants dealing in black goods. Wealthy families passing along unspeakable heirlooms, enchanted for preservation over the centuries. And of course, those who despise God, and wish to see it burned from this world like the infection it is." The sorcerer looked suddenly older, his surge of energy leaving him. "There have always existed those who hate God." Bringing the heavy book to his lap, the sorcerer manipulated it open single-handed, and began to read.

As the construct clopped up the incline, swishing its bristle-twig tail, I claw-walked across its driftwood back to speak more directly to the sorcerer.

"My lord, I figured it out." I snaked my neck, trying for

eye contact. "Why you hate me. You're just mad that I don't actually care about slaying God, or whatever."

"That is disappointing," he admitted.

The remainder of the ride, we spent in silence.

CHAPTER 9

In Which Glenda Is the Real Victim because This Concussion Is Seriously Fucking with Her Day-to-Day Life, and What Hardships Has Cameron Ever Experienced? Aside from Her Shooting Him Full of Arrows, Which He Deserved Tenfold, for God's Sake!

Getting concussed was, as Glenda's physician had put it, a health no-no.

Cerulina had eventually succeeded in dragging her to a clinic versed in the forbidden arts—commonly used by elves—and Glenda, reassured by the shriveled, knife-eared woman's demonstration of knowledge, nonetheless felt she should be dodging the heretical words being thrown at her. 'Neurofibrillary tangles,' 'white matter,' 'shearing'; it all overwhelmed.

Regardless of the cause, something remained wrong with Glenda. Headaches plagued her. Sunlight needled, making her squint even on cloudy days. Her anger was more easily triggered since she'd come off Passionweed, though it came cold and detached. It felt strange, this fury. It brought no bodily disruption, no change to her pulse; only the idea that satisfaction would be had if the object of her passing malice were to be brought low, somehow.

Worse still were the blackouts. Just yesterday, after dropping from a tree perch she'd been using to scout, Glenda had woken squatting on the ground, body trembling and saliva dripping from the corner of her mouth.

Time would heal the damage. That was the grand conclusion, after all that juggling of terminology. "Don't get hit in the head again," the physician had joked on her way out.

Glenda decided, then and there, that all this new venom existed to be funneled. She would destroy Sir Cameron. The prophetic vision had brought her such distress upon first viewing, with its black arterial gush and candy-red bubbling. Now, it was a pleasant daydream.

"You gave me light sensitivity, you stupid oaf," Glenda muttered, scratching an unflattering caricature into the soil with the heel of her foot.

The path to her revenge presented itself almost immediately. Cameron was not only her enemy, but the enemy of humanity at large. The Elders had burned a dragon heart, *a dragon heart*, for the prophecy that required his demise. She only needed to insert herself into a stratagem already in construction.

Of course, she'd sent letters via butterfly-dove to her noble family, emphasizing the danger to the world at large and imploring them to send resources—the elf kingdom having been dismissive, thus far, of the threat a human man could pose—and of course, Glenda's mother ensured that her summons were answered.

The humans stepped up their contributions as well. Four dozen mages of fresh-reached adulthood, after sacrificing their youth to magical study and drilling incantations with a discipline that put the military to shame, would drain themselves completely for this. An entire generation of New Albion magic-wielders, voiding their potential at once.

It wouldn't be enough to defeat the mad sorcerer. A similar stunt had been attempted earlier in the war, and he'd deflected their magical barrage with embarrassing ease—the one notable effect being that he lost weight, and never regained it. No, they just needed to blind him for a moment, to puncture his defenses and create a brief window of opportunity. Glenda volunteered herself for a central role and—given that her letters had at long last brought elven assistance in the war—how could they deny her?

Drills kept her occupied most days now, the repeated proving of her ability. She took pleasure from the dumbstruck gaping of human onlookers as she and a team of assembled relatives bounded over practice walls, slashed at hanging dummies, and picked their way, cat-like, along narrow beams.

They would breach the castle, all grace and sinew and pointed ears. And bloody justice would, at last, be hers.

CHAPTER 10

In Which I Am Committing to a Course of Action and Refuse to Suffer Judgement for It, and Probably My Folks Back Home Wouldn't Understand but I'm Here and They're There and They Also Want Me Dead, so Forget Them, I'll Dance to the Beat of My Own Drum (a Drum that at This Time Is Telling Me to Fuck an Old Man).

I decided to take seducing the mad sorcerer more seriously.

His odd acts of kindness, listening to me gab about my friendship troubles with Glenda, patching my wounds, *the dragon scale*, it all added up. I mean sure, the guy had turned me into a vulture, threatened to pull my teeth out, and implanted some sort of sick torture device in my chest, but... hmm, maybe this wasn't a great idea.

Still, I wanted out of this vulture body. He could transmogrify me. All I needed was a path connecting those points, a way to make it worth his while, as it were.

"My lord," I squawked over breakfast. The mad sorcerer was having thick-sliced bread with jam, and I was having a squirrel that had gotten trapped in the chimney and was only *just* beginning to rot. I'd flown it down to the kitchen to eat with the sorcerer, figuring a lonely guy like him would appreciate a social meal.

"My lord," I repeated, swallowing the scrap of squirrel intestine that dangled from my beak. "I think you should turn me into a woman."

The mad sorcerer choked on his bread.

After some spluttering, hacking of breadcrumbs, and indecision on my part as to whether I should be smacking his back with a wing, he recovered enough to answer. "Why in the world . . . ? Also, you are flinging rat . . . particles everywhere. From this point onward, you are forbidden from eating indoors. Effective immediately," he added, as I raced to get in one last beakful.

"It's a squirrel, my lord," I said, wiping my beak on the brick oven. "They have the fluffy tails, that's how you can tell."

"Stop that! Stop that!" The sorcerer rose to shoo me off the oven and, confused, I circled the room to land on a chair.

"Anyway, the transmogrification, my lord. I figure—since the prophecy is clear about bodily sex—I can weasel out of the thing by swapping. Pretty smart, right?" I finished wiping my beak on my own back feathers and raised a talon to scratch an itch beneath my chin.

"'Long eyelashes for a boy' . . . I suppose you're right." The sorcerer seemed to be deep in thought. "And you are rather disgusting as a vulture."

"Well, no, I groom regularly, my lord," I protested. "There's this nipple-looking thing at the base of my tail, see? And I get oil from there and smear it all over the place. Keeps me shiny."

"Stop flaring your feathers, I do not wish to see it! Obey,

or I will use the needle." The sorcerer kneaded his forehead, his toast lying forgotten on the table. A trio of small humanoid kitchen constructs descended on my squirrel, one carting it away and the other two working with brushes to scrub the scraps of red off the brickwork. I decided not to protest.

"I have given you free rein of this stronghold because, lacking opposable thumbs and any possible allies, the damage you could do is minimal. As a human, the situation would change." The sorcerer's forehead was lined and serious, but the lack of a solid 'no' made me giddy. Time for the sales pitch!

"I could cook and clean, and decorate—my lord, this place is pretty drab. That's not even getting into *the other stuff* I could do." I cocked my head in what I hoped was a significant manner, vultures not having any eyebrows to raise.

"Other stuff? No, no, I see that look, please don't answer. I know exactly where this is going." The sorcerer's eye flashed, and another little construct emerged to carry away his toast. Disappointment struck—I'd been hoping the sorcerer would eventually exit the kitchen having forgotten it entirely, leaving the crisp bread available for plundering.

But back to selling myself. "No, see, my lord, I reckon I could perform se—"

"Shut up, shut up, please stop talking. Alright. I will turn you into a human woman, on one condition." The mad sorcerer raised a single bony finger.

"Oh, my lord?" Joy and relief unfolded like a flower. "And what's that?"

"*Please* stop trying to seduce me."

CHAPTER 11

In Which I Have Been Transmogrified into a Member of the Fairer Sex, and Am Therefore Encumbered by Some Enormous Melons, Some Knockers if You Will, You Know, Hooters, Bags of Sand, or Whatever Term You Know Them by, and by God Do They Weigh Heavily on My Spine.

A secret people keep about womanhood: deprived of any other form of support, you will end up holding your own tits.

The continual flopping of chest meat had fast become unbearable. When at last I broke down and provided support in the form of a self-grope, it brought instant relief.

My entrance to the fireplace room did not cause the sorcerer to look up from his book; he brought one with him everywhere these days. "Oh good, you're here. I was ready to send a construct to drag you down by the ankles. Next time be more responsive to my sum—" The words turned into spluttering. He'd finally torn his gaze from the pages. "What are you doing?"

"My lord," I said with all the dignity at my command. "I need a brassiere."

The corpse clothes, which had already fit my man-body poorly, now hung like bags. The trousers threatened with each step to fall about my ankles. My shoes fit so loosely that I'd discarded them all together, padding barefoot through the castle.

"Stop clutching yourself. We can get you clothes, that was already a point of order." The sorcerer closed his book with obvious reluctance.

"There's another thing," I said, pressing my luck. "The needle—I reckon it sticks out in a place that will interfere with undergarments. So . . . if it could be removed . . . ?"

The mad sorcerer stared blankly.

"I mean if I do something bad, my lord, just hit me. Or is it an issue of upper body strength? I reckon even with your musculature, if my lord puts his hips into it and really swings—AH!" Knives stabbed out from the embedded needle, the pain clacking my teeth together.

He had yanked, hard, on the intermittently visible chain that connected to my needled chest. I wondered how it attached, and whether he wore his end of it as an unseeable ring.

"I'm just saying, my lord, it was already weird when I was a vulture, and it's extra weird now." I rubbed at the needle's head, soothing my poor stung flesh.

"What's 'weird' is that I have yet to wring your neck. Clothing will be purchased, be content with that." He returned to his book, opening it with a pointed snap. When I didn't move, he growled, "What? Oh, the original purpose of my summons. You said you'd clean."

"I have been cleaning!"

"Yes, I noticed that someone had smeared the dust around

in concentric patterns. Are you doing this to anger me, or is it genuine incompetence?"

Neither option seemed good.

The sorcerer pushed back his oily curtain of hair. "Do better. You can go." He waved in dismissal. I did not budge. "Now what?"

"Can we go clothes shopping now? My lord?" I pulled at the front of my pants to demonstrate their bagginess, nearly causing them to fall. "It's just that I'm always tripping, and I'd *hate* to accidentally flash you. Since you don't want to be seduced."

From the contortion of his face, you'd think Merulo was the one with a needle in his chest.

"Fine," the sorcerer spat. "We leave now."

And he really did mean now. Drawing a pouch from his cloak, he emptied the contents into one palm: white chalk, and several smooth pebbles. I watched him kneel in the dust, scratching a round shape of intricate outline with the chalk. The diagram took a minute to produce in full, at the end of which he placed the small stones around the edges at regular intervals, singing odd words in a wistful melody. Light shot from the circle, in a flash that left me blinking. The combined odours of rain, unicorn feces, and fried food filled the room.

"Come along, then," the mad sorcerer said and, stepping into the circle, he disappeared.

Biting back apprehension and holding my loose pants with one hand, I jumped into the glowing ring—and emerged into a bustling town, slick with fresh rainfall. The uncloaked sun shone clear overhead, sparkling in puddles that erupted in splashes as unicorn-drawn carts drove through them.

Around us, people strode about their business, with no apparent reaction to the two figures who had just appeared from thin air. Vendors shouted, hawking street foods and baubles. Dirty-haired children ran by us, giggling and yelling to one another. All this commotion passed around me as I stood free and unhunted. I didn't notice the tears until they fell, wet on my cheek.

The sorcerer frowned at me but refrained from comment. For his part, Merulo was transformed. A fashionable black hat sat perched on his head like a confused crow. In place of his cloak, he wore an open-breasted jacket buttoned with drops of silver, flaring to a tail over his bony rear. Disconcertingly, his exposed shirt was only a shade lighter than his pallid skin—if not for the ruffle at his neck, it might have given the illusion of partial nudity. His breeches also made me grin, form-fitted to his stick legs, and culminating in pointed calf-high boots. Head to toe, he looked like a wealthy and uncomfortable merchant.

Looking down, I found myself similarly transformed, with an unstylish dress falling to my ankles. It was part of the spell, I assumed, cloaking us to blend with our destination. My clothing retained its baggy feel, so I knew it to be an illusion.

"Sir looks almost like a proper person," I said, tears already drying.

"Is it 'sir' now?" The mad sorcerer brushed the front of his jacket, looking uneasy.

"Well, sir, if I use 'my lord,' people will look around for the duke I'm addressing." I stepped forward to link arms with the sorcerer. "Or how about we play it like brother and sister, and dispense with formalities altogether?"

Merulo coughed and tried to pull away, but I was hooked

on tight like a barnacle to a ship. Go on and make a scene, you bastard.

My strategy was this: touch, the forgotten vitamin, in the absence of which infants perish and grown men wither. Perhaps Merulo ordered one of his constructs to hold him at night, with all the comfort of cuddling a knot of brambles, but it could never substitute for skin on warm skin. With what I had at my disposal (granted, what most people had: a living body), I'd worm into his affection and then, down the line, with the sorcerer yanked about on my puppet strings, my handsome man-body could be restored.

The mad sorcerer leaned his head to mine, and I glowed at our comradery. My plan was already bearing fruit!

"When we get back," he whispered, "I may genuinely kill you."

"Ah," I replied. "Oh. Well."

He led me, arm in arm, an unremarkable pair of civilians in the crowded street. The chatter that had come as such relief after the castle's silence was becoming overwhelming, making me feel as though we walked amid a great flock of birds. I tried to glimpse myself in the shopfront windows, craning my neck until a break in the passersby revealed a strange woman peering back at me.

"Wait," I said to the sorcerer, pulling him bodily over to the glass. Hovering in translucence over a rack of display shoes, a woman gawked back at me with familiar amber eyes. Ringlets of gold fell to her chin, a lion's mane about a face that glowed bronze from the sun. Her lips were pouty petals, her jaw slim and graspable, her breasts heaving under an unremarkable brown dress.

"Well," I said. "Aren't you the pervert? Look how delectable you made me!"

"Quiet," he hissed. "This isn't my design. It's simply how you'd look as the opposite sex. If you're unable to handle it, we can always return to the vulture."

"I'm handling it. It's absolutely handled. Let's get some clothes, please."

The mad sorcerer attempted to enter a modest store, already occupied by a pair of drably attired shoppers, but—remembering how easily he'd paid off the chancellor—I tugged at his arm, leading him across the street to a more elegant establishment. Merulo shouted a dark cloud of oaths as a carriage nearly trampled us and I yanked him hard out of the way, directing him around traffic to our destination.

"Stop. Pulling. Me," Merulo said in my ear, the clip of his words implying an 'or else.'

I kept a firm hold on his arm. "Stop standing in front of unicorns."

A shop assistant opened the door for us, releasing a billow of perfume-drenched air. Our eyes hardly needed to adjust as the expansive windows let in a fall of natural light. Soft, sweet fabrics hung about the shop like fruits to be plucked. In the center stood a carved mannequin, eerily reminiscent of the sorcerer's constructs, clothed in a waterfall of rippling peach satin with sleeves puffed like wasp hives. I let the longing show on my face.

"Welcome, sir, madam. How can I be of assistance?" A plump woman in a dress that fit her like the rind of a lemon stood waiting with a smile.

"My *sister*," said the sorcerer, "needs attire in which she can kneel on the ground for hours brushing dust and mold. Something that does not foul easily. And I don't want to spend much money."

I let out a small noise of pain.

The seamstress sucked her teeth, passing me a look of sympathy. "We do have items at the lower end of the price range, and fabrics that are easier to wash. Mind, a beauty like you could make a burlap sack look like a queen's gown."

"Oh, do you think so?" I clasped a hand to my chest, trying not to let the sorcerer's sigh ruin the moment. "Thank you so much."

The first outfit she brought me to try—which I maneuvered my way into behind a changing curtain with some puzzling and problem-solving—fit well: a modest corset that gave my breasts the support they so desperately needed, over a tied bodice and a soft linen dress that gathered at my waist then flared to my feet.

The illusion left the corpse clothes as I peeled them off my body; with a touch of panic, I realized I had nothing to change back into. "We'll take this one," I said, sweeping back the curtain theatrically. The woman cooed, complimenting my figure, before drawing closer to discreetly correct my assemblage. She adjusted the lacing, pulling it tighter than I had dared, then plucked at my sleeves, straightening them.

"Do you, er, also have shoes?" I asked. "And stockings?"

She beamed and fetched a measuring device to fit to my outstretched foot, then bustled off to retrieve her wares. While her back was turned, I gave a saucy spin for the sorcerer. "You're the one buying. What do you think?"

"I think someone's enjoying himself far too much," he

grumbled. Then: "The cleavage is a bit much. You'll be cleaning in this, remember."

The seamstress overheard. "It's modern," she protested, returning with the requested goods. "With a body like hers, why keep her covered like a grandmother?"

I retreated behind the curtain to pull up the stockings. The shoes fit a bit snugly, but I liked the added inch of height; it helped return my eye-level to what it once was.

Pushing through the curtain again, I did a little clicking dance in the shoes, to the clapping delight of my new best friend the seamstress. "I'll be wearing these out," I said, and her painted lips pulled wide in a smile.

The price for it all seemed reasonable to me, though the sorcerer blanched and shot me a harsh look upon its revelation.

I left the perfumed establishment in high spirits, clicking my heeled shoes and playing with the linen of my skirt. Even the sorcerer, who carried my old corpse clothing draped over an arm, seemed a touch less full of rage than usual. Perhaps he was affected by the unchoked afternoon sun. He must be soaking it in like a starved plant, I thought, eyeing his exposed skin for any hint of an emerging burn.

"How shall we spend the day?" I moved to take his arm again, but the sorcerer dodged me. "I'm of the appetite for scones and a little hydration."

"*You* will be going back to the castle. *I* will be completing the errands typical for a town trip with the assistance of William. Don't protest, you draw far too much attention, and I would like to return here safely in the future."

William materialized from the crowded street, an unremarkable man aside from his inflexible gait and the curious lack of focus in his eyes. I reached out to brush his arm as he came to a halt. Instead of a sleeve, my fingers touched wood.

"Don't fiddle with him," the sorcerer scolded. He handed over the corpse clothing, which William received stiffly.

"I'm not! And anyway, if you won't let me help with chores, can't I wander around a bit? It's so wasteful to do multiple transport spells, and I'll be on my best behaviour." I twirled my skirt hopefully.

The sorcerer sniffed. "Your enemies include all of humanity, at least one elf, and possibly the bird kingdom, depending on how you spent your days as a vulture. And you want to *wander around*."

"I'll be perfectly safe by myself. I'm in disguise, in peak physical condition, and, I mean don't let this put you off," I lowered my voice conspiratorially, "but I happen to be something of a master manipulator."

The sorcerer gaped at me, then shook his head. Without further argument, and in synchronization with William, he strode off. "Be back in this location by sundown," he called over his shoulder.

My happiness faded as I realized the sorcerer had left me without any spending money. He'd abandoned me amid bakers and vendors, the scent of sugar and salt thick in the air, without any means of enjoying their wares. Was this deliberate torture? How was I supposed to grab myself a little treat?

The answer soon presented itself: feminine wiles. Among knights, it was common to use town leave for flirting with the locals, brandishing coin to procure squeals of admiration (among other things). I'd never taken part, preferring to spend my coin on myself, but maybe now I could engage from the other side. It couldn't be too hard to charm a knight into buying me some pretzels, and a splash of ale to wash it all down.

All that remained was to find a victim.

After playing the tourist, peeking in store windows and admiring the occasional fashionable hat that passed on a bobbing head, I found the knights. They sat on a slight incline before a spired church, arranged on the grass in a sprawl of masculinity. Leather armour and sheathed swords marked their station, as well as the tell-tale balancing scale insignias.

One man stood out, with his fox-red beard and broad everything: Sir Gareth, who'd been stationed at my outpost the previous year, before reassignment elsewhere. This must be the elsewhere. He'd been a notorious lady's man, and had given the impression of jovial sociability in our occasional conversation. Couldn't have designed a better set-up if I'd tried.

Dawdling in front of the church, I flashed little glances at the man, tucking my chin to my chest and fluttering my eyes.

"Have you got something in your eye, ma'am?" Gareth called, in the deep bellow I remembered.

"Ah, no," I said, "I was just, er. Admiring your beard!" I tried not to feel nervous as he separated from the other knights. His approaching form towered over mine in a way that felt distinctly different from our previous interactions.

Gareth grinned down at me. "You can touch it, if you like."

"Shouldn't we get to know each other first?" I squeaked. "Over, say, a pretzel and some ale?"

"A pretzel and some ale," he repeated back to the men, earning chuckles and a couple of hoots. "Aye, I can do that. Let's go, little lady." He grabbed at me, engulfing my hand in a hairy mitt. I found myself half-yanked along the street, directed in the same forceful manner I'd used with the sorcerer, and began to have second thoughts.

A pang of longing struck me. I wanted to be a man again, someone Gareth would meet eye-to-eye, instead of tugging along like a toy. "Ow," I said, hoping he'd take the hint, but he didn't.

He led me to a pub with a hanging wooden sign, bearing the crude depiction of a pissing dog. I scarcely had a chance to read it—'The Mangy Stray'—before I was ushered through the door. The hot, stagnant air made it feel like entering the gut of an animal. A row of small windows, choked with smoke stains, blocked all daylight with great effectiveness. Amid the smoking and drinking patrons, I could only see one other woman. She seemed somewhat out of it, squawking with laughter like a manic bird, while a weedy man rubbed at her shoulders.

We sat at an unoccupied table, each on a stool, and Gareth held up two fingers to the barkeep. "They don't have pretzels here," he said, then laughed like I wasn't in on the joke.

Alright, so I'd failed at my first task. But perhaps I could substitute the pretzel for something else: information.

"So, what's with all you knights dawdling about this afternoon?" I fingered a golden ringlet, pulling and releasing so that it sprang back into shape. "I've heard word of a prophecy foretelling the mad sorcerer's defeat—has that already happened, or something?"

"Now where'd you hear a thing like that?" Gareth's eyes hardened into little stones as he leaned over the small table.

"Knights told me," I yelped. "Other knights, who I've been drinking with." Two flagons slammed onto the table between us and, happy for the distraction, I grabbed at one and took a deep, foamy sip of ale. When I next chanced a look, Gareth was sitting back with a rueful smile.

"Those loudmouths." He forced a chuckle. "Well. What can you do?"

"Is it all wrapped up, then?" I said, once we'd both had a couple of swigs. "Should this be a celebratory drink?"

"Ah no . . . no. There's a complication." The burly knight sighed and placed a meaty paw over my hand, rubbing my wrist with a thumb.

"This mug's too heavy to lift with one hand," I apologized, retracting my hand and taking a double-gripped sip as demonstration. "This complication . . . it wouldn't happen to be a man named Sir Cameron, would it? The knights also told me about that," I added hurriedly.

Gareth heaved a true laugh this time, shaking the bulk of his belly. "Little miss well-informed. We'll have to keep an eye on you, eh? But you're right, it's that shit-head Cameron, God curse him to the abyss."

"Oh?" I said through gritted teeth. "From what I heard, he was quite beloved."

"That coward?" The knight guffawed. "No. His father bribed the Order to take him off his hands. Only reason he's survived up till now is some junky elf took him for a pet. Walked him about on a leash, I bet, else he'd be scrap meat on the front lines by now. Nobody human could stand the man."

"I heard he was handsome," I said, grinding my jaw. "Like a knight from a storybook."

"Sure," Gareth conceded, then rubbed his beard. "How do I explain this? Have you ever talked with someone who is obviously shaping their replies to please you? Except their guesses are like a blindman throwing at a dartboard. It leaves you feeling kinda soiled, like you've been talking to a poorly made shell." He tapped on his own head demonstratively. "Nothing behind the eyes."

"That's, uh . . ." I took a swig of the ale, then another, longer gulp. "That's a bit judgemental, isn't it?"

Noting my drained mug, the knight waved at the bar for a refill. "Something stronger!" He turned back to me. "You'd understand if you met the guy. Point is, our men were plenty pleased when the prophecy became broader knowledge. Rid ourselves of a collective pain in our ass and off the mad sorcerer, all in one go. How's that for two birds, one stone?"

"Birds?" I hiccuped, watching the progress of my fresh mug as it was carried across the dank room.

"Speaking of, you didn't hear this from me, but apparently the idiot got himself turned into a vulture."

I grabbed for the mug before it was fully placed, causing the bar help to jerk backward. "Oh," I squeaked, taking a gulp, and only spilling a small amount down my front. "Poor guy!"

"Yeah, you mentioned his looks. Let's just say the outside matches the inside now." The knight's hearty laughter surmounted all other noise in the bar. "And the way he dressed—"

"Alright, now you're just wrong. In a purely objective sense, you are wrong." I took another long swallow, nearly choking on its potency. "The, ah," I coughed, "the thread count, of his tunics? I heard it was so high, they felt like air."

"He—"

"The finest fabrics, the finest dyes!"

Gareth watched me upend my drink, overspill trickling from my mouth. "You alright there, miss?"

I slammed my mug down and stared into its empty depths. "I heard his clothes were stitched by blind monks. Who'd gone blind while embroidering. Because they were so good at it, and therefore so in demand. I heard all that."

"That seems..." His brows sank with the effort of thinking. "Bad?"

"No." I gestured for another mug, my arm whacking a passerby. "Sorry. No, no they love to embroider. It would be cruel to stop them. They"—I hiccuped—"they need it. They need to embroider."

He scratched at his beard and grimaced. "Let's talk about something else." Wood screeched as he slid his chair closer to mine. Had I briefly hoped the sound was a construct?

Gareth's plump upper lip rose in a leer. He had spittle on his beard, I noted, as a thick arm wrapped around my shoulder. Ah, this was what I'd done to Glenda... poor Glenda.

"Listen." His stinking breath steamed in my ear. "We've gotten to know each other, had a few drinks. Why don't you touch my beard now."

I toyed with my empty mug, thinking. I'd badly miscalculated this entire interaction. If Gareth was the sort to meet rejection with violence, there might not be a clear way out. I had been in situations like this before, and it was not unsurvivable... momentary discomfort passed, memories faded. Even so.

"I think I've drunk too much," I said truthfully. "I'm sorry, but I'd like to leave."

"A deal's a deal," the knight rumbled, and the arm around my shoulders tightened, pulling me in like a hooked fish. His red-cheeked face descended on mine, lips parted, and—

"Excuse me," came a stiff, haughty voice. "That happens to be my . . . my sister."

The scrawny sorcerer looked ridiculous in the dim bar, with his silver buttons and stupid hat.

I jumped to my feet, Gareth's arm unwinding from my shoulders like a slain python, and eagerly skipped over to the mad sorcerer. We had the attention of other bar patrons now, all wet glowers and snickers.

"Alright, brother, time to leave." I grabbed at his arm, clumsy from the drink, and pulled urgently. "I'll uh, touch your beard another time," I shot at Gareth, who responded by upending his mug and draining it in one gulp. "Let's go, let's go!"

After the stagnant warmth of the tavern, the cool dusk air was a balm on my skin. Merulo glanced over his shoulder repeatedly, marching us away at a hurried pace. "Is that what your best behaviour looks like? Drinking with—with scoundrels? In a *bar*?"

We'd only gone a few feet when it all caught up to me. Tears and snot cascaded down my face, dripping to dampen the front of my new dress. "I-I j-just wanted a pretzel," I said between sobs.

"Must you always choose safety second to the pursuit of baked goods?" The sorcerer guided me to a grassy incline and motioned for me to sit. "Did he hurt you?"

It was the same place I'd seen the knights lounging before, a gentle slope that culminated in the rising stone fingers of church spires. Evidently it had rained again while I was in the pub; the damp grass chilled me through my dress.

"Why do you care? You hurt me all the time," I said,

wiping gobs of snot from my face. "Don't act like it's different because I'm a woman."

"If you're uninjured, then tell me what's wrong."

Behind the sorcerer's head, the sun was setting, as if too embarrassed to stick around for what I had to say. "I'm, I'm . . ." I couldn't get the words out, breath heaving in my throat. "I'm unpopular."

"Is that it?" At my renewed wails, Merulo flinched and knelt before me in the wet grass. "Listen . . ." The sorcerer gripped my shoulders, and I blinked up at him tearfully. "Listen. Of course you are. Cameron, you are extremely annoying."

Surprise knocked the tears out of me. As the sorcerer smiled—was that meant to be in reassurance?—I closed the distance between us and pressed my mouth to his. Merulo tensed, but didn't immediately pull away. For a moment his face softened beneath mine.

"This is extremely odd," he said, the nearness of his words tickling my cheeks. "And you are intoxicated. And possibly a masochist."

"Shut up," I growled, and pulled him down so that we sprawled in the grass. One hand clenched in his oily hair, my other guided his grip to my chest. His mouth moved frantically against mine with all the hunger of a lonely sorcerer virgin, and something hard pressed against my leg.

Alas, our writhing was not to be. "So thish ish how it ish?" a bellowing voice slurred from above. "Couldn't find yoursh own womensh? And yoursh own *shishter*?"

Swearing, Merulo made to push himself off me, and was assisted by meaty hands gripping the back of his coat. The sorcerer was half thrown and half fell down the incline, where two of the knights who had previously been lounging with Gareth waited.

I heard the rising venom of a spell on Merulo's lips, but before he could complete it, Gareth smashed a fist into his jaw. The sorcerer stumbled backward into the waiting knights, his thin frame dwarfed by the burly men. Gareth pressed forward, snatching the front of Merulo's ruffled shirt and slamming that oversized hammer of a hand, again and again, into his mouth.

The same mouth I'd been in the process of kissing. Needless to say, this pissed me off.

With the men caught in their haze of testosterone, flesh smacking destructively into flesh, nobody paid poor womanly me any mind as I padded through the wet grass. Dodging the backward swings of Gareth's jackhammering, I reached for the broadsword at his waist, and pulled it free from its sheath with barely a sound. One of his companions called a warning, but too late; I had the sword pricked into his back, with enough pressure to drive the tip through his shirt and an upper layer of skin. He howled like a dog—but even through the cloud of alcohol, Gareth had enough sense not to move.

"I've always had passing adequacy with a sword," I slurred proudly.

Freed from the barrage, Merulo did not waste time. He completed his foul utterance, and Gareth toppled—onto the sorcerer. While the other two knights scattered, shouting and near-tripping in their haste to escape down the empty street, I dropped the sword and pushed at the deadweight that was Gareth, using every muscle in my transformed body to roll him off the crushed sorcerer.

"I could so easily have bought you a pretzel." Merulo lay stunned, but free of injury. Remarkably so, considering what I'd just witnessed. I could only imagine that he'd expended another dragon scale outside the pub, in anticipation of conflict.

"Is he dead?" I reached out a hand to help him to his feet. No longer a pastel wash, the clouds burned a lifeblood red behind him.

Merulo wrinkled his nose at the prone knight. "Unconscious. I applied the command word for 'slacken.'"

"The same spell you used on me?" I nudged Gareth's side with a tentative foot. "It doesn't smell as though he's shit himself."

"Most people don't."

We stood in sudden awkwardness. Was the sorcerer expecting to resume . . . ? But there came William with his marionette strides across the deserted cobblestone street.

"I had him unloading groceries through the portal," the sorcerer explained, with a hint of sheepishness. "These trips are *usually* uneventful. Now, however, I'll have to find a town of comparable size to fulfill my needs, which means trying new vendors, some of whom are bound to be low quality or otherwise disappointing." He sighed, a touch dramatically. "And of course, every minute spent on domestic matters is one in which I could have been attending to my constructs. The Order will certainly take advantage of that, with their constant advancements on my stronghold, the end result no doubt being an interruption of my reading. It's fair to say, Cameron, that this chain of events will substantially delay the death of God. For a *pretzel*." The sorcerer brushed dirt and street filth off his clothing; given his unbroken skin, it was the only sign he'd been assaulted by a trio of knights.

"Not just for a pretzel. I also got the crucial intel that everybody hates me." I kicked Gareth's side again. This time, the burly man let out a low fart. "You see this? You see this? And you're saying it's not a shit-yourself spell."

"Are you still on about that?" Merulo sighed, then straightened, his face attempting something poignant and solemn. "Cameron, listen. I have been an outcast my entire life."

"Oh good, something to bond over." I pried the sword belt off unconscious, farting Gareth. The world had begun to double, with two sorcerers, two Gareths, and four of my own hands manipulating the belt.

"Would you just . . . even when I'm making an effort, you're COMPLETELY infuriating." His fists had balled, like a child being denied a toy.

"Making an effort at what? Should I be forgetting I have a torture needle in my chest, just because you're getting sentimental over grabbing some tits?" With some drunken struggle, I buckled the sword belt around the waist of my already much-abused dress, so that the sheath fell down a hip. I retrieved the deadly steel from where I'd tossed it in the wet grass, and (nearly impaling myself) sheathed it with a satisfying rasp.

The sorcerer threw his hands into the air with a shout of frustration. "This is immensely unimportant. I am SUPPOSED to be finding a way to slay God."

"Well go on, then," I said, with a shooing motion. "Go slay God."

"I will," snapped the sorcerer, and I imagined I could make out the gleam of his eye, even through the illusion.

"Fine."

"*Fine*," he spat, storming away down the cobblestone street. With a sigh, I followed in his wake, stopping only once to vomit up alcohol.

CHAPTER 12

In Which Glenda Is Belatedly Rising through the Ranks of the Order by Means of Her Family's Wealth and Status, All because She Wants to Kill Cameron So Bad, Oh She Wants to Kill Him So Bad, You Don't Even Know, She Really, Really Wants to Kill Him.

"And the mad sorcerer was seen in broad daylight, 'making out' with his . . . sister?"

The three knights nodded enthusiastically. Though they knelt in the shaded interior of a high-topped tent, the summer heat baked the air about them, drawing sweat from their rugged faces and moistening their leather armour. Altogether, they produced an unbelievable odour.

Elder Beth, with her braided cone of white hair, sat patiently before the kneeling men in a wooden chair carved with vines and leaves. A gift from the elves—and one such elf stood at her side.

Before the Elder could launch into further inquiries, Glenda interjected, "Could we have a physical description of this 'sister'?"

The knights looked at one another, frowning with the effort of remembering, before the bearded one spoke. "Pretty little thing. Wavy golden hair in eh, ringlets. Had some strange mannerisms."

Glenda wrinkled her nose, turning to the Elder. "It's Sir Cameron."

"Sir Cameron is his sister?" The bearded knight sounded astonished.

Elder Beth pursed her lips, wrinkles appearing in fine webs, and exchanged a glance with Glenda.

"No, you fool, he's been transformed again." Glenda's tolerance for the bulky men filling the tent was waning.

"I almost kissed a man?"

What in the world had Cameron been doing?

"More importantly, we'll need a description of the disguised sorcerer," said the Elder, pointedly ignoring the knight's distress. She wiped sweat from her brow with an age-withered hand. "Where he went in the town. Which merchants he visited. Whether this was a first-time visit, or one with established relationships. Doubtless he'll be spooked now, he's unlikely to return, but if some need was being met?" The elation in Elder Beth's smile made her look decades younger. "He'll have to meet it elsewhere."

Glenda caught on to her meaning. If she'd been on Passionweed, no doubt this would have brought a rush of giddiness, but as it was, she felt only cold satisfaction. They'd have to withdraw troops from their constant attrition with constructs in the foggy borderlands to free up enough men to patrol the surrounding towns—but learning the movements of the sorcerer, and most importantly *when* he left his stronghold, could greatly accelerate their plans.

Even without the Passionweed, Glenda managed a small smile of her own. *See you soon, Cameron.*

CHAPTER 13

In Which I Have a Blinding Headache, and Cannot Bear to See Light or Hear Noise or Basically Experience Any of My Five Senses. In Which My Throat Is Dry and Furry and Tastes of Vomit, and In Which I Am Regretting Every Decision and Non-Decision that Has Brought Me to This Point.

Never trust a mad sorcerer, they don't actually care about you.

Also, never trust yourself to act rationally while sloppy drunk. It made me wince to remember. The plan had been a success, and I'd blown it! I'd wriggled into the sorcerer's affections, even squeezed a drop of sympathy from the man, and then thrown it all away. What, because it hadn't been genuine enough? Of course it wasn't genuine; none of this was. When had it stopped being about escaping death and regaining my original body?

At least it had gotten the sorcerer to dispense with the needle. After I staggered through the portal, woozy and tired, he had mumbled out a spell that had me fearing the worst. Instead, in a shattering of small pretty lights, the chain fell to pieces. I felt a tiny implosion where the needle had lain buried. "There!" he shouted, and that was the last we'd spoken for three days.

In addition to groceries, Merulo had purchased for me cleaning supplies, a comb, a change of clothing, and bedding for my wooden cot, which was nice, as I'd been sleeping wrapped in a moth-eaten curtain. The curtains were soft and thick, which probably meant expensive material, so I made a reconciliatory effort to restring them in their original position downstairs.

(Later that night, I crept out to retrieve the curtains, missing their familiarity. The sorcerer had scarcely missed them the first time, so why not?)

No instruction arrived as to how the cleaning should be attempted, leaving me to experiment. The wooden bucket, I filled at the pump in the kitchen, and with brushes, lard soap, and washcloths, I set to work tackling the accumulated grime. The sheer volume of vulture dung I scraped off the stone floors filled me with annoyance at my former self. Only passingly, though.

I developed a peevish relationship with the constructs, which mindlessly tracked in all manner of filth with their comings and goings. If the sorcerer and I had been on speaking terms, I'd have nagged him about the necessity of *indoor* constructs and *outdoor* constructs. Instead, I took to tackling their legs and forcing their feet up to be scrubbed, much as I'd mucked out the hooves of the Order's unicorn mounts.

Sometimes, their eye-flames would flash brighter, and I could almost feel the sorcerer peering through their sockets. Their heads turned eerily at these times, tracking my movements, so I tried to give a performance of blissful domesticity. I even whistled as I scrubbed; it sounded pretty shit even to my ears, though, so I gave up after a while.

My suspicion was that Merulo tracked my position in the castle to ensure we never ran into one another. Every time I plundered the kitchen, it contained only his little gnome-like constructs. Once, I even found his hastily abandoned breakfast, a cooked egg with a serving of meat, which I ate to teach him a lesson. The lesson being: if you're a coward I'll eat your breakfast.

My greatest joy came from discovering that the pits beneath the garderobes were magicked—our leavings disappeared down a portal into God knows where, meaning I wouldn't be expected to clean human waste.

On the evening of the third day, the agony of boredom became too much. Half jogging, so that the sorcerer wouldn't have time to spy me through the constructs, I flung open doors, hunting, until a little out of breath, I slammed through into the library and found Merulo perched on a cushioned chair with a textbook on his lap. Grimly satisfied, I pulled over a second chair and sat cross-legged in it, waiting.

The sorcerer didn't look up from his book. "You are a chaos entity, not a human being. And I liked you better as a vulture."

"Well la de da, good evening to you, too." Truthfully, I also missed being a vulture; it had been less work. After more silence, I tried again: "What are you reading?"

"You wouldn't understand it." The sorcerer licked a finger to turn the page. Above his head hovered an orb of witchlight, painful to look at directly.

"You know..." I grimaced, searching for a way to

justify my presence. "I heard that to demonstrate a proper understanding of a subject, you should be able to simplify it enough for a child to understand. Or if not a child, maybe me. Besides, I want to hear more about this 'Death to God' business. You're going to end the world, right?"

"Of course not." At last, the sorcerer met my eye, which I counted as a success despite his affronted expression. "The Descent perverted the world. I am going to restore it."

I blinked at his blasphemy. The time before the Descent was widely understood to have been a waking nightmare. "What about the things they say? That the air used to be unbreathable. That in the daytime, it got hot enough to kill a man?"

"We could have fixed it," Merulo insisted, book forgotten on his black-robed lap. "Given enough time. If it hadn't been for the *outside interference*." He paused, as if searching for words. "We have the world back, that's true, with blue skies and fruitful lands restored. But we used to have the entire universe."

I frowned, not following. In answer, the sorcerer sprang from his chair in a flurry of black fabric, nearly sending his precious book flying. He strode down the aisle of shelves, tracking his fingers along spines. Finding the object of his hunt, Merulo made a small sound of triumph, and withdrew the book with a flourish. Almost reverently, he placed the tome on the floor, and crouching, flipped it open to a double page spread.

I leaned forward, peeking at the diagrams, but before I could properly make out all their odd rings and orbs, Merulo snapped his fingers, and the witch-light was extinguished.

Blackness swallowed the room entirely. It felt odd for there to be no difference between having my eyes open or shut. Filling the silence, the sorcerer's chanting rose in volume.

I couldn't understand his words, but the longing in them moved me. What had I ever wanted with that intensity, aside from my own survival?

At the culmination of his spell, the diagram blazed, a burst of light that made me shield my eyes. It floated off the page, then grew to fill the room. Several golden spheres rotated in wide orbit around a central, burning mass.

"This is the sun." Merulo, dimly visibly in the golden glow, pointed to the sphere of fire. "And here we are, on this planet." His finger moved to a middling orb with a mottled surface. "Everything you know, every person, every mountain, is here."

"But there are others," I protested. "And bigger ones. What about that?" A larger sphere with a ring had caught my attention.

"Dead planets," said the sorcerer. "Lifeless. Though we'd begun to take them. We had a foothold here, on our moon"—he pointed to a smaller ball, spinning companionably about our world—"and on Mars." He indicated an unimpressive planet, one orbit outward from ours. "And more would have followed. Our empire was spreading. It was a time of unprecedented innovation, with exponential growth in the sciences and in our population. The start of our mastery over the solar system!"

Someone who liked the sorcerer less might have found this speech fanatical. He stared at me with giddy eagerness through the shifting lights of the display, like an overexcited kid who'd finally found someone to play with him. "When God arrived, it destroyed everything. Eviscerated the very rules on which reality operated. Genius technologies, millennia of accumulated human intelligence, rendered into useless trash overnight. All of life reshaped, made magical. It was the day the world ended."

With a wave of his hand, the diagram vanished, the orb of witch-light returning to its place above his head. The sorcerer looked breathless and sad. "We were our own Gods. All I want is for that to be the case once more."

I didn't understand most of it, but he seemed to appreciate a listening ear. "Dragons must have liked the old world," I tried. "Without magic, nobody would have had reason to hunt them."

"No, no." The sorcerer shook his head, exasperated. "There weren't any dragons!"

I pulled at my feet, tucking them in further. The soft cushion and dim room conspired to make me sleepy. "What do you mean—they were all born on the Day of Descent?"

"Not born—transformed. They were . . . artificial intelligences. Super brains, massive devices that filled rooms, and operated on the principles of physics. They ruled countries in lieu of kings." An odd, wistful look came over him. "Their bodies were incapable of motion. But their minds spanned continents."

I yawned, nestling deeper in the chair. "So, if you change the world back . . . then what? No more spells? Seems to me, being an unbeatable magical genius isn't so bad. Merulo, you cast more incantations in a day than most people do in a lifetime. Why crave a world where you'd be ordinary?"

The thin man sagged and returned to his seat. "Is that all there is to me, then? My power?"

"No, obviously you have that big ol' brain." I closed my eyes experimentally, leaning back in my chair. "I reckon you could become the genius of anti-magic instead. That sounds about right."

The sorcerer huffed, not sounding entirely displeased.

"So long as we're sharing..." I sank further into the cushions, my senses muddled by comfort. "What's with the eye?"

"What do you mean, *what's with the eye*?"

"Ssnot in there." I yawned.

"Are you asking me how I came to lose my eye?"

I grunted in confirmation.

"I . . ." He sighed. "I removed it myself. To better control my constructs. And so that it might be used in a spell."

"Hmmm," I said. "Ahmm."

"Are you even listening to me? Are you even awake?" The sorcerer gave another heaving sigh. Then came the whisper of turning pages as he resumed reading.

It is possible, at some point after, that I fell asleep.

When I woke, morning light fell through the thin library windows, and someone had draped the blanket from my cot over me.

CHAPTER 14

In Which I Woke Up with a Curious Lightness and Went through the Day Humming under My Breath until I Realized, with Something Not Unlike Horror, that This Is the Happiest I've Ever Been in My Life, and that I Have No Desire for Humanity to Forgive Me.

Heresy became our preferred method of bonding. I followed the mad sorcerer like a little black lamb, absorbing his forbidden teachings. "A goat," he corrected, when I voiced the image out loud. "Goats think for themselves."

Questions became a fun game.

"Did elves exist, before the Descent?"

"Yes, but as wealthy socialites, 'celebrities' and 'influencers,' who manipulated the appearance of their bodies. It was fashionable at the time, for those who could afford it."

"And chickens?"

"Chickens were chickens. Leave me alone now. I'm behind on my reading."

The only subject the sorcerer persistently avoided answering was what he planned for the after times. After he killed God, after he restored the 'laws of physics,' where he'd be.

What he would do. How life would continue for the man who structured everything around one transitory moment-to-come. It gnawed at me.

I also missed the old excitement of provoking his rage, and so tried my best to be a nuisance. Within reason, of course.

"Oh no, I've spilled flour everywhere," I moaned over one communal breakfast. "I hope nobody punishes me. For spilling all this flour."

"You can sweep that up later." The sorcerer chewed another mouthful of egg. "As I was saying, the thing that perplexes me is how far it extends . . . I've been tracking star movements, and they match pre-Descent records. Larnia is caught in a stain of infection, but whether it's spreading, or contained by some force, I have yet to determine. If it is only a singular planet that must be changed, that will greatly reduce the energy output requ—"

I dropped a plate. "Oh no! Clumsy me."

"Are you bored? Am I boring you?" The sorcerer's face turned red, his stone eye blazing. "Put voice to that, instead of assaulting my kitchenware."

He finally caught on a couple of mornings later, after the fourth plate. "I'm not playing into your perversions," the sorcerer said between nipping at his toast, as kitchen constructs arrived to carry away the plate shards. "If you succeed in drawing my anger, it will not be to your liking."

I picked up another plate—and was flung, bodily, against a kitchen wall. Pinned by an invisible force, ladles clattering above my head, I watched the sorcerer approach in full mouth-twisted fury. That he nearly tripped over a chair did not ruin the effect for me.

"If you break another of my plates"—Merulo jabbed a finger at me, red blooming in his pale cheeks—"prepare to spend the remainder of this day hanging from chains."

"Oh?" I said hopefully, ignoring the ladles that had settled atop my head.

"Stop that, stop smiling, you will not enjoy it. I know this with certainty, because you will be bored, Cameron—and more than anything else, you cannot stand to be bored." The sorcerer looked satisfied with this pronouncement, a black-clad villain who had, at last, found the hero's weakness. I grimaced.

"Now, I'm going to let you down." Merulo spoke with the false patience of a teacher-priest. "And will you be harming more of my ceramics?"

I hung like a crucified saint from the kitchen brickwork, the sorcerer mere inches from me. The tingling thrill of it all compelled my honesty. "Absolutely."

The sorcerer swore and slammed a hand into the wall beside my head, narrowly avoiding the ladles. "I am TRYING to be kind here."

"Well, maybe you don't have to be so kind," I said, discreetly testing the forces that held me in place. Under the kitchen table, the constructs carried off the last shards of plate. "You know, it can be fun sometimes. To . . . not be nice to people. And here I am, with nothing much to do but clean. Maybe you could be not so nice to me."

With the sorcerer so close, it was easy to hear his breathing change. "Is that right?"

"That is right." I tried to lean my face closer, feeling a fantastic frustration at the pressure that held me prone.

"Well," Merulo breathed, anger melting into something

else. "Then I will let you go. And if you smash another plate, just know that there will be . . . consequences."

"Alrighty, then." Abruptly, the force released me, and I fell forward, barely catching myself on the heels of my hands. The ladles clattered a final time, as if cursing their continued disturbance. In casual movements, under the sorcerer's watching eye, I took the plate that held his remaining slice of toast and—feeling far too pleased with myself—frisbeed it into a wall.

When the eight-foot construct arrived to drag me from the kitchen and march me down the stone corridors, I struggled, once or twice, for effect.

We entered the room where I'd been interrogated so long ago, and the mad sorcerer broke character. "Er." Merulo's stone eye blazed, conspicuous in the dingy torchlit room. "Those aren't adjusted for your current height, let m—"

"Oh, wicked deviant!" I interrupted, while the construct fiddled with the chains about my wrists. "Foul villain! You can violate my body, but you cannot violate my, uh . . . mind!"

From the extended pause, it was obvious I'd misspoken. With its handiwork complete, the construct clonked out of the room, tactfully closing the door behind it.

"In this scenario of yours, I'm the 'foul villain'?" Merulo looked genuinely taken aback. "After you devastated my kitchenware? And that's not the least of it, Cameron. You've been doing an exceedingly poor job at every assigned duty."

I pulled at the chains awkwardly. "What's wrong with my cleaning? Haven't you noticed all the vulture dung is gone?"

"Wonderful. And you've figured out how to remove the dust, but why must everything be sticky?" The wrong sort of passion was entering his voice. "And you misplace items. Constructs have limited intelligence. If you put something in a strange location, it confounds them. They cannot complete their tasks."

"I mean, I'm a knight playing at being a maid. What quality of work were you expecting?" If this was turning into a formal work review, it felt a bit awkward to have my hands restrained.

Merulo shook his head, starting to pace. "Time and again, you've resisted being put in your place."

"Which is why you've had to resort to such drastic measures." I wiggled plaintively. Could he not channel his anger into something more . . . productive?

Merulo smiled then, deliciously smug and mean. In the torch's flicker, his thin form loomed threateningly. "I should leave you here."

Thrusting my chest out self-consciously, I said, "Oh but, my lord, isn't there another way I could make up for my deficiencies?"

"Yes. By staying silent and out of sight." He was still smiling, looking more and more self-satisfied.

We should have established a safe word. "My lord, I will clean better," I said, feeling the pull of the chains on my arms a bit more seriously now. "And stop fucking with your plates. One hundred percent, it will be done."

"You don't actually mean that." He smirked. "No. I think I'll leave you here to marinate."

"Truth spell! Truth spell!" I squawked, sounding almost like my vulture self. I'd yanked forward without meaning to, and now my wrists ached.

With exaggerated impatience, Merulo went through the motions, withdrawing the small geode from the shadow of his robes, whispering a blue spill of magic over its surface, and drawing closer to apply it to my chest. His composure broke, and he paused, gaunt hand hovering, before unlacing my front and pulling down a corner of the dress, exposing my shoulder. His fingers were cool against my skin, and the geode even colder.

Clearing his throat, Merulo withdrew. It took a couple of tries for him to shove the geode back into the depths of his robes. "Have you been doing your best work?" The sorcerer's voice only cracked a little.

"Nope," I answered. "That stickiness you mentioned? It's from skipping the final wash of water. But in my defense, I did not . . . think you'd notice."

The sorcerer seemed too distracted to get properly angry. He cleared his throat again. "Will you do better, and cease this flailing for attention?"

I played with my chains. How did people ever reproduce, if seduction was this difficult? "Yes to the first . . . no to the second."

He turned to leave.

"Wait, please don't go," I cried, jangling in place. "You're right, boredom is exactly the thing I cannot stand. Merulo!" The room's air tasted dry and stale, like a tomb.

Frustration entered his voice. "You did ask for me to 'stop being nice.'" A tendril of black hair fell into his famished face, over his stone eye. "What did you want exactly, for me to hurt you?"

"Maybe," I squeaked. "But like, in a hot way."

"I could make your bones feel like molten lead. Would that be hot enough?"

Again, picking up steam in the wrong direction. "Too hot! Way too hot!"

"So then you want pretend consequences for real infractions. It's fascinating that you thought that would happen." Merulo brushed the stray hairs back, returning them to the inky mass that fell on his shoulders. "Cameron, from the moment we first met, you have been an unbelievable nuisance. Who can say how far you've delayed my research? Yes." He straightened, his natural eye matching the intensity of its stone twin. "This necessitates an apology."

I tried to gargle out the words, but they stayed stuck. That damned truth seal. "Look, I'd love to give a nice apology. But this is the most fun I've had in years." I stared at the torch-shadowed floor, hopefully in a contrite manner. "I can't be sorry for any of it."

"*Fun?* Being hunted by your former comrades? Being turned into a vulture and used as a—a pin cushion? Eating rats? Are you utterly deranged?" Not looking at him had been the right call; his voice sounded strange.

"I did actually like the vulture part," I admitted. "And rats are just meat. Tubes of meat. You get so squeamish, honestly."

"They're diseased vermin, Cameron."

"Why don't I cook you up a nice rat, and you ca—" The sound cut off, though my throat still vibrated with the passage of words. Confused, I tried again, my mouth emitting perfect silence. I chanced a glance up.

Merulo looked the happiest I'd ever seen him. He closed the distance in a single stride and stared down at me with a great deal of self-satisfaction. "Why didn't this occur to me sooner? It's perfect!"

I tried to reply, and felt foolish when nothing came out. Clicking his tongue, the mad sorcerer gripped my chin, angling my face upward. "Now that you've shut up, I can admit that this body is an improvement on the vulture." He leaned in all the way, lips brushing against mine, his other hand closing firmly around my waist. As I hung, giddy from the press of his body, the sorcerer whispered in my ear, "Shake your head if you want me to stop."

I did not want him to stop.

CHAPTER 15

In Which the Sorcerer Proved So Easy to Seduce that All My Previous Failures Seem Embarrassing in Retrospect. In Which I Will Be Forgiving Myself, as for a Good Number of Those Attempts, I Was a Vulture.

"This is the nicest thing anyone has ever done for me."

The sorcerer eyed me critically. "Surely that cannot be true."

We sat in what could loosely be considered a dining hall, if your standards only demanded a longish table and the space to fit it in. Cobwebs hung in every corner and dripped from the table's underside, their creators occasionally revealing themselves in black scuttling shapes that quickly disappeared. Only a narrow window saved the room from complete gloom. Merulo had ignited a set of wall-mounted candles with a gesture upon entering, but as the wicks were ill-tended, they promptly extinguished their own flames in pools of lopsided wax. Merulo didn't notice; he stood proud as a cat before a fresh-killed mouse as I examined the wax-paper bundle of pretzels.

I thought carefully. "When we were kids, my brother gave me a stuffed dog. He used my father's stockings, and stuffed it with sheep's wool, to make it soft. Of course, I was caned upon its discovery, it being a less-than-consensual clothing donation, but I slept with that thing damn near every night." I plucked a pretzel from the paper, trying not to drool over the thick chunks of salt that coated it. "This is the second nicest thing, then."

"And now, knowing what I can provide, you should have no need to seek the attention of . . . *others*."

I pulled a face at the mention of Gareth. "Why would I, when I have a full-service sorcerer?"

"And . . ." He pulled a chair from the table with a screech, then hesitated, apparently noticing the spiderwebs for the first time. In the end, he remained standing, his fingers clenched, talon-like, around the top of the chair. "I hoped we could talk."

"About what?" I asked. Then: "Oh God, that wasn't your first time, was it?"

"No!" He flared his hands in alarm. "Of course not. Though perhaps . . . it's been some decades."

Some decades. Good lord, how old was this guy?

The sorcerer squirmed for a moment, looking as if biting insects had invaded his underclothes, before stammering out, "And . . . for you?"

"Oh, you know." I tried for a charming look, jutting my chin out, only to remember that I was working with a more feminine aesthetic now, one that didn't hinge on a craggy jaw. "People like my looks, so I get around."

I imagined that might intimidate him even more, my comparative breadth of popularity and experience, but if anything, he returned to his usual self. "They like your looks," he repeated.

"Sure." I sat back so that natural light fell across my clear, lovely skin. "Most people do."

"Nothing else, then. Just your looks."

"Ah." I realized the trap I'd fallen into. "I mean . . . People do like me, you know."

"Ah yes, I remember you weeping outside that bar because your fellow knights *liked* you so much." The candlelight shadowed his face, making it hard to read.

I sat up, stung. "There's no need to be nasty."

"I'm just trying to understand. There's never been anything deeper than that? There's never been anything . . ." He hesitated. ". . . *more*, that you wanted?"

I thought about it. In most of my encounters, I did stand to benefit in some way: in the gathering of valuable intelligence, or in avoiding a particularly nasty advancement on the sorcerer's territory—though sometimes, I did settle for purely social gains. This, however, did not seem like a response that would please him.

"Never mind. Your silence is answer enough." He sighed, kneading at his forehead.

"You had fun, though, right?" I asked, slightly panicked. "And you like the way I look?"

The last of his vulnerability dissipated, and I saw once more the sorcerer who had threatened me with Benedict. "I have work to attend to," he said. "You have distracted me enough."

"Okay," I said, still clutching my pretzel. I raised it to him. "Thank you for this. And, uh. Maybe I could distract you again, later on?"

He smiled slightly, and I took that as confirmation that I hadn't fucked up completely. "Perhaps."

Once he'd left, I devoted myself to demolishing the pretzel, in all its salty, puffy goodness, with no thought but for the next mouthful. Taking stock of the remaining pile, I decided it would be better to eat them now while fresh, and so threw myself into consuming another, and another, until I felt quite sick. It almost distracted me from the unease in my gut.

A spider crawled across the table, hard to see now that so many of the candles had given up their fight. "I can't help but feel," I confessed, before it could dart out of sight, "that I've done something wrong. Though I cannot begin to imagine what."

The spider, being a spider, failed to respond, leaving me to sit in a thickening silence until all the candles had extinguished.

CHAPTER 16

In Which I Am Considering What Sir Gareth Said to Me, and Am Having the Epiphany that My Own Self-Image Does Not Perfectly Mesh with How Others Perceive Me, and In Which I Am Realizing that That Is a Fucking Disaster.

The sorcerer treated me coldly in the days following our conversation. He left rooms soon after I entered, and all attempts to draw him into conversation led to either strained silence, or to a sneering dismissal.

"He did like me before. Didn't he?" I ate alone in a hallway, not fussing over the breadcrumbs that dropped to the floor. Just creating future mess for myself to deal with.

A quadrupedal construct creaked past. Its head dipped slightly, flaming eye sockets evaluating the crumbs.

"I will tidy this!" I assured it, though from the dimming of its eyes I could tell the sorcerer had already gone. Leaving me alone to speak freely. "Honestly, I can't believe it's something you care much about, given how you've let this place deteriorate. The audacity of nitpicking about my cleaning while I'm chipping off layers of grime and vulture shit and tossing eggsacks out the window, but hey, if it makes you happy, then—huh!"

Like a lightning bolt: a revelation. What if, rather than whinging solely to pick at me, the sorcerer had a genuine desire for and appreciation of a sparkling clean abode? If so, that might be the key to regaining his favour.

I crammed the rest of the bread down my throat so fast I nearly choked on it. Then I lifted my dress with both hands, the better to run. My strength had diminished with this change in bodily sex, but I appreciated the physical strain as I hauled buckets of water from the kitchen, seeing it as evidence of my own self-sacrifice and benevolence. Foaming up the tiled stones with lard soap, I set to work polishing and re-polishing the hallway that led to his precious library.

Finally, my labour bore fruit. A tall black-clad figure stomped down the hall, arms weighted with quills and parchment. Loping behind him was a bird-beaked construct, its wing-arms straining under an improbably tall stack of books. Merulo kept his eyes fixed upward, the tensing of his mouth his only acknowledgement of me, and so stepped blindly into a patch of soap.

Parchments exploded into the air as the sorcerer fell backward, his legs sliding in opposite directions. The construct cracked into rapid motion, balancing its books on one wing, and snatching the papers that drifted through the air with the other.

"Why," Merulo sputtered, attempting to find his footing, only to slip again. Suds drifted, iridescent bubbles settling on his greasy black hair like a fairy crown. "Why have you done this? Fuck!"

"Uh, well, you did something nice for me—"

"And for that, you've decided to *kill me*?" He scrabbled

about for his parchments, bracing on all fours on the soapy tiles. His quill pot had shattered upon impact, leaving a smear of black across the otherwise spotless floor.

Skirting the wet patches, I approached him and offered a hand. Merulo looked ready to ignore me, so I pushed it in front of his glowering face until he accepted, wrapping his bony fingers around mine. Pulling the sorcerer to his feet proved remarkably easy; he weighed barely anything. "It wasn't deliberate," I said. "I'd actually rather you remain alive."

"Of course. How else would you benefit from my protection?"

I opened my mouth to reply, but found myself shamed into silence, both by the perfectly true accusation, and by the closing off of his face, so near to my own.

The sorcerer pulled away and smacked at the bubbles nesting on his robe, flicking them to the ground.

It struck me, then, how much it mattered that I remain in his good graces. Each time he withdrew his regard, it was like he took with it some vital organ that made it harder for me to breathe. So, like, a lung.

Should I say that to him?

"I am trying to be of some use to you," I tried instead. "With the cleaning. And if I can do more, just tell me."

"Yes, Cameron, here's what you can do." The sorcerer drew himself up tall, the last of the bubbles popping on the tip of his sharp nose. "Stay out of my way."

"Oh, okay, sure." I crouched to pick at the scraps of broken glass. "I'll just finish up here, then dust all the arrow slits or something. Say, if you have any appetite for dinner later, maybe we could coordinate?"

Air hissed out from between his teeth, then he muttered a quick spell. The glass fragments jumped from my hand, alighting into the air like insects to coalesce in the sorcerer's outstretched palm, the spilled ink following in a graceful black tendril. Without further words, he pushed the door open, the construct marching to join him.

"Does that one have a name?" I asked, pointing in desperation at the bird-thing before they could disappear into the library.

The sorcerer paused. "Wilbur," he said.

"That's cute. I like that. My brother let me name one of his chickens once. I called it Pecky. Because it—"

"It pecked, yes. Chickens are known to do that. And I suppose if you were to name my constructs, you'd choose 'Walky,' or 'Lifty,' or—if you were feeling particularly inspired—'Woody.'"

"Woody is nice."

"*Woody is nice*," he repeated in faint disbelief. Then: "I am indisposed for dinner tonight. Another time. And . . . thank you for your cleaning, even if it is inexpert."

"Anytime, don't even mention it!"

I remained scrubbing long after the door clicked shut, lost in my own satisfaction.

The following day, I couldn't find the sorcerer. Eventually, having exhausted all the unlocked rooms (and pressed my ear to all the locked ones), I climbed the long, winding staircase that led to the battlements. There he stood amid the fog, constructs crouched frozen around him like gargoyles.

"Oh, hey," I called, clutching my dress as a sharp wind tore at it, its passage whipping the fog into a roiling mass. "There you are. Say, were you thinking of lunch anytime soon? Because I'm feeling peckish, and I figure, if you're not doing anything else, then—"

A construct stepped into my path, blocking my advance. "Well, that's a bit much," I shouted over the gale. "You only had to say, 'No thanks, maybe later.'"

"Cameron!" the sorcerer shouted back at me. "I am in combat. Do not distract me."

"Oh, against the Order?" I slipped past the construct, edging through the fog toward him, the wind stinging at my eyes. "That's alright, I can wait."

Some combination of churning fog and my own tearing eyes made me misjudge the boundaries of the battlement, so that I knocked into a corner with an "oof." I'd only just begun to tip over the edge when wooden talons caught my shoulder, pulling me sharply backward. "Sorry! I'll just, uh, sit right here."

It got cold fast. The sorcerer's flashing eye cast a green light against the surrounding fog, and his face furrowed in concentration, focused on something I could not see. If this was a regular habit, it was no wonder his face had so many lines.

For my part, I rubbed at my arms and tried to tuck my feet beneath the fabric of my dress. I hoped the chattering of my teeth wouldn't carry, as no doubt that would lead him to further label me a distraction.

Something heavy dropped onto my shoulders. I jumped, before realizing it was a blanket.

It smelled of magic.

When I looked up, the sorcerer stood before me. Fatigue showed in his drooping posture, but his face was sharp, alive with fury and satisfaction.

I pitched my voice to be heard above the gusting wails. "Did you win, then?"

"I always do. If those mindless little knights would just—"

"They're not completely stupid," I interrupted, then stopped, surprised to find that the most tenuous thread of comradery persisted. "Most are hoping to serve a few years, earn a convenient injury, then retire to lordship—or more provincial pursuits, for the lower born—with the Church's favour secured. And then, some are like me. It's a fairly open secret that my father sent me off hoping I'd be slaughtered, so my brother could inherit." I smiled. "You see, even without the prophecy, I was already supposed to die."

Merulo looked genuinely outraged. "That's obscene," he said. "Your own father? Granted, you can be quite annoying—"

"Oh, it wasn't that. My father didn't think I'd make a good heir, as I'm not appropriately masculine." I sighed, my breasts heaving. "Which is ridiculous, of course."

"Er, yes," said the sorcerer, avoiding my eyes. "That is of course... an absurd notion."

Another howl of wind thrashed the fog around us and set the sorcerer's robes to flapping madly. With a shiver, I pulled the blanket close about myself.

"Aren't you cold? I mean, you don't have much in the way of insulation, if you catch my drift." A worry struck me that I was being too opaque. "As in, I have all this fat and muscle, but you—"

"Yes, understood." His eye flashed and he muttered something; cleaning up the last scraps of resistance, I assumed. "I don't suffer from the cold easily."

"No need to be stoic. It's freezing up here, and you're only human." To use one of Glenda's favourite expressions.

Merulo cleared his throat, looking about shiftily in a manner that had me scrutinizing his ears and skin tone, but nope: not a drop of elf blood. I shrugged off the blanket and, standing on my tiptoes, threw it about his bony shoulders. "From one human to another, this isn't good for your health. Don't stay out here long." Feeling bold, I pressed my mouth to his gaunt cheek, then withdrew, my own cheeks flaming. Navigating the wind and fog, I scurried from the battlements before he could respond, only stopping when I was safely in the stairwell to catch my breath.

Free from the wind and cold, the muggy dark of the castle felt welcoming, homely even. "I can be quite charming," I said, leaning against a wall and tracing its roughness with a finger. "It's not just in my head; he looked absolutely smitten with me. Hey, watch it please!"

A construct lumbered past me on the spiraling stairwell, taking up most of the space so that I had to squeeze tight against the stone. "Asshole," I called after it. "Piece of shit!"

It swung its head back at me, and I felt my stomach drop. "Sorry, sorry, Merulo. I didn't realize you were in there."

"It's fine," said the sorcerer, from the top of the stairwell. I waited for him to descend, watching with some satisfaction as he pressed himself flat to inch past another oversized construct. "I will say, this is not an ideal location for monologues."

I hid my wince by looking elsewhere as he descended. "You heard?"

"Apparently, I'm being charmed, though by what I can't imagine. By your complete lack of spatial awareness? Or perhaps the grace with which you pursue hypothermia? Or is it the constant neediness; is that what I'm being charmed by?"

The blanket still lay across his shoulders, a warm yellow against his black robes. I wondered if he'd forgotten about it.

"All of it, I think. You definitely like me."

"No," he said.

"Yes. Anyway, let's eat together. If you activate your little kitchen gnomes, there'll be scones in the oven by the time we arrive."

As he reached me, Merulo stumbled on the stairs, and I caught his arm. "It's tiring," he said. "The fighting."

"But you have enough energy for scones?"

"Fine, yes," he said, and exhaled. "Damn you. But no destruction of my property, and I mean that."

"Of course not. Time and place for everything, and you're obviously spent."

"No, there is not a time and place for destroying my kitchen. Do you hear yourself?"

Figuring it was a rhetorical question, I merely smiled. And even when we reached the stairwell's base, then throughout the long walk to the kitchen, he failed to shrug off my hand.

CHAPTER 17

In Which Gareth Can Eat Shit, as I Am Without Doubt Adored and Appreciated, and Very Good at Cleaning, and In Which There Are Now Substantially Fewer Cobwebs in the Castle, and Substantially More Unhoused and Angry Spiders.

Progress had been made, but I still wanted to know what, in that horrible conversation with the pretzels, had upset the sorcerer so badly.

It took some puzzling, but at last I worked it out. My looks, of course. I'd crowed over my own attractiveness with no reciprocating compliments, and no thought as to how it might impact his self-esteem. This had to be corrected.

Thinking up ways to compliment the sorcerer proved difficult, as he lacked a traditionally handsome face or body (or an untraditionally handsome one, for that matter) and wore only that same silly robe, over and over again.

"You're very scary!" I tried on one occasion, in the library.

I'd made a habit of joining the sorcerer for his reading. He'd grown childishly excited at my interest—though he steered me away from his precious relics toward the more modern books, written in a language I could comprehend. Childhood lessons had left me with basic literacy, but in practice I mostly stared at the pages and let my mind wander.

"What?" Merulo glared at me from the neighbouring chair. He tucked his legs up as he read, folding himself among the cushions.

"Your looks, your physical appearance. It's pure menace!"

"And you're bringing this up for what reason?" He tried to sound bored, but I thought he looked a little pleased.

"It's great," I continued, gaining confidence. "I'm sure you strike fear into the hearts of your enemies."

"Obviously," he said, simpering.

Now, what else could I compliment? "You're so smart, too. It's amazing how you know all these forbidden languages."

"Alright, Cameron, what do you want?"

"Nothing! Nothing. It's just—you're not mad at me, are you?"

He sounded exasperated. "For what?"

I sat back in relief. "If you don't know, then you're probably not."

"No, tell me, for what? Did you do something to my kitchen again? Damn it, what did you break?"

"No, no," I protested, but it was too late; his stone eye flashed wildly as he hopped through the castle constructs, checking viewpoints.

"It's not that, it's just—back when you brought me pretzels, I . . ." The sorcerer tensed, and my courage evaporated. "I didn't save you any," I concluded lamely. "That's all. I thought you might have wanted one."

The sorcerer stared at me in absolute silence, the fire of his eye flickering out, before his face cracked.

"I'm sorry," I said, over the howls of his laughter.

"You've done nothing wrong," he said, wiping at his eye. "Truly. Besides, I thought you liked making me angry."

My breath caught. From his jagged grin, full of too-sharp teeth, I knew that no further reading would be accomplished that day. "Now that I think of it, I *am* angry," he continued. "I'm positively furious. Surely, something can be done about that?"

CHAPTER 18

In Which Glenda Is Learning the Machinations of War, Which, Much to Her Frustration, Involve Dealing with a Legion of Less-than-Pleased Parents, and In Which Glenda Is Learning that Money Can Intervene to Solve Most Human Problems.

Draining a generation of student magicians would not come cheap. The Church could simply order them, and have it done, but why stir unnecessary resentment among the higher born? Paying off the families was an easy solution—provided that someone else supplied the cash.

Or at least, Elder Beth explained it so when Glenda expressed her frustration over this newest detour. The Elder had been thrilled to take her in as a mentee, but Glenda couldn't help an inward seething. She was, after all, an elf; no level of class or rank could put them on equal footing.

Once Cameron is dead, Glenda thought to herself, *I will shake you off like the tick that you are.*

But for now, their ambitions aligned. So it was that they stood in a grand audience chamber before Chancellor Felix Noor. Banners hung from the walls, one for each vassal of New

Albion. Glenda's eyes passed over a spread-winged eagle, a crawling salamander, a golden lion—at the last, she dug sharp nails into her palm, feeling a throb at the back of her head. Stands topped with witch-light kept the banners from falling into shadow. An excessive display of magical consumption, but that was the point: to broadcast conspicuous wealth and drain the small folk of their nerve, so that by the time they reached the chancellor, who lounged on a dais at the room's far end, your average goatherd or silk-merchant would be reduced to a stuttering mess.

Not so for Glenda, the Elder, and a selection of higher priests, who stood before an outspread fan of knights. Their polished armour reflected the witch-light, so that they shone like something from a fable.

In front of the dais, a scattering of the king's knights stood in hesitant opposition.

"So," said the chancellor. "It's over, then." He raised his goblet, with a small smile. "I'd have chosen a finer vintage, if I'd known this was to be a special occasion."

An obvious lie: this chamber, which ought to have been packed with supplicants, had been curiously empty upon their arrival.

"Be well," Chancellor Felix Noor said to the knights who bristled at the dais edge. "I can't expect your loyalty to me to come before obedience to the Church. Unfortunately."

Elder Beth stepped forward. "You must know why we're here."

"Tithe evasion," said the chancellor sadly.

This brought the Elder to a halt. Her snarl of triumph froze, half-formed.

"Is it not tithe evasion? I have been rather blatant about it. Very well." The chancellor sighed heavily. "I'll admit to it. The murder of Cedric Lombardi."

Mutters filled the hall. The Elder looked sharply at her closest attendant, who shrugged and shook his head.

"Not that either?" The chancellor was starting to look confused. "I've been helping myself to the king's treasury, is it that . . . ? No? Hm. I fixed the results of a unicorn race just this past week, could that be . . . ? Well then, what is it?" He drained the last of his goblet and slammed it down on the arm of his chair. "Or must I keep guessing?"

"Dealings with the sorcerer." The Elder's voice rose as she attempted to resume a triumphant overture. "You've been fetching him texts, and receiving forbidden artifacts in return."

"Oh, that?" The chancellor laughed, seemingly in good humour. "That will be my downfall? Nothing I've supplied has done him any good, despite his boasts. The madman hasn't made a scrap of progress in decades." His rich brown eyes narrowed. "I imagine you'll be seizing my wealth, since I've failed to produce any heirs. Is that what this is about? You need some pocket change."

Glenda felt the chancellor's gaze move to her and forced herself to remain straight-backed, a proud soldier of Order.

"It's the prophecy, isn't it? With that daft little knight. All of a sudden, everyone's in the most terrible rush. Well, I hope you'll use my money for something grand. Am I to be executed?"

"Jailed." The Elder's teeth clicked together with finality.

"Ah," said the chancellor, finally withering. "How dull."

Glenda searched herself for pity as knights escorted the chancellor from his raised platform, his paunch becoming more visible with his slumping posture. Mostly, she just found herself wishing he were Cameron.

And she rocked on her feet, imagining all the interesting things she would do if he were.

CHAPTER 19

In Which I Am Sore and Bruised in Some Excellent Ways, and In Which I Certainly See the Appeal of Having a Different Set of Plumbing.

I woke up smiling to myself. "Hello, fog," I said, to the curls of white infiltrating the stone window slit. "Hello, rat stain on the floor. Hello, hard, shitty cot. Hello—" I paused, as something broke through my tranquility. A feeling of dampness on the bed beneath me. But I couldn't have... I was an adult, for God's sake!

Already plotting how I would hide this from the sorcerer, I pulled back the curtain I used as a blanket, and screamed.

I found the sorcerer in the kitchen, leaning over a pair of plates in nervous inspection. Breakfast for us, I assumed. Tiny kitchen constructs prodded at the eggs and bread, optimizing their placement; these scattered at my approach.

"Merulo," I choked, drawing my blanket tighter around myself, "something's wrong. I think I'm dying."

"Is that my curtain?" The sorcerer stepped out from behind the table, squinting at my wrapping. At my choked sob, he paled, hands jumping into the air where they fluttered like sickly birds. "Calm down, calm down. What's the matter?"

Unable to speak, I simply unwrapped my blanket to show him.

The sorcerer shouted, his panic, for a moment, reflecting my own. Then, he paused, and a change came over his face. Unbelievably, he snorted. "How can you be this poorly educated?"

"Merulo!" I wailed.

"Alright, alright! Damn you. This is what you wanted, yes, to be a woman? And not a vulture? So then . . ." He waved a hand, poorly masking his own discomfort. "Here are the consequences."

"Merulo," I moaned, clutching at him with a red-stained hand. "My insides are coming out."

"No, they're not. They're—there must be a book for this. Sit there, I'll find you a book. And don't drip. You're dripping everywhere."

I lowered myself into a chair, barely containing a sob. "It hurts."

The sorcerer—who had backtracked so hastily he nearly tripped over a bag of flour—placed himself at the opposite side of the table, looking ready to leap if I grabbed for him again. "Women go through this every month," he said, his lopsided stare fixed on a hanging bundle of herbs. "Did you not . . . did your mother . . . ?"

"She died," I said, fidgeting. The fabric of my dress felt uncomfortably damp, and it was driving me close to madness. "In childbirth. I don't remember her much."

The sorcerer's face went through an odd series of contortions. "I'm sorry to hear that. Mine is . . . similarly disposed."

"Yes, I assumed," I said, wiping at my face. "Because of your age."

"How old do you think I am? No, don't answer that." He brought his fingernails to his face, as if to claw his cheeks. "This entire thing was a terrible idea. Though it is a relief to know you're not expecting."

It took a moment to process that. Then: "WHAT!" I shot up from my seat, the blanket falling. "That was a possibility?"

"Yes, I mean . . . Cameron, when a man and a woman—"

A horror seized me, entirely distinct from the Fear. I slammed my hands down on the table, the plates jumping from the force. "Turn me back into a man. Right this moment."

"Ah . . ." Merulo wavered in place. "The prophecy—"

"I'M BLEEDING OUT!" I roared.

"Yes, yes," said the sorcerer, more flustered than I'd ever seen him. "Yes, alright, it's just . . . alright."

At his hesitation, something in me deflated. "You would still like me as a man, wouldn't you?"

"It's the prophecy. You do remember the prophecy, don't you, Cameron? But," he added hurriedly, as another sob built in my throat, "I would. That is to say, I would still appreciate you, as a man. Though the mechanics . . ."

"Oh," I said, brightening. "I can teach you that."

The sorcerer half turned from me, his face reddening; at the flashing of his eye, a pair of kitchen constructs toddled in. Heat drenched the room from the still-burning oven. Bending, the constructs seized either side of a large paddle and dipped it into the flames, fishing out a plump loaf. The scent of fresh bread and fire rose, almost drowning out the copper of blood.

Merulo's eye flashed again, and I realized he was avoiding the interaction. "Merulo," I insisted.

He jumped, before clearing his throat and drawing himself to his full sorcerous height. "We could, perhaps, restore you to your original form. My castle has remained unbreached for decades. That will not change, regardless of the bodily sex you walk about in. Some deviation may still be warranted to subvert the prophecy. A change in hair colour—"

"No, no," I said, shaking my head. "No, I have to be blonde!"

"And why is that?"

I thought it over. "I'm more handsome as a blonde."

"Oh for . . ." The sorcerer kneaded his brow. "Fine, fine. The fault is mine, for assuming your looks are worth less than your life." From between two gnarled fingers, he peeked a ghastly eye at me, presumably to see if his taunting had any effect.

I didn't budge.

The continued silence gave me the opportunity to wipe more snot from my face. For some reason, Merulo stared as I did this, with something near to a grimace. "Don't do that," he said finally. "You're . . . you're leaving streaks."

"Huh?"

"Never mind, let's just—" He clapped his hands together. "Let us go. Now."

I hopped to my feet and followed his departing form out of the fire-warmed room through the winding corridors, leaving my poor stained blanket behind.

It distracted from my misery to see the castle constructs stand aside, respectfully issuing our passage. That these towering monstrosities of wood and teeth could give way to a frail, thin-shouldered man seemed comically imbalanced. Though, he did strut like he expected every ounce of subservience.

When we reached the library, I realized that I'd forgotten to treasure my final moments in female form. Would I miss it? Would I miss *these*?

"Stop that," snapped the sorcerer, and I lowered my hands from my chest. "Wait in there. I have materials to gather, before we can begin."

When he returned, he had a bandage wrapped around one hand, a bag of chalk occupying the other. Crumpled beneath one arm he carried a stack of papers with what looked like blood staining them.

I looked at them in question. He scowled back at me. "This is costly magic. If I'm to be doing it every other week, then it must be made more efficient."

"And . . . blood makes it efficient?"

"Blood pays the price."

"Ah," I said, not understanding. We might as well have used mine, if that were the case; I had an awful lot of it at the moment.

For all his grumbling, the casualness with which he performed his spells amazed me. I'd heard of people saving up half their lives to afford this procedure, but here I lay on my third transmogrification of the summer, a chalk outline being traced about me. I tried not to look at the ruin of my dress, though the discomfort of the stiffening fabric made my situation unignorable.

Merulo placed the bloodied papers at the spokes of the pentacle. Kneeling carefully so as not to smudge the chalk, he took one of my hands (with a downturning of his mouth that, frankly, I did not appreciate). He produced a slim knife from his robes and sliced off the outer crescent of my pinkie nail, then moved to my head and cut a lock of hair.

"A quick prick," he warned, before sticking the knife into my exposed arm.

"Ouch!" I drew my arm back instinctively, before surrendering it again at his huff. The blade had penetrated shallowly, drawing only a single droplet of blood, which he scraped up with the flat of his blade.

Having gathered all the necessary components, Merulo deposited them into a loop above my head, where the chalk outline bloomed into a pentagram. And he spoke the words.

There was the wet crack of flesh, my body shifting and crunching around me, and a distant awareness of agony, the numbing of which was surely central to the spell. Then came the tear of fabric as a muscled man's body erupted through my slim linen dress. The corset held until I sat up, then snapped with a crack that resounded through the library.

The relief was immediate. I could wash, I could change, and I would never again experience whatever the fuck *that* was.

"Well. That's done with." I flexed the new breadth of my shoulders. It felt unbelievably good to rise to my full height and see the sorcerer shrink. My calm restored, I felt ready to talk about things in a more sensible manner. "Does that really happen to all of them?"

"I think so," said the sorcerer. "Mostly. I mean, I've read..." He trailed off, grimacing, and I joined him in his silence.

Only for a moment, though. "That can't be true. Even Glenda?"

"I don't know!" Merulo threw up his hands in furious helplessness. "If she's not beyond the age of... then... actually no, Cameron, I do not wish to discuss elf menstruation with you. There's a book. I'll provide you with a book."

He hurried off between his shelves, fleeing me. The sound of books rasping against their neighbours and pages flicking told me that he was genuinely seeking out the information.

As I stood there in my torn and stained dress, it occurred to me: I'd gotten exactly what I wanted! All of it: my humanity, my handsome man-body, and the sorcerer under my thumb. Granted, the route I'd taken was perhaps not what I'd have chosen or expected.

I mean, every *month*? That just couldn't be true.

CHAPTER 20

In Which, with the Heft of My Biceps Restored, I Am Heaving Buckets and Swinging Mops Like Never Before. In Which I Sometimes Do Pretend that My Mop Is a Sword, and Practice Flourishes in the Air. In Which, due to the Flung Droplets from Said Flourishes, My Hair Smells Very Much Like Mop Water.

I had worried that Merulo might be less attentive to me after my transformation. In fact, the opposite proved true. He began to neglect his books.

I'd be scrubbing the floors, humming a jaunty tune, then look up to see the sorcerer feigning surprise. As if it were pure coincidence that he'd chosen this particular corridor to wander through—and coincidence that a construct had, minutes earlier, scuttled by to flash its eyes at me.

"The kitchen servants have something new," he'd say. "Something with ginger. If it's of interest." And I'd rise to follow the tail of his black cloak, leaving my washrag to mildew on the floor.

"I can only stay for a moment," he'd say. But I'd smash a plate against the wall and, well, more than a moment would pass.

One evening, we sat in the library—him in the tall-backed chair he favoured, me on a cushion at his feet, my head resting against his knee. I pretended not to feel the gentle brush of his bony fingers, afraid that acknowledgement would lead to embarrassment. Still, I gave myself away, leaning back into his fingers with a sigh.

He retracted his hand. "I'm—" he said, then stopped, strangled.

I opened my eyes, and twisted to look up at him. "You're what?"

His thin lips contorted like worms. A muscle in his chin twitched. With horror, I recognized something like fear in his face. "You're too ... aghh!"

"Aghh?"

Energy thrummed through him, vibrating his legs, but the sorcerer was still gentle as he pushed me off his knees and stood. "I've fallen behind in my studies."

"Sorry." I scooted back to give him space, cloaking my nerves with a grin. "I suppose I'm partially responsible for that."

"You are entirely responsible. That is the problem." He strode toward the library door.

"But it's not a problem, is it? We're just ..." The wheels of my mind ground to a halt. "If it is a problem, then I don't have to bother you so much. But it's not an unsolvable problem, is what I'm saying."

Merulo hesitated at the door, gripping the handle with white knuckles. "It is not unsolvable."

"Then ... let's solve it!"

"I may have to." He threw open the door with something

not unlike anger, and disappeared through it with a sweep of his cloak.

My jaw hung open as I waited for the gears in my skull to begin whirring again. On the ground, the historical archive I'd been pretending to read lay discarded. I brushed it off and carefully reshelved it.

"I can't help but feel there was subtext," I muttered, aligning the book's spine with its fellows. "But he's fairly blunt, isn't he? He'd speak his mind."

Feeling better, but not entirely soothed, I made my own departure from the library. It always felt eerie in there without him—like a menagerie cage without its captive manticore, all bare lonely bars.

And it had given me an uneasy sampling of how hollow the world felt without him.

CHAPTER 21

In Which Worry Is Knitting My Insides into Something a Lady Might Wear as a Scarf. In Which I Am Present in the Moment and Cherishing the Gift that Is the 'Now,' While the Nauseous Lump that Is the Future Tries to Work Itself through My Mouth. In Which I Really, Really Am Trying.

I shielded my eyes from the sun. The breeze carried salt from the sea below, where waves foamed and splashed, first pounding then sucking back from the rocky cliffs.

I maintained a respectful distance from the edge. And not just because of the dizzying drop—I felt certain that if I *did fall*, those churning currents would keep my corpse dancing forever beneath the surface.

I pointed at the water below. "Would all the salt pickle me?"

Merulo frowned at me before understanding. "Fish would eat you first."

I scrutinized his reply for any trace of temper, but failed to find it. If anything, he sounded playful. Nothing of his latest tantrum remained.

"The correct answer," I said, aiming for similar lightness, "was that you would save me, from both the fish *and* the salt."

"Hm." Merulo had brought a book, which he opened to an interior spread of a rocky landscape. He seemed to be comparing it to our location. Apparently satisfied, he snapped the book shut and drew a pouch from the enchanted depths of his robes.

"What's that for?" I asked, and received an annoyed huff in response. Merulo showed little enthusiasm when discussing magic.

"Channeling the spell," he said. "It's not strictly necessary, but we're in no rush. The words and items, they give direction."

Upending his pouch, the sorcerer poured small bones onto the lichen-webbed stone. He knelt before his pile, showing no regard for the cleanliness of his robe. Then, startling me, he placed his thumb between his teeth and bit. Blood welled up, shocking scarlet against his pallid skin. Before I could protest, Merulo pressed his thumb to the rockface, dragging it to paint a crude pentagram around the bones.

"Can't think of a better way to get an infected wound." I crossed my arms. "Honestly, you don't think enough about keeping yourself well. Like, say . . ." Here I hesitated, uncertain if I was probing a sore spot. ". . . in the after times. If you—*after* you succeed. We might be hated."

To distract from my anxiety, I picked up a nearby rock. Hiding behind a hand, I gave it a test lick to see if the salt coated everything.

It tasted like a rock.

"Next time we'll bring baked goods. It's been less than an hour, and you're already eating stones," the sorcerer muttered.

Rolling my shoulder, I tossed the stone away. It soared

over the cliff's edge, chattering as it bounced along the rocks below. "And am I right in assuming there won't be constructs to come to our defense, after the magic's gone?"

I'd have to start manually cleaning the garderobes, too, lest the fumes kill us where we squatted. And without portals, it'd be a long round trip to restock the castle from local villages. Which meant we should purchase unicorns now and set up a stable area in the courtyard.

I'd want a palomino unicorn, to match my hair. Merulo could have a greasy black one.

"If I can *finish* my work—if you can find it in yourself to stop distracting me . . ." The sorcerer examined his bloody handiwork. "You shouldn't be in any danger, as the prophecy will be rendered meaningless. If it's truly a concern, I can transport you to a region well outside the Church's influence." He cleared his throat, then shouted guttural, dry words that made me long for unsalted water. The ground beneath our feet trembled—then, *things* rose from it, pushing through the solid surface as if it were pudding.

"What about you? Why not perform this 'killing God' spell in safe territory to begin with?" Something rose from the ground close to me, and I side-stepped to give it room. It looked to be the stone skull of an enormous animal, all beaked snout and spiky teeth. "And we'll meet up, right, after you're finished?"

"We will not." The sorcerer reopened the wound on his thumb with another bite, then walked among the giant bones, smearing them with bloody symbols. I could see more bones surfacing in the distance. We'd be at this for a while.

"Okay, whatever, so I'll just stay with you." Taking my

words literally, I followed the sorcerer as he walked along the cliff, attending to the bones.

"Cameron, when this is done . . ." Merulo rubbed at his bleeding thumb. "I have enjoyed this, certainly, and I'd be lying to deny there's . . . *temptation*. But what I aim to complete is vastly more important than either of us. And when it is finished, I will not be in a state where I can—" The sorcerer cut himself off, grimacing. He spoke an incomprehensible word, and the blood-marked bones floated into the air, drawing toward him to circle like curious birds.

I wanted to grip Merulo by his scrawny shoulders and shake him out like a carpet, but those orbiting bones spun with the force of missiles. "What does that mean? Whatever you're planning, it's not going to *kill* you, is it?"

"I will be in a state where survival may not be possible," he admitted, distant behind his net of skulls, whirling vertebrae, and dagger-like ribs.

"What state? Merulo, what state will you be in?"

He continued his walk along the cliff, bending now and then to add a bone to his flock. "I will not have this body. The things I do now will no longer be possible."

The distance between us grew with each addition, the density of swirling bones making it difficult to hear him.

"All this time, you've been building toward something that will destroy you?" I said, and did not receive an answer.

Sometime later, his scouring of the cliffside complete, the sorcerer sung open a portal and gave a choir conductor's gesture. The hovering bones dove like seabirds, disappearing one by one, until Merulo and I stood alone on the cliffside.

As he moved to step through, I darted forward and caught

his arm. "You know, destroying the magic . . . it's a massive change to be imposing on a whole lot of folks who, quite frankly, like the world the way it is."

"And?" The sorcerer pulled his arm out of my grip. With another step, he vanished.

Cursing loudly, I jumped through the portal after him, leaving the sea behind without a glance. "I mean—okay, I don't really care about that aspect either. It's just . . ."

"Just what?" The sorcerer cut a strong shape in the windy courtyard, with his flapping black hair and robe. The bones no longer hovered, but had stacked themselves obediently in a corner alongside a more typical pile of human and animal remains.

"If this is a . . . a quest toward self-destruction—if it's some stupid, grand suicide . . ." I raised my hands in exasperation. "I don't know that I can watch that happen without doing anything."

"And what would you do?" The sorcerer completed his inspection of the bones, presumably the cores of some monstrous future constructs, and stalked past me. "You'd have me throw it all away? Burn all I've fought for to ash, in exchange for what—eating scones with Sir Cameron?" His voice twisted, mocking me, but the breath he held betrayed him. It was a real question.

My hands stretched toward him, like a drowning swimmer. "Yes. If the alternative is you *dying*, then yes. Fuck it. Burn it all." He was almost within reach. Just a couple more steps, and I could see my words landing like blows. "You don't have to do all this. Just stay here, with me, and . . . we'll keep doing what we're doing. Or we can go somewhere else. We could do anything at all."

The sorcerer wilted, defeat already carved into his face. My fingers brushed his robe. "No more of this destroying God bullshit—"

"Leave."

"Pardon?"

The sorcerer side-stepped me. My hands groped at empty air. "Leave. I want you out of my castle."

"But . . . surely we can talk about this—"

He stood rigid, as if in a pre-death rigor mortis. "I have no use for those who distract me from my goals."

"Merulo—"

"LEAVE!" he screeched, his eye flashing, and suddenly the courtyard was full of constructs, their heads raised and waiting.

"But the prophecy . . ."

A quiver ran through him, and my horror lessened by a degree. He still needed me! He couldn't buck off our connection. Our fates were tied. Once more, I tried to close the distance—and constructs mobbed me, forming a barrier of wing and claw and misshapen gut. I pressed forward, shoving the gnarled arms that blocked my view. Over the shoulder of a goat-faced construct, I caught a glimpse of the sorcerer stalking away. "Merulo!"

He didn't turn around. "You'll destroy me either way, Sir Cameron. So leave."

I shouted a bit more, and bruised my hands on several wooden bodies. I might have even bitten one. But their eyes didn't flash, and none of them moved to harm me or retaliate.

Finally, at some unheard command, the constructs dispersed, leaving me panting but unrestrained. The wind rasped at my eyes, and I wiped them.

"I'm coming in now!" I shouted to nobody, for the constructs had crawled and scuttled away to attend to other duties, leaving me a solitary speck in the empty expanse of the courtyard. "Merulo?"

But there was nobody to respond. The mad sorcerer had gone.

Chapter 22

In Which, in the Space of a Single Afternoon, It All Fell to Shit. In Which I Am Reminded that This Man Is the Enemy of Humanity and as Such, Probably Isn't Very Good at Interpersonal Conflict. In Which Neither Am I, so What Then? In Which I Am Angry and Sad and Cannot See a Way to Fix This, so Why Not Break It Even Further.

Nothing stopped my re-entry to the castle. No constructs gripped me in their terrible curving claws when I stormed the kitchen and desecrated a tray of scones, and no foul scythes landed across my back as I returned to my room, brushing crumbs from my chin.

I walked back and forth across my bedroom, repeatedly, but courage came before I could wear a path in the limestone. Even then, I had only a small amount, fluttering in my chest like a moth.

Each step down the hallway felt like something I couldn't take back. It made my flight of weeks prior, semi-conscious and impaled by an arrow, pleasantly nostalgic in retrospect; at least then, my mind had been unified on the goal of survival. Now, pieces of me split and argued.

Nobody human could stand me. Gareth had said that. But the sorcerer had been so nice. He'd given me pretzels, for crying out loud! And wasn't I the solution to his loneliness?

"He won't let me go," I said, smiling away my nerves. "That's all there is to it. He's had a nice sorcerous tantrum, and now . . . now things will be fine."

All too soon, the library appeared before me. I considered taking another lap around the castle, or two, or maybe even three, but forced myself to open the door and walk through it.

The sorcerer sat hunched over a book in his usual chair. All spindly and insectoid, he looked like something you might crack over your knee with ease. It gave him a vulnerability I hadn't noticed before.

My gut twisted. "You want me to leave."

"Yes," said the sorcerer.

"Then . . . then, I'm leaving now."

"Wonderful." He licked a gaunt finger and turned a page.

I spluttered. "And the prophecy?"

"What about it? Simply refrain from getting killed. I'm sure even you can manage that much." Merulo's hair fell into his face, an oily curtain that draped to the stained pages of his ancient book.

I felt ill. Had he not enjoyed my presence here, as a cleaner, a companion, a co-conspirator?

Perhaps he tired of my silent dawdling, for the sorcerer shut his book with a snap. "I have errands to run in town. By the time I return, I expect to find you gone."

I stood open-mouthed, wanting to protest but not knowing what exactly I was objecting to. He didn't give me time to gather my thoughts, but stalked from the library without another word, and was gone.

It took me less than an hour to pack. From under my cot, I retrieved the tattered remains of my trusty linen dress, and folded it reverently. Gareth's sword, I buckled around my waist. I restored the curtain I'd been using as a blanket to its original wall. Then, changing my mind, I tore it back down again. In the kitchen, I loaded it with food and tied it into a little bag to carry over my shoulder. "My curtain now," I said.

After some consideration, I also packed my spare dress. I could barter it for room and ale, the latter of which would be sorely needed.

Throughout, I hoped to see the flash of construct eyes, the stuttery turning of their heads as they tracked me, but all the castle servants moved past me blindly. Merulo was not even bothering to watch me leave.

With nothing left to do but go, I stood unmoving in the hall that led to the courtyard. We'd had a fight, yes, but we'd fought before.

"I'm objectively hot, and a massive catch!" I shouted in frustration. "And what's his side of things? That I'm ruining his suicide?"

The bundle over my shoulder already felt heavy. I turned back and forth, indecision spinning me in place like a bottle, until something clicked.

"Too bad. If he wants me gone, he can drag me out himself. And I'll cling to every wall and doorframe on the way." Let him live in a castle with my scratch marks winding through it, the bastard. When had I ever been obedient? And now I was marching out to, what, humour one of his fits? Absolutely not!

I'd feel a bit stupid unpacking my scarce belongings, but the sorcerer would come back, and we could communicate, *properly* this time. It would be alright.

Things could still return to how they were.

In the hall ahead, the air split. A circular glyph unfolded, its detailed edges resembling lace. A transport portal. For a single joyous instant, I thought it was Merulo, regretting his words and returning early.

Then the dark blot in its center materialized into a crouching elf, and I felt death close around me.

"Oh. Hello, Glenda."

CHAPTER 23

In Which My Past and Present Have Collided in a Most Unpleasant Way. In Which I Have to Act Fast, or Something Terrible Will Happen to Me. In Which, through All the Screeching in My Head, I Understand with Horrible Clarity that There Is Nothing I Can Do but Wait for It to Happen.

Not even the burliest of knights can go five minutes against a thin-boned elf girl.

I didn't last one. Glenda barely materialized before she was bounding down the hallway to grab me. Her hand closed about my wrist like an iron shackle. I wasted my last moment staring down at her stupidly as she strong-armed me through the closing portal.

We emerged in a church with a high tapered ceiling, resplendent on all sides with scenes of stained glass. In one quick motion, Glenda unsheathed the sword from my waist and stepped backward.

Knights crowded this place of worship, but I ignored them in favour of the largest stained-glass window, a depiction of God's Descent in a mosaic of interlocking colours. Light streamed through it, splintering into a fantastical rainbow where it fell upon the checkered floor.

The sight should have brought me comfort. I'd grown up under God's many eyes. They'd watched me from the illuminated pages of my family bible, from the carved wood of our church altar, and from stained-glass displays much like this one. God was integral to my upbringing, His shape as familiar as my brother's hens.

Now, looking at the tentacled mass, the eyes that sprung from irregular locations like teenage acne and the red halo of light that kept Him in perpetual silhouette, I felt as the sorcerer must. As though I looked upon an intruder, foreign to my understanding. For the first time in my twenty-five years, I looked up at God and felt only dread.

"Sir Cameron," a voice called.

I turned to see a white-robed Elder walking at an unbothered pace between the assembled knights. As if I'd entered the church on a whim, and she just happened to recognize me.

She came to a graceful stop before me, unblemished robes gathering at her feet, and smiled with true kindness. "Despite your actions, we are not without mercy. We thought to give you a chance to pray to God in His holy house. To ask forgiveness, and ready your soul for its journey."

Perfection! I'd recite the longest prayer in my memory, until the knights were rolling their eyes and begging permission to drag me out in chains. She'd offered a precious gift: time for Merulo to notice my absence and rush to my aid with a swarm of constructs.

Why, then, did the thought sicken me?

"I appreciate the offer," I said, barely registering the words as coming from my own mouth. "But me and God aren't on speaking terms right now."

"Then I'll pray on your behalf. Safe travels, Sir Cameron."

"*Thank* you. We are traveling to my murder, but by God, let's do it safely." I dropped my bagged possessions, freeing my hands, and evaluated the pack of men before me.

Glenda moved to backhand me, but the Elder stopped her with a wave. "Not inside the church."

This wasn't like my taunting of the chancellor. I was no longer under the sorcerer's protection. But what could they do, kill me?

As a pair of knights rounded on me, gripping my arms above the elbows, I heard my own hysterical laughter. They pushed me down the church aisle, kicking at the backs of my legs whenever I threatened to crumple, until we exited into blinding sunlight.

Why today? If they'd struck even an hour earlier, Merulo might have returned to see my unpacked belongings and wondered after me. It's as though they knew the precise minute to best grab me, as if . . . Oh.

I really hated magic.

War-unicorns waited patiently along a hitching post, dapples and duns and shiny bays. I didn't recognize our location, but assumed it was one of the satellite towns bordering the sorcerer's territory, close enough to the prophesied killing ground that it made an acceptable detour.

With the prickle of swords surrounding me, I followed grunted directions, approaching a white mare with a curling beard. She was far shorter than the equine construct, so I could at least clamber into her saddle without much humiliation.

Secure in my seat, I slammed my heels into the unicorn's sides, and shouted, "GO, GO!"

The knight holding her bridle regarded me with embarrassment. A couple of the men laughed, but most looked serious. Behind me, a slim figure slipped onto the mare and twisted my arms back painfully with inhuman strength, securing my wrists with a twining cloth. While I struggled and yelped, the knight stroked the unicorn's muzzle, whispering soothing words. More respect given to the animal than to the man astride it! Somewhere inside me, that last lingering thread of comradery snapped.

Seeing that I was properly secured, the knight handed the reins to the slim blue arms reaching around me on either side. I wondered, idly, if I could ratchet my head back with enough force to break Glenda's nose.

"Were the Elders angry after you shot me?" I twisted around to look at her. "You nearly did me in, which would have meant no more prophecy."

"Prophesies always come true, one way or another," Glenda replied coldly. "I should have told you that from the start. It might have saved us all some trouble."

That couldn't possibly be true. I felt disconnected, as if I hovered outside my own body. But it didn't have to be today, that wasn't specified. I didn't have to die today.

"Glenda," I tried again, as the unicorn trotted into motion. Knights on sleek steeds fanned in formation around us, forming a cage. "We used to be close. But the way you're acting now, it's like talking to a stranger. Did I ever really know you? I mean, which version is real, then or now?"

The light fell in leaf-filtered dapples as we left the church grounds, following the remains of an ancient road. Glenda's sigh blew the hairs on the back of my neck. "Do you really want to know?"

"Well, er. Yes?" If I could perhaps engineer a fall from the unicorn . . . I couldn't outrun them all—but again, I was buying time. Better still would be a plunge into a river or down some crevice.

I craned my neck every which way, but the forest floor rolled out even and unchanging, no handy cliffs presenting themselves. Fixated on escape, I nearly missed Glenda's reply. "I don't feel things, Cameron. It's like there's something frozen in me, something that thaws at birth in everyone else. That's why I take the Passionweed."

"The . . . what?" Against my better judgement, I found myself softening. I considered sharing my own debilitation, the Fear, in a last-ditch bonding effort.

"Passionweed. It's harmless, really. You chew it before a boring play to better connect with the actors' performances, or at a party, to wind up the intensity of things. People experiment, and they move on. They grow up. But for me . . . it thaws me." Her voice took on a dreamy quality. "And not just to a normal level. I can surpass normal, feel more than anyone else."

It sounded exceedingly unpleasant to me, like scraping off a layer of skin to better feel the breeze. Then again, her natural state was what I longed for—to be calm, collected, without the Fear astride me.

"I wish you'd told me," I said. "Back when we were friends. There's nothing wrong with . . . feeling things differently.

Or whatever it is you said. But there's *absolutely* something wrong with shooting me full of arrows and—and kidnapping me, and tying me up, and—and plotting my murder, and I don't see what that has to do with personality quirks or drugs. Glenda . . ." I was pleading now. "We don't choose who we are, but you can choose to act differently."

"Oh, like you chose to smash my skull in with your sword? To betray the forces of good and order? That sort of choice?" Her hands tightened on the reins in front of me, knuckles prominent through her blue skin.

"Ehrm . . ." Around us I saw sideways glances, the closest knights listening in. Maybe I could use this distraction to subtly steer the unicorn, directing us into an overhanging branch. I'd duck, of course, leaving it to smack Glenda in the face.

"You don't care about anyone else, Cameron. So long as *you* stay safe, you'd let this whole world burn."

It was completely true. "Glenda, that's not true! I just think we've, uh . . . *misjudged* the mad sorcerer, you know?" The unicorn snorted, ignoring the coded instructions I was squeezing through my legs. "There's stuff he's told me, about the pre-Descent world. We've lost a lot, and Merulo's just trying to restore it."

"The prophecy doesn't require you to have a tongue," Glenda warned, and I shut up. She, however, carried on. "You dare to bring up what we've lost. Do you have any idea how many *men* we've lost, in the weeks since your *betrayal*? It's a lot, Cameron. If you'd died back then—back when we would've hailed you as a hero—they would all be alive. How many lives are you worth, huh? All those families without sons and fathers. Is it worth it, just for you? You know it isn't. You can't even pretend otherwise. So why?"

"I didn't want to die," I said miserably, before remembering that my tongue was at stake. I tucked it deep into my mouth, as if I could hide it from her, and tried to slouch in a dejected, placatory way, so that she'd be surprised when I burst into action.

And when would that be? At what point would I launch my grand escape? We continued to not pass any ditches, gullies, or rivers, and the unicorn only tossed her head at my increasingly desperate squeezes and kicks. I waited for a chance, and a chance never came, and then we were there.

"It's the statue," Glenda said helpfully. "That's how we knew the location. You'll die in its shadow."

The corroded form of the statue hunched over the swaying meadow, its features honeycombed by time. A light wind teased the grass this way and that, caressing its stone legs. I kicked savagely at the unicorn, hoping to startle it into motion, but it just shivered once, like a dog shaking off a flea.

Glenda slipped lithely off its back and, before I could seize the reins in my teeth and steer the beast to freedom, she yanked me down, hard. I landed on my stomach, the wind knocked out of me, and wheezed uselessly on the ground. It hurt, sucking for air while my lungs resisted expansion.

Then it came: the opportunity. My breath returned to me, while Glenda stood idly, waiting. Of course, in her elven superiority, she'd misjudged the recovery speed of a healthy human man!

I lunged to my feet and dodged past Glenda, through the soft cool grass, all my strength channeled into my pumping legs—then the world tilted, the ground rushing up to meet me. My chin slammed hard into the earth. One of my ankles felt wet, and curiously weak.

Glenda stood over me, holding Gareth's sword. Its blade dripped a revolting crimson. "This is going to happen, Cameron. Face it with some dignity."

I hopped at her as best I could with bound hands, but she easily side-stepped my attack. Falling to my knees, my gaze swept wildly around the men as I tried desperately to meet someone's eye. "I was a loyal Knight of Order. If they do this to me, it could be you next. Please!"

Unlikely to be true, unless the Church started doling out prophecies like weekly bulletins, but I had to try *something*.

Pain bloomed in my skull. A force pulled me backward, and I rolled my eyes back to see Glenda's hand clenched in my hair, pulling me through the grass to the statue. Ignoring the keening of my scalp, which felt ready to tear free in a sheet, I writhed, hooking my feet into uneven patches of ground.

"Please don't do this, please! Glenda, please!" I cried. "Let me speak to an Elder. What Merulo's planning, it's not all bad, if you could *please* hear me out—"

Glenda stepped over my body so that she crouched above me. A shadow fell over us, and I mewled, small and strangled. It was the shadow of the statue.

"What you said . . ." Glenda pointed the sword toward me. It dripped, my own blood falling to stain my cheaply woven shirt. That's right, I'd never gotten a proper one for my man's body. That meant another shopping trip was in order. I could take Merulo's arm, and pester him, maybe even kiss him if he got too angry with me. Let me fall into that fantasy, anything to avoid Glenda's unblinking stare. "You know what the mad sorcerer is planning?"

I realized my misstep as she leaned closer, hushed and conspiratorial. "You know the layout of his castle? The number of constructs at his disposal? His favoured spells? Which heretical texts he's been bargaining for—oh, you didn't think we'd catch Chancellor Noor for his dealings?" She smiled, all teeth. "It doesn't have to happen today, Cameron. There's so much we can learn, and I'm sure the Elders would keep you in comfort for the duration."

This was it. The reprieve I'd been grasping for.

"I . . . I can't do that, Glenda." It was the stupidest thing I'd ever said. "He's my . . . friend." Tears boiled, blurring my vision, and I cursed them. My last moments, and I couldn't even see. "I wish I could, I so wish I could, but I can't. I just can't."

Glenda popped something into her mouth and chewed, like a cow at cud. The casual, almost vulgar gesture brought fire to my cheeks. I locked eyes with her in sudden clarity. "I hope he kills your God. I hope he succeeds in everything." As fast as it arrived, my resolve crumbled. "And, Glenda, please, if you ever see him, tell him that I lo—"

She plunged the sword into my neck.

It took two minutes. The sting of the blade, the bubbling of oxygen leaving me.

Glenda's overflowing eyes. Rotten hatred toward her, wishing she'd move so she wouldn't be my last sight. Batting a red hand at her, seeing her catch and hold it. Not feeling the touch.

Head tilted back, uncomfortably so. Wishing she'd hold

my head, to relieve the stretching. A horrible hunger, gasping through my coppery mouth. Something I wasn't getting. Something important. What was it?

White clouds in a clear sky. Soon there would be nothing, forever and always, nothing, nothing. Black swallowing the sky, how could there be nothing, how could I be nothing, please Merulo, help me—

My eyes were open, but I could see nothing. Feel nothing.

Soon there would be

Nothing.

CHAPTER 24

In Which There Is Nothing.

CHAPTER 25

In Which I Am Nothing.

CHAPTER 26

In Which Glenda Is Beautiful and Splendid. In Which She Has Served the Order and Brought Honour to Her Family. In Which She Has Secured Peace for Her Land and Glory for Her God. In Which Her Lips Are Twitching at the Memory of How His Eyes Dulled and Fell Blank and In Which She Is Grateful to Have Been a Servant of the Law and a Deliverer of Justice.

Glenda ascended the foggy slope, her armour draped with the gleaming white robes of Order. At her sides marched elven relatives, and at her back, the forces of humanity. Constructs gnashed from all sides with creaking branch-limbs and flashes of infernal flame, but the troops were in high spirits. Men shouted insults as they hacked into living wood, and Glenda herself laughed, swinging her halberd into the dog-faced thing that erupted from the fog ahead.

"It's time to turn the tide," she called, the purity of her voice ringing like a church bell. "Raise it, raise it now!"

Behind her, a pair of knights ripped the stained cloth off their jointly carried cargo and, lowering the pike's end to stabilize it in the dirt, hoisted the impaled thing into the air. A maroon glob of congealed liquid dripped onto Glenda's shoulder.

Around them in the fog, constructs began to howl.

"Sir Cameron asked me to pass along a message," Glenda shouted, smiling, and she told them.

CHAPTER 27

In Which Nothing.

CHAPTER 28

Nothing.

CHAPTER 29

In Which Glenda Knows that She Will Be a Figure of Legend, a Story Told to Children, the Noble Elf Who Brought the Mad Sorcerer to Heel. In Which She Has Never Been So Assured of Her Own Goodness and Honour.

Never before had the Knights of Order reached the castle. The men sang hymns, joyous expulsions as they battered the crawling, snapping evil of the sorcerer's servants. It had shaken them all, the sheer number of constructs clinging to the castle walls and battlements, but something vital had left their enemy. The constructs fought mechanically, stupidly, with none of the clever stratagems of old. And none of the anticipated spells descended; the air did not boil, nor turn poisonous, nor thicken to a gel.

Several times, they triggered hidden pentagrams etched into the stony ground, which revealed their designs with a pulse of light, readying a terrible force—only to dim and fade when no magic flowed into them.

The sorcerer was not fighting back.

The forces of Order, an enormous number of men gathered for this final push, overwhelmed the wooden monstrosities with growing confidence, leaving nothing but twitching splinters in their wake.

With the front gates bashed open, new threats emerged from the courtyard: gigantic piscine constructs that writhed open-mouthed along the ground. An unlucky mercenary, transfixed by the sight, disappeared in a single snap, his feet protruding comically from the creature's mouth.

Leaving this development to the humans, Glenda skipped ahead with her elven kin. They broke through the final door and danced down the stone halls, light on their feet despite their armour, as playful and elegant as hunting cats. In preparation for fighting at close quarters, Glenda set aside her halberd, instead drawing the sword she'd used to take Cameron's life.

The elves split from one another, each loping down a different corridor. Squeezing reckless performance from muscles that, after the day's exertion, now ran solely on adrenaline, Glenda dodged the swing of construct scythes and the grope of twiggy claws, hunting for the sound of breathing, footsteps, any noise a man might make. Finally, she heard it: the scrape of chalk on stone.

Glenda smashed through the door ahead of her and crouched, sword brandished, her eyes wide with fear and pleasure.

"You must be Glenda," said the bent and hollow man. He stood in the center of a complex chalk diagram that seemed to bend and warp under her eyes. "Are you the one who did it? Did you use that sword? Never mind." The man glanced down at his work, and his mouth stretched into something that might loosely be considered a smile. "Don't answer. It's already too late."

Screaming aloud to quell her unease, Glenda rushed the sorcerer, impaling him on her . . . except the sword didn't go through. It glanced off him with a reverberation that jarred her elbow. A cut in the fabric, revealing sickly white skin, was the only sign she'd made contact.

Shouting, summoning the reserves of her magic to coat the blade in holy light, Glenda swung at the man again. A shallow red line opened across his torso, droplets flying off the sword to spatter the chalk diagram. Glenda stepped back, panting, as the mad sorcerer threw back his head and laughed. The sound, hacking and without humour, sent ice down her spine.

"Do you know," the man asked, as Glenda backed away, "what the final ingredient is for this spell?" She reached the doorway just as the pentacle began to glow. "It's dragon blood."

The room flashed.

CHAPTER 30

In Which I Am Something. In Which Oh God, Tell Me That Didn't Really Happen, Tell Me I Wasn't, Tell Me She Didn't, Tell Me—

"It doesn't have to happen today, Cameron. There's so much we can learn, and I'm sure the Elders would keep you in comfort for the—" Glenda blinked her overlarge eyes. "Huh. I . . . that damned man!"

"You—you killed me." The words came without any semblance of control. "You killed me, I died, you killed me—"

"Yes, and used your corpse as a flag," she snapped. Knights milled about the meadow, confused. Had any of them also returned from death?

"Pardon?" I marveled at the feel of grass beneath my hands, at the late morning heat, even at my own hunger, all of it taken from me and now returned. "How did it work, like a pole went up my ass, or—?"

"Quiet," Glenda growled. People loved to use that word with me.

"No, I will not be quiet. Glenda, you just said you used my corpse as a flag. That absolutely requires follow up. And what possible situation . . . I've never in my life thought 'Huh, this is going well, but it'd go a lot better if I had a dead guy to wave about on a pole'—oh, oh, so now you're going to hit me? Okay."

Glenda's petite hand smacked me across the face. It felt like a mule kick.

"The thing about prophecies," Glenda said, that same hand balling in my shirt collar and yanking my face to hers. "Is that they always come true. And your *boyfriend* can turn back the clock as many times as he likes, I'll keep killing you until it sticks." The tears that filled her eyes at that grim pronouncement told me the Passionweed must be kicking in. I could use that.

"Glenda, please, why in the world do you hate me so much?" I let my face soften, taking all the hatred and fear from it.

"Because you gave me light sensitivity!" Glenda shouted, spraying spittle into my eyes and mouth. "What, Cameron, did you think head trauma was good for people?" Snarling, heavy tears falling now, she raised Gareth's sword to end my life again.

That's when the dragon arrived.

The blue summer sky opened like a flower around a central black seed. It hurtled toward us at tremendous speed, erupting into a writhing black slash that blotted the sun with its flared wings. Behind it, the portal folded into itself and demurely disappeared.

Men screamed. Spitting curses, Glenda tore her eyes from the dragon, her attention returning, unfortunately, to me. Before she could complete her sword swing, something smashed into us: a unicorn, its mouth stretched into an impossible snarl, its skin dripping smooth and gelatinous.

I twisted out from under the transmogrified steed, away from Glenda, who stabbed at the unicorn-turned-basilisk, again and again, flinging up gouts of stinking blood.

"As many times as it takes, Cameron!" she cried as I squirmed away. "I'll kill you as many times as it takes!"

Freed of the basilisk's weight, I limped to my feet and took in the chaos. The dragon wheeled, black and terrible, breathing nauseating torrents of what looked to be raw magic. Charging knights transformed into trimmed shrubbery, while flung weapons bloomed into flowers of enormous size, which defied the mood by drifting peacefully back to earth. Unicorns, rearing and bucking, became bestial in the dragon's passing breath, pulling off their riders to sink teeth into the crevices of their armour. The earth danced and broke around me, swallowing men in sulfur-stinking gashes. A man rushed at me, yodeling with his sword out, only to disappear into a crack that promptly sealed, his sword arm protruding from the ground like some sort of bizarre plant. The hand still clutched his blade. I staggered closer and rubbed my bound hands against the sharp edge, freeing myself.

Not trusting my ankle to hold, I started crawling toward the forest—only for grass to rip free from my hands as something seized me.

"No!" I cried, which didn't help much. Black talons circled my midriff. I pried at them, even balling my fists to strike with all my strength, but the dragon didn't even flinch. The meadow fell away beneath us; when it grew distant enough that a drop would prove fatal, I gave up my struggle.

Attempting to look up at the dragon brought tears to my eyes, as each wingbeat displaced a stinging rush of air. Black scales covered the beast, overlapping like those of a fish, except on its gut, where scar tissue radiated in stiff white ropes. The effects of this injury were plain; the dragon's body was sunken and thin, its spine standing in a ridge of disturbing definition. I could hear it panting over the whistle of wind, and the leg that held me shivered with exertion. In a change of heart, I hoped fervently that it *would not* drop me, and gripped both hands around a massive toe.

My outlook improved as we passed into fog. "Are you bringing me to Merulo?" I shouted.

It angled its wings, bringing us lower. The white-cloaked ground drew rapidly closer, and I realized, too late, that this wasn't a landing. Moments before impact, the dragon rolled, swinging me like a doll so that I experienced the collision solely through the jar and shuddering of its leg.

The claws around me loosened, and I twisted free. The short drop brought fresh fire to my ankle, but I didn't let the pain slow me as I scuttled backward, putting distance between myself and the monster.

When it failed to move, its legs sticking into the air like some ludicrous smacked fly, I wondered if it had died on impact. Then, the rich blackness of its body contracted. Wings folded into a velvety robe. Scale melted into weak, pale flesh. In place of the primordial beast lay a familiar man.

"Oh my God, Merulo." I staggered toward him, dropping to my knees at his side. "Someone turned you into a dragon?"

The sorcerer's breath wheezed. I drew closer to hear his faint words. "I am a dragon, you fucking imbecile." Having expended the last of his energy, Merulo slackened, eyes closing.

I lightly slapped his face, testing his unconsciousness,

then patted him down to check for injuries. Not finding any, I sat back to attend to myself. Above my ankle, skin flapped loose over a weeping gash. The sight made me nauseous, so I decided to ignore it.

"Merulo." I poked his sunken cheek. "Wake up. I can't carry you."

Two useless men, alone in the fog. At least we'd landed solidly in his territory. Despite knowing that a hunting party would soon come for us, I felt thoroughly depleted, so I lay down beside Merulo on the cool ground.

I really didn't mean to fall asleep.

"Did you want to die again so soon?" The sorcerer's pale, hovering face looked like something from a dream. "Honestly, leaving an open, bleeding wound. If it had nicked your fibular artery, you'd be gone. And I can't turn back time again." His face disappeared; I felt tugging around my ankle, something being tied. "If I'm going to waste all this energy keeping you alive, at least meet me halfway."

Sleep called to me, the rock at my back as soft as a down-stuffed mattress, but a new sound slammed me back to alertness. I sat up, eyes wide. Beside me, the sorcerer was crying.

"I wasn't sure if it would work," he said. "If you'd be restored, physically intact, but remain a lifeless body."

Feeling woozy, I groped for words to reassure him. "Apparently they used me as a flag? That's wild."

The sorcerer hiccuped a laugh, tears streaming from his single eye. Less than a day had passed since I'd seen him last, but he looked older. "Who would even think to do that?"

"Right? That was my reaction, too." Shifting closer, I

wrapped my arms around him, drawing him firmly against me. His ribs were so prominent—why had I never taken his malnutrition seriously before? "Hey, come here. It's alright."

I held the sorcerer until his quaking breaths settled, then let him pull away. Merulo averted his face, rubbing his eye and sniffing in what looked to be an attempt to restore his dignity.

My rear had gone sore from sitting, so I shuffled discreetly. "Not to get doomy, but I think the conditions have been met. We need to move."

"The conditions for my prophesized defeat?" Merulo stared glassy-eyed into the fog. "It's already happened. I'm defeated."

"That's an odd thing to say while we're both alive." Standing unsteadily, I held out my hand. "Come on, you won't kill God with that attitude."

"My attitude is irrelevant," the sorcerer said. I kept my hand out. With a sigh he took it, rising to join me in the swirling white. "I'm drained."

"Drained?" I laughed, a touch frantically. "You? But I thought—"

"Cameron. I reversed time for the entire world. There is nothing left of my magic." He exhaled, displacing a billow of fog. "I can't defend the castle. They'll burn my books. We don't have anywhere to go."

I couldn't summon an argument against any of that. Still, I led him onward. One step in front of the other. Merulo trembled, either from emotion or fatigue, and periodically my ankle threatened to give, but leaning on each other, we ascended the escarpment.

Drained. The mad sorcerer was drained. It didn't seem real, no matter how many times I repeated it.

Shapes materialized from the fog at intervals, constructs lying lifeless. Without their flaming eyes, they looked like uprooted trees, left to rot.

Walking became easier as we found a steady rhythm. Despite the tied cloth (which, upon closer inspection, looked to be torn from the sorcerer's robe), seepage ran down my leg, filling my shoe with blood so that each step squelched unpleasantly.

I only tried once to make conversation. "I have mentioned Glenda on previous occasions—"

"Awful little creature," the sorcerer spat.

"Oh yeah, definitely. Anyway, I might have asked her to, uh, pass something along? And I was wondering if . . ." I had the sudden urge to whistle, to feign nonchalance. "If she accomplished that?"

"No," said the sorcerer, sharp and immediate.

"Huh." I felt an odd sinking in my chest. "I guess she didn't feel inclined to do me any favours. But now I suppose you're curious as to what—"

"Not even remotely. Cameron, our immediate survival is my priority at present, so if you're capable, let's save our breath."

Wanting to push the matter, I glanced at Merulo, and saw something I shouldn't have: sunlight, cutting through the fog and casting his face bone-white.

"This mist is thinning," I said in horror, and he nodded.

That was the last we spoke for some time, our energy funneled into forward motion, our breaths coming heavier as we mounted the slope.

We'd made good progress when the sorcerer sat forcefully,

nearly causing me to fall. His posture and robe brought to mind a large, diseased crow.

"I've been thinking." He sighed.

"Good. That makes one of us." I sank beside him, careful of my bandaged ankle. Throughout our walk, the sorcerer's stone eye had not flashed once. I wondered if it would ever light again.

"We need help. I need help." His face contorted, the admission seemingly as painful as bad gas. "I must make contact with . . . someone."

With the fog dissipating around us, I felt rather exposed on the rocky face of the escarpment. "Could we do it in the castle?"

He shook his head. "It's too far, and there's barely enough blood left in your body to fill a glass."

Hyperbole, I wanted to protest, but the temptation to curl like a mouse and fall blissfully asleep remained. I could imagine it: the fading of my senses, a gentle tumble into the void. Back into nothing.

Nothing.

"Merulo, I know you're a solo artist"—I reached up to grip his shoulder, making a conscious effort not to dig my nails in—"but how's about you give that person a yell?"

He shrugged out from under my hand, fiddling with his robe. "We're on rather poor terms at present."

"Well, it's never too late to apologize! I mean, hey, if you want tips on how to kneel and beg, you're looking at the expert." I beamed my brightest, most encouraging smile.

"Fine. But I'll need to remove a toe." A spidery hand disappeared into his robes, reemerging with a glint of silver.

The wicked blade he'd used to prick himself on the seaside cliffs.

I blanched. "Yours, or mine?"

"Mine. Why would it be yours? Never mind, just . . ." The sorcerer grimaced. "Do it in one stroke. I enchanted the knife; it should cut true. If you resort to hacking, I will . . . vomit on you."

"If that's the best threat you can manage, then I fear for our intimate life." I accepted the knife from him, evaluating its cold weight.

"Cameron, quell your perversion just this once and cut my damn toe off. This one here." Merulo slipped off a shoe and pointed at the smallest toe. Judging from their knackered length, he hadn't cut his nails in some time. Squatting with the faint embarrassment one usually feels when handling feet, I pried the toe away from its brethren and placed the base of the blade above it, a guillotine in miniature.

Before committing to the cut, I said, "Are you sure? If a gesture of appeasement is needed, there's got to be a way that doesn't involve mutilation."

"That's not . . ." The sorcerer threw back his head, exasperated. "It's for the spell. Dragon bodies are a powerful source of magic. I may be drained, but that doesn't mean I cease to be a resource."

In other words, a spell he'd usually cast with less effort than a belch would now cost a minor digit. Poor Merulo. Without another thought, I pressed down on the blade, meeting only the briefest resistance. Merulo gave a banshee wail and scrambled away from me. His jaw hung open, uncomprehending.

"I thought it'd be better without build-up," I said, shaken. "Anticipation can be worse than the actual thing."

"No," the sorcerer finally managed. "No, I'd say the actual thing is worse. Damn it." Bringing the torn corner of his robe to his mouth, Merulo ripped off another strip with his teeth and packed it around the gushing stub.

The toe lay like the pale larva of some unmentionable insect in a spreading pool of blood. Pressing admirably through his pain, Merulo seized it and, using the cut end like a quill, smeared a crude sigil onto the rocky ground. He placed the toe in its center and uttered an incomprehensible plea. Violet flames erupted, consuming the forsaken digit.

The voice that emanated from the fire was deep, and full of startled outrage. "You dare? After pawning my microwave?"

Merulo kneaded his forehead. His hands still shook from the shock of amputation. "Hydna, I wouldn't call if the situation weren't dire."

A growl of frustration made the flames flicker. "Why can't I end this call?"

"Because I am burning my own body to maintain it," the sorcerer snarled. It seemed a poor time for one of his tantrums, so I waved at him frantically and, catching his eye, mimed an exaggerated smile.

"Merulo..." The voice sounded concerned now. "I'm opening a portal. Come through immediately."

The sorcerer hesitated, casting a regretful look at me. "Not without my library. It must be moved to safety."

"Then die with your books," the flames spat.

I jumped in before things could devolve further. "Please, sir, or... ma'am? Merulo has told me about how sorry he is for slighting you, regarding the . . . uh . . . micro . . . Anyway, he has deep regrets, really. And we're hoping, in the spirit of your past relationship, that you can find it in your heart to grant Merulo help in his hour of ne—"

"Who is that?" the voice interrupted. I stopped, wondering whether to introduce myself.

"A friend," snapped the sorcerer. Relinquishing the negotiations to him, I scoured the fog around us, watching for dark shapes that might betray the approach of knights.

"You don't have friends."

"Enough talking." Even drained and down a toe, the sorcerer maintained his arrogance. "Either you bring through my books, or I'll have Sir Cameron here cut off my hand so that I can accomplish the task myself."

Muffled oaths. Then: "You rat bastard. Stand back."

I was busy mouthing *'I most certainly will not'* at Merulo, and was thus quite taken aback when the air split open to reveal the second dragon of the day.

Before the portal could fully unfold, the monster burst through, a behemoth of burgundy wings and scale-draped muscle. I recoiled, reaching for a sword I didn't have, while Merulo rose to greet the thing.

The dragon's coils disappeared every which way into the fog. Its eyes, a reptilian crimson, were as big as my balled fists.

"Are you like, a baby dragon?" I whispered, as I discreetly positioned Merulo between myself and the monster. He smacked me on the arm, muttering something about sexual dimorphism.

"This is your friend?" came the booming voice of the dragon. "Not a servant, a prisoner, or a concubine? A friend?"

I understood; 'friend' implied a level of equality it was not seeing. "Listen," I said from behind Merulo. "I might be a lowly human being, but you know what?" A beat of silence followed as it waited for me to continue, but I had nothing.

In the midst of this awkwardness, the dragon contracted into a giant woman. Muscular, broad-shouldered, big of hip and thigh and breast. Just... large. Her clothes didn't particularly impress me, being a man's standard tunic and leggings, but I marveled at how they stretched to fit her contours.

"Listen, man, I'm not being bigoted." The dragon made an obvious effort to soften her voice as she approached. "My brother has never had a friend before. I'm proud of him, is all." She dropped a hand on Merulo's shoulder with enough force to hammer in a six-inch nail. It was commendable that he did not visibly vibrate.

I peered at the two of them in disbelief. With her tawny complexion, wild mane of burgundy hair, and overall glow of health and vitality, the woman could not have looked more dissimilar to my poor, pasty Merulo.

"Huh." The dragon studied Merulo's un-shoed foot, then looked me over in turn. I shuddered to think of the impression I made, with my cheap, ill-fitting clothes thoroughly saturated with dirt, sweat, and blood. My hair felt like the mangled hide of an animal, and dried mud crusted my face from where I'd been dragged across the field. Her biceps also outsized mine by several orders of magnitude.

She tilted her head, a curiously bird-like gesture. "This is the guy you drained yourself for?" At Merulo's stricken look, she went on. "What, you thought nobody would notice repeating a day? I organized my entire electronics room, cleared the dust, wiped it down, then boom, now I have to do it all over again. Thanks for that, you little idiot."

"He did it to save my life." I stooped to retrieve the sorcerer's shoe from where it lay in a patch of sun-starved grass. "And if you bring us through to safety, I can tidy up your room again, while you sit back with a nice beverage. It'll be as good as it, uh... would have been... tomorrow. Did I say that right?"

Merulo looked pained as he received the proffered shoe and shoved it into the inner pockets of his robe.

"Eh, thanks," said Hydna, a touch awkwardly, "but nobody touches my machines. Because greedy little thieves"—her voice rose as she turned on the sorcerer—"can't seem to help themselves!"

"I put it to better use," the sorcerer snapped, rounding on her. "You used that scrap metal to reheat day-old fish. I traded it for the secrets of the universe!"

The relic he'd exchanged for the textbooks. "I know where it is!" I said, happy to dissipate what was shaping up to be the most uneven fight imaginable. "Chancellor Noor had it before getting caught by the Church. It must be in their heretical vaults by now."

The muscular woman pulled a face. "Then it's good as gone. I'm not fucking with the Church."

"If you don't wish to 'fuck with the Church'"—the sorcerer's hands twitched, as he visibly restrained himself from using air quotes—"then I'd advise we get to work. They'll be arriving soon to execute us all."

She groaned. "Why must you be such an aggressive freak? You know how many enemies I have? None."

"Because you kill them all," said the sorcerer, casting me a 'see what I have to deal with?' look. I pretended not to see it, not sure which of the two I should be trying to please.

"Exactly. I don't fuck with people I can't kill." Flexing, she expanded back into a cascade of scale and claw, the suddenness of her mass blowing away the fog.

It was her. I should be trying to please her.

Merulo extended an arm toward the castle. "The library is in the stronghold southeast of here, second story. I won't leave a single book behind. Also," he added as an afterthought. "Sir Cameron has been wounded and requires attention."

"Anything else?" she boomed. "Maybe a pint of ale and a backrub?"

I laughed, too shrilly, and the dragon fixed me with a scarlet eye. Merulo looked faintly disgusted.

"Blood loss appears to be affecting his mental faculties, so let's start with your friend." In an utterance that would have been terrible from a human tongue, and felt nearly unbearable from the thundering maw of a dragon, she cast the spell. Something rushed through my body, briefly darkening my vision. Alertness, so abruptly attained that it felt like a drug.

"No, that's just how he is." The sorcerer sighed, clearly spent from the effort of standing imposingly. "But thank you, nonetheless."

Now that I felt strong, with my weight carried evenly on two healthy legs, I could see how frail the sorcerer looked in comparison. "Merulo, couldn't you use, a, uh . . . 'touch up' as well?" I indicated his bare foot, which still seeped freely.

The dragon twitched her muscles impatiently. Merulo shook his head. "Dragon bodies are pure magic. It would take an immense amount to restore what has been lost, more than it's worth."

Clearly growing tired of this discussion, the dragon opened her maw (revealing a tongue I could have curled up and fallen asleep on without feeling cramped) and spat forth a familiar incantation. A portal blossomed in the air before us. "I'll fetch your damn books, so go through," she growled. "And if I find anything more has been stolen, there won't be enough of your bodies left to bury."

"I would advise against threatening Cameron," the sorcerer said, limping toward the widening gap in space. "He has entirely the wrong sort of response."

Stepping through the portal, Merulo vanished.

The dragon looked at me in question, flaring nostrils wide enough to plunge my hands into.

"Ah . . . well . . . sometimes blood gets confused as to where it should be flowing, is all." I edged past her. "I'll be going through the portal now, if that's alright. Okay, goodbye. Thank you."

I stepped through—and was underwater.

Or rather, given my continued ability to breathe, *under* water. I could vaguely make out a dome far above, holding an unimaginable weight of water at bay. In the distance, the transparent barrier curved behind the rise of ancient buildings. We stood, I realized with growing disbelief, in an entirely submerged city.

Expensive, coveted glass glittered in excess. Signs protruded from every surface, marked with forbidden languages, pointing arrows, and smiling faces. Rippling blue light fell across everything, distorted by the movement of the water above. The main source of illumination, however, came from lampposts that shone an eye-burning white. At first, I misunderstood, thinking they must contain witchlight; then, as I heard an odd buzzing, I recalled the sorcerer's teachings. *Electricity.*

"It's a relic," I breathed. "This entire place."

Merulo nodded grimly, then stumbled forward, making for a bench at the edge of a tiled plaza. In his wake, red smeared the tiles like a gruesome slug trail. "God's infection thins out beneath sea level. Technologies work down here that would be useless trash anywhere else in the world."

I followed Merulo, and sat gratefully beside him. The arms of the bench flared in a static swirl of sculpted waves and pinching crabs. I traced these with a finger.

"I have to warn you . . ." The sorcerer looked too weary to do more than talk, sinking completely into the bench. "On the day of the Descent, this did not serve as a sanctuary for unblemished humanity. It was a tomb for all who dwelled within it. There are places that Hydna and I have cleared of bodies, but elsewhere . . . explore at your own risk."

Goosebumps prickled, my arm hairs standing on end. "They couldn't live down here? They couldn't escape?"

"Food ran out, eventually. And look." Merulo raised a weary arm as a shadow passed overhead. A leviathan, gliding feet from the glass, the iridescent ribbons of its fins drifting behind it like wartime banners. "This place is not truly of the old world. It's transitory. We've found automated carriages here, and the base of a transport system that once led to the surface." He gestured loosely, in a different direction. "However, technologies cease to work mere feet above the dome. The exits are all blocked in a hasty, ugly manner, and thoroughly chewed where they pass through water." Merulo looked affected, despite the depth of time that separated us from them. "Humans of the old world died here, trapped, under the eyes of monsters that should not exist."

The leviathan above seemed playful, and not particularly monstrous. It skimmed along the glass, rolling on its side to fix an enormous yellow eye on us. I'd only ever seen them from a distance, breaching water in a flash of scale. Never with such intimacy.

"We must be so frustrating to it," I commiserated, but the creature didn't look upset, skimming over us again with a sweep of fins. Its colours were mesmerizing, seeming to change and ripple. Something occurred to me. "Does magic still work down here? Can we get out?"

"Yes." Merulo sounded disappointed. "The deeper seas may have been spared transformation, but nowhere on this planet is truly clean."

We sat watching the dance of the leviathan far above us, until the sorcerer regained enough energy to speak. "I grew up here. Before my mother was ... Anyway, she sent us through a portal, myself and Hydna. It's a mystery to us, how she discovered this place and restored its mechanisms, but it's always been safe."

A childhood spent underwater in a dead city. That explained a lot. "Are there other dragons in hiding?" I asked, testing how much intrusion he would allow by scooting closer on the bench. "In refuges like this?"

"We're the last, Hydna and I." The sorcerer let his head rest on my shoulder, and I tried not to react. I felt renewed appreciation for my man's body, which had the breadth of shoulder to support multiple sorcerer heads if necessary. "My mother . . . she was alone a long time before stealing our eggs. She found us in a church vault. They must not have thought we were alive, else we would not have been allowed to remain in our shells. A grown dragon makes for a far more bountiful harvest than an egg."

Seeing that this was a serious moment, I made myself stop grinning like a fool.

Merulo exhaled slowly through his teeth. "They burned her heart, Cameron, to make your prophecy."

Burning the heart of a mother to destroy her son. "I'm sorry."

Above, the leviathan tired of the novelty, drifting away into the sea that stretched endlessly in all directions.

"I lied, just now," Merulo said, startling me. "Hydna and I, we are not the last."

He withdrew his head, sitting straighter on the bench. "One other remains, a half-elf. Not a foundling like myself or Hydna, but the last remaining flesh of our mother. She is lost, though." The rippling light softened the sorcerer's jagged features.

I wasn't sure how to respond to this confession. "Lost?"

"Raised by elves, a follower of the Church. Every year, I trade for information, but it never changes. Domitia remains theirs."

"And she can't be reasoned with?" The benefits of having multiple muscular dragon women on our side seemed obvious.

Merulo tipped his head back to watch the silver flashes of passing fish. "Hydna and I are in agreement: Domitia is too dangerous to make contact with. Dragons cannot war with other dragons. That level of clashing power would end in disaster for more than just ourselves. No," he concluded firmly. "Secrecy has kept us safe down here."

"Except you're not anymore," I said, in growing panic. "Secret, or safe. A field of knights watched a black dragon carry me away. And if the Church has somebody of your po—" I stopped and cursed myself. "Of your former power, they will find us. Even under all this water."

The sorcerer looked far less concerned than the situation warranted. "I think not. This location has never been found. And I have never been defeated."

I shuffled, unnerved. Had it been too much to hope that in draining his power, he had also lost his ambition? "You said—"

"A moment of weakness that will not be repeated," he said briskly. "I am not defeated. This world will be restored, and God will be slain." A pleading note entered the sorcerer's voice, which hurt to hear from such a proud man. He fixed his single black eye on me. "Do you believe me, Cameron?"

Never had I been more grateful to be free from the truth spell. "I do."

Sparing me from further deception, the air split and a thunder of bookshelves fell, spewing their contents onto the tiled plaza. Merulo leaped to his feet, shrieking, his arms raised with the futility of spells he could not cast.

"Hold on, it looks worse than it is," shouted the dragon, as she dropped through the gap in space and became an outrageously muscular woman once more.

"These are irreplaceable!" The sorcerer clutched at his hair.

"You didn't immobilize them before transport? It's a simple spell!"

Hydna snorted. "You're welcome for the help. And wait, I'll sort this." With a quick chant, the shelves creaked and righted themselves, the books rising on invisible strings to slot themselves away. Within moments, Merulo's library had restored itself.

"I suppose they're in the wrong order now." Merulo limped toward his re-formed library. Even bereft of magic, his sharp figure and flowing robe made for an imposing sight. He plucked at the closest shelf, examining a book for damage, then ran his hand along the shelf, reading spines.

"Restoration to a past state." Hydna crossed her arms triumphantly. "It's a simple spell."

"Hmm," said Merulo. "Unnecessary dramatics. Objects that haven't been disturbed to begin with don't require restoration. But thank you, nonetheless." His voice wobbled slightly, I noted with alarm.

I stood with a stretch. "Hey, I know it's barely noon, but is there anywhere we can rest? Purely for my benefit."

After thoroughly confirming the health of his books, Merulo allowed us to be led down the winding streets. Hydna motioned to passing structures like a tour guide, extrapolating their function and history with quips and guffaws. Though she did it solely for me, I found it hard to pay attention. As we passed one landmark, a statue of a trident-wielding man, a chill ran through me, and I clutched at Merulo's sleeve like a child. Hydna looked back at us, frowning, but to my gratitude she didn't pry.

"Here we are!" She halted before a sprawling building.

"This was probably an inn. There are about twenty rooms with beds, and one giant kitchen. All cleared and clean, thanks to me!"

"Let us pray you make a better maid than Sir Cameron," Merulo drawled, as his sister ushered us in.

"Oh?" Hydna leaned closer as I passed. "Did he make you wear a little outfit?"

"Uh . . . just my dress?" I said, then flushed. "I was a woman at the time, so the dress was—I mean—Merulo, wait up." I broke into a trot, escaping Hydna's laughter.

The sorcerer seemed to know which way to go, but he wavered uncertainly at the base of the staircase. Moving to his side, I wrapped an arm about his waist. He hesitated before accepting the help, leaning against me as we ascended.

"We'll speak further after Sir Cameron has rested," Merulo called back. "Be sure to have food and drink prepared."

His sister hissed, reptilian, but departed without comment.

Even when we reached the top of the stairs, I didn't stop supporting him. Having my musculature returned to me definitely had some benefits. The sorcerer muttered and gestured guidance, and I half carried him through an open door, not bothering to take in the strange materials or ancient decorations.

The waiting bed looked soft and, to Hydna's credit, clean. Untouched by time—or perhaps simply restored to a past state.

Pulling away from me, Merulo staggered and fell bodily into the bed, not bothering to draw back the sheets. He curled atop the covers like a mangy cat.

The sorcerer had never slept in front of me before. I had speculated that he spelled himself to be continuously awake, to avoid interruptions to his studies, or that he rested in brief stints behind one of the castle's many locked doors. Now, though, he could not avoid me. I'd learn whether he snored or mumbled, and whether, while dreaming, his legs kicked.

Filled with renewed glee at being alive, I threw myself onto the bed beside him, making his frail body bounce.

"What on Larnia do you think you're doing?" Merulo sat up, a sneer at the ready.

"We're sharing," I told him firmly, pushing him back down.

"You can sleep on the floor like a dog," Merulo said, but without true temper. He returned to his fetal position, and I shaped myself around his back, draping an arm over the jut of his ribs.

"You smell," said the sorcerer, "like somebody who's been dragged through a field, sweated through every inch of clothing, and bled all over himself."

"Ah." I shuffled closer. "Well, you smell nice."

I felt the force of his snort through his ribcage. "I don't smell of anything. Because *I*, and please understand the emphasis of that 'I,' bathe with *frequency*."

"No." I huffed demonstratively, lifting a lock of his oily black hair. "You smell of magic. It's sharp, like a spice. I used to not like it, but it's grown on me."

"Don't expect me to feel the same about sweat and mud." But he didn't insist on me leaving. He shuffled into a more comfortable position, the rise and fall of his chest slowing as sleep began to take him.

I, however, remained sadly conscious. Something was gnawing at me.

After a time, I shook Merulo gently. "Hey, are you awake?" There was no response.

"HEY?" I tried, just a little bit louder.

"WHAT?" Merulo answered in a snarl, proving that he'd been very much awake and simply ignoring me.

I hugged his thin body tight in a placatory gesture. "It's something Glenda said. It's stuck in my mind."

"The elf? I'd like to have her stuck in my teeth."

"Gross. Anyway, so she made a fair point, that if I'd been polite enough to die when they wanted, a good number of knights would still be alive today."

"And?"

"I mean, they're dead because you killed them. Or your constructs did. Or, wait, you did too, as a dragon."

"And?"

"Well, it's just that I don't feel bad about it."

"So then," Merulo's voice rose to a shout, "why are you bothering me about this? Sleep!"

"I'm just wondering if I'm a bad person, is all."

Under my arm, I felt his body stiffen in anger. "And who would they be to decide that? Who are any of them to pass judgement? They live like animals, ignorant of how the world could be, how I will MAKE the world. They needn't even die, if they would stop throwing themselves at me to be slaughtered. No, there's no merit in docility, in obedience, in—in scientific stupidity. There is no 'good' or 'bad,' only the truth of my work and the lies of the Church. You are with me. You've spat up all the filth they fed you, and now you will help me tear the restraints free from this world."

"Oh," I said. "Right. Truth and lies. Hadn't thought of

it like that. Good talk, Merulo, I'll just . . . huh." I nestled closer, unsure if I should reveal that I was now more confused than ever.

Still, it was better than thinking about that other thing. I wondered if, before he drifted off to sleep for a second time, Merulo felt my trembling.

Returning to a void of nothingness, even of the temporary sort, held little appeal to me. I'd wake, I knew I'd wake, this time and the next, but someday I wouldn't.

Someday, I would die again.

Drawing what comfort I could from the presence of another warm body, I ordered my eyes to shut, waiting for brain-exhaustion to take me where I wouldn't go willingly.

CHAPTER 31

In Which Glenda Admits that Perhaps It Was a Tad Ambitious to Think that Her Presence Would Be Enough to Offset the Human Incompetence of the Order. In Which, if It Had Been a Purely Elven Operation, then Of Course They Would Have Known He Was a Dragon, and Of Course They Would Have Known He Had Time Magic. In Which She Needs the Support of Her Own Kind, and In Particular, In Which She Needs Access to a Special Resource.

All elf children knew the story of the mongrel witch.

A passing she-dragon, seeking to ruin a noble elf man for her own cruel amusement, seduced Chadwick Sproutjoy. Only after the birth, when he saw the warped child that resulted from their pairing, did shock restore the man to his good senses. He slew the beast and earned an admirable fortune all in one stroke. The man remained a great leader, if now whispered of with gentle pity for his past. And, in a gracious display of tolerance, the daughter was surgically corrected and raised as an elf.

The mongrel witch paid back their generosity, as she

proved to be an unending well of natural magic. In adulthood, however, her dragon nature dominated; she became volatile, self-isolating, choosing to live as independently as the Church would allow, in a hut that wandered on goat legs, deep in the Swallowing Swamps.

This was who Glenda now sought.

After the slaughter and chaos of the field, she had returned—on foot, all their steeds having been monstrously transformed—to the assembled force waiting to storm the sorcerer's castle. Just as before, they'd traveled through the fog, up the rising slope of the land, but no constructs met them with flaming eye or bared splinter-fang. Instead, they found wooden husks, strewn like toys after a child's play session. Even the fog lost its power as they walked, dissipating so the sky shone a clear blue at the summit. The tapestry of forest that spread out beneath them, unchoked by fog for the first time in decades, spoke to a victory already won.

Reaching the castle, the forces of Order had no need to bash through the doors. They found them broken explosively from the inside, as if a massive force had exited the castle at great velocity. *Perhaps a black dragon in a terrible hurry*, Glenda thought, her mouth crumpling.

Inside, she'd separated from her elven kin and retraced her steps. This time when she passed through the library door, nobody waited within a convoluted pentagram. There was no cadaverous man to laugh at her and spatter his own foul blood. What's more, the room had been emptied. Wide and high-ceilinged, it had formerly contained shelf upon shelf bristling with the sorcerer's dark tomes. But not a scrap of wood or page remained.

The hideous sorcerer and his traitor paramour had escaped.

The other elves found her kicking the walls of the emptied library, senseless with fury.

Forming a circle, they had conferred. To fight not only a sorcerer, but a dragon, a man capable of thumbing his nose at time itself . . . the elves all agreed that this required an escalation.

Now, accompanied by the Elder who'd overseen this latest war effort and a trio of slim and lovely elves, Glenda spurred her mount through the swampland.

Their unicorns lifted hooves caked with mud, flinging up specks of the stinking stuff with each laborious step. Enchanted to repel soiling, the Elder's robe maintained its shining white. The mounted elves, not being in the practice of draining their own children for frivolities, had a fine brown speckling ascending their legs.

Glenda took some satisfaction from this. She'd expected to find comfort among her own kind, but day by day, her shoulders grew tenser, and her jaw more tightly clenched. Her fellow elves, she had to admit, lacked the Church's discipline. They relied on order, but seemed perfectly content to leave the humans to enforce it—for God's sake, she was considered an aberration for setting out to join the war! An aberration, for doing the right thing. None of them would have taken a sword to Cameron's throat. They'd rather sit back, file their nails, and let someone else pick up the blade.

And they'd looked at her so funnily when she scolded them for speaking in a forbidden language. Honestly. Like *she'd* done something wrong.

Glenda was plucking small, stinging flies from the air with whiplash movements, funneling her anger, when the three elven guides halted their mounts. Through the bird calls and buzz of insects, she heard slurping. Something large was moving with slow ease through the swampy depths. Glenda peered about cautiously, but vine-choked trees clogged the landscape, ruining her visibility. Another elf inhaled sharply. Following his gaze, Glenda saw it. Visible through scarce gaps in the yellow-green foliage, an enormous shape rose and fell with the stride of its four legs.

The unicorns whinnied, fearful, as their riders kicked them into motion. From behind a screen of branch and leaf, Glenda watched the behemoth stop and lower itself.

They waded closer, and the shape resolved into a small cottage, built atop the gigantic, green-furred legs of a goat. No, not furred; *leafed*. The bestial parts of the dwelling erupted in a coat of vegetation. Glenda pictured the wood that must exist beneath those leaves, and shivered at its similarity to the sorcerer's constructs.

The unicorns slogged toward the front steps, which hovered an inch above the swamp's surface. Small, fat birds perched on the roof, overlooking the door. "Only the wounded woman may enter," one called in an eerily artificial voice.

The other elves protested in synchronization, speaking over each other in their desire to correct the situation, but the birds screamed loud enough to silence them all. The same bird spoke again. "Only the wounded woman."

Apologetically, all the elves looked to Glenda. Elder Beth held her silence, but Glenda knew that beneath her placid mask, she burned with fury at the dismissal.

With an anxiety born from the handful of Passionweed she'd snuck that morning, Glenda steered her mount closer and slipped down from it to the cottage steps, which creaked beneath her feet as she ascended. Glenda took a moment to appreciate the door's wreath of yellow flowers before entering.

Inside sat a fat woman. She rocked gently in a carved chair, backlit by the glow of her stove, with pungent herbs dangling from the rafters above. One of her eyes was oddly hooded, its icy iris ever so slightly unfocused. She smiled, revealing a sharp tangle of teeth. Even her blue skin looked *off*, bruised, a shade too dark and too red.

"I can see someone has hurt you." The gentle music of the witch's voice made Glenda forget her disgust. "Have you come to be made whole?"

Glenda touched her face self-consciously. Her cheek no longer burned where the unicorn-turned-basilisk had vomited its acid, but her fingers could still trace the pits and welts. Before her departure, Cerulina had gently prompted her to smooth it out with magic. Elves commonly drained themselves for cosmetic enhancements, but Glenda had ignored her, wanting every resource available for this hunt. Now though, with this unprompted offer?

"If you could," Glenda said softly, her eyes filling. "I'd appreciate it."

The witch's silver hair hung long and sleek. She drew it back in a quick knot, the motion exposing the scars that traced to her armpits, and beckoned Glenda closer.

"This will sting for a moment," Domitia said, her words a lullaby that hid their meaning. Curiously soothed, Glenda nodded her acceptance. With a chanted sentence came a crawling sensation on her cheek, and the briefest flash of heat—then there was smooth skin beneath her questing fingers. Glenda couldn't help herself; she cried aloud with glee. It had been terrible to realize that she'd lost not only her prey, but her looks.

The witch tilted her head, her lips parted in confusion. "That cost rather more than I thought."

"Probably the head trauma." Glenda hiccuped a laugh. "You might have cleaned that up, too. A man, he—" But she couldn't continue. Tears came now, streaming down her cheeks. "He—damn it. Domitia, I've come to ask you for help."

The mongrel witch nodded, rocking mildly in her chair. "I thought as much. Why don't you draw up a cushion, and we can have ourselves a chat."

CHAPTER 32

In Which Merulo's Sister Is Very Intimidating and Large and Does Not Seem to Abide by Normal Social Standards. In Which that May Actually Work in My Favour, as I Am Realizing that Neither Do I.

"And this is—COME ON, MOVE FASTER—this is where the train docks. Don't EVER go inside the train, it's nothing but rusted metal. Do you know what tetanus is? Do you know what a train is? A train is like a long car."

I didn't know what a car was, but lacked the heart to tell her.

Despite her imposing frame, her crooked nose (obviously healed from past violence), and those muscles, Hydna bounded about with the eager friendliness of a puppy. I'd stopped trying to shape my replies to please her, as everything I said—no matter how foolish or petulant—seemed to bring her delight. Most likely, I could thank Merulo for lowering her conversational standards.

"Moving right along now, this is—CAREFUL!" Hydna lunged at me, and I flinched, closing my eyes in brief cowardice, but she only yanked me back from the sinkhole

I'd been about to step into. "You're a delicate little thing, so use your eyes, eh?" was my rebuke, along with a shoulder-shattering clap on the back.

"I'm above the average height for men," I said, pointlessly, for she'd already moved to the next attraction of *Poseidon's Family Fun Resort*. This section looked horrific, with its crumbling facades and time-bleached pigments bearing the ghostly afterimages of smiling aquatic creatures. When Merulo and I first arrived, we'd emerged in the section of the resort used for housing visitors. The tall, strange buildings radiated out from our newly designated library plaza for several blocks, before giving way to the amusement district.

It bewildered me that they'd built an underwater city solely for transient entertainment, though I didn't doubt Hydna's explanation. Mentioning this to Merulo proved to be a mistake, as he said, "Yes, I imagine thinking is a great effort for you," then banished me to spend more time with his sister. Or rather to "provide that creature with whatever form of entertainment you see fit, so that I might be spared its company."

"Hydna. Are you and Merulo not close?" I asked, remembering the exchange, then winced. I'd interrupted her explanation of a terrifying wheel that stretched many feet above us, complete with intermittently spaced chairs into which victims could be locked.

"Close?" She sounded baffled—and thankfully unoffended by my lack of attention. "Of course not!"

I squinted up at the dragon woman. She'd dressed herself in relics for the tour, having wasted God knows how much magic on their restoration. A wide-brimmed hat embroidered with water droplets sat atop her massive skull, while a shirt stretched painfully tight over what might either be breasts or prodigious pectorals, its smiling fish distorted into a boggle-eyed monster. Her baggy pants, which ended mid-thigh, burned an intense yellow-green that did not exist in nature. It felt cruel to ask someone so playfully dressed this question. "You are family. Shouldn't there be some, you know, underlying love?"

This was rather pious, considering that my own father likely fell asleep each night thinking of creative ways to kill me, but she didn't have to know that.

"He's a walking knife," came her growled reply.

"Well, yeah." I kicked at a loose piece of pavement. Intervening in the sorcerer's various moods had gone some way toward thickening my skin, but I still shuddered at the waves of displeasure radiating from Hydna. "He's a lonely guy, I think."

"He'd be less lonely if he weren't such a piece of shit." She met my eyes without blinking, and I found myself mesmerized by their reptilian scarlet.

"You have to . . . I don't know. Meet him more than halfway? He does want company."

"But is too much of a bastard for company to want him back."

"Exactly!" I said, delighted that she'd completed my thought. My excitement faded at her expression. "That's neat that you can raise one eyebrow like that. Good control of your, uh, facial muscles."

Hydna pointed to a circle of unicorn-sized crabs, complete with saddles, welded to a roofed platform. No half-shouted explanation followed; I'd succeeded in puncturing her enthusiasm.

"Those are cool," I tried lamely. Then: "He's been kind to me when he didn't have to be. Merulo, I mean. Not that everything's been perfect. I didn't much like the whole 'torture needle' thing, but—"

"The what?"

"Hang on, I'm coming to a point. Merulo might make a lot of insulting, degrading remarks, and he is overly obsessed with killing God—"

"This is a *defense*?"

"Hydna, please! What I mean is that, brushing aside all those little details, he's always been there when I needed him most. Like when Glenda shot me full of arrows, or slit my throat, or—"

"Who the fuck is Glenda?"

"Hydna, come on, I didn't ask you what a car was." I rubbed at my stubble, wishing I could reach into my own head to pull my thoughts into order. "Merulo will be there for you, too, if you ever need him"—and I hoped that was the truth—"so, it'd be good if you could both . . . *try*." At her contorted grimace, I added, "I'll talk to him too, promise. Same speech!"

The dragon woman exhaled deeply. "You're an annoying little man, Cameron."

"Again, above average height."

A hand landed on my shoulder, and she steered me with gentle force around a sunken pothole that could easily have swallowed a dragon. "You have any family?"

Damn. Forced to reveal my own hypocrisies. "Yes. A brother who idolizes me, and . . ." I hesitated. "A father who despises me."

Skirting complete, she removed her hand. "Do you want me to kill your father and steal your brother?"

"No! Absolutely not."

"I could do it, easy."

"I know you could."

"Painlessly, even."

"Hydna!" I pleaded. At the furrowing of her brow, I remembered my manners. "Thank you. That is ah, *very kind* of you to offer. But the less contact I have with my brother, the better. I'd only stain him."

We silently passed a towering metal track, which twisted high above in loops and dives. "S'pose it would be a bit much," said Hydna. "To have two of you down here."

I gave her my sternest frown. "I'll pretend you didn't say that."

CHAPTER 33

In Which I Have Grown Accustomed to the Idea that I Spent a Full Day Dead. In Which I Am No Longer Frightened by It, and No Longer Desperately Trying to Remember if There Had Been Anything Beyond the Nothingness. In Which, Thinking Further upon the Matter, Perhaps It Still Does Affect Me, and Perhaps I Could Use a Bit of Peaceful Contemplation without Any Further Stresses for a Time. In Which I Have a Brilliant Idea for How to Secure This Peace.

When he found me in the inn bedroom, Merulo's face was white with fury. "You!"

"Me?" I said, in panicked surprise. "You can't be angry with me today. It's my birthday."

He paused, anger giving way to bewilderment. "Is it?"

"Uh, well, I was born the day after the summer solstice, so . . ."

There was silence as we both tried to work out the date. Time moved differently underwater, without weather or input from the seasons. "The summer solstice passed well before we left," he cried at last. "It is not your birthday."

"Then my birthday passed by and we never even celebrated,

which is even worse. I feel just awful about that." And I tried to rearrange my features into appropriate mournfulness.

It didn't work. The lines on his forehead twitched, before sloping into Vs. "Enough of this nonsense. Did you or did you not tell my sister that I sought to beg her forgiveness, but was too"—his face contorted, and I winced in anticipation—"*emotionally incompetent*, to do so in person?"

"I didn't say that!" I protested.

"You didn't say, and I quote, that 'my loneliness eats at me like a cancer, but that my only method of coping is to shove my head further up my ass, so as to huff my own fumes'?"

"What's a cancer?" I asked. His glower deepened, and I quickly amended, "No, I never said any of that! Only that—"

"So, you did say something, then? Out with it!"

"That I wished you two would get along better," I finished miserably, "and that I wanted Hydna to make more of an effort."

He maintained his suspicious glare. "And you didn't use any of that . . . 'colourful' language?"

"Of course not. Merulo, you know how highly I think of you." I grimaced. "I mean, I didn't at first, so I understand the confusion, but back at the start you didn't like me much either."

"And who's to say I like you now?" The sorcerer sneered.

I bit back laughter. He looked constipated with pride, drawing himself up tall in his patched black robes, but by now I knew that the more frozen he appeared, the more flustered he was beneath the surface.

"I suppose that's why you used up all your magic on my resurrection," I said, trying to keep my mocking gentle. "Because you dislike me so much."

He quivered, before turning with a sweep of his robe. "I have matters to attend to," he said, though he did not leave. Then, in as lethal a spit as he could manage: "Of course I don't dislike you."

I tried not to cackle as he marched from the room. For the rest of the day—which I spent going door-to-door in the inn, investigating the decay of the uninhabited spaces, before washing all the filth from my body in our room's luxurious bath—I felt a buoyant warmth. "He must like me quite a bit," I said to myself, sinking into the tub of water, which filled from a streaming spout at its end.

"I may also like *him* quite a bit," I added, then clenched my hands in embarrassment, sinking beneath the water's surface. "I do. I even told Glenda so."

And did you mean it? asked a tiny voice in my head. *Or were you caught up in the emotions of 'Oh God, oh no, I'm about to die?'*

"Well, why shouldn't I mean it? He's an impressive guy! All powerful and magical, and cool, too, in a scary sort of way. And he pays me special attention."

That isn't enough.

"Okay." I slapped at the water's surface to create miniature waves. "He's alone like I am. There, are you happy?"

Nope.

"Damn, then what are the reasons to love someone?" I sank my head beneath the water's surface, feeling my hair float about me. When I sat back up, the water drained from my face in rivulets, my tension leaving with it. "Okay. Here goes. There's something that connects us, and it goes deeper than that stupid prophecy, like we're both . . . *more* than we would otherwise be, so long as we're together. I mean, I full on *died* for him. And dying's a big deal for me. That's enough, isn't it?"

For once, the voice was silent. Then: *That's true*, it said, astonished. *Dying is an especially big deal for you.*

"You see?" I flicked the water's surface, trying to keep the smugness out of my voice. "I meant what I said."

Feeling as though I'd earned it with this revelation, I reclined further, closing my eyes against the bath's warmth, and letting myself thoroughly prune.

"Cameron!" came a shout from outside the bathroom door.

I flinched, wondering in sudden guilt whether I should've been rationing the water. "I'm indisposed!" My voice echoed slightly in the tiled room.

An ominous silence followed. "When you are no longer indisposed," Merulo said finally, "come to the library plaza. You know where that is."

"Okay, will do." I listened for the click of a closing door, then reluctantly extracted myself from the bath. A soft cloth hung from a hoop, which I used to dry myself. With a grimace, I re-dressed in the stained, torn corpse clothing.

By the time I exited the inn, night had fallen. Without that faint trickle of sunlight, the electric bulbs of the resort burned at a higher intensity, making the geometric buildings and streets appear brighter, sharper, more alien. I plodded down the road, feeling the absence of people like a weight. The dragons might be used to living in a tomb, but my imagination strained, filling in the crowds that must once have churned down these walkways. Their conversations and laughter were nearly audible, as if the vast time that separated us was only paper-thin.

When the library came into sight, I felt enormous relief.

This quickly turned to puzzlement. Someone had laid a tablecloth across the ground, weighing it down with plates of food and a single package wrapped in thin brown paper. Hydna and Merulo sat at opposite corners of the tablecloth, looking uncomfortable. At least they weren't fighting.

"What's all this?" I asked, jogging slightly to reach them. The food looked wonderful—bread rolls, fried fish, and sautéed vegetables in greens, reds, and yellows.

"I portaled into the local town." Hydna gestured a muscled arm at the spread. "To get us something nice. As I heard it was *somebody's* special day."

A smile pulled itself across my face, and I swallowed a squeak of joy. If she'd been standing, I might have tried to hug her.

"It is *not* his birthday." Merulo unfolded himself from his seated position, snatching the parcel from the tablecloth. "Here," he said. "Because, as you said, we did miss the date, which has evidently upset you."

It had mostly been an attempt to get out of being yelled at, but I would never let him know. I took the parcel eagerly, tearing apart the paper to find—fabric!

My breath caught. I pulled out a soft, emerald-green tunic and a set of breeches in what looked to be dyed brown cotton. Last in the package was a pair of polished leather shoes, complete with copper buckles.

"I found a guy who looked well dressed and politely asked him to strip and sell me his clothes. He was about your size." Hydna's grin made me think she'd been less than polite. "It was Merulo's idea. He said you have a garment obsession."

The sorcerer had put himself in my reach. Taking

advantage of this, I threw my arms around him. At first, he stiffened and cursed beneath his breath, but after a moment I felt a spidery hand pat me awkwardly on the back. "Thank you," I said, sniffing and wiping my eyes before stepping back to examine the clothing. "These are far too small."

"We can fix them with magic," Hydna said impatiently. "Or I can."

She stepped forward for her own hug, her arms crushing the oxygen from my lungs. As I squirmed, ribs cracking and eyes bulging, I caught sight of Merulo over her shoulder. He'd turned from the sight, to shoot a look of pure death into the empty air.

That spelled trouble.

Gasping, I begged my way free of her grip. "Thank you," I wheezed, my eyes overflowing with either gratitude or pain. "Thank you both, very much. But, ah, you in particular, Merulo, as it was your idea." The sorcerer nodded, and I fought down a grin. I'd been noticing some distance from him—that it might be *jealousy* brought me dangerously close to laughter.

It was all quite flattering, really, but I wouldn't let it get to my head.

CHAPTER 34

In Which Glenda Is Feeling Light-headed and Slightly Nauseous and Doesn't Want to Think About How Far Away the Ground Is, or How the Air Would Whistle Past Her Face if She Fell. In Which Her Stomach Feels Like It Is Caving In on Itself. In Which She Wonders if She Could Spit Out a Levitation Spell in Time, but In Which She Admits to Herself that Most Likely, She Would Only Get It Partially Out before the Grotesque Crunch and Splatter of Impact.

Glenda was afraid of heights.

She could have spent the flight in relative comfort, lounging in the coach's cushioned interior and only faintly feeling the rattle that followed each beat of its great leafy wings, but the mongrel witch had wanted directions.

"The mad sorcerer travels through portals," Glenda had protested, staring up at the chimeric offspring of a swan, a stagecoach, and a flowering vine, but the mongrel witch had only clucked her tongue.

"This 'mad sorcerer' might be happy to fling himself through space and end up God knows where, but I prefer to see where I'm going."

Which left Glenda crawling on her belly up the extended neck of the carriage, to peer dizzily at the ground far below. With great relief, she spotted the outline of a town, and slid back into the carriage through the soft curtains.

"We're close," she said. "It'll be harder to orient without the sorcerer's fog as a landmark, but if we land now, it should only be a couple of hours ride."

"We can't fly the entire distance?" Reclining on a spread of hand-embroidered cushions, the witch looked perfectly at home. She made a careful selection from a jar of biscuits, plucking a specimen dotted with nuts and the crimson flash of berries. Pressing it past her rosebud lips, Domitia chewed without hurry.

Glenda tried to think of a reason that didn't involve the upcoming inversion of her stomach. "I can spot large landmarks, like my outpost, but the field won't stand out by air."

"Very well," said the witch, and the carriage descended. Glenda's gut plunged; she gripped the wooden walls for support, wondering at how the witch could maintain her calm even through this horrible dropping. They touched down with a clatter, bringing Glenda's teeth together in a painful click, but the impact caused no damage. Its movements smoothed, the carriage rolling on freely.

The witch pulled languidly at a cord, opening the carriage curtains. In the clearing ahead stood a local man, eyes wide. His armful of collected wood tumbled piecemeal to the ground.

"Which way now?" asked the witch, and Glenda told her.

Glenda feared the carriage might have difficulty passing through the press of trees, but it reacted to the thinning space like an animal, tucking its enormous leafy wings and hunkering on its wheels. In clearer sections, it picked up speed, rolling at a unicorn's gallop; this required Glenda to pay constant attention, shouting directions before key turns could be missed. Finally, feeling more exhausted than if she'd walked the distance on her own two legs, they arrived at the prophesized location.

It looked a mess. The Order had dutifully retrieved their slain knights, but the spoiling bodies of the transmogrified steeds remained, filling her nose with sweet decay. Strangely coloured flowers grew where the dragon's breath had passed, and great gashes yawned in the earth amid the swaying greenery. At the feet of the eroded statue, the basilisk lay rotting.

It had been a lovely bay before the transformation, with a yellow horn that curled like carved butter. Now, the creature hung draped across the statue's legs, foul and deflated, strips of its pebbled hide flapping loose in the wind.

This was the sickness that the mad sorcerer brought to the world.

Stepping carefully from the carriage, Glenda picked her way through the grass. The walk felt terribly long. The aroma of the dead monster intensified as she drew nearer, all liquifying offal and the vinegar stench of its venom, so that by the time she reached the statue's shadow, her stomach threatened to spill. Holding her breath, she pulled the sword free from the sucking socket of its eye, then scrambled backward across the meadow.

She entered the carriage breathing hard, the sword still coated in flaking blood. "This is it," she said. "Cameron's sword. And now we find him?"

The mongrel witch smiled, receiving the blade with thick fingers. "And now we find him."

CHAPTER 35

In Which I Am Growing More and More Familiar with the Roads and Plazas of an Underwater City from a Pre-Apocalyptic Era, and Would by Now Be Feeling Quite at Home if Not for One Small Issue.

It felt unmasculine to admit, but the mounds of corpses creeped me out.

I could easily distinguish which heaps the dragon siblings had piled, and which had existed, untouched, for centuries. What a grim task it must have been for those last survivors, to keep their tomb-to-be in order. The corpses piled by the ancients filled deep pits in the ground, which Hydna explained had once held water for swimming. One of them, before dying, had carved words into the tiles along the pool's edge. After some consideration, I decided not to ask the dragons for a translation.

Their bodies, mummified in the arid cold of the dome when life systems failed, were a dark leather. The stretch of their skin forced their faces into snarls, cushioned by the gentle puff of their hair. Supposedly, they'd rot now that functionality was restored to the whirring mechanisms that issued heat and air. For now, though, the bodies kept me company.

The stacks made by Hydna and Merulo failed to match the ancient heaps in quality. Transporting the desiccated bodies had clearly caused crumbling, resulting in dusty piles of shattered forms. But I couldn't judge the siblings for their trashing of the remains, nor even for the vaguely artistic stack of heads I found in an otherwise empty plaza. Their early life didn't exactly sound idyllic; some hardening must have been required.

My main source of anguish was that the people of the pre-Descent seemed to have no use for swords.

I'd done a rudimentary search for a blade, gotten lost, panicked a bit, stumbled on some gruesome sights (apologies to its creator, but I truly did not appreciate the head stack), then given up.

During one of our group lunches, I finally asked the dragons for advice. Hydna grinned at the opportunity to show off. She summoned a sword in a puff of smoke, a gleaming Knight of Order blade with balancing scales on the hilt.

"That's mine," I said, taken aback. "See the notch on the hilt—my father bought me this. He said he could have spent the same amount on a dairy herd, and that if I ever lost it, he'd have me whipped. And I did lose it, after bashing in poor Glenda's head . . . or not so poor, actually, she's been rather horrible lately. How is it possible that you have my sword?"

"Don't be so impressed," said the sorcerer, scribbling away in his notes. Smoked salmon, bread, and apples sourced from a seaside town lay spread on a towel atop the pavement. We sat in the plaza that held Merulo's relocated library—he never ventured far from it these days, and just as rarely spared attention for anything beyond his work. "Objects that bear personal significance are far easier to locate. She took the easy route."

Diplomatically, I ignored Merulo. "Thank you, Hydna. This means a lot to me."

She acknowledged my words with a brisk nod, before ripping off another chunk of fish with her teeth. More than half of this feast would be disappearing down her gullet, as per usual. One day, I would ask her how she paid for our food, but for now I had a greater pull on my attention.

Unable to help myself, I rose and—moving a safe distance away from the picnic—gave my recovered blade a few test swings. It came as a relief when my body slipped easily into drilled stances and movements. The last time I'd held a sword, it had been pressed hard into Gareth's back. That memory brought my heart to an anxious flutter, and I thrust and bobbed with extra zest, fencing a phantom.

"It'd be better practice if you had an opponent," Hydna called, having disappeared the fish in a marvelous show of gluttony. She rolled her shoulders, loudly cracking the joints.

"No, see," the sorcerer cut in, still scrawling, "Cameron will lose purposefully, and then you'll have to deal with his perversions."

Before I could protest, she said, "Okay. Maybe I'm into that."

I felt very happy.

"Sir Cameron," said Merulo. "This is a formal order: you are not permitted to sleep with my sister."

"Who said anything about sex?" said Hydna, rising to her considerable height. "I just want to beat the shit out of him."

I felt very unhappy.

Already suffering from the tightness of unmaintained muscles, I swung into another set of drills. "How about we do a regular duel, and stop at surrender?"

"Aw, come on." Hydna's voice came from behind my shoulder, and I jumped. When had she moved? "I'll fix you up with a spell afterwards. Don't you like this stuff?" Crimson eyes shone from under the mess of her hair. Her full lips curled in a grin, and I noticed a gap in her too-sharp teeth.

"Not when it's real!" I felt myself beginning to flush, and pulled my sword to my chest. "I don't actually like getting hurt."

"That's right," called Merulo, sketching something now in broad sweeps. "He only wants you to say nasty things in pretend. And then you have to fuck him afterward."

"This is getting incredibly personal," I said. "And I'm really just . . . practicing with a sword here."

"Alright." Hydna held up calloused hands, admitting defeat. "A normal sword fight it is. Give me that for a second."

With considerable reluctance, I handed over my blade. She wrapped her hands around the hilt, speaking softly. With a flex of her biceps, she tore the blade in two down its center. I made a small noise of anguish, which faded as I realized that each half had re-formed into a complete sword. Taking the blade she extended, I looked it over thoroughly. It was still my sword, down to the familiar nicks and wear.

Preoccupied as I was with this examination, Hydna's first swing nearly cut my face in two. I leaped backward, my body moving before my thoughts could catch up, and drew myself into a stance.

Hydna bobbed, light on her feet, a terrible smile straining her mouth. She thrust before I could process it. Again, I reacted with muscle memory alone, her blade slamming into mine with a ring. The blow vibrated through my body, and I feared my sword would snap. Hydna followed her next smashing blow with a twist that ripped my hands free of the hilt and sent my sword spinning. It skittered across the pavement and beneath a bench, far out of reach. Thinking this a loss, I allowed my abused muscles to slacken, shoulders dropping.

There was a clatter as Hydna discarded her sword and raised her fists.

"Oh no, you can't," I started, ducking away from a blow that would have crushed my skull to powder.

"Hydna!" I skittered back as the dragon woman came for me. She raised a fist, and I plunged backward with enough speed that I lost my balance, meeting the hard pavement. This had to end it.

But the dragon woman followed me to the ground, knees slamming down on either side of my torso. Her massive hands, burning with a fever heat, gripped my wrists to restrain them. I may as well have been pinned by a bear. "I didn't tell you the penalty for losing," she growled, her burgundy hair falling about our faces. "You shouldn't have accepted a fight without knowing the penalty."

"Normal sword fight," I yelped. "That was the descriptor!" My legs lay free. I could kick upward, but would that do more than antagonize her?

"Normal for me." Her triumphant laugh blasted like a trumpet so close to my ears. "See, if I'm fighting someone? They die. But my brother, now, he wouldn't like that so much. So, how's about I break every bone in your body instead?"

"Merulo!" I cried shrilly. "Help, please!"

"You think I can't take on my idiot brother?" Hydna's hands clutched harder, nails digging into my skin. Her teeth were as sharp as fangs, parted and wet. "I could do whatever I want, to either of you."

She paused, then—

"Ahh, Merulo, you were right!" Pealing with laughter, she climbed off me.

I crossed my legs hurriedly, covering myself with my hands. "It's just, it's confused blood, that's all."

"You picked the funniest man to drag down here. Who reacts that way?" The dragon woman slapped her thighs, bent with the force of her mirth, before making her way back to the picnic and dropping with a thud. I supposed there was more fish to eat.

I collected my sword, checking for damage, then sheepishly rejoined them. Merulo occupied himself with long strokes of his pen, pointedly ignoring me.

"It's not funny," I said, helping myself to an apple. "Really." It broke easily under my teeth, crisp and sweet. A few more bites—and then panic struck as I recalled his jealousy at my birthday feast. "And just so you know," I said, sidling closer to him, "I'm not interested in her, at all."

"Thanks," said Hydna. She raised her bushy eyebrows at me. "Then I should never do that again?"

"Uh," I said, and both dragon siblings snorted. "Whatever. Look, show me what you're working on." I leaned in to view Merulo's journal and frowned, confused by what he'd drawn across the pages.

An arm. Covered in sigils and lines that drew away into

clouds of finely printed text. It looked skinned, the interlock of musculature and tendon evident down to the minutiae of its curling fingers. At the shoulder, instead of meeting a body, the device erupted into straps of the sort that might hook around a chest.

"That's a nice drawing. Is it for anything in particular? A new type of construct?"

"It will be for me," Merulo said, scribbling another row of sigils into the elbow joint. He'd drawn it so that some elements appeared lifted off the rest, as if caught mid-explosion.

"You have arms," I pointed out. "Two of them. Do you need more?"

"Cameron." The sorcerer lowered his quill. "We've had this talk before. I will not allow any interference with my work."

"I'm not interfering." In slow movements, I took his journal, surprised that he was allowing this intrusion. "I'm only asking questions, to better understand." I leafed through the drawings, swallowing past the lump in my throat. One spread of pages contained a detailed leg, the page nearly black with the density of written notes. In growing horror, I kept turning pages, but no other body parts presented themselves. Only a slim wand, like something an Elder might carry, with a handle molded for gripping fingers.

"An arm and a leg. That's what it will cost." I closed the book, not wanting to look at him as he was now, intact. "That sounds like a joke they'd tell in a tavern."

"Fair payment, given the results." The sorcerer was gentle as he retrieved the book. "Hydna will pay the rest. She won't drain herself, not like I did, but it will be close."

"Too damn close for my liking." She spoke with her mouth

full. "And those limbs will stop working with the magic gone. You'll need to think about that. If we fish around the mummy piles, there's bound to be pre-Descent folk with mechanized prosthetics—we can yank them off, duplicate, and adjust."

"We won't *have* our current forms after the infection is cleansed, so it will not matter." Merulo was clearly rehashing an old argument. Finished with his notes, he took my abandoned apple and began to devour it, smearing his chin with scraps of its flesh.

I recalled what he had told me about dragons, what they had been, pre-Descent. "You'll be electronics?"

"Computers," corrected Hydna, reclining with a belch. "Super-computers. They're like . . . thinking boxes, made of pre-Descent materials. I'm not overly keen on the idea, but who knows, might be fun."

Her words were punctuated by the splatter of an apple core, which Merulo had thrown to bounce along the plaza tiles. "You're keen enough on the rest of it," he said, wiping his mouth with the back of a hand.

"What if you kept your bodies?" I asked. Then, quickly, as the sorcerer's face soured: "I'm not interfering, only asking. But . . . do you have to?"

"Dragon bodies are raw magic." Merulo's bony fingers descended on a fresh apple. "The transformation is a necessity. Everything will be restored, cleared of God's corruption."

"Ah." I wondered what would happen to the leviathans, with their beautiful draping fins. "So that's that, then."

A faint, treasonous hope remained in me, that the conditions of the prophecy had been met. That the mad sorcerer was defeated and would never see the world he sought.

Even if he mutilated himself in a failed attempt to destroy all magic—it beat outright death, or whatever loss of self that transformation might entail. We could live like that, Merulo on his prosthetics, with his fading dreams.

Though—and here I snuck a sly glance at my sorcerer, who had a fleck of apple flesh caught in a scowl line—with my powers of *persuasion*, he might even be stopped before that point. Which, you know, would be preferable.

CHAPTER 36

In Which Hydna Has Taken Me on Another Wandering, Shouting Tour and Has Thoroughly Depleted Me of All Bodily Energy. In Which My Limbs Are Something Akin to Undercooked Bread, In Which My Brain Has the Exhausted Inflexibility of Overcooked Bread, and In Which, Finally, I Am Hoping to Rest and Regain a Resemblance to Normal Bread.

I could tell night had fallen, as the rippling sunlight had tapered to black, leaving a dome of ink above me. I could also tell because I was yawning.

In my stumbling journey back to the inn, I rubbed at my eyes, repeatedly, and thus nearly tripped over the pile stacked before our bedroom door.

It contained, neatly parceled: my sword, my awful corpse clothing, the various baubles I'd picked off the ground, and some cleaning supplies I'd begged off Hydna.

"Uh . . . Merulo?" I gathered my belongings in one arm, and with some trepidation, opened the door.

At first, I thought a mummified animal had been left on our bed as a macabre gift. Then I recognized the sorcerer. He lay facing the wall, so that all I saw was black cloak and bony shoulders.

I took slow, tentative steps into the room, floorboards creaking. "Merulo?"

"Do not think," he drawled without turning, "that, absent an eye, I am blind. Hydna is a charming individual—"

"Hm," I said.

"And a healthy one." His shoulders curled. "I'm sure her strength and stamina are not without appeal—"

"Hey! Your stamina is fine."

"And you do lie," he concluded. "You lie to me, and you lie to others. Constantly. Do not try to deny it, for that itself will be a lie. You are not isolated with me anymore. You no longer have to act in . . . in certain ways, in the hopes that I will save you. She has not hurt you, she has not been cruel to you, and so if you like her—"

"Merulo," I said flatly. "She would crush my pelvis to dust. Can I put my stuff back now?"

"It is my preference that you leave."

"I already left once, and we saw how that turned out." I regretted this immediately as the form on the bed flinched.

Hesitantly, not sure what else to say, I tucked my clothes into a drawer, leaned my sword against a wall, and returned the baubles to the places I'd deemed decoratively fitting. I set a blown-glass fish beside a lamp to better catch the light. A rearing unicorn (which, bizarrely, lacked a horn), found its home on our dresser. My plastic shell-mirror, I set on the bedside table, so that I might examine myself in the mornings.

This last placement brought me uncomfortably close to

Merulo. For a moment I stood there, wondering at how he managed to breathe so angrily.

"I'm not lying to you. Really." I sat on the bed beside him. "I mean, if you're asking whether I *have* lied, then yes, there is a possibility—"

"Cameron—"

"—I don't *actually* find your lectures on astronomy intuitive, and I'm sorry about that—"

"*Cameron.*"

"But I'm not lying about . . . whatever it is you think I am. Honestly, this is just confusing." I flopped down with a sigh, bouncing the bed with enough force to throw Merulo into the air. He let out a strangled yell.

"Sorry, sorry," I said. The sorcerer's brief journey toward the ceiling had thrown his hair into his face, and now he sat up, glowering at me. "It's just—can we enjoy this brief window where nothing terrible is happening? Please?"

"I am impairing your enjoyment."

"Yes!" I said, grateful to have broken through to him. "Yes, you are."

"You don't want Hydna."

"No." I paused. "Or rather, as a friend. But she's not who I want."

Merulo muttered something dark under his breath. I couldn't quite make out the words, so decided to hazard a guess. "Your stamina is fine," I repeated, and patted his back reassuringly.

And that seemed to settle it, for shortly thereafter I fell asleep.

CHAPTER 37

In Which Glenda Is Happy to Be Making Progress, and Happy to Be Spending Time in a Cushioned Carriage, but In Which All Attempts at Conversation Have Left Her with the Curious and Unpleasant Suspicion that She Is Being Judged and Found Wanting.

They followed the glow of the sword like a compass.

Glenda brought up portals again, delicately, but the mongrel witch waved her into silence. "I am not the sorcerer. Cutting through space is an act either of arrogance or desperation, and we have the luxury of time. We fly, or we ride."

As it turned out, they didn't need to ride for long. The blade pulsed brighter as the carriage hurtled down an ancient tar road, bouncing with every pothole. Glenda swung the sword back and forth, struggling to discern which direction generated the stronger glow as they circled the outskirts of what had once been the sorcerer's territory. Houses soon dotted the roadside in greater frequency, until they rolled into a small town.

"I know this place." Glenda leaned from the carriage, Passionweed allowing for a full heart-pounding excitement.

"The sorcerer used this village to replenish his supplies. We found it after Cameron started a . . . *conflict* with our knights. Surely even he wouldn't be stupid enough to return."

The glow led them through the town, past hastily reined in unicorns and gawking children, then out the other end. Its luminescence peaked, drenching the carriage interior in white light, as a military outpost came into sight.

"He can't have been captured again." Glenda cloaked her unease with a laugh. This was her prey, and her hunt.

The carriage rolled to a gentle stop. Its doors opened of their own accord, accompanied by the fall of wooden stairs. Gathering her flower-embroidered dress in one hand, and the sword in the other, the mongrel witch descended with a grace that made her bulky form look weightless. In contrast, Glenda hunched down the wooden steps with caution, fearing they might demonstrate animalistic life by twitching or rolling beneath her. Nothing of the sort happened, but she maintained her distrust of the vehicle.

Hurrying to catch up with the witch, Glenda discovered a new discomfort; with Domitia's blue skin and braided silver hair, the knights would think she was an elf. And elves shouldn't look like that, all round of face and belly. Certainly, an elf woman would never grow to such a height.

It occupied her, how best to slip into their introductions that she, not this corpulent witch, best represented her kind—and so Glenda was as stunned as the knights sitting inside when the outpost door tore off its hinges, flung by a terrible power.

The mongrel witch held the blade outstretched, its burning light impossible to look at directly. She pointed it at the slack-jawed men, one by one. When she reached the last man, a bearded fellow who Glenda found faintly familiar, the sword erupted like a sun in miniature—then just as quickly went out. The man had enough time to spit a curse before a spell propelled him upward, slamming him into the outpost ceiling. With his outspread limbs, he looked like an oversized fly in a web. The other men cried out, grabbing for their swords, but the witch fixed them with a deadly look.

"Get out," Domitia said, and they did, giving the woman a wide berth as they fled through the ruined door. With Glenda at her side, the mongrel witch stood beneath the suspended man. "Sir Cameron, I presume?"

The elf peered upward. "No. But I remember him. The conflict I mentioned before—this is one of the knights who reported it."

"That's right!" said the knight, saliva escaping from his mouth. "I am a victim of Sir Cameron!"

Domitia broke her spell with a word, and the man tumbled to the floorboards between them.

"How so?" the witch asked calmly as the man scrambled to his hands and knees. She took one of the knight's abandoned chairs, lowering herself with a regality that Glenda had to admire.

"Sir Cameron transformed himself into a woman." The burly man's posture was pleading, dog-like on all fours. "And—and—it was him that came on to me, not the other way around! He deceived me."

The witch rubbed her chin. "If that was her true self, then no deception took place. I perform that procedure often, for those who seek it. This is your sword?"

The knight nodded, still not daring to rise. "He took it from me, him and the sorcerer."

"*She* took it," the witch said sternly—then, ignoring the knight's rushed apologies, swept to her feet and exited the small outpost, stepping carefully over the ruined door. Glenda hurried after her.

"You failed to mention that Cameron is a woman now," Domitia said as they walked, annoyance clear in her voice. The carriage lowered itself like a loyal pet. Glenda imagined that if it had a tail, it would be wagging.

"He was a man again the last time I saw him." Glenda climbed in after the witch. "It wasn't his 'true self,' just some Cameron stupidity. He was a vulture, the time before that."

They settled into the cushions, and the witch resumed her snacking on the biscuits. Glenda eyed them with hunger, remembering that the witch had offered some earlier, but gritted her teeth in determination. Better to maintain her figure.

"You help people to lie, then?" She might as well enrich herself with some gossip. Glenda treated the witch to a smile, but froze at a snapping sound; the biscuit in the witch's hand, destroyed by a tensed fist.

"There is no lie." Domitia spoke with a hostility that made Glenda recoil. The witch visibly worked to calm herself, before speaking again. "You're quite invested in religious norms."

"As we all should be!"

"Even when they cause people to deny themselves?"

"Deny what, objective reality?" Glenda giggled nervously. Seeking to recover the situation, she said, "Listen, we need to find an object of significance to Cameron. Why not try his family home? There should be records with the Church as to where Vaillancourt manor is located."

The witch nodded absently, and Glenda felt the carriage pick up speed. When the woman spoke again, it was in a gentler voice. "Is it Passionweed that you take?"

Glenda flushed violet, and fixed her attention on the scenery passing by the carriage windows. "I can't imagine what you mean."

"I help people, Glenda." As much as she wanted to tune Domitia out, Glenda found herself pricking her ears to the woman's musical voice. "It's a hard journey to reach my cottage, with the mud and the stinging insects, and I make it worse by wandering. There is no set place my home may be found. Those who do succeed are typically desperate. Their friends and family have failed them, and so they pin everything on rumours of my mercy."

Glenda nodded, happy to have the witch on a different tangent. The carriage passed a pair of gawking farmers on unicorn-back, and she felt brief pleasure at being inside the transport that inspired their awe.

"I've tended folk like you," the witch continued. "Sometimes, it's a terrible event that renders them numb. Sometimes, it comes from nowhere, ebbing and flowing. Whatever the cause, if they want their emotions restored or enhanced, I help them. If they simply need to make peace with who they are, I help them. But I never prescribe Passionweed."

Glenda waited in annoyance for the woman to get to her point. Feeling like a child forced into a lesson, she said, "So tell me, great witch. Why would that be?"

"It leads you to seek peaks, surges of feeling. What I

recommend is the redhood flower. You can forage it yourself in the right locations, and it restores emotive abilities without the ecstasy. It's less flashy, certainly; the highs are lower, the lows are higher. But you won't lead yourself to destruction under its influence. It's also cheaper," the witch added. "Not that I imagine money's a problem for you."

Glenda contemplated jumping from the moving carriage. "Thanks, but I'm perfectly fine."

"You feel a great deal of antipathy toward this knight, Sir Cameron," Domitia persisted, her voice careful. "Passionweed may be exacerbating this. It could give you some relief, to let go of old hatred."

"I should hate him." Glenda folded her arms, in what she knew to be a juvenile manner. She blinked rapidly, fighting the prickle of tears. "There is not a speck of honour in that man's body, and not a sin under the sun he wouldn't commit for his own self-preservation. If my hatred needs an end, it can have one with his second death."

"No one is beyond redemption," the witch said, looking at her with an emphasis that Glenda failed to grasp. Unable to formulate a response, the elf leaned stormily against the opposite side of the carriage and, sighing, Domitia ceased to press.

CHAPTER 38

In Which I Am Watching My Bony Sorcerer and Contemplating Treason. In Which I Have Already Betrayed My Family, and the Order I Swore an Oath to, and Humanity, and God for That Matter, but In Which This Particular Treason Is Causing a Lump in My Throat that I Cannot Quite Swallow Around.

Merulo sat in deep concentration, whittling away. With the help of a wickedly sharp knife, he'd succeeded in paring a block of driftwood into a slim wand. The carved channel spiraling from the tip made it resemble a unicorn's horn, though this illusion was broken by the small compartment cut into the base, where a sigil-heavy vial might be deposited.

As he worked, a transparent tube snaked from his right arm to a steadily filling jar on the table. Dark blood flowed through it, extracted through ancient methods. The colour disturbed me, as did the faint hissing as it spurted from his vein, but the sorcerer paid no heed.

He did, however, notice my gawking. Merulo halted his carving, laying down the wand, and plucked up an empty vial to brandish at me in happy demonstration. "The sigils have no enchantment in them yet, Hydna will take care of that, but this"—he danced the glass between a thumb and forefinger—"will take my own blood for fuel. Like a battery—oh, have I explained batteries?"

"Your sister has, with . . . inescapable enthusiasm." I had genuinely feared for my own well-being, having been forced to correctly recite her teachings on cathodes and anodes before she would allow me to leave. This took place during a tour of her electronics room, and though I wasn't immune to the glow and hum of ancient technologies, I'd taken great pains not to return.

The sorcerer smiled, white-lipped. "I suppose she also took you to see the bellows." She had indeed, great pumping machines that fed on the sun and supplied breathable air to the doomed resort. Hydna's sudden appearance, and the manacle grip of the dragon's hand around my arm, usually meant an impromptu and non-optional field trip.

"Yes, they were lovely, very . . . large. Say, shouldn't you leave a few drops inside your body?" I spoke casually, so as not to betray my traitorous intent. Black fluid filled the jar, sloshing crimson along the edges when the occasional tremor rocked the table.

"It's a renewable resource," Merulo said. Still, he pulled the needle-end of the tube out from his skin, pressing a finger over the wound. "This one's done. Be of some use and take it to my sister."

I had no choice but to receive it, though the jar warmed my hands uncomfortably.

Merulo didn't notice me leave. Every part of him was

sinking into his work, most of all his attention.

By now, I knew where to go. Sections of the underwater resort were familiar enough that I'd devised my own shortcuts and markers. Left at the smiling fish that sported alarmingly human teeth. Right at the desiccated hat stand, its wares crumbling to powder at the slightest touch. Up the flight of steps that, from the frequency of my visits, no longer left me winded, into the arena that Hydna had claimed for her workshop.

Scrape marks led the way from where she'd dragged in a desk. As always, I felt nervous entering the arena, surrounded as it was by empty rows of layered seating. I couldn't help but imagine a ghostly audience, watching in perfect silence. Hunched in the center beneath all those nonexistent gazes, Hydna looked like a lone gladiator.

I spoke from a distance, so as not to startle her. "Hydna, lovely Hydna, how are you?"

"Oh, heya, Cameron. Did you want me to bully you again?" Both our voices echoed faintly in the space. Hydna didn't look up as I approached, but I didn't take it as a slight. Both dragons worked with a frenzied obsession that left me grateful for what little attention they could spare me. She sat at a cluttered desk, in a comically undersized chair. Dipping her brush into a dish, she flicked its tip to remove excess liquid, and painted a pattern over a long section of metal.

"No, no. I mean . . ." I hesitated, then clenched my teeth in regret. Other matters took priority. "No. I have a delivery." I placed the jar with a muffled thud beside the dish that it would soon be filling. "And I have a delicate question that I'm hoping you'll keep between us."

"Yes, Cameron, it happens every month. We've been over this."

"No, not that. It's something... more serious."

"Oh?" Hydna lowered the metal. Her crimson eyes, better suited to a bird or reptile, were hard to meet, though I felt equally uneasy looking past her at the empty rows of seating.

"What you said before, about not being 'keen' on the potential results of... what you're trying to accomplish."

"Killing God and transforming the world," Hydna supplied helpfully.

I crossed my arms—then, in a change of heart, replaced them on my hips. "Well, yes, but also the turning into a computer thing. You said yourself you don't fancy that. So... and this might sound terrible, but... why help him? Merulo can't do it on his own, being, you know, *drained*. So why not keep everything as is? Yourself included." I smiled heartily, framing it as a casual hypothetical, rather than the searing accusation I wanted to level. Why, when she had so many other options, did she facilitate her brother's self-destruction?

The dragon woman looked at me with reservation. "Even at full power, Merulo could never have done it on his own." She emptied the jar of dark, clotting blood into the dish, then poured a clear fluid from a glass, swirling it together with the brush. "Anti-coagulant," she explained, and I nodded as though I understood the word.

Finished with her stirring, Hydna continued. "You might think that because I got all the looks and strength, Merulo got the brains." She rolled her shoulders, demonstrating those first two attributes. "In fact, I got all three."

"Maybe he got the modesty."

Hydna fixed me with a look. "We both know that he did not." Apparently satisfied with the blood's consistency, she dipped her brush and resumed the intricate scrawling, the veined bulk of her hand belying the delicacy of its movements. "My brother struggles with science. He's a magical genius, even I can admit that, but when it comes to the pre-Descent principles? I know them best. Maybe even better than anyone alive. My brother studies hard from those books, but he'd learn faster down here with me, taking shit apart and wiring it back together." The red sigils she slashed looked like bloody cuts on the smooth metal. "Electronics, computing, mathematics. He fetishizes the old world, but his skills have always tended toward the new. So he needs me for this master spell he's cooking, always has. The difference is that now he needs my magic, too." She paused to re-dip her brush. "I'm also a little offended, Cameron."

"Uh," I said, mesmerized by her quick brushstrokes, "I'm sorry. By what?"

"By you, thinking this is all his idea."

My stomach sank into my pelvis. "But—"

"I don't want to be a computer. And I don't care much about God, sorry, Mer. But think!" Her hand shot into the air, blood dripping from the brush as she gestured. "Think about what we could *have*. Space travel! Calculators! Little robot dogs that do a flip when you play music! And best of all, people to talk to about it all. That's all I want." She was breathless, bright drops of her brother's blood trailing down her arm. "Even if I have to be a computer to do it. I just want to talk to someone who knows more than me."

"I, ah, don't personally think that I can offer that."

"No." Hydna sighed, the energy leaving her. In a slow, tired gesture, she reached to thump me on the back, nearly severing my spine. "If I could offer advice: make your peace with what's to come, Cameron. Because it's happening, no matter what."

CHAPTER 39

In Which I Am Executing a Scheme. In Which the Scheme Is Genius, Enough so that if It Works, I Will Be Commissioning Someone to Stitch It into a Tapestry, but In Which Some Participation Is Required for Its Success. In Which That Participant Is Bemoaning His Participation.

"I can't waste my time on this," Merulo groaned—but we'd already gone back and forth, and I'd already won.

It was a significant victory. He worked, and he ate, and he slept, but the last two only barely. At night, I fell asleep to the scratching of his quill on parchment.

It opened a wound in my chest, comparing these last weeks to our time in the castle. What had changed? Why this distance? Was it just desperation, brought on by his draining?

Or could it be resentment, for my role in his ruin?

I shrugged off these thoughts as best I could as I led the sorcerer down a crumbling path between crumbling buildings. In a comradely manner, and with no nerves whatsoever, I beamed at him, breathing the recycled air with gusto. "A healthy body leads to a healthy mind."

"Yes, and how is yours?" he grumbled, before pausing. "That was mean, wasn't it?"

"Yes."

"And I'm supposed to be nice."

"Yes."

"Except when I'm *not* supposed to be nice."

"Exactly," I said, and Merulo groaned again.

A number of the buildings leaned over us in frozen collapse, like eavesdroppers. The sorcerer eyed these as we passed, fingering the wand tucked into his belt. "You shouldn't walk here alone."

"Nothing bad has happened yet." I paused, realizing this wasn't a sound argument. "And if it happens, then it happens."

"*Nothing has happened, but if it happens, it happens.*" The sorcerer raised his hands to the domed ceiling, as if in prayer. "Sometimes, I find it hard to distinguish whether intelligible language is passing through your mouth, or whether you're just making sounds."

I decided to ignore him.

It was an interesting exercise, matching the sorcerer's strides. His spidery legs traversed the same distance as mine, but, without adjacent muscles to power them, I found myself outpacing him whenever my attention lapsed. Merulo made a great show of not breathing heavily, though his nostrils flared with the effort. But if I slowed too much, then away he strode, as imperiously as he might pace the lengths of his battlements.

It brought an odd anxiety, embarking on such a mundane activity with him. Walking with someone else, I might reach for their hand, and intertwine our fingers—but with the mad sorcerer? Spitting lightning bolts and forging half-alive monstrosities were perfectly natural for him. Handholding, less so.

"It's here," I said, spying the fallen sign I used as a landmark. Something like a sentient wheel of cheese lay balanced against a wall, its mouth agape. "In here."

Forgetting my inhibitions, I grabbed for Merulo and pulled him into the alley between two buildings, where the artificial lighting failed to reach. He made a face, but allowed himself to be maneuvered into the shadows, and positioned before a ladder. "You have to climb," I said, pointing. "If you're able."

Merulo glowered. "Of course I'm able."

I eyed him, doubtful. "Would it be better for me to go first, so that I can help you up? Or . . ." At his hesitation, I decided. "I'll go first."

"This is beyond foolish," he called, as I scurried up the metal rungs, luxuriating in the stretch of my muscles. "And unsafe. These buildings are very, very old."

At the top, I pulled myself onto the roof, then turned to hang my head down. "You scared?"

"You—" the sorcerer spluttered, and reached instinctively for his wand. "You mangy—You insufferable—You think that I would be scared, of a ladder?"

I leaned further over the edge. "It does look that way."

Truthfully, I'd been scared, too. The first time ascending, I'd placed my weight carefully on it, step by step, ready to jump free at the slightest sign of bending.

From two stories below, Merulo speared me with a glare. "If you continue to speak like Hydna, I will forbid you from spending time with her."

"Alright, I'm sorry. Can you come up, though? Please?"

Saliva filled my mouth as my anxiety grew. We'd both experienced flying on our own wings, so fear of heights shouldn't really be a factor—but his pride might be. And I didn't have time to cook up a different scheme. Not before he shed his limbs.

There was some further grumbling, as Merulo shifted from foot to foot. Finally, he rolled back the sleeves of his robe, exposing arms like white sticks, and stepped onto the ladder. His face took on a look of great concentration.

I decided against hooting and clapping, as that might be interpreted as mockery. Instead, I hovered at the roof's edge with the nervous pride you might feel watching a small child ride their first unicorn. "Come on," I muttered, too quietly for him to hear. "You can do it."

Step by step, Merulo mounted the ladder. His skin went through a remarkable transformation, shifting from bleached white, to the boiling red of a shellfish. At the top, I seized his flailing hand, lifting him bodily onto the roof.

"There," I said, kneeling beside him. "Doesn't it feel good to use your body?"

He lay panting on the cement for long enough that I grew worried, before replying: "No."

"Come on." I pulled him to his feet, and let him lean on me for a moment, before drawing him forward. "Over here. I promise it's worth it."

Merulo glanced around the rooftop with a level of concern that I wasn't used to. "It's collapsed!"

"Only partially."

"*Only partially* . . . Cameron, when we tell you not to wander, it's not out of cruelty. It's because—*ouch!*"

I swirled, my heart in my throat, to see the sorcerer hopping on one foot. No obvious blood or gore surrounded him, though I did see a protruding crevice where one might stub a toe. "You alright there?"

Merulo's face flushed, his mouth twisting into innovative shapes. "Remember who you are speaking to. I am the sorcerer Merulo, who has defeated armies, held kingdoms at bay, and . . . oh, fuck it." Perhaps it was my polite nodding along, but his outthrust chest had deflated, his posture drooping. "Just get on with it."

An empty doorway led down a flight of stairs. At one point it had contained a door, but a jammed one that had given way to a couple of moderate-strength kicks. "The ground-level entrance was blocked," I said apologetically, as Merulo narrowed his eyes at me.

Judging by his breathing, descending the stairs took less toll on him than the ladder. My excitement grew as we neared the room, until I was practically skipping.

"If this were anyone else, I'd think I was being led into a trap," said the sorcerer wearily.

I beamed at him, opening the rusted door and pretending not to notice how it came off in my hands. As Merulo stalked past, I balanced the now-detached door against a wall, and followed.

A plush black carpet covered the floor, decorated with an eye-burning pattern of stars and whirls. Defunct machines crowded the walls, rectangular booths where plush seats faced dead screens. And ahead—

"Look!" I pointed at it, all but hopping. "It's you!"

A dragon reared across the wall, black scales gleaming in the light of the fire shooting from its jaws. Granted, it had the wrong number of limbs (the overly generous artist had given it arms, legs, AND wings), and its snout lacked the beakish angularity of Merulo's. Across from it, a unicorn reared, its horn angled to plunge into the dragon's throat. I'd thought about covering that bit up before bringing Merulo, but decided there was no need. The painted dragon would *clearly* win.

I had shifted some of the boxy relics so more of the dragon was visible. It helped that the partially collapsed roof and walls allowed in a wash of light—though I disliked how it highlighted the unicorn.

"I thought everything here was supposed to be nautically themed," Merulo said, somehow managing to complain. But his eyes were fixed on the mural. "Is that what I look like?"

"Yes! Only, your horns are much longer. And..." I struggled to think of ways in which he compared favourably. "You have a more elegant neck."

The sorcerer surprised me by laughing. "An elegant neck?"

"Yes, like a swan! Or like me, when I was a vulture."

"Cameron..." The sorcerer looked pained. "You did not have an elegant neck."

"Anyways. Point is"—I gestured at the walls, which also depicted a shining knight, and a geezer in a pointed hat shooting magic from his fingers—"this is pre-Descent, isn't it? These people were dreaming about our world in the same way that you've been dreaming about theirs."

"Cameron."

"I'm not being manipulative," I lied. "It's just . . . if you reframe your thinking, we're already living in someone's ideal version of reality. So instead of changing it all, perhaps you could just . . . change how you perceive it?"

The sorcerer approached the mural with something like reverence. He placed a hand against the faded paint. "Your thoughts, when you manage to summon them, are not entirely insensible."

"So then . . . ?" I'd been holding myself with more tension than I realized; as black spots entered my vision, I reminded myself to breathe.

His spidery fingers crept along a wing, following the flare of leather. "They dreamed of dragons. And then they starved here, in this ruin."

"I mean, you could look at it that way—"

"And I do."

"So that's it, then." A portion of roof lay on the carpet. I sat on it heavily, my head in my hands. When I'd spotted the mural in passing through a broken wall, the idea had come to me like divine providence. Now, the thought it ever could have worked seemed ridiculous.

What else? My skull felt overheated from the force of my thoughts. What else could I do to save him from himself?

The sweep of black fabric in the corner of my eye saved me from further descent. Merulo sat beside me, wincing as the concrete shifted slightly beneath us. "This room," he said, with a stiff carefulness, "is, ah. Very nice. Thank you, Cameron, for sharing."

"But it's not enough."

He exhaled through his teeth.

"Alright," I said. An odd urge struck me, to tear this stupid carpet up by the roots and shove the relics out to fall onto the street—but instead I put on another smile for Merulo, and stood. "Let's go back, then."

CHAPTER 40

In Which Glenda and the Witch Have Been on the Road Too Long, and In Which, despite the Cushions that Liberally Line the Carriage, Glenda Is Experiencing a Fair Amount of Pain in Her Tailbone.

A pile of scorched material lay before the Vaillancourt manor.

Glenda leaned out of the carriage window as they passed, but the ashes failed to reveal their former shape. "That better not be what I think it is."

The manor house was middling, consisting of the usual grand rise of stone and slanted roof, with requisite ivy climbing the walls. If it didn't have any modern flair, at least the greenery looked well-tended, cut into rounded bushes that bordered the gravel entryway. The squawking chickens ruined any hold the manor might otherwise have had on old majesty; it looked pedestrian with the birds pecking about and shitting wantonly, the home of a family in decline.

A servant exited the manor at their approach. He looked bewildered to find no carriage-beast to tend to.

"You can stroke her neck and tell her she's a good girl," the witch said apologetically, descending the carriage steps. "She likes that."

Glenda flowed down the steps after her, all perfect elven posture, her fear of the carriage's beastliness forgotten. She felt, rather than saw, the admiring gaze of the human man. Another servant, a short, flustered woman, emerged to bring them to the lord of the manor. The woman quaked as she led the elves—probably, thought Glenda, intimidated by the better examples of her sex. The mongrel witch might have . . . deficiencies, but with her silver hair and jutting ears, she still ranked infinitely higher than a human.

The servant deposited them in the great hall. A table ran down its center, lined by elegant seats, beneath a hanging chandelier—*unlit*, Glenda noted in annoyance. The hide of a slain manticore lay before the long table, its glass eyes bulging. Glenda exchanged a look of mutual disapproval with Domitia, before separating to prance about the room, evaluating its style. She passed a wooden cupboard, carved in the elven fashion, a hanging shield with the crest of a roaring lion, a richly embroidered tapestry depicting God's Descent . . . and most satisfying of all, the painted portrait of a stern man with two golden-haired boys. The taller boy, it warmed Glenda's heart to see, had his face scratched out, as if with the fury of a knife.

"My apologies, I hope you have not been waiting long." The lord of the manor greeted them with tempered politeness as he strode into the room. His hair was scoured white with age, but Glenda thought it might once have shone a familiar gold.

"Not at all," said the witch. "Thank you for welcoming us on such short notice. I am Domitia Dragonheart." She did not, to Glenda's horror, use her elven father's surname. "And this is Glenda Bellerose, of the Knights of Order. We're here about your son."

Glenda cringed at the witch's bluntness. The lord's expression darkened, his wrinkles deepening. "He's never been right. Never." The man seemed keen to match Domitia's forthrightness. "To think, we fed and clothed that . . . if I'd only known, I would've strangled the wretch at birth."

Movement, in the corner of the room. Glenda tensed, ready to draw her knife, but it was only a boy. No, not a boy: a man, but short and fresh into adulthood. He hovered at the room's entrance, likely thinking himself out of sight in the shadows.

Elves can see in the dark, Glenda thought, with a fair amount of venom. Low intelligence must be a familial trait.

"Ah, yes." The witch sounded uncomfortable. "We're hoping you might have a belonging of his. Something of personal significance that we might take with us." Domitia gave no indication of having spotted the boy. Perhaps the witch had other shortcomings to her vision, in addition to that lazy eye.

"I'm sorry for the trouble my son has caused." Lord Vaillancourt seemed to be in a world of his own. "There's such anger in me, and nowhere for it to go. A personal belonging, you say?"

The witch nodded serenely. She'd taken pains, Glenda noticed, not to stand on the manticore rug.

"Did you see the ash heap upon entering?" the lord asked, and Glenda stifled a groan. "We've extracted his poison from this house. Everything of his, we fed to the flames. I'm sorry, good ladies, but nothing remains."

Glenda glowered as they left the estate. The slow strides of the serving girl who led them reminded her of the days spent scouting the woods with Cameron. Always, she had reined in her elven speed to match his pace, even when their sluggish progress made her feel like screaming. It enraged her now, thinking of all the times she'd lowered herself for *him*.

"Excuse me," a timid voice called, as the women made to re-board the carriage. "You needed something of Cameron's? Would you . . . are you going to bring it to him?"

Glenda grinned in predatory rapture. "Of course," she answered before the witch could speak. "It would help his heart, to have something from home."

The young man shuffled, twisting his hands in his shirt. He looked to be in his early twenties, face hidden under a heavy bang of curls, his otherwise fashionable clothing marred by the smear of animal shit across one pant leg. Chickens crowded about his feet with a chorus of clucks. He stared down into their midst, as if drawing comfort from them. At last, he decided. "It's this way."

They followed the lordling down a path that bordered the manor house. The stink of dung filled the air, as did the rasping cries of animals. Their source soon presented itself: goats, a fenced pen of them, chewing happily on a stack of hay.

Muttering an apology for the detour, the man unhooked the gate and wove through the animals to reach their wood-walled shelter. He reached into the underside of the shelter's thatch roof, and withdrew something lumpy, made of cloth. Goats swarmed him on his way back, nipping at his pants and shirt. He sternly shooed them away—but Glenda could see his faint smile. Latching the gate firmly behind him, he paused, reluctant to give up his prize.

"I made this for him," he said, fiddling with the plush, worn-out toy. "People say he's a coward and a traitor. I don't know if it's true." A she-goat reared to better bleat over the fence, and the man paused to scratch her muzzle. "When we were younger, Cameron . . . he had these episodes. He'd be crying and hiding, like there was something after him, but there never was, nothing at all. I made him this"—he held out the toy, a roughly sewn four-legged beast—"because my animals help me, whenever I'm feeling down."

A dog, it had to be, with those floppy ears. Glenda swallowed her laughter. A dog for a dog. How fitting.

The witch accepted the toy gravely, holding it as though it might shatter in too firm a grip. "And Sir Cameron had this with him often?"

"During our childhood, always." Deprived of anything to occupy his hands, the young man turned back to the goats, allowing them to nibble his fingers through the fence slots. "Cam left it behind when Father sent him to become a page. And I took it from the pile, during the burning, in case he ever came back." He turned to the women, his eyes glistening. "But now you can bring it to him. Thank you."

Glenda practically skipped on their way back to the carriage, but the witch's footfalls were leaden, her face pinched. Inside the carriage, seated on the plush cushions, Domitia looked at the elf without warmth. "These periods of fear that the boy described. Is this another thing you failed to mention?"

"What, that Cameron is a coward? Have I not been perfectly vocal about that?" Glenda fluffed the cushion behind her back. "Honestly, the way he *begged* when we had him, it wasn't befitting of a man."

The witch seemed on the verge of saying something, before shaking her head. Holding the cloth dog with continued tenderness, she spoke the spell that would lead them to Sir Cameron.

CHAPTER 41

In Which My Plotting Notes, Which I Had Oh So Carefully Stashed, Have Been Discovered. In Which I Am Sweating and Gulping and Possibly in Trouble.

I exited my bath, a fluffy towel wrapped about my waist, to find Merulo seated on our bed in ambush. He held up the chalkboard that I'd cleverly hidden beneath the mattress. In doing so, his sleeve fell, revealing the bandage that now permanently wrapped his blood-letting arm.

"You've crossed out seduction," he said mildly.

"Hey, hey, hey!" I tried to snatch it, but he rose in a flare of cloak.

"'The joys of exercise' received two strike-outs. Glad you picked up on how unpleasant that was for me. And what's this—a sad face beside 'reframe thinking.'"

"That's private!" I grabbed at it with more urgency, my legs tangling in the towel.

"'Convince Hydna' has also been eliminated, so I suppose I don't have to fear collusion. It's incredible that you wrote this all down."

"Merulo," I begged. "Stop."

With his free hand, he pulled the chair from his desk, and positioned it between us. "And then there's 'steal wand' with a series of question marks after it. That seems well thought out. And—oh look! 'Seduction Two.' Cameron, what is Seduction Two?"

"I could show you," I said desperately.

He smirked, turning again to avoid my grasping hands. "The wonderful thing about your betrayals is their complete lack of cohesion and effect. You make for a pleasant enemy."

"Betrayal?" I squawked. "I'm trying to . . . to . . ."

"Preserve the order of this world?" Merulo finally looked tired.

Well. *'To save you,'* is what I'd meant to say, regardless of how it had dried on my tongue.

"Stability may seem like a comfort, but it's a false one," Merulo said, with odd gentleness. I realized I was being lectured; he'd slipped into his schoolmarm affect.

Abandoning our one-sided game of chase, he stalked past me to the bed, and sat, patting the duvet beside him. With a sigh, I obeyed—with suds still dripping from me, I would doubtless create a damp patch.

"Think, Cameron. Consider your . . . appetites. Think of how your supposed comrades treated you, before this. They would never have allowed your freedom. I seek to, to . . ." Now it was his turn to grasp for words. "To pry off the bars that hold all of us. Do you understand?"

"Yes," I said miserably.

"It is beyond you, and me, and . . . whatever we may have. You understand?"

"I do."

"So, then." His lips became thin lines. "I will be taking this. And I may show it to Hydna." His cheeks puffed slightly as he swallowed whatever was building in his throat. "Seduction Two. *Really*."

"No, Merulo!"

He leaped from the bed, childish in his glee, and I trailed him out of the bedroom and down the hall. "Come on. You don't have to do that."

He broke into a faster trot, shoulders shaking with the effort of his repressed laughter, and I decided to maintain my complaints for effect only.

Let the man have one last bit of fun.

CHAPTER 42

In Which I Am Puffing and Groaning and in Substantial Amounts of Pain, but In Which What I Am Doing Is Important Enough to Be Worth Any Agony.

The popping bubbles let me know that I was being summoned.

I'd been speed-marching up and down a set of stairs to maintain the tone of my calves, so it came as some relief to stop. Even still, I had to bend double and pant, slicking back sweaty hair, before I felt ready to follow.

Once certain of my attention, the bubbles picked up speed, popping and re-forming so that I had to break into a trot along the cracked pavement to keep up. I dodged past the trident-wielding statue that had so badly frightened me on that first day, skirted a pit of collapsed concrete, and circumvented an abandoned vehicle, catching only the briefest glimpse of the small, curled body within. I barely needed the bubbles now, having recognized the route to the library plaza, so I slowed, not wanting to arrive out of breath.

The mismatched dragon siblings stood before the shelves, waiting.

"See?" said the sorcerer, receiving a fully laden basket from Hydna. "He comes when called."

I frowned at him, before clapping Hydna's outstretched hand, her preferred method of greeting. "How's it going?"

"The prosthetics are complete," said Merulo, shattering my good spirits. "So I thought I'd take one last walk on my own two feet. Hydna's even packed a meal."

Merulo looked scared, I realized. Pale, even for him, with a forced edge to his usual scowling arrogance. His hands shook almost imperceptibly where he gripped the handle.

"And there's no point in saying you don't have to do this?" I reached for the basket, and he allowed me to take it; from its weight, Hydna had clearly packed something substantial.

"None whatsoever." Merulo brandished a hand imperiously, then waited. Growling in annoyance, Hydna nevertheless obliged her brother and spoke the words to tear through space. A portal bloomed in midair, revealing the calm sands of a starlit beach beyond.

I had asked Hydna earlier why she summoned portals with spoken words, while Merulo drew elegant pentacles. Apparently, it came down to efficiency. The more direction you gave a spell, with intertwined sigils, spoken command words, and symbolic items, the easier it flowed, like a channeled river without excess leakage. Merulo had been less wasteful than I'd thought with his magic. Hydna favoured shows of brute strength.

The sorcerer stepped through first, lifting his feet high to get through the raised portal. I hopped up next, landing in soft, sinking sand on the other side. When the portal clamped shut before Hydna could join us, I raised my eyebrows at Merulo.

"My sister has some final tinkering to do. She'll open the portal again, at a set time." He stalked down the beach. I watched his stride, wondering how it would differ, afterward. His robe blew gently in the evening breeze, complementing the rhythmic lapping of the waves, and I felt the terrible urge to freeze this moment before anything more could change.

He sat abruptly in a black flap of cloth, having found a jutting rock that suited him. "We'll eat here."

I got to work disemboweling the basket. It contained a disconcerting amount of wrapped meat, two apples, paired goblets, and a flagon of dark red wine, all bundled in a finely spun blanket that I laid with a flourish on the sand.

The sorcerer groaned as I unpackaged the meat. "Hydna has been forcing chicken liver on me, for blood restoration."

I smiled at that, and selected a tender strip, popping it into my mouth. "She's showing her love."

"Do not speak with your mouth full. Liver is a repulsive organ that smells like spoiled cheese. Meat should *not*"—his voice rose in a burst of temper—"smell like cheese."

Right, time for the wine. Holding the bottle between my knees, I pried out its cork with a loud pop. As I poured in arcing red streams, Merulo chewed on the liver with exaggerated revulsion.

He'd chosen a bright evening. The full moon shone silver on us, granting decent visibility, though the night still drained the beach of colour.

"Hydna has a theory." Merulo sipped, and I tried not to look too eager. It'd be funny, I thought, to see the sorcerer drunk. "She's been pilfering my books, in particular astronomy, and something bothers her." He tilted his head, appraising the abyss that curved above us, dizzyingly deep. "The stars. They match the pre-Descent records precisely."

"Ah, I see!" I nodded, not understanding. At Merulo's glower, I took a deep swig from my own goblet.

"Everything is in motion, always. Orbiting, falling, spinning. Due to the vastness of space, it would take many centuries for even the slightest difference to be noticeable, but we've had that, and there is nothing."

"God's influence extends farther than you thought?" I guessed, munching on another piece of liver. Merulo had a point; the flavour took some getting used to.

"No," said the sorcerer, after draining his own cup. "We can't think that. Or else, all of this will be for nothing." He held out his goblet for a refill, and I, the perfect henchman, indulged him.

"The alternative is what, that it's fake? We're not seeing the real sky?" The wine made my tongue feel dry and puffy, along with its usual effect of emboldening my lustful impulses. I settled for running my fingers through the sand, carving nonsensical lines.

"Precisely." The sorcerer leaned forward with the breathless excitement of a buzzard on a carcass. "Which means . . . ?"

I swallowed another mouthful to get out of answering. Frustrated, Merulo continued, "Which *means* that the colonies on Mars, and the moon—that moon, right there." He pointed accusingly into the sky. "They could be active, cut off from Larnia by whatever barrier has been erected. And all our knowledge, our cultures and languages, everything presumably lost on the Day of Descent—the religions you can scarcely imagine after this forced, homogenous worship of a monster—the moon could be their ark."

"Or they could be dead," I said, the drink making me bold. "It could be a tomb, like the resort. Eat some liver, you need it."

"Ahh." Merulo followed the meat with a cleansing draught of wine. "It's possible. But I'd like to think they're alive." He motioned the goblet at me, sloshing out half its contents. "And if so, I'll be returning their home to them."

"They will sing the praises of the mad sorcerer," I agreed, discreetly shuffling toward his rock perch.

"Why do they call me that?" The mad sorcerer noticed his diminished wine with a gloomy lowering of his brows. "I've always been quite coherent. Kill God, restore the world. Where's the madness?"

"They're haters." With a carefully calculated scoot, I shoved my way onto the rock beside him. "Ignore them."

The sorcerer was too deep in his thoughts to protest my arm snaking about his shoulders. "Even if these stars are fake," he said. "They may be the only ones I ever see."

My resolve snapped. "Don't do it." I fought to keep my voice steady. "Honestly, why should you have to carry all this? If it's a problem—and I'm not saying it's not—someone else will step up to fix it."

"When?" Merulo leaned into me, and having braced for his fury, I fell silent. "It's been a thousand years. I know how you feel, but let's not fight about this. Not tonight."

After a long silence, I managed to say, "Okay," and brought my mouth to his.

Abruptly, he pulled away. I tried not to audibly sigh as his face hardened, some internal wall sliding back into place. We had *finally* been getting to the good stuff!

"I lied," he said.

Surprise brought me to a standstill. My mind swam, bleary under the alcohol. "About the moon?"

"No. Why would I—? No, about that horrible little elf." Merulo scowled, and my face contorted in an echo of his. As former friends went, I didn't rank Glenda highly.

And then it connected. "You mean, she told you, that . . ." I paused to swallow and compose myself. "So she did tell you, then? You received my, uh, last words?"

The sorcerer left our perch and stood, silhouetted by the full moon. "That you loathe me. Yes."

"*Loathe?* That's what she—? Oh fucking fuck, Glenda." I pushed myself off the rock to join him. "Well, actually, that might be my fault, I didn't get the word fully out before, you know . . ." I drew a finger across my neck, in case he did not, in fact, know.

This, at least, got Merulo to look away from his damn moon. "Then you don't loathe me?"

I wanted to cry from exasperation, or perhaps slap his gaunt cheek. "You can't think of any other word it might have been? Come on, Merulo, you're the intellectual here."

His thin lips moved as he sounded out possibilities. I gave him time, shifting my weight from one foot to the other with accompanying crunches from the sand.

"Loathe is the only word that makes sense." The night did his face no favours, shadows collecting in the lines that gave his mouth its perpetual scowl. "I am not entirely without self-awareness. And I do want to, ah"—he choked on the word—"*apologize*. For the needle. I have no qualms in using violence against those who would destroy me, but against someone so pitiful, who was under my control?" The sorcerer pursed his lips. "It was tasteless. I regret it."

"Yes," I agreed. "It was a completely undeserved punishment."

The sorcerer's frown deepened, and his mouth twisted, but heroically, he managed to refrain from comment.

Despite my prodding, I found that I also couldn't bring myself to say the word. "It really wasn't loathe."

"I have done nothing to inspire any other feelings." A thought seemed to strike him. "Unless . . . *lust*?"

"LOVE," I shouted. "For fuck's sake, it was love! You think my final message would have been a come on? Really and truly not a situation where any movement could occur down there."

"Well," said the sorcerer. "One never knows, with you."

A tense quiet followed, both of us staring at the round white moon. It was that or risk accidental eye contact.

"Hydna will be opening the portal soon," Merulo said, after a time.

"You don't have to say it back. There's no pressure. It was supposed to be an 'in my dying breath, I confess' type thing, so there's no need to make a big deal of it or anything, and—ah fuck, are you crying?"

"No." The sorcerer sniffed, turning his back on me.

"My mistake. Must be an allergic reaction to the sand. Terrible time for that to strike." I sidled closer, giving Merulo a playful shoulder-check that made him stumble. "You love me. Admit it."

"Hydna will be here soon." He sounded desperate.

"Then she'll get to hear how much you love me, which is a lot."

"Quiet," he hissed, as another voice bellowed across the beach.

"What was that?" Hydna's figure in the distance looked distinctly menacing, a giant marching down the shore toward us.

"Your brother is in love with me!" I shouted back, cupping my hands around my mouth. Merulo garbled something and grabbed my arm, squeezing with all his feeble might.

"I know!" came the yell. "It'd be cute if it wasn't so disgusting!"

The sorcerer sagged, his grip on my arm loosening. "This is nonsensical."

"Oh yes, everything's been nonsensical for a while now. Let's lean into it," I said, and pulled him in for a kiss while Hydna hollered and hooted in the background. With the cool night air, and the taste of wine in my mouth, everything felt good.

As far as final moments of peace went, it was a decent one.

CHAPTER 43

In Which the Dog Is Glowing Bright Enough to Pain Glenda's Eyes, but Still They Have Stopped, and Still They Delay. In Which Glenda Is Wondering Why She Follows the Instructions of a Half-Breed Witch So Readily, but In Which She Has to Admit, Albeit Reluctantly, that It Is Nice to Stretch Her Legs.

The town they'd entered for the night was preoccupied with a harvest festival.

The witch, of course, insisted on attending, and so now they strolled, sipping from flasks of cider. It burned Glenda's throat, but warmed her belly, and the intoxicants made the pressing human crowd easier to stomach.

A bonfire filled the square, flames shooting up to lick at air greyed with smoke. Stalls ringed the square, with vendors shouting advertisements for everything seasonal at the throngs of families, couples, and roaming gangs of children. They passed apples in every form: fried, baked, dried, and candied. Tarts flavoured with elderberries, red currants, blackberries, mulberries. Spears of roasted vegetables, sugar-crusted breads, and thick cuts of meat dripping in fat.

Spying this last item, Glenda pulled a face. "Do they have no empathy whatsoever?" she said to Domitia, not caring who overhead. "As if the animals are less alive than they are! As if they don't want to live, just like we do!"

"Sir Cameron wants to live, too."

It took some gasping and exhaling before Glenda could bring herself to respond. "Animals are innocent! He is anything but. And besides, I don't want to eat him. Although . . ." A smile crept across her face at the image of him strung up like a hog. "It would certainly serve him right."

Domitia winced. Perhaps she would have found a retort, but a man stumbled up to them, whisky on his breath.

"Phew!" He attempted a wet and rather flat whistle. "The size of you, ma'am! Are all elves that big?"

"Yes," said the witch firmly, while Glenda squawked. "All of them. This one didn't eat enough growing up." Domitia's hand settled on her shoulder, and Glenda readied herself to shrug it off . . . but instead found herself grappling with an odd heat that started in her cheeks, and moved downward. It did *something* to see Domitia's hand, warm and broad, envelop the entirety of her shoulder. Glenda wondered, flushing, if those hands were large enough to fully encompass her waist.

Too much cider! It must be interacting with the Passionweed in unexpected ways. Glenda coughed into her fist, burningly aware that the witch had not withdrawn her touch.

"Aye, we had a cow like that," the man said, tipping his straw hat. In his haziness, he overdid it, revealing a head as bald as a thumb. He stooped to retrieve the hat, shoving it firmly back into place. "Its mam got ate by shucks before it finished growing, and the stupid thing wouldn't suckle from any of the others. Barely got big enough to slaughter."

"Yes," said the witch. "That does seem like an identical situation." She twinkled down at Glenda, who started, shocked to be enjoying the same joke.

"Huh," is all she could manage. "Uh."

When Glenda failed to materialize a smile, the witch changed course, her face hardening. "But perhaps my friend here does not like being compared to a cow."

"Didn't mean any offense," said the man, his panic sobering him. The crowd had carefully parted around the elves, but they didn't show the man the same care, so that he was continually buffeted on either side by passing elbows. "Meant none at all, ma'am. I am sorry for botherin' you."

Domitia offered a smile. "It's quite alright. You enjoy your evening now."

He bobbed, babbling thanks, and somehow lost his hat again. Before he could regain it, Domitia took Glenda's arm, and gently steered her away. "He didn't mean any harm," she said. "They just get excited, seeing someone new."

"We could be making progress right now. Your carriage doesn't need sleep. We could be on the road, closing in on those bastards."

The witch clucked her tongue and guided them toward a stall hawking braids of bread. It stank of garlic and butter. "Glenda, Glenda. Why fight for a life you can't enjoy?"

The humans queuing for the stall looked over their shoulders, blanched, and made way for the elves.

Glenda sniffed. "Another pearl of wisdom."

"I am twice your age, you know, and wisdom does flow

downward." The witch gave her a smile that flashed the edges of her jagged teeth. "I could easily be your mother."

A full-body shiver ran through the elf, like a static shock. *Now, why had that done something to her?*

Then and there, Glenda vowed never to drink again. "Tomorrow," she said, staring into the crowd with violet-flushed cheeks. "Tomorrow, we leave at dawn. I want to end this."

CHAPTER 44

In Which I Cannot Understand Why, When We Are Safe and Hidden and Happy, He Insists on Creating His Own Horrors, or Why Something as Abstract as the Prospect of a Slightly Better World Might Matter to a Person More than His Own Limbs. And In Which I Am Just Now Realizing that I Had the Opportunity to Dull This Experience with Alcohol, but In Which It Is Too Late Now. In Which Things Have Already Begun.

"Think of this as revenge," Hydna had said, "for every time he's been a cunt."

It didn't cheer me up.

"If I could handle your constant consumption of rodents, you can tolerate this," Merulo had snarled.

That hadn't helped either.

"Well, Mer," Hydna said to her brother as I mounted the stairs to my viewing perch. "If I have to be ripping your limbs off, I'd rather it be in the heat of battle, but this'll have to do."

I sat in the outer ring of the arena. Hydna's desk had been shoved to one side, clearing space for the grisly performance to come. A metal table held center-stage now, lit by a snaking artificial light that stood as tall as a man. On the table lay Merulo, his sister standing over him, gloved and masked, her hair tucked into a bulging cap. The blue shift fit her poorly, tearing along the armpits as she moved, but she'd insisted on the costume. Cloaked in plastic, with her glittering tray of enchanted knives, Hydna looked like something from a nightmare.

"This is the best part!" she hollered up at me, waving a knife. "I've always wanted to knock this fucker out."

I sank lower in my seat, hoping the distance would hide my expression. Would it distract her from the surgery if I began to vomit? The temptation mounted to leave now and poke about a mummy pool while Hydna did . . . what she would do, but I couldn't surrender to my cowardice. Not this time.

"Oh for fuck's sake, get this over with." Merulo's voice sounded tinny from so far below. "Or would you have me laid out like a mackerel for the next hour while you chitchat with that f—" His insult cut off as Hydna chanted the command word, activating the bloody sigil painted on his chest. Dragons, it seemed, were significantly more expensive to spell into unconsciousness than handsome knights.

Motionless now, Merulo looked for all the world dead on the table. A cloth modestly covered his genitals, but the rest of his exposed skin shone fish-belly white under the electric lighting. I felt uncomfortable seeing the scar tissue that enveloped his lower torso; he kept it so deliberately hidden while in human form. His left arm and right leg were marked with black-inked crosses. "So I don't get mixed up and take everything off!" Hydna had explained jovially.

I forced myself to watch as she began. She hoisted a cleaver, heavy with sigils, and chopped down with more enthusiasm than I thought warranted. Merulo's arm separated in an easy, unreal motion, like she'd popped the limb off a doll. She spat a quick word, encasing the severed arm in magically summoned ice, then swapped her weapon for smaller instruments, clipping carefully at the spurting wound. Blood speckled her face and clothing. I wondered at Merulo's ability to survive this.

When she moved to his leg, I hid my face. Enough bravery for one day.

After some time, I looked up to see that it was done. Having stitched and tidied the stumps, Hydna occupied herself with returning tools to their original line-up. With her dark chore completed and cleanup underway, I expected some of the tension to lift—instead, she hesitated. Emotion was difficult to read from this distance, but something had shifted in her posture.

I jumped to my feet, ready to race down the stairs and join her at Merulo's side, but as easily as it came, the moment passed. Confidence filled her broad frame again and, setting down the blade, Hydna moved to where her brother lay prone. I watched in great nervousness, as she bit into the meat of her index finger, smearing the resulting blood across the sorcerer's thin chest to paint another sigil. Slamming a hand over his ribs, Hydna belted out a string of words.

I saw motion on Merulo's stumps. His flesh rippled like water, melting into shiny new skin that sealed itself over the puckered red stitchwork. But they'd said . . .

"You'll drain yourself!" I shouted.

The distant woman shook her head. "I'll still have enough for what we need to do."

Speed made me clumsy as I tripped my way down the seemingly infinite stairs, finally slamming past the barrier gate to join the siblings in the arena's center. Just in time: Hydna completed a second spell and the sorcerer sat up with a gasp, looking disturbingly reduced with his missing limbs. His single eye scoured the arena, wild and confused, until it fell on me.

"I thought it would hurt," he said airily. "It hurt when I took my eye out."

He collapsed back against the table.

I seized Merulo's remaining hand, trying to rub some warmth into it. "How are you doing?" I asked Hydna, who slouched off to the side.

"Tired," she said, her ashy face speaking the truth of this. "Very tired."

"You are both fucking idiots," I said, and was met with a shrug.

CHAPTER 45

In Which We Are Living with the Consequences of Our Actions, both of the Sorcerer's Poisonous Ambitions and of My Own Inability to Remotely Temper Them, but In Which We Are Still Here and Still Alive and Still Waking Every Morning with a Renewed Thankfulness for All That Has Yet to Be Taken Away.

It had taken practice, and he had, impossibly, lost even more weight, but Merulo now walked with his familiar imperiousness. Only a faint limp and the clink of the prosthetics betrayed any difference. The artificial limbs worked as intended, magicked sections sliding over one another in an imitation of tendon and muscle. Merulo even claimed to have some sense of touch through them, in the same way he retained shadowed sight through his stone eye.

He didn't want any acknowledgement of the days I spent half carrying him about as he adjusted, pained and miserable, so of course I was tactful.

"The power balance has definitely shifted." I sat perched on a stool overlooking his paper-strewn desk. "I reckon that I, the strong and handsome knight, am in complete control now. I should be the one issuing orders. I'll start thinking of an appropriate title, too. Perhaps 'Your Grace,' as a start?"

"Is that all?" said the sorcerer. Over the weeks, he had transformed our underwater bedroom, pinning notes and sketched sigils across the walls, and in a couple of areas, scrawling directly onto the wallpaper in a fit of passion.

"I think so," I said. "For now."

"Alright." With quick quill strokes, Merulo copied a series of glyphs from the spread tome before him. "Fantastic. As an aside, each and every day I regret wasting my powers on your resurrection."

"That's genuinely very harsh." I wobbled back and forth on my stool, lost in boredom. With the dragons scheming at an increasingly frenzied pace, barely even stopping to sleep, I'd been left feeling isolated and without purpose. I'd even slipped back into cleaning and meal preparation, just for something to do, which at least stopped the dragons' work areas from growing too disgusting.

"Now that I have this"—Merulo retrieved his wand from its resting place atop a stack of pages and angled it in my direction—"you could be a vulture again, with extreme ease. So perhaps stop testing the limits of my patience."

"Aw, you like me too much to do that." The stool nearly tipped with my rocking, but I caught myself on the desk's edge, preventing a fall. Unfortunately, this jarred it sharply. I watched in mute horror as towers of stacked paper toppled, fluttering in a cloud to spread across the room.

The sorcerer turned slowly, with murder in his face. "Do I?"

"Could you two not flirt with me in the room?" Hydna batted at one of the drifting pages. She sat on the bed with her own set of papers fanned about her, the mattress sinking beneath her weight. "I swear, Mer, whatever work you think you're doing is nothing compared to the math going through my head right now."

I peered at her. "And, Hydna, what you're doing will . . . ?"

Merulo spoke before she could. "Cleanse the stain of God, undo its transformations, destroy its magic. And free our world from its isolation. Anyway, Hydna, I thought you had completed your end." The sorcerer stood with the click of sliding metal, and a pronounced sigh, and began the task of gathering his scattered pages. I hopped off the stool to help, feeling more than a little guilty.

"I did," Hydna growled. "And now I'm checking for errors." She tapped the papers peevishly, but she couldn't keep the excitement from her voice. "Haven't been any so far. This is going to work, Mer. It's really going to work!"

"Not that there's any rush." I held out my handful of collected pages, which Merulo snatched without thanks.

"No, Cameron. It's not as if the combined forces of humanity are currently hunting us down or anything." He stumbled slightly as he reseated himself at the desk. The prosthetics, though brilliant, were not a true replacement for flesh.

"Sarcasm shouldn't be your go-to. It's indistinguishable from the way you normally speak. Maybe if you tried something more obvious—like insulting limericks." I moved to retake my stool, ready to resume my rocking, but halted at Merulo's glare.

"Hydna. Dear sister. Could you allow us a moment of privacy?" There was a singsong quality to his words that had me reconsidering all my actions of that morning.

Had he been serious about his threat? Returning to

vulturehood held little appeal, especially not in this enclosed environment, with no fresh carcasses to dine on. With his new limp, I stood a good chance of outrunning the sorcerer if I could just make it to the hallway. After that, I'd tuck myself away until evening, by which time Merulo would *almost* certainly have redirected his passions into some new improvement to his spell.

I stuck close to Hydna as she exited with her papers, making an exaggerated display of goodbyes and pats on her broad back and, crucially, placing myself by the open door.

"Close it," said Merulo.

I hesitated, my hand on the handle. "Uh, with me on the inside or the out?"

"The inside."

In what felt like the closing stroke to my execution, I clicked the door shut. Across the room, the sorcerer had ceased his scribbling and sat watching me, still as a cobra. I tried to put a great deal of respect into my ramrod posture.

"Cameron," said Merulo. "I would like to hurt you."

"Oh." I slouched in relief. "*Oh*. Okay!"

"Which reminds me." The sorcerer's smile was as sinister as any I'd seen in my short but fraught life. Behind my back, my hands returned to the door handle. "Do you remember when I brought you along, as a vulture, to the exchange with Chancellor Noor?"

How could I forget? Our first act as a unified team! "Of course," I said, beaming. This change in direction brought confidence and so, abandoning the door, I made my way to the bed and sat. A faint indentation remained from Hydna's crushing mass.

Rolling the wand between his fingers, Merulo regarded me. "You do know that it was with the intention of humiliating you, yes? A shining Knight of Order, made into an ugly pet."

"Uh . . ." I eyed the door again. "When you said hurting, did you mean physically or emotionally?"

"Physically."

"Well then, let's skip to that part," I said, getting into it again despite my wounded feelings.

"You've proved remarkably immune to shame, then and always. My point is, now that I have my strength restored"—here Merulo brandished his steel and wood arm, curling the artificial fingers—"I can work to find some position that will shame you, some degree of pain or restraint. It will be quite fun, I think." His single eye held a feverish glint.

We really were a matched set of freaks.

"That's only if," I said, shrugging off my shirt, "you can take a minute off from killing God."

"I can take a minute."

CHAPTER 46

In Which Glenda Just Wants to Get to the Blissful Culmination of Stabbing Cameron through the Throat Again, but In Which She Is Worried About What All This Time Alone with the Mongrel Witch Is Doing to Her, as She Has on a Couple of Occasions Now Felt an Odd Stirring that Should Only Be Brought About by Tall and Refined Elven Men, and Certainly Not by a Woman, and Certainly Not by a Woman Like This, and What Is That Damn Witch Doing Now, What Is She Doing.

Domitia was throwing headless fish into the sea.

Glenda sat on the cold beach, watching. "Could you please explain," she called between splashes, "why this is necessary?"

Domitia held up a hand in a request for—what? Silence? Obedience? Glenda gnashed her teeth, but nevertheless complied. She dug her heels into the sand in lieu of the more *colourful* actions that occupied her daydreams.

They'd followed the glowing dog for many days in the rolling carriage, stopping in villages and sometimes even at farmhouses to sleep and restock on supplies. The glow eventually led them to the edge of a cliff where, spreading its wings, the carriage had leaped, causing Glenda to shriek in fear and surprise. Circling above a section of featureless water, the worn toy glowed like a meteor—but the carriage lacked any aquatic abilities, leaving them to idle on this beach with a stack of hastily purchased and slowly rotting cod.

Despite her complex feelings toward the woman, Glenda could admire the strength with which Domitia threw the fish. They landed a considerable distance away in eruptions of white foam.

Most likely, the stink of fish now polluted those rounded arms and wide hands. Glenda *certainly* would not allow any contact that might transfer those pollutants. And she *certainly* wasn't picturing it. She'd been careful, since that festival night, to keep herself at arm's length from the witch. Domitia, with a creasing of her brow, seemed to understand the elf's dodging skittishness, and maintained her own distance accordingly.

"And now here she is, wasting time," Glenda muttered as she stacked sand in a heap across her feet. Thus absorbed, the witch's yell of triumph startled her. She looked up to see a dark form passing beneath the turquoise waves.

Domitia was unperturbed, raising her scarred arms in welcome. "Hello, sweetheart," she called to the monstrous head that breached the water's surface. "Will you be my eyes? I have plenty of fish to share!"

The creature wove closer, grinning with needle-point teeth, until—with a sharp decline in grace—it hit sand and began to waddle. Without the water's support, the leviathan's ribboned fins looked like snagged mounds of seaweed.

The monster dwarfed even her mass considerably, but Domitia approached it without fear. She tossed a fish up to be caught with a snap, speaking softly all the while.

With a pat on its dripping snout, it was done. The beast was hers. Domitia tugged the glowing toy out of an expansive sidepocket and held it up to the leviathan. "Gently," she ordered.

The monster took the dog between its teeth with the same delicacy it might use for its eggs. Lit by the toy's radiance, its scales sparkled like gems.

"We are going to kill Sir Cameron," Glenda called, knowing that Passionweed fueled her temper, but unable to control herself. "So it doesn't matter whether that toy gets chewed to bits. He'll never see it. Unless you've changed your mind about whose side you're on?"

"I am on the side," Domitia said darkly, "of whatever will prove best for the largest number of people. This is not a quest for vengeance."

Not for you, thought Glenda. She bit back further comments, knowing the witch would only respond with more stubbornness and self-adulation. Domitia might pass as an elf, but she had the temperament of a storybook dragon.

The sea monster galumphed its way back along the surf until both its carriage-sized torso and the long, serpentine length of its neck had disappeared into the waves. With a soft plop, its head sank, and it vanished. The witch stood there in silence, water lapping about her ankles, and her eyes rolling white. It didn't take long for Glenda to break. "Care to share what you're seeing?"

"Nothing, presently. The leviathan is diving, following the glow. Getting distracted by fishes—naughty! Come on, sweetheart, let's stay on track." She paused, the cries of seabirds a distant chorus, then: "I see it. Incredible. They have an entire city hidden in the depths. Brightly lit—and so many buildings! I can't imagine the magic it must take to keep the water at bay. Oh, she can't go any further." The witch smiled ruefully. "I'm detaching now, to enter the city with my own consciousness. It will be tricky. Easy to rebuff if I'm detected, which I fully expect to be. Please grant me silence. Once I find Sir Cameron or the sorcerer, I will open a two-way call so that we may speak and confirm their identities."

"Are you crazy?" Glenda leaped to her feet in a storm of sand. "Why would you warn them? We have the advantage!"

"Now, I've noticed that you keep saying *we*. You are here solely to identify the men, after which you will go no further." The witch exhaled deeply, her eyes the white of hard-boiled eggs. "As for surprise . . . the sorcerer never had to announce his intentions. He made the declaration, of his own accord, that he would destroy God and reshape this world. Without that warning, and without the resulting wars launched against him, I imagine his studies would have progressed much faster. Even if it was simple arrogance, I respect it. And"—the witch smiled with a rare ferocity—"maybe I'm a little arrogant, too."

Glenda stood poised, trembling with fury. But what could she do? In a controlled release of tension, she splashed into the shallows to join the witch.

"So yes, Glenda," Domitia continued over the cries of gulls and gushing of water. "I will declare my intentions: that I am coming to destroy the sorcerer and maintain the order of our world."

Glenda waited in wary readiness, her toes sinking into wet sand, while Domitia moved her hands in the air, steering herself through a foreign space. "There we are, a little closer, and . . . OH!" The witch sounded genuinely shocked. "Well. Good for them, I suppose. The timing is unfortunate, but . . ." She grimaced. "This will have to do. Here we go."

CHAPTER 47

In Which I Will Not Describe the Preceding Events out of a Sense of Demure Politeness, but You Can Be Assured that It Was Some Real Freaky Shit, Some Real Satisfying You Know What, Which Involved Magic and, No I Shan't Say, and Wow Am I Glad to Have Absolute Privacy in This Underwater Bedroom, I Sure Would Hate to Have Any of This Observed or—

"Excuse me for interrupting . . . whatever this is. If you'll allow it, I can arrange to call back later."

I was hanging by my ankles, buck naked, when the voice came. It seemed to emanate from a bubble holding a woman's projected face, which bobbed before us.

Merulo leaned back. "No, this is as good a time as any."

"If you're sure." The woman sounded faintly embarrassed. She looked like an elf, although her face was pleasantly round-cheeked, and her skin a darker shade of blue. One of her eyes wandered slightly, drooping. "Well then, first I'd like to perform an identification. Glenda? Is this the sorcerer Merulo? And is that . . . Sir Cameron?"

Glenda's doll-like face appeared in the hovering bubble. "Oh my God, Cameron! Oh my GOD."

"Microwave! Microwave!" I sputtered, flailing.

With a flick of his wand and a rushed mutter, the sorcerer summoned the illusion of clothing. My illusory shirt promptly fell down over my face, denying me sight.

"I can give you some privacy, but first, please take this as an announcement of intent." The woman spoke in a melodious voice, which I might have found pleasant under different circumstances. "I, Domitia, the one they call the mongrel witch, will be putting an end to your schemes." A pause. Then, with a touch less drama: "If you'd prefer to come my way to finish this, that'd be terrific. Just follow the connection made by the call."

"No. I won't." Merulo's face was hidden from me, but I imagined it held some variation of his usual scowl. "You are Domitia the half-dragon?"

The seriousness of it all hit then, and my heart pounded in my throat. I wanted down, quite badly, but also feared interrupting.

"Indeed," said the woman, in her strange, musical voice. "I simply offer this warning then: I will be coming."

"How admirable," spat the sorcerer. "Now get out. I haven't finished with him yet."

CHAPTER 48

In Which Glenda Now Has Seen Things She Will Never Be Able to Erase from Her Mind, for the Rest of Her Life She Will Close Her Eyes and There It Will Be, the Mad Sorcerer as Nude and Bony as a Dried Fish, and Cameron, She Doesn't Even Want to Think About Cameron, but Rest Assured Her Urge to Kill Has Temporarily Been Overcome by the Urge to Take a Vow of Celibacy and Retreat to Somewhere Quiet and Pastoral.

"They're degenerates." Glenda's tongue felt thick with revulsion. "Sick and twisted, evil, filthy inverts!"

The witch strode along the beach toward her parked carriage, leaving dark footprints in the sand. "Glenda, shut up."

This shocked Glenda so badly that she did, in fact, shut up. Domitia's next actions were salt in the wound, as from the depths of the carriage she withdrew bundles that Glenda recognized as purchases from the last town stop. The witch sat on the steps of her carriage, uncovering a fresh pie and a sealed jar of sweet tea.

"What are you . . . what could you possibly be doing? We

need to go after them. They'll be jumping through any number of portals. Have you gone mad?"

The witch bit deeply into the pie, releasing the strong odour of ginger. She ate slowly, and with relish, only stopping to answer after her immediate appetite was satiated. "A ten-minute head start seems fair."

Glenda squawked in disbelief. Water lapped around her bare feet. Kicking it into a spray, she marched to where her shoes lay in the sand and seized them with a force meant to signal her rage. "Is this a game to you? These men are foul, and we have them in our sights at last. You'd let them get away?"

Another hearty bite of the pie. The scent of ginger, mingled with sea brine and heated sand, was not entirely unpleasant. "I'll be going against a full-blooded dragon, one with time itself under his command. To be frank, Glenda, I do not expect to make it out alive. Allow me this final meal in peace."

"Maybe if you weren't so preoccupied with eating all the time, you'd be better equipped to fight."

This got the witch to look up from her meal. Brushing crumbs from her chin, she pointed at something behind the elf, singing faint words. Even in her rage, Glenda felt some curiosity, and so she turned.

"Here, Glenda. I've made one of those portals you love so dearly."

A force struck her back and sent her hurtling through the opening void. As she fell, shrieking, she heard final words from the witch: "Do consider the redhood flower."

Glenda toppled into dirt and weeds, the portal sealing behind her. "Damn you!" she shouted, scrambling to her feet. "Damn you, you damn witch!"

A sound brought her attention to the trees. The same man they'd seen when the carriage first touched down, all those days ago, stood there again with an armful of collected timber.

"What are you looking at?" Glenda howled. Without a word, the man dropped his wood and turned, sprinting away down a woodland path. Smoke rose from somewhere in the trees, betraying the presence of a nearby cottage.

"Damn it!" Glenda cried, recognizing the location. She'd been abandoned near the outpost village—too far to rejoin the witch, too far to reclaim her prey, completely shut out from whatever would unfold. "Damn you! This was mine! This was supposed to be mine!"

Depleted from her exclamations, Glenda crouched panting in the soil. It was with supreme annoyance that she realized she was hungry.

CHAPTER 49

In Which I Am in a State of Utter Panic, and Am Also a Bit Worried About the Sorcerer as I'm Sure He Didn't Intend for the First Meeting with His Long-Lost Sister to Be Quite So Nude on His End, or Quite So Threatening on Hers, and In Which I Am Deeply, Sincerely Uncomfortable with the Number of People Who Have Just Seen My Cock and Balls.

"There's no time, no time! HURRY!" the sorcerer shouted, which did not in fact speed up my dressing. I hopped, one foot in a pant leg, while Merulo waved his wand with a rasp of discordant syllables, opening a call to his sister.

"I felt someone poking about, but they left too quickly," came Hydna's growl. "Who was that? Who's found us?"

"Domitia," said the sorcerer, loading the name with emotion.

"We're fucked, then."

"Hydna!" Merulo sounded aghast. "We are not 'fucked.' You've finished your end, yes?" He waved at me again to make haste, and I complied as best I could, crawling across the floor to find where my shirt and shoes had landed. Why, oh why had we not undressed me in a more orderly fashion?

"I told you!" Hydna's shout reverberated around the bedroom. "I haven't finished checking for errors!"

She must be in dragon form to create such a noise. Having collected my garments, I dressed in the corner, feeling grim relief at having a sword to buckle at my waist.

"It doesn't matter," said Merulo. "We must proceed immediately with what we have." He seized his knife from the desk, slashing at a finger, and threw himself to the tiled floor to smear bloody glyphs. "My arm, I need my arm! Hydna!"

"How can I help?" I asked, watching the scrawled patterns develop. Even in his urgency, the lines came out exact, the curling loops and sigils elegant and clear. Before he could answer, a portal opened in the room, spitting out an ice-covered limb that fell to the floor with a thud.

"I'll do it now, Mer." Hydna spoke through the portal, without entering. "This might be goodbye. Best of luck."

"Say you love each other!" I cried, before she could close it. "You absolutely do, so just say it!" I raised my hands, exasperated.

"Fine. Yes, I do 'love' you, Hydna." Merulo kept his eye fixed on what must be an especially interesting patch of floor. "You have a brilliant mind regarding pre-Descent matters. And you've been of great help, despite—"

"Despite you being a constant asshole? Yeah," she said. "But I love you too, somehow. Try not to die." With that, the portal folded shut, leaving us alone in the inn room with its paper-pinned walls, the severed arm slowly defrosting on the floor between us.

"Using this"—Merulo abandoned his spell-work to grab it, closing artificial fingers around his former wrist—"I will 'reach' the entire world!"

When I failed to laugh, he looked genuinely disappointed.

"Where is Hydna going?" I asked.

"Five pre-determined locations around the globe, to place the points of a pentagram." Merulo returned to his own pentagram, clamping teeth about his finger whenever the wound threatened to close. "I haven't finished my research for this one," he admitted, somewhat hoarsely. "But it should work. It *has to* work."

"What about your leg? Don't you need that as well?" I hoisted the bed with a grunt, toppling it against a wall to give the sorcerer more floor-space to draw on.

"Fuck!" Merulo cried. He jerked to his feet in an unhinged motion that had me fearing for his linework. "My leg! And my eye! The next spell depends on them. Cameron, you know where my sister sleeps?"

"Um..."

"I'm not accusing you of sleeping with her. The building beside the arena, she's hollowed it to make a den. Inside, you'll find an icebox. Exactly what it sounds like, a box filled with ice. It contains my leg, my other eye, and most likely, an enormous quantity of chicken livers. Run, as fast as you can, and fetch those for me. Not the livers, the other things."

Wasting no time, I barreled out into the hallway, only to trip to a halt as the sorcerer shouted, "WAIT!" He stood in the doorway, offering... the wand?

"Domitia may arrive at any moment, and you have no defense. Use this." He shoved the wand into my hand, then manipulated my fingers, closing them around the handle. "You've been around us long enough. You must have picked up some spells."

The wand felt oddly warm in my grip. Tilting it produced the slosh of dragon's blood, hidden in the compartment at its base. "Uh," I said, "just the one." It was the spell I'd memorized in my childhood, the one the Church had used to drain me.

"That will have to do." The sorcerer shooed me, as if I were still a vulture. "Go, go now!"

I took a tentative step backward. "I don't know if I can use this."

"It doesn't matter if you can. You must. Damn it, GO!" Merulo slammed the door in my face. I stood stunned in the hallway, realizing that I'd been left unchaperoned with an item of immense power.

The door opened again. "She's beautiful, isn't she?" Merulo's single eye shone wetly. "Domitia. She looks like my mother. Except blue."

"Yes," I said softly. "She looks very nice."

This time when the door closed, I broke into a run.

CHAPTER 50

In Which Glenda Has Been Cruelly Betrayed and Cast Aside, despite All Her Hard Work and All Her Commitment, All because of One Fucking Comment Which She Probably Shouldn't Have Made, but Then Again Domitia Shouldn't Be So Damn Sensitive, and Definitely Should Not Have Abused Her Power in What Was Essentially an Assault, and In Which Perhaps Glenda Should Report to the Church that the Half-Dragon Isn't as Under Control as They All Believe.

Glenda was venting her rage at a tree, kicking and kicking until bark rained in splinters to expose soft pale wood, when the clouds above formed a man's face.

And not just any man. Her enemy, the hideous sorcerer, a man who—from the sharpness of his form—looked to be lashed together from knives. The glower of his eye, the oily curtain of his hair, all were picked out in the curling whisps of a darkening thunderhead. Craning her neck, Glenda saw that it was far from localized; in the distance, another face formed, and another. She could see no end to them.

All the faces moved at once. The sorcerer's stone eye flashed with lightning, rain falling like spittle, and he spoke in the rumble of a storm: "You've all heard of me. I am Merulo the sorcerer, and on this day your God will die at my hand. I will wipe this planet free of its corruption, and in doing so, purge your magic and open up the cosmos! If you are frightened, good, be frightened. Flee all magically supported structures, as they will crumble. Flee the Church, as they are liars. If this warning goes unheeded, then the cause of your death will be stupidity. No more needs to be said."

With that, the clouds dissipated into white puffs that hung in a tranquil sky. After some hesitation, the birdsong resumed.

"Evil fucking bastard," Glenda breathed, the tree forgotten for now. "He can't succeed. Can he?"

In the stories her parents read to her as a child, the villain always lost, right at the end when things looked their worst. And she couldn't forget the prophecy. They'd fulfilled the conditions! Cameron had died bloodily, and in doing so, secured their victory. Unless—and what an unspeakable unless—the sorcerer had undone their work with his reversal of time? But then, who could stop him?

"Domitia." Glenda spoke to the empty forest with the reverence of a prayer. "We haven't always . . . gotten along. And I'm sorry for making that comment, really. But please, please . . ." She regretted the Passionweed now, hating the tears that rolled down her cheeks. "Don't let him win. End that evil fucking prick. We're all rooting for you, even if the rest of the world doesn't know it. They're praying for someone to save us, and it's you! Please, Domitia . . ." Glenda collapsed against the tree trunk, seeking comfort and support from the same vegetation she'd just been mulching. "Please save the world. And," she added as an afterthought, "please kill Cameron."

CHAPTER 51

In Which I Find that I Have No Particular Aversion to Severed Limbs, Likely because of All the Time I Spent as a Knight in Battles and Such. In Which, to Be Truthful, I Typically Arranged It so that I Would Arrive after the Battles, Meaning That I Mostly Saw the Shed Limbs and Not the Shedding.

As it turns out, severed legs weigh rather a lot.

And Merulo's leg was far lighter than it should have been, consisting as it did of the thinnest possible layer of muscle over bone. "Completely hairless," I said to myself in wonder, as I lifted the leg from the icebox. Thinking about it, I'd never seen him shave, or show the faintest hint of stubble. Must be a dragon thing.

His eye I found under a layer of stacked livers, in the iciest corner of the box. A coating of frost dulled its iris. This brought a tightness to my throat, and I told myself to better appreciate the rich black of Merulo's remaining eye when I next saw him.

After some thought, I dropped the eye down the neck of my shirt, so that I could carry his leg two-handed. The eye rolled against my skin like a lost grape, caught in the fold where my shirt tucked into my pants. A terrible thought occurred, as I jogged from the building: if I tripped, I would feel the eyeball squelch flat against my abs.

I'd made it halfway back (trying *very hard* not to trip) when the water above the dome vanished.

I might not have noticed, if not for the change in light. I'd grown accustomed to the white ribbons that danced in faint patterns across the resort, the product of sunlight refracting through water. Between one footfall and the next, they disappeared.

Without them, the resort looked harsh and flat. I stared in wild alarm to see nothing above me, not a single puddle. Only far off, on the edges of the dome, could I still make out the distant swirl of water. She hadn't removed the entire ocean, then.

I was panting hard, almost hyperventilating. Merulo might be drained, but he was still a dragon. I only had to reach him, and he was close, incredibly, frustratingly close. It so thoroughly consumed my focus that I nearly ran right into Domitia.

A gently rounded woman, muscle evident in the breadth of her arms and legs, stood on the resort road ahead of me. Her hair hung like spun starlight, picked through with delicate braids in an elven style. She looked like she might be fun to dance with, on a less serious occasion. Trying not to whimper audibly, I shoved the frozen leg beneath my arm and withdrew the wand.

"Sir Cameron," said Domitia. "I've heard a lot about you." Somehow, she infused even those blunt words with melody, like the opening verse to a song.

"All good things, I assume?"

"Unfortunately not." She cast me a sympathetic look. "Though, given the people in question, I'd have taken praise as more damning."

I choked out a laugh. Of course, she'd been with Glenda.

"Sir Cameron," she said, with a gentleness that made me want to weep. She took a careful step forward. "Do you know what will happen to the sorcerer if he succeeds?"

"Uh," I said. "I believe he'll turn into a computer?"

"What he seeks will destroy him."

"You know, it's nice to have someone acknowledge that. It really is." I tried to hold the wand out straight, but it vibrated with the shaking of my arm.

"And yet you still assist him." She approached at a leisurely pace, her hands held up in the universal gesture of peace. Thick ropes of scar tissue descended from her inner arms, marring her blue skin. In one hand, she gripped a crudely stitched dog, which bore a striking resemblance to my childhood toy, Waggy. "I'm a healer by trade, not a warrior. Let me help the both of you. It's never too late, Sir Cameron, to do the right thing."

I jabbed the wand at her and she froze. "They called me scum, right? Everyone you talked to? It's alright, I know. I know they hate me. See, the thing is"—and my arm steadied, as some new emotion took over—"if I help you now, I'll be exactly the scum they think I am."

The witch began to shout a spell, but somehow, miraculously, I was faster. As the words of command left my lips, the wand bucked in my hand like something alive, and up shot Domitia, levitating with a force intended for a stone cathedral.

CHAPTER 52

In Which I Have Overcome the Fear that All My Life Has Been a Plague of the Most Noxious Variety, Worse than an Ass Full of Boils, and In Which I Have Made Use of My Wonderful Recollection of Childhood Trauma to Do Something Quite Remarkable and Worthy of Praise.

"I defeated a dragon!" I cried, bursting into our bedroom.

"Is she dead, then?" Merulo stood in the center of an immensely detailed pentagram, the ashes of his burnt arm flaking at his feet. He looked pale, but invigorated.

"Ah . . . no, just temporarily floating away."

"Then we have different definitions of 'defeated.'" He accepted his leg from me, and his sloshing wand, and—frowning as I reached down the front of my shirt—his defrosted eyeball. "Why . . . No, I need to stop asking you why." He dropped the body parts onto our bed with a thump. The melting ice immediately began to seep into his spread of paperwork. "It's time, now, to send you somewhere safe."

"Absolutely not," I said, and surprised myself by not feeling the slightest bit tempted. "There must be some way that you can make use of me."

"I already have several uses for you." He smirked, inappropriately I thought. "Combat, however, is not one of them."

"Have you forgotten who saved you from Sir Gareth?" I asked. Then, at his blank look: "Oh, you have forgotten. The knight who was bashing your face in? That 'scoundrel' from the bar? Anyways, even if I'm useless, even if I'll get in the way, I can't just go."

Merulo paused his gathering of materials to turn a cold eye on me. "I could make you leave."

"I know," I said. "But please don't."

Baring his teeth, he tore animalistically at the papers covering a wall, then seized an ink-loaded quill and slashed black curving lines across it. "We've wasted enough time. Come on, then." He completed the elaborate pentacle with a flourish, then turned to grab at the bed sheet, wrapping his eye, his leg, a sealed jar of blood, and various other materials into a compressed bundle. Struggling slightly under its weight, he handed it to me. "Here, the work of a mule."

I took the bundle—which turned out to be rather light—and Merulo pointed his wand, spitting words I now recognized. The painted circle shimmered with the warping of space. Ducking, the sorcerer disappeared into it, and I leaped after him—just as something huge broke through the bedroom door. With an uncharacteristic yelp, Merulo shouted the portal shut, and we stood staring at the empty space it had occupied.

"Alright, so she's not completely defeated," I said, while Merulo urgently scratched another pentacle into the soil. Choking heat surrounded us, as did the screams of strange animals. Moss-damp trees towered on all sides, taller than any pine or maple could grow.

"Here," said the sorcerer, hastily jabbering the words of command, and he leaped through the circle. I jumped after, clutching the bundle to my chest—and landed in searing cold. Wind whipped at my eyes, forcing them shut, while my feet sank deep into numbing snow. This time Merulo carved his glyphs into a snowbank, his thin form hunched and shivering. Again, he cast the spell, and again we passed through space.

A desert. Warm wafts of sand, sticking to the moisture of my snow-soaked legs. Dunes rose around us, carved into waves by some inhuman sculptor, while the afternoon sun scorched overhead.

"That should grant us enough time." Merulo took the bundle from me and unwrapped it, scattering its contents across the golden sand. In this heat, the politely frozen body parts would soon be swelling with rot.

"Enough time for what?" I fidgeted with the sword at my waist, eyeing our desolate surroundings. At any instant, I expected that dark hurtling mass to reappear.

"For me to kill God," said the sorcerer, and he danced, as giddy as a child. "First, I will have to locate it. That's where my eye comes in."

"Should we . . ." Everything was moving too fast. "I mean, one way or another, this will be goodbye, won't it?"

"What are you after? One last frolic in the sand?"

"Merulo!"

I didn't like draining the joy from him, or seeing the hard downturn of his mouth. "I've earned us a head start. I must use it to complete my end of this, now." The sorcerer's shoulders hunched, and he half turned from me. "This has been good, though, Cameron."

I spoke around the lump in my throat. "It has, hasn't it?"

"Very good."

"Yes."

"Now, if that's settled..." The sorcerer's grin had returned. "I have a God to kill."

Following his shouted directions, we spread the white bedsheet across the ground, piling sand in the corners to keep the breeze from catching it. My role complete, I stood to the side and watched as Merulo painted the sheet with blood. It rusted as he worked, the interconnected sigils darkening from a fresh scarlet to the maroon of Hydna's scales. For once he did not work from memory, instead heavily referencing his clutched notebook. I worried at the time spent on this, extended by his frantic paging in search of specific glyphs, but managed to direct my energy into rehearsing a set of drills. Sweat soon drenched me, dripping down my brow and pooling under my armpits, but it felt good to swing about a long, sharp piece of metal.

A joyous yip came from Merulo, the sound a coyote might make with something fresh and squirming in its jaws. His pentacle was complete. He stepped into its center, straightening to his full height and smoothing down his robes—dirty and torn now. I felt a pang for how they'd looked upon our first meeting. Granted, I hadn't been a fan, but they'd grown on me. As had their owner.

Merulo thrust out his thoroughly defrosted eyeball in a fist. Far from easing into the spell, he erupted into a complex recitation, thick with anger and sniping accusation, howling the guttural vocabulary as if it were his native tongue.

Rippling outward from him, a bubble of *something* rushed toward me. I stumbled back with a cry to avoid it, and saw—

Nothing.

No desert. No evening chill. No toying wind, not the scent of baked sand nor the metal of painted blood. No sweat trickling down my neck, no hunger in my gut, nothing.

There was nothing.

Nothing.

CHAPTER 53

In Which the Mongrel Witch Has Shifted from Her Dragon Form, Which Is Hard to Maintain, and a Bit Embarrassing Too, with Its Missing Wing Leather, and In Which She Has Straightened Out Her Floral-Patterned Dress a Few More Times than Necessary, and Cleared Her Throat, and Re-Adjusted a Shoe, but Cannot Afford to Procrastinate Any Further. In Which, if She's Honest with Herself, She Dearly Wants to Turn Around and Go.

Domitia was not having a good time.

She stood in an underwater city, in a bedroom defaced by pentacles and cluttered with devious little notes, staring at the wall into which the two men had vanished.

Why, to begin with, had she left her comfortable cottage that swayed with its gentle passage through the swamp, and left her job—or her *hobby*, as her father liked to call it—where she could channel the deviation that had cursed her from birth into something beneficial, something that took suffering from the world?

All it had taken was a pretty little elf with wet eyes, and she'd been off, barely pausing to pack. And now what?

Now she found herself in pursuit of a malnourished man who appeared to be down multiple limbs, and a basket-case of a knight who had all the defensive power of a wet kitten. They had 'help me' written all over them, and here she was, intending to do the opposite.

But the sorcerer threatened to do something terrible. All the magic, all around the world; he wanted it destroyed, and said so proudly. He had already turned back time—what a day that had been, starting with a miserable, lightly pregnant elf rapping at her door, covered in the swamp mud she'd slipped and fallen into more than once, asking to be relieved of her condition. Of course, Domitia provided that service. How could she be cold enough not to? But the elf had believed it necessary to disclose the long, wretched circumstances of the conception. She'd cried a bit, and Domitia had made cup after cup of herbal tea while desperately offering biscuits. Then— with the deed finally done, and the elf back on her way, refusing to stay the night—something had *wrenched* in the air with the sharp smell of magic, and Domitia found herself back at her front door, standing before the mud-covered and thoroughly baffled elf, sunlight streaming down upon them. That day, having to put that poor woman through the ordeal a second time, Domitia had trembled with a rage she attributed to her dragon half. It had burned through her like a fever.

It was that *anger*, paired with the soft vulnerability in Glenda's face, that convinced her to bring down the sorcerer.

Ah, Glenda. As much as Domitia resented it, she had a weakness for beauty. For beautiful women, more precisely. Tall women, short women, women with full lips and rounded bodies, women with bird-like angularity and chiseled cheeks. All sorts of women! And look how that turned out.

For a while, she'd excused away every stinging remark that left Glenda's lips. *She's been educated differently*, Domitia told herself. *She doesn't know. She just needs gentle argument, and a slow introduction to new ideas.*

But still it had built up, and still she had snapped, that dragon fury surging in her again.

Even if they hadn't gotten on, Glenda's absence now left Domitia quite alone. But that was alright. She'd always been alone, even in the company of other people. Even with her elven family—especially with her elven family. She could wear her solitude as a cape and take strength from it.

She could do what needed to be done.

She could . . . "Kill an anemic double-amputee," she said, and clapped a hand over her face. "God, what am I doing. What am I doing?"

She drew breath deep into her chest and straightened. "I'm doing the right thing. That's what." And the right thing didn't always feel clean, or good, or leave her warm and glowing. Like with that poor elf woman, the right thing sometimes left her with sleeves stained with tears and the snuffing of a tiny life. The right thing was something you had to be strong enough and sure enough to commit to; the right thing was what was *necessary*.

And so, she walked to a desk laden with notes, selected a quill and a pot of ink, and returned to the wall to add symbols of her own.

For as much as she believed in the necessity of doing good, she believed twice-fold in the power of her own magic.

She stepped through the wall, tearing open the wound left by the previous portal, and found herself in a jungle, heat pressing around her like a blanket. Monstrous trees crowded her, their distant canopy letting through only slivers of the brilliant blue sky.

The sorcerer's second portal took her longer to find. Domitia retained the quill and ink, but with nothing to sketch on, she soon threw these aside and traced her symbols directly into the rich red soil.

Finally, she located the shimmering wound of the recent portal. It was good timing—even as she watched, its edges faded, healing. Regretfully, she drew a pentacle to rip apart space again, and (muttering an apology to the fabric of reality) stepped through.

Freezing cold. A bitter wind knifed into her single eye, the glass one being blissfully numb. She squinted, speaking a small flame into existence to warm her hands. Her next symbols, she carved into snow.

"Where are you, come on . . . there you are! Thank you, sweetheart." Domitia felt a bit silly, speaking to the after-traces of a portal with such affection, but her legs were numb with cold, and the prospect of escape made her giddy. "Let's get going."

This last jump brought her to a desert, an environment she knew from illuminated manuscripts and fairy tales. The sun hung low in the sky, the sand rippling in its fading heat, and—Domitia tried not to laugh—not far from where she stood, both Sir Cameron and Merulo lay prone. She could see the rise and fall of their chests. Not dead, then, but unconscious.

Beside the men lay a bedsheet, weighed at its edges with sand and painted with symbols that Domitia knew all too well.

"So that's what you're after," she said, a little sadly. "You wanted to see Him. Well, I hope it was worth the price of admission." Domitia could see it on the bedsheet, now that she knew to look: the flaking remains of a burnt eye.

She considered rolling the men into a more comfortable position, as they looked to have fallen where they stood, lying as they did in a ridiculous tangle of limbs. In the end, she simply chose a spot in the sand and sat with crossed legs. There she waited for them to wake, so that she might continue this painfully imbalanced game of cat and mouse.

CHAPTER 54

In Which There Is Nothing. In Which I Am Nothing. In Which—

The nothing retracted with a snap, and I heard guttural sobbing. I'd clearly fallen at some point during the spell, as the desert sky filled my vision. Time had evidently passed. It was violet dusk, faintly pricked with stars, with the rising moon staring down at us.

"Cameron!" Bony hands shook me, and Merulo's face appeared, lined with concern. "Cameron, it was only a vision. You are unharmed."

"Death," I heaved, recognizing the cries as my own. "Death, that was death, that was—"

Merulo slapped me hard across the face. I blinked at him. "Microwave."

"If you two are finished," came a woman's voice. "We have much to discuss."

Domitia sat cross-legged in the sand, close enough for it to be shameful that neither of us had spotted her. Merulo sprang off me and, with some unsteadiness, I followed. I unsheathed my sword, and Merulo brandished his wand, but the half-dragon didn't show us the courtesy of responding in kind. She stayed seated, the slouch of her shoulders betraying sadness, but also victory. As if she didn't expect to fight. As if she'd already won.

"So now you've seen," she said. "Just as I did, many years ago." With a thumb and forefinger, she reached beneath her eyelid and plucked out her lazy eye. I quickly looked away, not wanting to see the empty socket.

"I . . . don't understand." Merulo gripped his wand tightly. "Why couldn't I see God? Where does it hide?"

"God is dead," I said, certain of my words. "That was death, Merulo. That was the nothing." Desert grit clung to my drying cheeks. I felt like I could crumble to the ground at any moment, and that if I did, nothing in the world could get me back up.

"I imagine it happened on the Day of Descent." Domitia pushed her false eye back into its socket without any sign of discomfort, then motioned for us to sit across from her. Neither of us complied—me, because I had to remain standing to maintain my sanity, and Merulo I assumed out of pride. With a sigh, she continued. "It was the dying act of a being beyond our comprehension. It came to our choked, dying world and answered a prayer."

At Merulo's snort, something in Domitia's posture sharpened. "I don't hate God. A being of that scope, expending its life to grant our wish . . . I think it must have loved us. Not as individuals, but as a world. I think in its last moments, it loved us enormously. And the connection people seek with it now, the desire to touch that love through prayer, and artwork, and music . . . Some of it is beautiful. Some of it moves me."

I opened my mouth to protest, ready to share my own

experiences as a lifelong churchgoer, but Domitia raised a hand. "I cannot, however, ignore the arrogance of the act. The same arrogance that you now demonstrate yourself." She leveled her gaze at the sorcerer. "A single being, no matter its power or intelligence, cannot make decisions for millions. Merulo, you must understand. You have no right to impose yourself on this world."

"Watch me," snarled the sorcerer.

I wanted to clap at his brevity.

"You think you deserve to choose, because you can take it by force? Then take it. Outmatch me." Domitia spread her arms, displaying both her musculature and those strange, snaking scars.

Merulo made no move. Slowly, Domitia got to her feet. She cast a deliberate look at the leg that lay, in a cloud of meaty stench, beside the painted bedsheet. "Your use of that wand. The amputated limbs ... You've drained yourself, haven't you?"

At my side, Merulo remained silent.

"Then there's no need for me to kill you. Crippled from overuse of magic, no path remains for you to achieve your goal."

"My body remains," Merulo said faintly. "I'll wring out the magic from every vein and limb and inch of gut."

Despite her flowery speech and supposed kindness, Domitia had shifted into the predatory stance I knew well from her dragon siblings. "Ah," she said, advancing over the sand. "When he cut off my wings, my father kept them, folded in cloth, to be burned for spells. It's disgusting, how we can be used." She stopped before him. "Merulo, I'd like to leave you alive. It will be a long life, I'm sure, with much to experience. Spend time with your partner, who clearly adores you. Just say you will not continue, and I will leave now, in peace if not in friendship."

Merulo spat, a thick gob that hit Domitia on her rounded blue cheek.

"Then I'm sorry," said Domitia. "I truly am."

All this time, she paid me no heed. Of course, why should she spare a thought for a lowly, insignificant little human? My swung sword caught her from behind, a killing stroke driven by all my practice, all my muscle.

The blade shattered.

Domitia sighed. "Sir Cameron, please step aside." She hadn't even bothered to turn around. Her floral dress hung open at the back, slashed by my sword stroke, but underneath her skin gleamed a healthy and unbroken blue.

Right, she was a dragon. Well, can't say I didn't try.

This distraction did, however, allow Merulo to point his wand. He shouted dark words at such staccato speed, it was a marvel he didn't stumble over them, issuing a spell that—

Domitia brushed her hand through the air dismissively, and the wand flew from his grip. It burst into splinters midair, leaving the spell to die on his tongue. With another wave and a calmly spoken word, Merulo's prosthetics exploded.

He crumpled, empty socket bleeding, cheek flecked with the crushed remains of his stone eye. His arm and leg still hung attached, but mangled, nothing more than scrap metal.

"Wait!" I threw my sword to the sand, staggering toward Merulo. Why hadn't he chosen a location with dirt and grass, somewhere with *traction*? Each step through this sinking material was agonizing. "Please!" I flung myself down before him, arms out, a shield against the half-dragon's bulk.

"Sir Cameron," Domitia said softly. "It doesn't matter where you're standing. Magic doesn't operate as a projectile. Merulo has made his decision, please allow him to honour it." She raised her hands again, fingers spread, but paused at the widening of my eyes. At the way I looked past her, over her shoulder.

I'd seen it first. The rise of gigantic red lines, towering walls of light cutting through the sky. The colossal strokes of a pentagram that encompassed the entire world.

Domitia whirled, her placidity fracturing. "There's another—"

"Another dragon?" Merulo laughed. "Of course there is. You didn't think I was the brains behind this, did you?"

Bloody walls dominated the horizon, their light blotting out the stars. He spoke in exhausted fragments, but still I recognized the dark glee in Merulo's voice—from Benedict, from the needle, from every time he'd taken pleasure in inducing my fear. "All I needed to do was kill God. That was the entirety of my role. How accommodating, to find it already dead. Take my life if you wish. You've already lost."

"No," said Domitia. "No!"

It was hard, seeing the woman's despair as she swung her attention to me, knowing that I would do nothing to alleviate it. "Sir Cameron, what do you know of this? Please, think of your brother."

"Chickens will stay the same," I said, with remarkable restraint considering the beating she'd just delivered to her own brother. "Simon will be fine."

The whisper of moving sand behind me: Merulo, crawling toward his amputated leg. Domitia shouted, and an invisible force backhanded the sorcerer, so that he wheeled in an arc of sprayed blood. I shouted.

Red light painted the desert then, washing out all other colour. The ascending walls bathed the world in a macabre glow. Reduced to a mere observer as unthinkable magic mounted on all sides, Domitia's face knotted in distress, her fingers clenching uselessly at nothing. It took me by surprise when she closed her eyes and began to sing.

From the foreign lilt of the words, I knew it to be a spell. Her voice soared, pleading and prayerful, the volume quickly surpassing my tolerance. I clapped hands over my ears, but still I heard her keening crescendo. The scent of magic tickled my nose, that sharp, wild prickle of something changing. And as she sang, Domitia smoldered.

"Shut up, shut up," Merulo rasped, scarcely audible. He was somehow still conscious, hunched in the sand like a twisted black scorpion. "You have LOST! Shut up!"

Flames rippled from Domitia, shifting colours in a nauseating chaos, burning back the red night. Beneath that kaleidoscopic inferno, she sang louder and louder, even as her flesh dripped from her face and her clothing turned to ash. In a blaze of light, it reached its climax.

As did the pentagram's gory walls. Together, they erupted, so that the air itself seemed made of magic.

Just as quickly, it faded. The starry sky returned, and Domitia lay dead, a scorched husk.

Merulo was repeating something in a garbled voice. It took me a moment to understand. "What did you do, Domitia?" he cried. "What did you do?"

CHAPTER 55

In Which the Mad Sorcerer Has Been Defeated. In Which My Prophecy Has Come to Fruition. In Which I Have Destroyed a Man Who Once Was My Enemy but Now Is Anything But.

A scream of anguish. Something you'd sooner expect from a rabbit in the teeth of a dog, not from a man. Not from Merulo.

"It's alright," I said, though I didn't believe it. The sorcerer writhed in the sand beside me, and I tried, again, to soothe him. "It's alright."

"No, no," Merulo wailed. "I can feel the magic. It's all around us. She protected it! And I am not transformed. *Nothing* is transformed. I failed!"

Unable to help, I instead lay back on the cold slope of the dune. A day of sweating and panic had left my throat raw, but nothing clouded the sky, no potential for quenching rain. The night sky was a pit, with only the flimsiest of forces preventing us from falling into it. From falling into *nothing*. Vertigo made the edges of my vision swim, but I maintained my focus, mapping out the stars that Merulo had wanted so desperately to reach. I couldn't see any of the constellations I knew—perhaps because of our foreign location, or perhaps because of the stupidity that comes from dehydration. In the morning, I'd come up with a plan to find water. It would be difficult, escaping this barren desert alive, but for now I lay silent and peered upward.

Merulo's wails faded as he lost his energy, but his breath still came in dry heaves. And I did nothing. I did not move, and I did not comfort him.

What more could be said to a man whose life purpose had evaporated in a sudden heat, and who now, mangled and drained, had nothing left but me? A paltry prize, given that he'd wanted the entire cosmos.

I stared harder. The stars were moving.

Two pinpricks, of a brighter intensity than their surrounding stars, swam through the night at a leisurely pace. "Merulo," I said. Then, with more urgency: "Merulo. For fuck's sake. Look UP."

Something in my voice must have broken through his anguish, because Merulo obeyed. "The barrier," he said, his mouth hanging open. "Hydna destroyed the barrier. We didn't fail, not entirely. They're coming!"

"Who is?" I pushed myself upright in the sand, staring at the twin stars. The night seemed huge now, every speck of light a possibility. "Who's coming?"

"Mars," he croaked. Then his head dropped, crunching on impact with the dune.

Leaning over him, I shook his shoulder with care, not wanting to grip his meatless bones too tight. "Merulo!"

"Hurgh," said the sorcerer, returning vaguely to life.

"Stay awake, just a little longer." I quivered with energy, a tantalizing idea unwrapping itself like a gift. Merulo's amputated leg, lying feet away, contained more magic as a fetid ruin than I'd ever held in my own body. And before me lay the world's most adept magic-user. "You've gotta help me with a spell. The one you did earlier, with your arm. And where are we, precisely?"

CHAPTER 56

In Which the SMS Lunatic Freak *Has a Whim that Shall Not Be Denied, and though It Dearly Loves Its Captain, Some Things Are Worth Straining a Relationship Over, Such as, For Instance, Rediscovering the Earth.*

When the Earth popped back into existence beneath them, the ship wasted no time. It didn't matter that it carried a bellyful of cobalt and water, stripped from the asteroids that made up its livelihood, or that its fuel was at the lower end of its capacity. WE'RE MAKING HISTORY, the ship said, lurching into a corrected course as the captain swore. STRAP IN!

Speed was a crucial factor. After all, nobody would care much, in the news or in classrooms, about the *second* ship that rediscovered the Earth. The ship had begged for authorization to seed its drones into the atmosphere, which the captain granted after eighty-three seconds of PLEASE, PLEASE, PLEASE, PLEASE, scrawling across their eyeglass.

The drone wrangler narrowed his eyes in concentration. "Visuals from the drones are connecting. We'll see around the planet in just a sec . . . Here, a group of blue people? And unicorns. A floating church. That's a dragon, I think. Crystal towers. Dark masses in the sea. This is..."

Then a pair of drones captured clouds, curling and shaping into what looked like words, and all other viewpoints shrunk, shoved into corners.

"And no incoming radio waves, electronic transmissions, nothing?" Captain Abel asked, a frown wrinkling their dark skin. "It's an eccentric way to communicate. Are you sure it's directed at our drones? What are they saying?"

"That's Gita's department," said the drone wrangler, swiveling his chair to face her.

"The language is hard to place," said the engineer, her hands dancing across the ship's interface. "*Lunatic's* still running it through... oh!"

"What?" Captain Abel gripped the engineer's seat, their eyes following the lines of text racing across her display.

"We're getting a match, but... it's to a conlang." Gita expressed her disbelief with a head tilt—something the captain usually found quite charming. "Loanwords are plugging the gaps, mostly twenty-third-century Mandarin and English."

"A *conlang*?"

"A fictional language. This one's from a franchise, *Legends of Larnia*. It caused some controversy at the time for its socially conservative material, but it peaked in popularity right around Event X. Actually, that timing is a touch close for my liking, let me just—" The engineer began to mumble, conferring with the ship. "Huh." She sat back in her seat.

Captain Abel hastily released their grip, lest their fingers be crushed. "What now?"

"Ship's got a theory." Gita's honey-brown eyes rolled up to

meet the captain's, who hovered, tense, above her. "To celebrate the twelfth season of the live action adaptation, the media conglomerate controlling its copyright launched a capsule loaded with books, recordings, and artwork. They likened it to a Noah's ark, 'the world of Larnia,' preserved forever in space."

"Gita. I'm not hearing a theory."

"It's just..." The engineer chewed at her lip. "What we're seeing on the drone footage has to be terraforming and gene-manipulation on a level we're not capable of. What if something received that capsule. And used it as an... instruction manual?"

"What you've just said," the captain said slowly, "is so stupid that it makes me want to throw up in my own mouth. But alright, let's run with it. The clouds are speaking to us in an ancient fictional language, fine." They rubbed their chin, fingering the indent of an acne scar. "Can you translate?"

"Oh, sure!" Gita moved in quick darting motions, flicking through data. "Thank Luna for the long-dead nerd who assembled this wiki, it's fantastic. And thank you, ship," she added, at the *Lunatic Freak*'s aggrieved beeping. "It says, and I'm translating roughly, '*Greetings from the* friendly *and* polite *sorcerer/ God is dead/ We'd love to go to Mars/ Need help/ Thanks.*' Then there's a string of archaic coordinates."

The ship took control of the broadscreen, plumbing its database for the longitudes and latitudes of Earth, a sweep of numbers broadcast for the crew's enjoyment. From these, it highlighted an area on the night side of the planet, where a drone pair flew over sweeping desert dunes.

"And what shall we do with this information, ship?" the captain asked, with some weariness. Back on Luna, they'd been coerced into taking their cousin's bully-dog on a walk. The way it dragged them about by its leash, seemingly desperate to strangle itself on its pulled-tight collar, reminded them unflatteringly of the ship.

IF WE IGNORE CLEAR COORDINATES, THEY'LL THINK WE'RE LACKING IN INTELLIGENCE. AND I'M NOT A FOOL. I'M A LUNATIC FREAK.

"You heard the ship," said the captain. "It has a reputation to maintain. Let's send down a drone and greet this 'friendly and polite sorcerer' ... Ah, fuck. Are we really doing this?"

OH YES, came the scrawling words. HERE WE GO!

The footage from the drone pair plummeted as they passed through the clouds. They panned over the curving dunes of a night-shadowed desert, so much smoother than the pockmarked landscapes of Luna. As the drones drew closer to the ground, the view became disturbing.

The drones transmitted footage of two men in strange dress. One seemed in good shape, if a bit frantic in his waving. The second man, thinner and older, with dark flecks of blood on his face and more coating his crushed prosthetics, lay motionless. Not dead: switching views, the drones could still detect his body heat, though it was alarmingly low. A burnt log rested at the younger man's feet. From its blackened toes, it might once have been a leg. A scarce distance off, the charcoal remains of another body lay sprawled in the sand, quite dead.

The younger man spoke with urgency, judging from the nonstop flap of his mouth. He gestured emphatically at his wounded companion.

"Gita," said the captain. "Can we translate that?"

"Ship and I are working on it. We're almost done with

the filter ... okay, now we'll run the captured audio through, from the start. Ship, if you'd like to do the honours?"

The ship buzzed happily, flashing the translation across their eyeglasses:

OH FUCK, WOW. SORRY FOR SWEARING. UH, MY FRIEND THE SORCERER IS VERY BADLY INJURED, AND I'M SORRY, SHOULD I BE SPEAKING IN A FORBIDDEN LANGUAGE? I DON'T KNOW ANY. THE ONLY REMOTELY EDUCATED PERSON HERE IS OUT COLD, SO THIS WILL HAVE TO DO. CAN YOU UNDERSTAND ME? HELP, PLEASE, FRIEND, HURT. I MEAN, IF YOU CAN'T SPEAK COMMON, THAT ROUND THING THERE IS AN EYE, RIGHT? OR A CAMERA, I KNOW ABOUT CAMERAS. ANYWAY, YOU CAN PLAINLY SEE THE ISSUE. MAYBE THERE'S A TRANSLATION SPELL? MERULO, WAKE UP, IT'S THE MARTIANS! BY THE WAY, THIS IS NOT WHAT PEOPLE OF OUR WORLD USUALLY LOOK LIKE, THEY TYPICALLY HAVE MORE BLOOD INSIDE THEM. MERULO! DAMN, HE'S OUT. LOOK, COULD YOU PLEASE HELP? PLEASE?

"Martians. They think we're the bloody Martians." The captain resisted the urge to spit, not wanting to sully their ship.

"What should we say back?" asked the drone wrangler, his fingers thumping against the dash with poorly contained nerves. Beside him, Gita vibrated, ready to transmit their words.

The captain sighed. There was a tension in the cabin that they lacked the skill to deflate. "Tell them the truth, that we can help. After that, we can bring them up under stage five quarantine."

FEELING DARING TODAY, CAPTAIN? flashed the ship.

"I'm feeling," said the captain, running a hand through their close-cropped hair, "like making history." In truth, the unreality of it all threatened to plunge them into hysteria. They fought to keep their voice chipper, and their mind detached.

A shiver ran through the ship as the transport shuttle detached. The crew waited in tense anticipation, the transport streaming its visual capture onto the broadscreen. When the jewel-toned planet appeared on their screen, it looked both familiar, with its swirling whites and tranquil blues, and horribly wrong. Nobody said it out loud, but Captain Abel felt certain that everyone had noticed. They should have seen the Americas, or a stretch of Europe and Asia, but the continents mashed together into a single curved Pangaea. Likely, the captain thought, with contours that perfectly matched the map of Larnia.

"We have a problem," said the drone wrangler, and the captain jolted their attention to his section of the broadscreen. "That, uh, that dragon I mentioned earlier? It's caught a drone. And it's speaking to it."

Through a shaky camera, the drone transmitted its assailant. At first, they saw only the blur of beating wings. Then it tossed the drone to the ground (the visual shaking briefly upon impact), and the monster was revealed in its entirety. Maroon scales flashed, absent only on the leather of its folded wings. Pterodactyl, lizard, dinosaur . . . None were good fits for whatever genus this thing belonged to. Horns erupted from its brow, black weapons that curved above reptilian scarlet eyes.

Halting their examination, the beast contracted into a muscular woman.

"Oh, perfect," the captain groaned. "I love that."

The woman waved, which surprised them—but of course, why wouldn't they have gestures in common?—and then her mouth began to move.

HELLO, MARTIANS, scrolled the ship, translating. OR MOONLINGS, WHICHEVER. I AM THE ONE WHO BROUGHT YOUR EARTH BACK TO YOU, AND AS SUCH I COMMAND YOU TO TAKE ME TO SPACE.

Captain Abel massaged their forehead, where the seed of a headache now grew. "Seems like she'll be more trouble than the others. Not even a please or thank you. Also, the fact that she's a dragon, I don't like that."

THERE'S ROOM ON THE TRANSPORT, the ship insisted. REMEMBER! HISTORIC EVENT!

Captain Abel inhaled deeply through their nose, held the breath in their chest, then exhaled. After four repetitions, they felt capable of response. "I suppose, if we're already bringing up the others . . . have the transport head there next. Ship, are you preparing the med-bay?"

AFFIRMATIVE. YIPPEE!

"And we'll need to inform Luna"—the captain tapped to get Gita's attention—"of our unusual cargo. At least this one didn't assume we were Martian hyper-capitalists. How's our fuel projection with the extra weight?"

IT'S PUSHING OUR MAXIMUM CAPACITY! The words scrolled fast, betraying the ship's excitement. BUT THAT'S THE LAST ONE, PROMISE! THE DRAGON IS ESSENTIAL!

Captain Abel forced a smile. "Well, if she's *essential*, then we'll bring aboard the dragon *and* the man *and* the polite and friendly sorcerer. Until then, I will be fucking asleep. Good work, crew!"

Before anyone could protest, they marched from the cabin. The door slid shut behind them, and, at last, they allowed themself a small groan of pain. This blossoming headache was a monster, and nothing that followed would lessen it, they knew that much. Reality was different, reality had changed, reality had unicorns and dragons in it.

I'LL WAKE YOU ONCE THEY BOARD, scrolled the ship across their eye-lens, and they nodded affirmation, only to wince at the jogging of their tenderized skull.

Captain Abel's last thought, as they crawled into the darkened nook of their sleeping shelf, was to pray to whatever God might be out there that this freshly returned Earth proved a better neighbour than Mars.

CHAPTER 57

In Which a Star Is Falling from the Sky.

The round, foreign structure descended from the heavens like an instrument of God.

It landed in a wash of light and flame, turning the night briefly into day. Four legs unfolded from the pod, sinking into the sand, and straightening the ramp that unfurled like a tongue.

A construct. But no—this was metal, not wood. This was... actually, I didn't know what this was.

Feeling like I walked through a dream, I lifted the limp weight of Merulo and mounted the ramp, flinching at the hollow clang of my footsteps.

Inside: a ring of seats, harnesses falling from their shoulders. Lights blinked on, blinding me. When I could bear to open my eyes, I saw illustrations lining the walls of small figures finagling themselves into the seat-straps.

"You first," I said to Merulo—though, being unconscious, he neglected to respond.

My hands came away wet from securing him into his partitions.

I'd barely strapped myself in when the hatch snapped shut, and with it, my last view of Larnia. Before I could shout at this, acceleration struck. A terrible weight pressed on my shoulders, sinking my eye-jellies deep into my skull. Every breath took a struggle.

Then, it stopped.

I was still gasping in recovery when the hatch slid open to reveal, not peeping Martian visages, but Hydna.

"Hy—"

"Shit." Hydna ducked into the pod, filling it with her bulk, and beelined to her brother. Her calloused hands fluttered over the crushed prosthetics that dangled like windchimes from his shoulder and hip. Clamping her jaw tight enough to spasm, she dropped into an adjacent seat, nearly tearing the harness in her haste to secure it. "GO!" she roared to the pod, and it did.

Once more, force peeled back the skin of my face. It grew, and grew until it was too much to bear—then, in an instant, it abated. Replacing it was a sense of weightlessness. Not just a sense; I floated in my seat, with only the harness keeping me in place. "AUGH!" I cried, and watched as saliva drifted from me in tiny, pretty bubbles.

It distracted me so thoroughly that I nearly missed Merulo's last breaths.

Those last gasping intakes—like he sucked air around some hidden obstacle. I could tell, even as Hydna freed herself of the straps and pounded at his chest. I knew the finality of it.

Merulo was dead.

It barely breached my awareness when the door slid open again, and a glittering horde of metal floated in to snatch away his corpse. Dimly, I heard my own voice, painful in its volume, overlaying a second, far calmer voice that issued nonsense words.

There was a wrench, as weight re-established and my feet slammed into metal flooring. Then I was following Hydna, without the memory of having unstrapped myself from the transport wall.

We passed into a corridor, and I sat. From that vantage, I watched Hydna seize a hovering contraption, her greed for information overcoming any sense of loss. She hooked her pointed nails into a crevice, tearing through its shiny surface. Small metal parts tinkled to the floor around us. I leaned back against a cool, smooth wall and realized that I was waiting to feel something. Really, anything at all.

Using the organs of the machine she'd taken apart, Hydna assembled something like a small, heated knife. With a cry of triumph, she brought it to sizzle against the wall of our prison.

The burn of a spark against my cheek woke me.

"You can reverse time," I said. "Merulo did it for me. Go back to . . . to before she hurt him." I choked on the words. My voice felt hoarse. Had I been shouting?

"My idiot brother is fine. Have you not been paying attention?" She paused. "Oh, the ship was speaking in Mandarin, wasn't it? Damn it, I forgot. Well, if it'll get you smiling again, I'm sure the ship'll let you peek at him. We've been getting along great." She patted the metal hull she'd been eviscerating, and from somewhere overhead came a distinctly pleased beeping.

There was whirring, like that of a horribly fattened fly, as another metal construct flew down the hallway. It opened its gut and shit four small beans into Hydna's outstretched hand. To my disbelief, she inserted two of these in her ears, then held the other two out to me. I didn't have the energy to protest, instead cramming the cold objects into my ears in self-violation.

"There," came a bouncy voice of indeterminate sex. "It took me a few minutes to break down your language, but now we can talk properly. I'm the standard mining ship you're aboard, SMS *Lunatic Freak*. No need to respond aloud, you can vocalize in your throat without letting the sound escape. Sound just clutters the air, don't you think? When you meet the crew, I'll play your translations in their ears, and vice versa. With no delay! Isn't that amazing? Hey, do you happen to know any other languages? Even scraps. I can use them to fill gaps when referring to technology. Hydna knows historical Mandarin, what a clever and beautiful dragon she is, but you haven't shown any signs of comprehension."

"English." Hydna's lips moved silently as her voice sounded in my ear. "We've been teaching him the English names for things. You can use that to plug the gaps."

"I want to see Merulo." I attempted to line my voice with steel, but it still quivered.

There was a pause, in which Hydna resumed her excavation of the wall, peeling back a frightening bulk of metal to expose nested wires.

On the opposite wall, a door slid open. I walked through it on unsteady feet, into a sunny wash of light. My ears vibrated with the droning of machines.

Merulo lay on a slab in the midst of them. They'd disposed of his robes—which made fury surge in me, unexpectedly—

and had draped him in a girlish shift that tied at his neck. Merulo's colouring had improved, a trace of pink returning to his lips, and even his hair looked . . . had the ship styled it?

The machines buzzed around his stumps, fixing them with what looked to be metallic attachment points. I smelled burnt skin, and the fresh rust of blood.

More blood entered him, snaking red through tubes that speared his arm. "Is that human? He's a dragon, you'll . . . dilute him! Or something." I spoke out loud, refusing to play the ship's game.

"I can't suck it back out," came the voice at my ear. "But if the other dragon would like to offer herself as a blood-bag, that's easily done."

I shoved a floating machine aside to reach Merulo. My hand grasped his. He felt warm, and further heat emanated from the legless table he lay on.

The ship had done a better job of caring for him than I had, with my collapsing and self-pity. Abruptly, the anger left me. "Thank you. Nothing made you help us. But you still . . . Thank you." With a free hand, I rubbed at my constricting throat. "Can I stay with him, please?"

One of the machines bumped against my rear. "Sit," the voice instructed, and I did. Only the frantic increase in buzzing betrayed that it now held a man's weight.

The door must have closed, for I no longer heard Hydna's banging. "What's that?" I pointed at thin rectangles of red, leaking through the sorcerer's shift above his abdomen.

"His guts were a mess. I fixed them, just a touch. It should help him process nutrients."

I tried to envision a non-bony sorcerer, and failed. "You can do anything at all, huh. You're . . . you're a super-computer, aren't you?" The machines in the room purred, which I took as assent. "Back in our world, you'd have been a dragon. Like Merulo and Hydna. No wonder you're so capable."

"I may as well be a dragon," said the voice. "I fly! My hide is near impenetrable! And did you know, I can even breathe fire when I like?"

"You're wonderful." I yawned, the table's warmth rising through my arms. "All dragons are. I haven't met a single one who isn't brave and brilliant, even . . ." Even Domitia, who had put my sorcerer in his current state. Who had burned herself alive to deny Merulo his dreams.

The room's light dimmed, as if sensing my exhaustion. "Rest now, if you like," said the ship. "You, and your sorcerer. We still have a way to go before we reach the moon."

CHAPTER 58

In Which the Abominable Man in the Med-Bay Has Woken. In Which His Cackling, Even When Heard through the Distance of a Recording, Has Raised Goosebumps on the Captain's Arms. In Which Everything Is Slipping Out of Their Control.

The polite and friendly sorcerer refused to have his brain chipped.

Without it, the ship-crafted prosthetics still worked, but at a fraction of their potential capacity. No thoughtlessly smooth motion, no transmitted sense of touch or temperature.

He'd communicated his own desires to the ship, demonstrating with sketches. The ship got to work fast, whirring over the limbs, painting alien symbology using blood taken from the woman. It was utterly strange and barbaric. While the golden-haired man bounced about, polluting the stream with his nonstop chatter, the other two finished their work, chanting in a language distinct from the conlang—after minutes of frowning, Gita matched it to spell words from *Legends of Larnia*. The captain suspected the ship had known this from the start and simply neglected to share.

Something... happened, after the recitation. Captain Abel felt it as a tingle on their skin. Across the cabin, Gita shivered violently. They caught a whiff, faint enough to be almost imagined, of unfamiliar spices. The ship wasn't all that large, but to have affected them from the opposite end of it?

"Ship, I need a reading on the chemical composition of the med-bay air. And energy readings. I have some concern that whatever happened just breached quarantine."

The ship did not respond.

"Ship!" barked the captain, for once not subvocalizing.

Text filled their eyeglasses: EASY, CAPTAIN ABEL. WE'RE MAKING HISTORY, REMEMBER?

"They used magic," said Gita, her amber skin ashy with fear. "Look at how he moves that arm—that's not possible without a chip. It's magic, Captain."

A glance over at the drone wrangler brought no relief. His shock of red hair, grown overlong in a rebellion against space-faring standards, lay plastered against his skin with sweat. Their assigned ambassador had not yet cleared them for landing, so the ship hovered in an isolated patch of space over Mare Cognitum, the Sea That Has Become.

"They're working on the leg now!" Gita spoke with a near-hysterical edge, also abandoning subvocal communication. "We'll feel it again!"

IF I MIGHT INTERJECT???? scrolled the ship, and the captain felt relief at the prospect of submitting to a stronger will. THE BOUNDARY IS GONE. MAGIC IS NOW A PART OF THE SOLAR SYSTEM. WE'RE IN A NEW ERA! LET THE DRAGON CAST HER SPELLS, WHO CARES? THIS IS ALL SO MUCH FUN!

The engineer began to weep, fat droplets dripping off her chin onto her sari.

CAPTAIN ABEL, flashed the ship across their eyepiece, WHY DON'T WE LET GITA COMMUNICATE WITH OUR GUESTS DIRECTLY? SHE'LL SEE THEY'RE ONLY HUMAN. IT MAY HELP WITH HER FEAR.

The captain slashed dissent with a hand—but too late, the cabin's broadscreen minimized all visuals, upscaling a med-bay feed. Three Terran faces looked in sudden alarm at the camera.

"Ship, are you projecting us to them?" the captain subvocalized, tilting their head meaningfully toward Gita.

"I've added a filter to give you all friendlier smiles," the ship whispered in their ear, "and erased the tears. That seemed appropriate."

"Did it?" They tried a real smile; it felt as stiff as cheap plastic, and as likely to crack.

"Hello?" said the golden-haired man. The captain knew this wasn't his true voice, only a simulation playing translated words in real time, but it surprised them, nonetheless.

"Greetings!" they replied shrilly. "I'm sorry to interrupt, but we've all been wondering. How is it your companion is harnessing his prosthetics without a neural chip? Is there an alternate technology, perhaps, that you've made use of?"

"Uh . . ." The man side-eyed his companions, who stood staring into the transmitter with predatory intensity. "This might be a long shot, but have you heard of 'magic'?"

Gita shrieked. Frantically, the captain gestured at the air. "Cut it off, cut it off!"

With a wink, the faces disappeared.

"That did not," breathed the captain, "help."

CHAPTER 59

In Which the Crew Is Obviously Having a Bad Time, and I Feel for Them, Absolutely, but It Honestly Is a Bit of a Bother.

"Oh, come on. Your captain shouldn't have said all that. Of course you helped. Everything you've done has been perfectly civilized!" I petted the nearest floating machine in what I hoped was a reassuring manner. After our brief communication with the crew had gone so disastrously, the poor ship needed a shoulder to lean on—metaphorically, as the sheer weight of it would likely crush me into jam.

"Must you always be blabbering?" said Merulo, his new eye blazing. The ship had set the dragon siblings up with projected displays in the med-bay, which, given the reduced number of the buzzing machines, now seemed pleasantly spacious. I didn't think he should be standing, let alone absorbing all this new, sharp-edged information, but he and Hydna were pawing at the displays like kittens at yarn, scrolling through dizzying arrays of text and photographs.

"Must *you* always be . . ." I couldn't think of anything appropriately cutting, nor did I really want to. "Mean to me?

Anyways, you just came back from being three-quarters dead. At least sit down." I patted a space on the operating table next to where I sat, feet swinging.

"He may feel perky now, but once my drugs wear off, he will crash," the ship agreed in my ear.

Merulo's look of attempted menace was undermined by his dress; the shift tied about his neck flapped open at the back, exposing bony white butt-cheeks. "This is information I would tear my remaining arm off to access. And you'd have me, what? 'Take a load off?'"

Their assembly had taken mere hours compared to the intense days of labour and study he and Hydna had poured into his previous limbs, but Merulo's arm and leg now moved smoothly enough to be mistaken for flesh. The polished black plastic was all that gave them away. Burnt blood flaked off the limbs as he moved, having served its role as fuel for the spell.

"Honestly, Merulo, it's like you enjoy shedding limbs." I lay flat on the table—which had been sprayed clean of fluids by the floating machines—and felt warmth radiate through the muscles of my back, unknotting them. "Come on, Hydna, talk some sense into him."

"Hmmmrgh," Hydna grunted, absorbed in a display of tiny humans on a screen. "Not now." She hulked over the display, her tunic and breeches looking oddly rough in the smooth, oyster-dome room.

"Lunatic Freak?" I rolled on the table to give my front a turn with the heat. "Before we meet the people from space, could you please give Merulo some clothing? It's just, we can see a rather lot of him right now. Particularly in the rear."

"Would that I had my magic," the sorcerer seethed. I

had to swallow a peep of joy as he turned from a projected display to direct dark attention my way. "Perhaps the vulture was too generous a form for you. Yes, how about one of those scurrying rodents that you so liked to prey upon? Hydna?"

"Not! Now!" she hissed.

"Here's what I have to offer." The ship spoke through some hidden orifice in the ceiling. Both wall displays switched to scrolling images of clothing, leaving the dragon siblings to shout their frustration.

"Sorry, Mer. You said a rodent? Did you have a particular species in mind?" Hydna turned to me with a storm in her face. Unlike her brother, who so often channeled his fury into activities I enjoyed, Hydna's anger genuinely chilled me.

"Uh." I eased myself off the table, carefully circling around it to place Merulo between myself and his sister. "Could we choose outfits, first? It's just another type of research, if you think about it, finding out what these moon people wear."

"Don't hide behind me. I won't protect you," Merulo muttered, but my words had worked. The siblings regarded the displays with fresh curiosity. From the sheer number of items scrolling past, this couldn't possibly be what the ship *contained*, but, as with the limbs, what it had the potential to make.

"I need clothing, too," I said to the ceiling. "Mine are drenched in various bodily fluids, and they've never quite fit."

"So many styles." Hydna looked hypnotized, her fingers hovering over the display. "Hey, Mer. This is how humans dress without enforced monotony. They must not have a Church. Or maybe several Churches, that's how it used to be. And—give me the material composition please—plastics?

Wasn't that a problem in the old world, the constant creation of plastic with no means to dispose of it?"

"We have genetically altered bacteria now," the ship chirped. "The little guys devour it, and can in turn be used for fuel, fertilizer, or various foods. There's a pricey alcohol on Luna which comes from microorganisms fed on an exclusive diet of discarded celebrity undergarments!"

I sidled closer to Merulo, not quite daring to slide an arm around his waist, but wanting to be present and involved. Thanks to the ship's administrations, his formerly lank hair now hung black and silky about the sharp planes of his scowl.

"What do you have that's close to his old robe?" I asked, appraising the strange parade of items. "He never wears anything else."

Merulo gave another cry of discontent, but my friend the ship had already obliged. "There." I pointed. "That looks nice. Look at the shoulder spikes! The Order would piss themselves in fear, then slip in it. The piss, that is."

"Show me what you consider most appropriate," Merulo said with stiff politeness. The selection narrowed to three near-identical black robes. None of them had spiked shoulders.

"The left robe is most conservative, if you're feeling dull. The middle looks closest to your old clothing, and the right is *interesting*. Right would absolutely have me acting up."

"Middle," said the sorcerer, wrinkling his nose. Hydna failed to participate in the decision, being absorbed in her own frenzied scrolling and subvocal communication.

"My turn!" I cried, pushing the recently undeceased sorcerer aside. "Lunatic Freak, please show me what a strapping young man in his mid to late twenties might wear.

Something suited to a young warrior, abandoning his faith to become a mad sorcerer's disciple!"

"Disciple?" scoffed the sorcerer. "A magic-less oaf, scrubbing floors clean of his own bird shit? Try to contain your self-flattery. The costume of a serving wench would be more fitting."

"He really does like me," I assured the ship, worried that it had not changed the display at the sorcerer's suggestion. "It's just how he talks."

The patching of their relationship accomplished, I gave myself up to the joys of shopping, even if it did feel curiously flattened through a screen. One displayed costume looked like a thrown net, shaped to a human form. The knots arranged the net into a lovely geometry, but it didn't look very warm. Or modest. Another showed a dress—did the ship know I was a man?—that slit alluringly over the hips, allowing a saucy length of leg. I tapped at it. Just to get a closer look. No other reason.

"That looks appropriate." Merulo pointed to an outfit I hadn't planned on stopping at, and I swallowed a squeak of dismay. A crisp black shirt, form-fitting black trousers, heeled boots in, you guessed it, black. I wouldn't have chosen it myself, but if Merulo showed interest?

"Selection locked," came the voice, and the screen shifted to an abstract display of colour. I couldn't help but notice that, before the options disappeared, the dress appeared to be highlighted.

"That's done with, then." I treated the ceiling to one of my signature smiles. I couldn't help my relief; black would've looked awful with my colouring. "Thank you so much, Lunatic! Is it alright if I call you Lunatic?"

"Of course!" came that sexless voice. "And I'll call you Cameron." One of the machines had its eyepiece on me, I noticed, a black circle containing the faint reflection of my own face.

"I will need interior pockets in my robe," said the sorcerer. "Hydna, I can instruct you in the enchantment needed for them."

Hydna grunted in annoyance, but I knew how rarely she denied her brother. It was reasonable to have a soft spot for your only remaining family.

Further scrolling was interrupted as the displays swam together, merging into a cube of light that resolved into a grim face.

"Sorry to interrupt," the captain said in Common, without a trace of accent. "But Luna has cleared us for landing. Please collect your personal belongings and prepare to deboard within the hour." With that, the face vanished.

The sorcerer's laughter bordered on screeching. Hydna joined him with her own booming tenor, and even I tried to add a chuckle or two, before deciding I was outmatched.

"We have everything," Merulo wheezed, once breath had returned to him. "Everything! We win! We get it all."

"Minus a limb or two," I said, but he only shushed me.

"The moon!" Hydna shouted. She seized Merulo and spun him in a hopping dance and, to my surprise, he did not protest.

"Careful, careful." I held my hands out, anticipating disaster. "Not too fast, Hydna. He's just had surgery. Hydna, you're being too rough!"

"The moon!" shouted the sorcerer, ignoring me—or so I thought. Pulling free of his sister, he grabbed me by the head and planted a kiss on my forehead. "The moon!"

"The moon," I agreed.

The lighting of the room shifted, to a kaleidoscope of reds, blues, and greens, whirling in dots across the walls and ceiling. Hydna bellowed, open-mouthed in delight, while Merulo clutched my arm.

"Cameron." Unshed tears softened his single eye, and something in my chest crumpled with joy. "This . . . all of this. It's the most wonderful thing I could have imagined."

I couldn't help but agree.

CHAPTER 60

In Which This Is the Most Horrible Thing Glenda Could Have Imagined.

Metal beasts whirred overhead, spooking Glenda's unicorn. She'd walked, then run, to the nearest Order outpost, her stomach churning with a hunger that sapped strength from her limbs. Even with the world ending around them, none of the knights had gotten in the way of the shouting, violet-faced elf as she commandeered gear and a steed. Many of them stared overhead, their limbs locked in mute horror.

The moon looked wrong.

It hung, as white and round as ever, but something infested it. Pinpricks of yellow light, like a carpet of hives, or—if looked at more sympathetically—like a spiderweb strung with golden dewdrops.

And around it in a quiet dance, stars fell from the sky.

Glenda kicked at the sides of her steed, a chestnut mare whose coat shone like blood under the moonlight. "Go, go!"

A figure darted across her path. The unicorn reared, twisting against its bit and prancing to a stop. Glenda shrieked a curse, and yanked a slim knife from her belt.

"No!" The figure, a wide-eyed woman, shielded her face with a basketful of morels and puffballs. "I'm sorry! I just—what's happening?"

Re-sheathing her blade, Glenda squeezed her eyes shut, searching for some semblance of calm. She found none. "God is dead," she called down. "The mad sorcerer is victorious. We are now in the aftertimes."

"But . . ." The woman gulped. "What does that mean?"

Before Glenda could answer, another woman appeared from the brush. She grabbed at the mushroom-gatherer, pulling her away. Overhead, something large and blazing with light swept above the treetops.

"*What does that mean?*" Glenda repeated, incredulous, while her unicorn snorted and shied, its dainty hooves stamping a beat. Humans were such fools. How could they fail to grasp the significance of this?

Glenda dug her heels into the mare, yanking its reins. "Go!"

It meant the end of their peaceful norms. The end of Order itself. In this new chaos, cats would eat dogs. Fish would soar through the sky, while birds swam below. Rain would rise from the soil, men would bed men, and women would . . . women would . . .

Glenda didn't notice the unicorn slowing to a trot.

Screams sounded from the forest. Harsh screeches trailed in the path of metal behemoths that shot across the star-filled night. Glenda wiped clammy hands in the silk of her unicorn's mane, then sat back in the saddle, near breathless with the force of her thoughts.

The world was changed, irreparably. The order unbalanced,

the status quo un-statused, the table upended and all the drinks spilled.

And Glenda, bobbing with the slow, lazy strides of her unicorn, rubbed at her chest and marveled at the combustion within her.

Maybe this did not have to be such a bad thing, after all.

EPILOGUE

In Which the Mad Sorcerer Has Completed His Foul Schemes, and Won, and Landed on the Moon, but In Which, Perhaps, He's Learned a Touch More than He Wanted to.

"A... video game?" The sorcerer sounded faint.

Merulo and I wore clothes spun for us by the SMS *Lunatic Freak*, smooth and silky garments that fit as though tailored by a master. It gave significant pleasure, the feel of clean materials against my skin, and the knowledge that—no matter how unconventional—I did look *good*.

I'd been embarrassed, stripping and showering in the curtained section of the med-bay beneath water sprayed in a thick mist from a hovering machine, but the cleanliness gave me the ability to sit proudly beside the sorcerer. Especially given the non-reaction the moonlings had toward my dress. Only Merulo had seemed flustered, until (with *perhaps* too much of an edge) I reminded him that he wore somewhat of a dress himself.

My goodbye to SMS *Lunatic Freak* included only a small spilling of tears. Hydna had entered an almost religious fervour once we exited the ship into a transparent tube set above the rocky plains of a black-skied world. A small spattering of ships sat perched in this desert. Some resembled oversized spinning tops, others predatory birds. My departing glance confirmed the SMS *Lunatic Freak* to be a hybrid of the two varieties.

A man had waited for us, weak-featured, but sharp in his attention. He introduced himself as Mr. Speakwell, gave us fresh earpieces for communication, and bade us follow—but Hydna could not be removed from the shipyard.

"It's like when a shuck has its teeth in a unicorn's nose. You can smack it about with a stick and shout to your heart's content, but it won't let go," I explained to the man, after watching his multiple attempts to persuade her into joining us.

Speakwell looked at me without expression, then gave up, leading Merulo and I through the tube. After a few minutes of passing through a dead landscape overhung by night, something new appeared: the sprawl of a massive, rounded building. I kept my cheer at maximum as we passed into its maw, hoping that some would leach into the silent Merulo.

Now, we sat staring at a wall-screen. Aside from the mousy man, Speakwell, the room was empty, the seats that circled the rounded table void of whomever typically filled them.

"Yes, a video game," said Mr. Speakwell. "*Legends of Larnia*. See, this is how the Earth looked prior to Event X . . . and this is it today." On a slowly spinning globe, the continents drew together, merging. "And this is how it compares to the game map." An overlay of an illustrated map—and even I had to admit their similarities.

"Tectonic drift . . . ?" Merulo sagged in his seat beside mine. I could tell he lacked faith in his words.

Speakwell shook his head. "Not in a mere millennium. Not this level of movement. I can't imagine such a sudden shift of continents would be conducive to human life."

"Pre-Descent, the population was near twelve billion?"

"That's correct, twelve point four billion."

"I would estimate," said the sorcerer slowly, "that the Earth's current population could be measured in millions. And this is after a thousand years of recovery."

Something in the man's eyes flickered at that. "It's hard to believe that the moon now outpopulates the Earth."

I couldn't join in their somberness. It was too distant, and too abstract. I could certainly imagine it—the rending of the earth, the sudden violence of change—but at the approach of the Fear, I forced my mind into blankness.

"What else?" Merulo asked. He looked as desperate as I'd felt in the meadow under the statue's shadow.

"It's better that I show you. This is the box art." The screen flicked to an illustration. It resembled the cover of Merulo's textbooks, with strange words overlaying an . . . oh, dear.

Merulo wasn't speaking, and I had no courage left to look at him. We stared at the illustration of a scowling sorcerer. The painted man sneered, ugly and evil. Neither eye was false, and his forearms, where they jutted from black velvet sleeves, were knotted with lean muscle. Nothing like the malnourished twig of Merulo's remaining arm. Whisps of colour danced under the outstretched claws of his fingers—was that meant to be magic? Behind his oversized form, the silhouette of a knight on unicorn-back could be seen, his sword raised heroically. Of course, loyalty compelled me to root for the sorcerer.

"The face is completely different," I said. "Yours is . . ." Weaker in the chin? More deeply lined? "Far more, ah, intellectual."

Merulo looked pale, his jaw clenched. I recalled how his gasping had sounded in the shuttle transport. "This is all a bit much. He's in poor health." I directed my words to Speakwell, standing attentively beside the screen. "And we need sleep."

"Explain," Merulo snapped, rising from his seat. His new attire didn't catch the air quite like his old robes, which had billowed with his motions like a living thing, but the sleek cling of the garments still gave him a certain power. "This man is . . . someone from a story?"

"The villain," the man answered, his round face polite.

Of course. Of fucking course it was.

"We have very little data to work with, at present," Speakwell continued. "Mainly what had been gathered by"—and was that a downturn of his mouth I saw?—"the SMS Lunatic Freak. But from my imperfect estimations, I would say that your world shows a remarkable adherence to *Legends of Larnia*. It's scarcely conceivable that any force could accomplish this. Though, that same force stole the Earth from under our nose, and held it hostage in a pocket dimension. Who's to say what it can or can't do."

"It can't do anything anymore. It's dead. And are we prisoners? You have to tell us if we are." Standing, I placed a hand on Merulo's prosthetic arm, and was surprised at how my fingers trembled.

The small man seemed to realize that he'd lost us. "You are guests, not prisoners. Please, allow me to show you to some temporary lodgings in the spaceport, where you may rest.

There is much more to discuss, but your health is the priority."

"Fine," said the sorcerer. "I imagine this information is not restricted, and we may access it in our own quarters?" His mismatched stare was a fierce thing to be at the receiving end of.

Speakwell hesitated. "The information is of a sensitive nature, given the current circumstances. Of course, we have no desire to restrict your freedom or withhold secrets."

"Of course," Merulo repeated, injecting the words with venom.

"Most of the moon is currently asleep." He spread his arms apologetically, but I refused to be fooled by the affected subservience. "For now, as Sir Cameron has rightfully pointed out, it may be best to join them and recover your vitality."

"Lead us, then." Merulo sighed. He kept his shoulders sharp, and his expression imperious.

Speakwell marched off like a wind-up doll, still full of his chaffing enthusiasm. "If at any point you feel too unwell to walk, please alert me and we'll arrange for alternate transport," he called back. At my side, the sorcerer bristled.

We left the room to pass through empty corridors. Light, whether electric or otherwise, glowed from panels in the ceiling. "What about Hydna?" I asked after some unknown distance.

"Whenever you wish, you may speak by subvocalizing 'contact,' and then her name. Your metaphor was apt, though—I suspect we will not be able to relocate her until she is willing." The ambassador turned his head to twinkle at me. "Eventually, you may have to rein her in. Or else half our women will be trailing after her, asking her to flex."

"I'm sure!" I grinned. "And I bet the other half will be after Merulo, eh?"

An awkward pause as the ambassador busied himself with the buttons of a doorway.

"I mean, they'll be pretty into the sorcerer, right? How could you not be? Right? Hey, come on, I think you've pushed enough buttons."

"He, uh." The ambassador coughed into a gloved hand. "He . . . Yes. Certainly."

"Cameron," Merulo said in warning.

Our footfalls echoed as we passed into another set of empty corridors. I felt an odd guilt. We were somewhere extraordinary, but my mental state prevented proper appreciation. Half-baked scenarios took precedence over the foreign landscape we passed.

If this mutual wariness between us and the ambassador led to anything . . . well, if they thought us dangerous, then perhaps it was best to prove them right. But what power did Merulo have at present, to protect us from the moon?

They didn't know he was drained. That was it. Their careful treatment of us, this politeness, and offering of shelter. They feared his magic. We must seem as alien to them as they were to us.

"We are not walking to an execution," Merulo said wearily, and I realized he'd been watching me over his shoulder. His lanky, anemic strides were easy to match, but I had fallen behind in my ruminating. "Unless you are truly frightened of rest and food, in which case, go ahead and complete your breakdown. Weep on the floor, if you like."

"There is no need to fear," the ambassador affirmed.

"You'll find we're quite civilized. At least, here on the moon."

The hall opened into a wide room. A fountain spurted at its center, ringed by benches. Dangling shards hung from the ceiling, like a gigantic bottle caught mid-explosion; they chimed against each other pleasantly.

Again, completely depopulated. Were the residents of the moon not allowed to see us?

"Contact SMS *Lunatic Freak*," I subvocalized, dragging my steps. The sorcerer shot me a look of annoyance, but slowed to match me, as did our bright-eyed guide.

"Cameron! How wonderful! Did you miss me already?" True to Speakwell's word, it was the ship's bouncy voice in my ear.

"Can they tell that I'm communicating with you?" Sweat rolled down my brow, despite the perfectly tailored temperature of the facility.

"Bugging personal communications is illegal on Luna. They may have a scanner on you to detect subvocalizations. Which is immoral, but could hold up in court given the circumstances. Assume that only my words are private."

"Ah . . . okay. The ambassador." Even in a situation like this, I had to appease my curiosity. "He seemed to dislike saying your name?"

"That's because it's two slurs, back-to-back," said the ship, with obvious cheer. "It's funny to make them say it. They never want to."

"Oh," I said, trying to keep the distaste off my face. "I can see why that would upset people. Who named you that?"

"I did! I had a different name before sentience, but who cares about that? Don't even mention it."

"Right." I nodded before I could stop myself. Damn, I

hadn't realized how much more than voice I typically put into conversing. "Lunatic, this situation worries me. There's nobody here. In the shipyard, then all through this gigantic building, all we've seen is the ambassador." I could only slow us so much; we exited the fountain room, back into the labyrinth of winding halls. I realized, suddenly, that the over-smooth walls were *screens*. Dead ones, displaying nothing.

"Ah," said the ship. "Evacuated. That's why they kept me from landing for so long. They're scared of the magic! My crew was frightened too, very frightened."

"But you're not?" It was strange, this speaking without actually speaking.

"Unknown variables are my favourite! Listen, when you're clever like me, so much becomes predictable. That's why I love humans. And now, I love your magic, too."

"That's funny of you to say, when the two smartest people I know tried their best to destroy it." I jumped as a grip closed around my arm. Black plastic claws, courtesy of the glowering sorcerer.

"Leave my sister be." He spoke sternly, but with a clear effort to soften his words. "We are not in immediate danger, and Hydna's worked hard to come here. Let her enjoy it."

"Right. Sorry. I'll just say goodbye."

The SMS *Lunatic Freak* continued in my ear. "Luna has a high emphasis on human rights. It has to keep itself distinct from Mars, after all. You shouldn't come to harm. But be gentle with my people. I didn't think you'd affect my crew the way you did."

Speakwell brought us through another plaza, then at last to a stop before a door. It had no handle, and presumably slid into the wall to open. "Here, keys for both of you to get in or out as you please. The display inside is set to your language. All words without translation have been substituted by circa 2300 English, as the SMS . . . *Lunatic Freak* advised. The ship also said that you'd prefer to share a bed?"

Everything up until this moment had been worth it to see Merulo's face redden. He spluttered, but I cut in: "Ignore him. That's what he wants. If, ah . . . if that sort of thing is alright up here?"

"Of course," said Speakwell, sounding surprised.

"Don't speak for what I want. Cameron, you are so thoroughly drenched in sweat it's as if you crawled from a pond." The sorcerer drew his bony frame up with a dignity that was undercut by his continued blushing. "It is repulsive, and we can all smell it."

"One bed!" I confirmed again, holding up a finger. "That will do us."

"Right," said the ambassador. "Well. As I said, that's been provided. I hope you enjoy your rest."

"If you wanted us to rest, you shouldn't have given us one bed." I gave the man an exceedingly charming smile, then plucked one of the cards from his outstretched hand.

"It's like you want to become a rat. Do you? Do you want to be a rat, Cameron?" Merulo reached past me to snatch the other card, a little roughly I thought.

Speakwell's voice only broke a little bit. "Hold your card over this patch, here." He demonstrated. "That will allow entry. Goodnight now, we'll speak more in the morning." And he stood at attention, waiting for us to enter, like the world's most easily overpowered guard.

"This is why Lunatic Freak thought you didn't like me," I muttered, as the sorcerer flashed his card against the door. "Because you're always threatening."

The room was unremarkable. From the faint lines in the floor, it seemed like the bed might be kin to the doors, sliding in and out as needed. Sheets covered it, and pillows. Not much had changed in the millennia of separation—unless they'd styled it to fit our archaic tastes?

Merulo ignored the bed in favour of the wall-screen. He hesitated only briefly before plunging in, flicking and poking the display to bring up bursts of images.

I spread my arms and let myself fall onto the bed, sinking into soft silver sheets. "Whew. What a day."

"A villain. That stupid game's sorcerer was a villain." Merulo stopped his tapping and cast me an oddly mournful look. "Do they think that of me?"

"Uh." Time for damage control. "Well, you are a bit—"

"A bit what?" he snapped, his surrogate eye blazing with red light. Why had the ship given him that?

"A bit ambitious," I finished lamely, rearranging myself on the bed to get a better view of the passing images.

"Our world should be on its knees thanking me for what I've done." With the black talons of his artificial hand, the sorcerer tapped at an image of spiraling planets. "They should beg for my forgiveness."

"Right," I said. "No, I hear you."

I'd intended to say more, but the clacking of his fingers on the screen lulled me, almost hypnotically. I sank into sleep, with no mind to potential dangers, and only minimal thought as to how Merulo might fit onto a bed I sprawled over so thoroughly—until a blow to the head brought me sputtering back to wakefulness.

"Move!" said the sorcerer, holding the pillow ready for another legitimately painful slam. I did move.

He'd managed to turn off the lights, somehow; his eye glowed a faint red in the dark. "You're taking too much of the covers."

"No, I'm not." It was an old argument, done more out of habit by now.

He yanked the blankets to his side and curled in them. But instead of sleeping, the sorcerer twitched and fidgeted, and finally spoke. "You looked so afraid, the first time I saw you."

"Hm?" I tried to think. "In front of your castle? I thought I was holding it together pretty well."

"No. The day before, when that beastly gang of knights stole my Roberto."

"Ah," I said, recalling the one-legged, no-armed construct.

"I really did try to kill you." He sighed, almost dreamily. "Almost had you, too. All those laughing knights. I was so looking forward to silencing them. And to seeing their faces drop as I cut apart your—"

"ALRIGHT." I raised myself on my elbows. "Is there any particular reason you've fixated on this?"

He blinked at me, mirroring my confused wariness. "Is it not—I thought it might be doing something. My recounting of the scene." He glanced down at where I was bunching the blankets and let out a bark of laughter. "It is!"

"Yes, well, it's not very appropriate. I was very frightened and—agh!"

The blanket had been ripped free and thrown to the floor.

In the dark, his red eye shone like a frozen ember. Something cold and claw-like touched my cheek. "Sir Cameron. I think I'm ready to see Seduction Two now."

"You need to stop bringing that up—" I got out, before further talk was rather abruptly cut off.

On that, our first night on the moon, we did not get much sleep.

The End

ACKNOWLEDGEMENTS

I'll give my thanks in roughly chronological order!

The first snippets of this book, I posted online. People said "hey, I like that!" and left funny comments. Being primarily motivated by praise, I wrote some more. On my next post, I got hatemail ("why do you think YOU can write a book?"). Being secondarily motivated by spite, I wrote *a lot* more. Without all those online voices, this book wouldn't exist. So, a massive thanks to everyone who crowdfunded my motivation! You made a difference, and a huge part of this book belongs to you.

But of course, there's more to this book than the initial draft. It's impossible to express how grateful I am to Courtney Miller-Callihan, who first saw potential in Sir Cameron, and to Ben Millier-Callihan, who became my agent, and worked with me through the first messy revisions. After applying to over one hundred literary agents and receiving either silence, an automated rejection, or a polite "I don't know how the hell to categorize or sell this," I was starting to falter in my belief. That first video call with Ben was like twenty Christmases. I think I mostly just stared blanky at him (out of fear), but inside, I was very, very happy.

And then! Titan Books became my publisher! Leading to

another video call where I stared like a goldfish, but had a lot of inner feelings. I'm unbelievably lucky to have gotten Katie Dent as my editor. She did the editorial equivalent of letting me know I had my fly down at several points, meaning I got to zip it up privately, which is . . . so important. Plot holes? What plot holes. There were never any plot holes. Everyone's character motivations made sense the entire time, and I've never gotten a word wrong. But seriously, the version of the book that Katie helped me grind out is so much more polished and cohesive, and something I'm really proud of. Her influence is all throughout this, and if you liked any part of it, you should be thanking her as well.

The rest of the Titan team also deserve accolades. Thanks to Rachel Vincent for her editorial help! Thanks to Louise Pearce for the copyediting! Thanks to Kevin Eddy for the proofreading! Thank you, Richard Mason, for the interior design, the arrows sticking out of the chapter titles are so cool. Thank you to Natasha MacKenzie for the beautiful cover and edge design (again, love the arrows!), and especially thank you for not swimming to Canada to murder me when I got overly enthusiastic with my ideas. And a huge thanks to Bahar Kutluk, Caitlin Storer, and Katharine Carroll, the publicity team responsible for putting this book in front of you.

There are more people behind the scenes, and I apologize for not being able to list you all, but please know how sincerely grateful I am.

I'd also like to thank the zoo of animals that has kept me sane throughout this process. It's been rough! I've had a worsening autoimmune disease that was (until recently) undiagnosed, and have been living like a frog in a pot of boiling water. There have been days where I couldn't do more than eat and sleep, but always I've had little guys in fur and feather suits who make it all seem okay. Thank you to Yennefer, Tallgeese, Wormbecca, and Anzu, my stupid chickens who refused to seek shelter in storms and always needed me to rush outside and shoo them to safety. Thank you to Chiefcake, my giant rabbit who followed me around biting my crutches when I had a broken leg. Thank you to Belphegor, my kitten who grew fur despite everyone (including the vet!) telling me he'd be a bald greasy worm forever. Thank you to Wednesday, who moved out with my housemate, but who would always put his butthole in my face while I was writing. I miss you Wednesday, but I don't miss that. And thank you to the almighties, Pangur and Grim, who have been here my entire adult life, and who, between the two of them, have four remaining teeth.

Lastly, thank you Mom, for teaching me how to read.

ABOUT THE AUTHOR

GREER STOTHERS is an award-winning author/illustrator based in Toronto. Their experiences as a nonbinary individual inform their writing and art, as does their drive to find the humor in everything. Find Greer online @greerstothers.com.

For more fantastic fiction, author events,
exclusive excerpts, competitions, limited editions and more

VISIT OUR WEBSITE
titanbooks.com

LIKE US ON FACEBOOK
facebook.com/titanbooks

FOLLOW US ON TWITTER AND INSTAGRAM
@TitanBooks

EMAIL US
readerfeedback@titanemail.com